PRAISE FOR

REPRISE

Reprise is nothing short of a whirlwind. Novikov's complicated science of time travel and time loops is original and engaging [...] Full of tension and twisting storylines, *Reprise* is a sci-fi novel that feels almost real. Its characters must follow the rigorous trials of the scientific method, as well as the terrifying possibility of the Shadowrealm, all while sorting out the complicated relationships forming between Eddy, Mara and François. This book is a breakneck journey, a loveletter to being a nerd, and a good time. — Genevieve Hartman, *Independent Book Review*

• • •

Pitch-black satire that never forgets the human frailty at its heart ...

Reprise is a contemporary Gothic, a taut, claustrophobic psychosexual drama about three compelling characters trapped in each other's orbits and by a highly thematic bit of technology — the Instance Device, which allows a limited form of time travel to revisit a past moment in one's life. They seduce each other, murder each other, and they bring each other a sort of joy that one can only experience when one has thoroughly convinced oneself that joy is no longer an option. It's a dysfunctional romance with world-scorching possibilities and it's an examination of academic politics and depression. I should also add that it's much funnier than I just made it sound. Massively funnier.

If you like your pop culture nerdy, your queers messy, and your time travel criminally clever, this book is for you. It was certainly for me.

— Rachel A. Rosen

REPRISE

A post-modern comedy of manners

Zilla Novikov

The BumblePuppy Press

OTTAWA, CANADA
2023

The BumblePuppy Press

Reprise is published by:

The BumblePuppy Press
PO Box 4814 Stn E
Ottawa ON K1S 5H9
Canada

National Library of Canada cataloging in Publication Data:

Novikov, Zilla, 1979 -
Reprise / Zilla Novikov
ISBN: 978-1-7387598-1-1

Ebook: 978-1-7770944-9-2

First edition

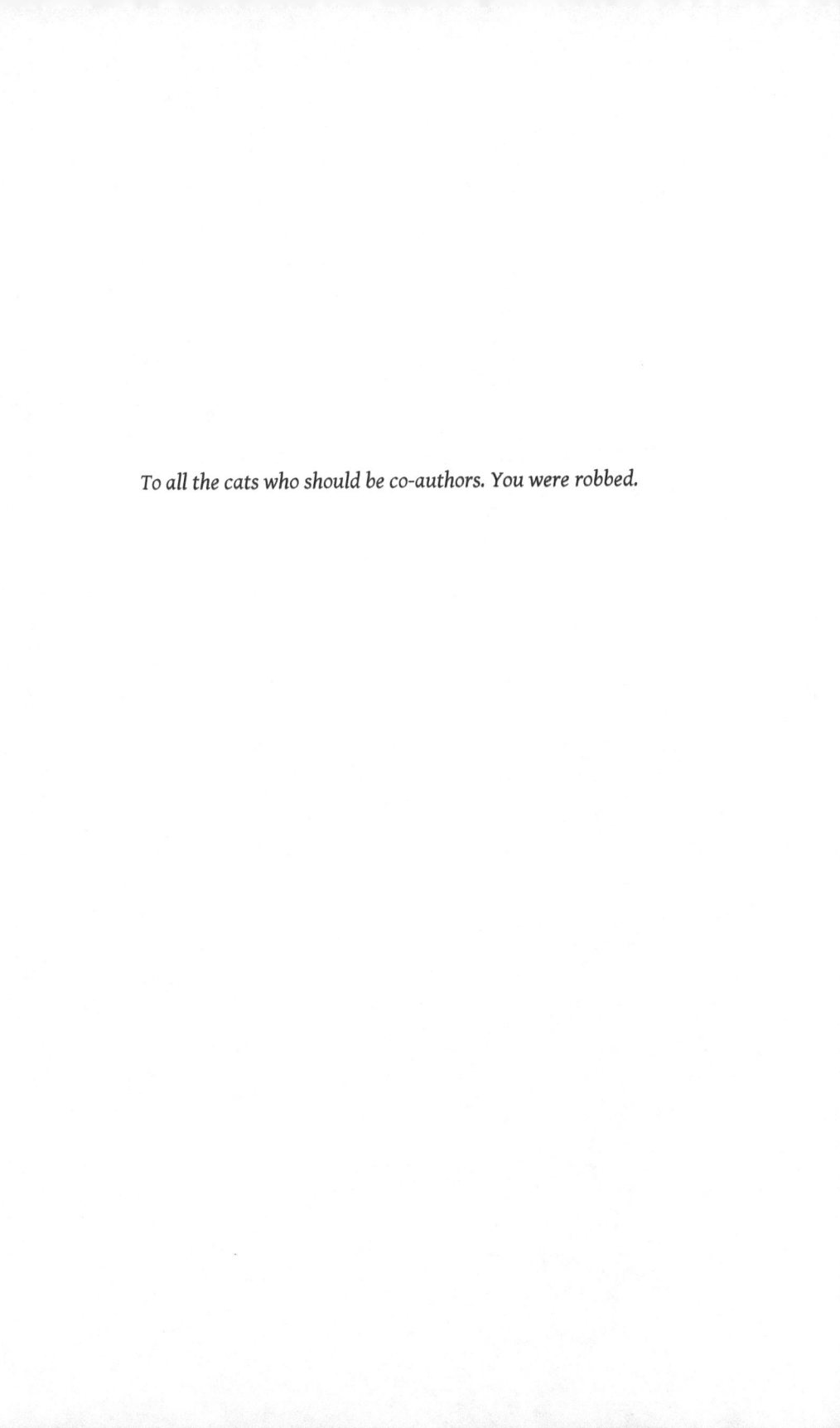

To all the cats who should be co-authors. You were robbed.

*E*ddy is dying again.

At least anaphylaxis is a novel diversion, and they say a change is as good as a rest. Eddy's throat itches. It starts as an annoyance, her maroon turtleneck sweater is too tight and she discreetly tugs at it, but soon she can't stand the pressure on irritated flesh. She tears at the collar until she finally gives in and pulls the whole thing off, lab safety and workplace etiquette be damned. Even that gives no relief. Eddy scratches at her neck, digs her nails in as if puncturing the skin could relieve the pressure. She's written about localized pain to the throat on countless patient summaries on countless clipboards—or the same clipboard in countless Instances—but she never thought about how much it would hurt. Eddy's thinking about it now.

François pushes a chair against the back of her calves and she collapses onto it gratefully. Tears blur her vision and she can't see anything when she checks her watch.

"Not long now," he reassures her, his voice soothing, his hand on her shoulder. She lifts her head to watch him but his figure is muddled, her vision won't snap into focus. His outline is cloudy and without form, a dark shape haloed by the fluorescent lights of the lab. His hand squeezes her shoulder and it's the only sensation left other than pain. "I'm here with you. It won't be much longer."

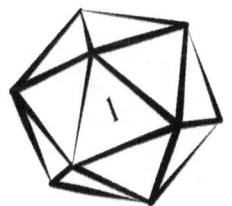

Dr. Gagnon came by when Eddy was drinking her third glass of wine on an empty stomach. He was the fourth person who'd made the trek to her session's corner of the conference hall, where Eddy's poster hung on the back of a fabric divider, behind a pillar. Time loops were a hot research topic. Theoretical studies on posited brain-wave changes during time loops, on the other hand, were about as well loved as *Attack of the Clones*. His grey eyes skimmed over her words, then over her — black pencil skirt, black blouse, black heels, like the reanimated corpse of a sexy librarian — and he smiled, bringing a warmth to his angled cheekbones and square chin.

Within moments, they were performing the traditional mating dance of academics in the wilds of a convention center. Eddy's internal monologue narrated in its best David Attenborough impression as Dr. Gagnon asked her to describe the poster and listened to her elevator pitch. He asked questions about reproducibility, she answered with statistics, and finally they were done with foreplay. He shifted in, closer to her, and she could feel her pulse race. It was time to talk science.

"Why do you discount the possibility of measurable changes to brain waves during Instances?" Dr. Gagnon asked, shoulders set as he faced her, confident in his challenge. Eddy met the intensity of his scrutiny with her own. "There were a number of subjects who experienced altered functioning of the occipital lobe when they returned to the regular timeline."

He paused, giving her a chance to respond. Before her mouth carried her away, Eddy saw something in his expression and paused, realizing, several beats too late, that he was talking about one of his own papers. That he expected her to have read.

Well, she hadn't.

Eddy was eight months away from failing to make tenure, currently living on her credit card and hopelessly behind in her marking. No one — not even the esteemed Dr. Gagnon — got to see her sweat. Despite everything, Eddy smiled back.

"We need to develop reliable methodologies for reporting," Eddy said, blithely sidestepping answering his question and offering him a word salad somewhere in the ballpark of the topic. It worked on her undergrad students. "It's fine if no one knows how the Instances work — that's a problem for engineers and philosophers. But we need to be sure that what subjects report from Instances is consistent with their experiences."

Dr. Gagnon's eyes twinkled as she spoke, as if he saw through her act and didn't care in the least. Eddy took a sip of her wine, a Malbec with a faint metallic aftertaste, but a lifesaver after standing this long in heels. She looked like a collected, highly professional academic, and not at all like an imposter conducting metastudies on other people's data, compiled from papers she'd barely skimmed.

"Ground-truthing gets cited well, but the funders don't care about it. You'd want to link it into a pre-existing study and use it to add value. Or say you're running a physiological study to compare what people admit to doing in a timeline without consequences to what they actually do. But getting a study to spy on people's inner lives through an Ethics review would be a nightmare."

His words made more sense than hers had, but it was his tone that got her, a conspiratorial whisper, something just for the two of them. She smelled his cologne, red brick, cypress, and rust, felt the heat of his breath on her skin as he leaned in. He must have been flirting with her.

"Ethics never lets us have any fun." She tilted her head at him, considering how to best cut through the Gordian knot. "You only need Ethics if you plan to publish."

"True," he agreed. "Industry loves their NDAs. But their money is less prestigious than the Research Councils. You want to have both." His words were technically accurate, but entirely irrelevant to the situation at hand.

Eddy laughed and hoped none of the bitterness came through. "You've got all the best kinds of problems." She glanced at her poster. "I don't need Ethics for theory."

It didn't really matter; the conference wasn't meant as palliative care for Eddy's critically ill research career. The point of attending was Wahid's coming out, her shy, brilliant PhD student forced to introduce himself to the bright lights of the field after a quietly delivered but intellectually stunning talk. She'd put money on him winning a best-talk award. As for her, she had Wahid's drink tickets to round out her own, and the unexpected bonus of someone interesting to talk to during her session.

"You will, when you test it," he said with too much assurance.

Eddy studied the certainty written on Dr. Gagnon's face. Part of her must have realized the situation the instant he asked his first question but understanding took its sweet time to filter through the rest of her wine-muddled brain.

Dr. François Gagnon had access to the Shadowrealm. Not computer simulations and anecdotal reports, but the real thing, Instances themselves.

Jealous anger bubbled up in her and she stepped back, out of the warm circle they'd formed, into the cold of the over-air-conditioned convention center. He'd dared enter her corner of the poster hall, come slumming to see how the peasants applied statistical models to his supplemental tables, a king watching them reach for the crumbs he distributed after a feast.

"It's a fascinating study. It would be a shame not to publish it," he said, like she was a PhD student nervous about rejection, not a professor with students of her own. Assistant professor, and student, singular. But Wahid was a very good one.

Eddy squinted to read the blue LEDs of the clock on the front wall. She still had two drink tickets left, thanks to the free glass from some company or other, and only another forty-five minutes of poster session left to endure. Wahid was meeting up with friends in town for dinner, which left Eddy blissfully free to eat a pizza-like food substance from room service and watch *Night Beats* reruns. To enjoy the good parts of travelling to a conference, such as they were.

"I'll put you down as a reviewer," Eddy said lightly. And her mother had thought she'd never learn tact. "What session are you in?" she asked, because he hadn't intended to tread on a raw nerve, and changing the subject was the thing an adult would do.

"I ran the session on Pharmaceutical Innovations this afternoon. Everyone wants to apply Instances to experimental drug testing. Allergy medication is the only thing we've gotten approval to run so far, but that's the tip of the iceberg," Dr. Gagnon said, waving expansively. "I'm sorry you missed it — I'd love to know your impressions. But these big conferences have too many parallel sessions."

He was wearing a navy jacket and a slate-blue collared shirt but had foregone the tie. A casual session chair. When she got home, Eddy was going to spite-read his papers, which was similar to normal reading but involved more swearing. His eyes searched hers, lingering, waiting for her answer, and maybe he wasn't lying.

"Allergy meds are a good start. I didn't think anything would be approved after the Washington incident," Eddy said with more regret than the statement deserved; she was just an educated bystander here. "It's too easy to falsify results, and there's so much money at stake."

"And lives," he added.

Eddy shook her head. "Do you count that? It was horrifying, but it established that if Dr. van Asshole plugs himself into a time loop and kills the Instance-version of you, you don't die in real life. It's not the instrument's fault — the real problem happened in the main timeline, not the pocket universe or a lucid dream or a parallel dimension or whatever happens when the subject isn't now. Isn't then? Wasn't now? Grammar is hard with time travel."

Eddy drank from her glass, only to notice that Dr. Gagnon's hands were both empty. His pinpoint-oxford shirt sleeve was a perfect half an inch longer than the end of his jacket. His nails were neatly trimmed, and his left hand sported a gold band.

"Indeed." And then, stupidly for such a seemingly intelligent man, he added, "If your Ethics Board is giving you trouble, I'd be happy to look over the paperwork for you. I'm curious what happens when we test your hypothesis."

He put a friendly hand on her shoulder, the weight of his fingers through her blouse somewhere between professional and familiar, suggesting more than an academic interest. He might still appreciate her scientific prowess, though; he understood her study, called it fascinating. Eddy went with flattered, not furious.

"It fails," she said earnestly. Intrigued, Dr. Gagnon raised his eyebrows, dark under salt-and-pepper black hair. "I'm sure of it. But I can't test it. My department can't afford to purchase an instrument for me, and the Research Council facility likes researchers with prior hands-on experience using known methods, not crazy people turning up and flipping switches."

"I've seen crazier." His fingers pressed more firmly through her clothing before pulling away. "And with less purpose. You should come to Ottawa and use mine. What semester are you free?"

This conversation was the closest Eddy had been to Instances since she'd watched a demo at a conference two years ago, one in a crowd of scientists eager for a glimpse at something that felt like magic. She'd had enough promising research conversations in her life to know that this one would come to nothing, but it was worth celebrating anyway. People without access to the Shadowrealm were forced to live in the moment. Eddy downed the rest of her glass of cheap red and pulled two drink tickets out of her badge with a flourish.

"Can I get you something? My treat."

"They don't have anything worth drinking," Dr. Gagnon objected, smiling. My, what big teeth he had. Straight and white, a man with a good dentist. "American beer and Californian wine."

"The selection by the industry booths was okay. I didn't look where it's from, but the wine tasted old enough to hold up its own head," Eddy offered. "They've got Prosecco too. Though I figure bubbles are wasted space."

"You're right," Dr. Gagnon said, smiling as he conceded the point, and Eddy felt a thrill of victory. "That's Reid Curtis, the defense contractor. He's celebrating his company's twenty-fifth birthday, and he won't serve something he wouldn't drink, but he's not willing to go bankrupt for the Ivory Tower. Though I'd argue a few academics are worth the expense of a good bottle." He held her gaze as he said it, eyes bestowing his favour. "The place across from the conference hotel has a decent selection."

As a scientist, Eddy excelled at pattern-recognition. For example, just then, she knew that she was taking the first step towards a poor life choice. "Sounds great."

"It's impossible," Eddy objected, loud enough that the black-clad waiter turned his head to check they didn't need anything. "Neural changes are physical changes. It doesn't matter when the fMRI says they occurred during the process. If they occurred in simultaneous but offset time, then eating would work too and whatshername from MTV wouldn't be dead and Ethics wouldn't require a full novel to get a haircut in the Shadowrealm."

François took a sip of his wine, hand pressed against the glass, the stem held firmly between two fingers. "The Shadowrealm?" he asked, and Eddy flushed. She hadn't meant him to catch that.

"The Instances. I teach my students using examples from *Night Beats*."

She was not going to tell him that her cat was named Lilith, because she had some dignity and a professional reputation to maintain.

"You don't reference the first time-loop episode? It's the same fundamental principle as Instances. And there's more ghostly shenanigans than the Fae plotline. They practically dropped Brent in the second season."

Given the massive popularity of *Night Beats*, it shouldn't have been so difficult for Eddy to find someone to talk to about both pharmaceutical testing protocols and the physics of the show. There was something faintly pathetic that at forty, Eddy still couldn't find any work friends who shared her extracurriculars. A situation that would shortly solve itself, when tenure review came up and she didn't make it. She took another sip of wine, finger idly tracing the delicate curvature of the glass. It was better even than the stuff the industry reps were giving away. She'd count tonight as a perk of the job, to balance out the mountain of essays she'd be coming home to.

"Monica Keeling," she said, remembering. "That's the name of the MTV host who died of hypoglycemia. I tell the kids — the students — it's like eating in the Fae Kingdom and I show the clip of Jane switching from salad to cake. We don't know if Ms. Keeling took her glucose pills in her Instance, but it didn't work if she did. It couldn't work."

The waiter was refilling Eddy's glass before it emptied, so she had no chance to count her drinks. It didn't really matter. She'd committed to this bad idea, and she intended to see it through.

François nodded and said, "I should try that analogy. Though perhaps not when I'm doing outreach." He lifted a slice of bruschetta and pushed the plate towards her with his other hand. "Brain scans show the subject responds to Instance stimuli."

Eddy shook her head at his statement, but she picked up a slice and moved it to her plate. He smiled at her, satisfied, and she might have tried to unravel the smug edge to his expression if she wasn't distracted watching his mouth on his wine glass, the movements of his throat as the liquid disappeared. Watching him return the glass to the live-edge walnut bar top with sinuous hands, carefully adjusting its position as if to fulfil some unfathomable requirement of etiquette.

"Only when they're evaluated after the patient returns, and the subject's account of their experiences can be incorporated in the output. If it actually worked, someone would've figured out how to make it predictive so they could anticipate what the patient experienced before they came back," Eddy countered, deploying the fraction of her brain still focused on the meaning of his words rather than the shape of his mouth.

"Isn't that what your study suggests? Modelling the brain-wave outputs to visualize the experiences in real time."

It was nice to meet someone nerdy enough to reciprocate her incomprehensible technobabble. There couldn't have been more than a full dozen people deep enough in Eddy's niche subfield for that, and François had broad shoulders and liked *Night Beats*.

"I suggest it, but only because when it fails it'll prove my theory right." Eddy frowned, picked at a stray tomato that had escaped its bready habitat, and caught François' eyes following her motion. "I can't afford to buy the instrumentation, let alone run it. But it wouldn't be too difficult to add the tests on top of whatever you're doing anyway, and if you can afford Instances you can afford an MRI machine. It's just time to analyse the data, and I've got that. Like you said, it's value-added." She'd have time soon, anyway. The world was full of bright sides.

When they finished drinking and eating — mostly drinking — François didn't show her the bill, just put down his credit card and wrote a tip. In some distant memory, Eddy remembered that she'd offered to treat. Instead, she leaned towards him, fingers reaching for his clean-shaven cheek as her mouth sought his. Only to be gently rebuffed.

"I'm married," he said, his hand out, his golden ring flashing like a talisman.

It was late, and the restaurant was dim; he might have missed seeing her back stiffen as she jerked away, her face redden with mingled confusion and embarrassment. Maybe it would make sense when she was sober.

Eddy took a deep breath in, running her eyes down the boxy edges of the Instance hardware in Dr. Gagnon's lab. A glossy touch screen graced the sap-green metal casing which enclosed the wiring heart of the machine. A series of twisted black cords snaked out from plastic edging and linked it to the desktop computer, another to a fist-sized box with a joystick and a handful of buttons. The chair in the centre was worn, creases on the black fabric marking the passage of scores of grad students into their own pasts. It was one of the most beautiful things Eddy had ever seen. Her hand came up, as if to touch the raised lettering of the company logo, but she saw Dr Gagnon watching her, grey eyes bright, and she brought her hand back to her side.

Eddy hadn't listed him as a reviewer when she submitted the work from her poster as a scientific manuscript, but for all she knew he'd been one of the anonymous reviewers. Less than a week after it was accepted, François had emailed her and asked if she could recommend someone for a short-term postdoc position, examining time-loop responses from a psychological perspective. Eddy's list had her own name at the top.

"I can't let you try it yet," he told her with something almost like regret. "There's insurance, and the warranty, and Ethics approvals to consider." His mouth quirked up in a smile, and he was exactly as hot as she remembered. "There's much less red tape if you take the job."

Eddy grinned, her gaze drifting from his face back to the hardware. The controller waited, resting in the middle of the black seat, enticing her. "When do I start?"

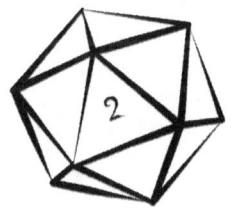

*E*ddy looks down at her empty hand, but that's meaningless. She let the ball fall before she entered the Shadowrealm. What matters is that it's not bouncing on the floor. Beside her, François explains which buttons to press, the sensations to expect, and she shushes him with an impatient wave.

"I know. You already told me."

François falls silent, watching Eddy explore. She checks the time on her phone — three minutes behind what it said in the Middlerealm — and her watch — one minute behind. Her watch running fast didn't matter to Eddy before François gave her access to time loops. She pulls out the pin to reset her watch but stops when she realizes François is chuckling.

"There's no point trying to change anything here. You have to do it in real time." Despite his playful tone, Eddy's embarrassed, betrayed by her instincts. She knows she can't change anything. She also knows that her embarrassment is nonsensical. François won't remember what Eddy did in the Shadowrealm when she gets back to the Middlerealm. He holds out the fluorescent green ball to her. "Give it another ninety seconds or so before you drop it. It'll still be going here when you leave, but it'll have run out in real time." He's a patient teacher, or the time loop gives Eddy the illusion he is.

"Tell me something," she says as she takes the ball. The faux-rubber texture is vaguely unpleasant. "Something I don't know in real time."

He laughs again. Normally clean-shaven, there are hints of grey stubble coming through. Between marking, lab inspections and preparing to host Kit's external examiner, he's had a long week. "Where to begin?" He pauses for a moment, considering, before, "The Departmental sign-off to let you use the Shadowrealm hasn't come through yet."

Eddy grins, delighted at his use of the term, and drops the ball.

"I'm throwing a defense party for Kit at my place," François told Eddy. "Thursday at 7. You're welcome to bring a partner." A partner rather than a husband. How progressive of him. Someone had dragged Howard Stark all the way to the early 2000s. Eddy had avoided post-work socializing with her new group for three weeks, but she couldn't put it off forever.

"Just me," Eddy said. "What can I bring?" She'd gotten a bottle of champagne for her first MSc student when he graduated. The authentic stuff from France, though Eddy was only a co-supervisor. A box of David's Tea for her first and only solo supervised MSc. If Eddy hadn't left, eventually she would've figured out something for Wahid. Fancy flavoured coffee, maybe. She still might. The university hadn't let her continue to supervise as a postdoc, let alone one employed at a different institution, but Wahid had sent round a manuscript to edit and her name was second. He hadn't even acknowledged his new PI. And Eddy thought she'd always be the least politically astute person in any room.

"Don't worry about it," François responded, casually generous, and she nodded. No one expected Eddy to go to any great lengths for someone else's student. She had only met the girl a couple times at group meeting, anyway. It was pointless to guess her tastes.

The gunmetal grey of François' shirt brought out the colour of his eyes and complemented his burgundy sweater vest. Eddy should have been ashamed of herself. His outfit screamed Tory, and she was still there for it. Maybe the colour was a subtle hint he was a red Tory, and Eddy's questionable taste in men wouldn't bring quite as much dishonour to the empire. The woman beside him — presumably the wife he'd claimed at the conference — noticed where François was looking and gave Eddy a smile. It was warm and full, but didn't quite reach her brown eyes, as deep and mournful as a Margaret Keane painting. She hovered close to François, graceful fingers tucking a strand of dark hair behind a delicate ear before adjusting red-framed glasses. François leaned in to kiss her, before placing his hand on her back and moving them both to Eddy.

"This is Mara, my wife," he said, running a hand around the waist of her periwinkle skirt as he introduced her. "And this is Eddy." His tone was cordial but professional. Eddy reached to shake Mara's hand and was met with a jolt of static, a spark of electric resonance bridging the space between their skin. Eddy should have pulled away at the shock of it, but her hand lingered for a moment, remembering the sensation as they shook.

"We have cheese," Mara declared brightly and slightly incongruously, startled, perhaps, at the sudden connection. "Unless you're vegan. We still have cheese if you're vegan. But you can't eat it." She turned her face to François. His expression softened as he met her gaze. "François, you didn't tell me what she eats, she can't just have celery sticks and ranch dressing. I don't think ranch dressing is vegan either." Her voice got faster and breathier as she spoke.

François pet the pastel yellow shoulder of Mara's sweater, the gesture familiar to Eddy by now. "I would've told you if there was anything to worry about. Eddy is perfectly agreeable."

"I eat everything," Eddy lied, since the odds of okra or mozuku seaweed showing up at the snack table were very low. "Point me at the cheese and let me loose."

Mara shifted her weight, centering herself. When François released her, his hand slid along her hip as if unwilling to let go. The pleated layers of her skirt settled back into place once he was gone, without a crease or wrinkle. Alone, Mara drew inward, tightly held within herself, giving nothing away.

"This way," she motioned to Eddy, playing the part of a gracious host. "You're his new postdoc, right? He's always talking about you."

"That's me," Eddy confirmed. Their house was tastefully decorated with oak furniture and grey chevron curtains, exactly as Eddy would have expected if she'd bothered to think about it. "His group's massive but I'm the only postdoc. You must be sick of throwing parties, with all the thesis defenses."

Mara's smile lasted only an instant, a fractional break in the tension she carried. "I always wonder, what do I do if they fail? But then they never do." The cheese selection was as grand as Mara had implied. The celery sticks were obviously an afterthought, their greenery out of place among the white, orange and blue. Even the napkins, bearing stately charcoal sketches of birds, belonged in a magazine photoshoot. Mara looked critically at her creation. "I always want more vegetables. They're working on medicines, they should know how to be healthy. But no one eats them."

Eddy took a stalk. She dipped it in baked brie on the way to her mouth, but it still counted. It took strenuous chewing to overcome the fibrous strings. She'd forgotten that she also hated celery. "They're young and invincible. Besides, they still think they'll invent their own cures." Eddy was going to make it through this celery stick. Afterwards, she was never going to pick up another one, no matter how glad Mara had been, the edges of her face softening to reveal a pleasing roundness.

"They won't, though." Overcome by her own certainty, Mara backtracked at once. "I mean, they're not the kind of doctor that prescribes things." She looked down at her hands. "I'm sure your work is very difficult."

"Not really," Eddy said with more honesty than she offered to students or funders. "Most of it is less complicated than programming a

VCR." Eddy grimaced. "I made the mistake of using that as a reference in one of my classes, you know. A bunch of the kids didn't even know what it was. I've never felt so old." Not-teaching was a definite perk of Eddy's demotion. There was something luxurious about only doing research, navigating the political whims of an individual instead of committees, completely ignoring the existence of undergrads except when they held up the lines at Tim Hortons. François wanted her to manage the next cohort of Honours projects, but at least by fourth year most of them had worked out how to do their own laundry. Besides, that was ages away.

"Kids do that," Mara commiserated. "Joseph — my son — he's fourteen. He wasn't born when the planes hit the Twin Towers. He doesn't know that Sharon visited the Dome of the Rock or about the Russian invasion of Chechnya. All these times that seemed so important and he doesn't understand." Mara picked up a celery stick and took a bite, her face perfectly relaxed, raising the frightening possibility that she actually liked the things. She hadn't even put dressing on it. The woman had superpowers, and Eddy was in awe. "But then, he's lucky not to know. A clean slate." Mara finished the stick and automatically took another. Maybe she wanted something to do with her hands, but she was eating the stalks, not holding them. Eddy couldn't look away, nude lipstick against pale green, teeth cutting through fibrous sinew, a satisfying crunch.

"Seriously though, you could do anything we do in the lab. You'd be as good as any of the grad students." Eddy let her gaze cover the range of students milling around the sound system and by the liquor cabinet, as well as the banistered staircase above which Joseph was presumably sleeping. Not sleeping. What time did fourteen-year-olds go to bed? At fourteen, though, he'd be starting to think of himself as an adult. Maybe he didn't have a bedtime. Eddy shuddered internally. "Better. There's studies. Video games rotted their brains and they don't know how to focus without an achievement bar to grind towards. They need something shiny to validate their existence."

"If they want a gold star, I have plenty of stickers left from Library

Reading Hours. It works for preschoolers." Mara kept her voice low, but no one was listening to the middle-aged women who'd absconded with the greenery.

"I'll take you up on that," Eddy promised, because it was a hilarious idea, because it was a reason to contact Mara again, and because it would probably work. Going for broke, Eddy added, "Have you ever been in an Instance?" Eddy, Queen of Solid Life Choices, suavely asking her new crush on a date to her other crush's workplace. Who was also her husband. Relationships were even more convoluted than time-travel grammar. "I could use a lab assistant, and it's fun."

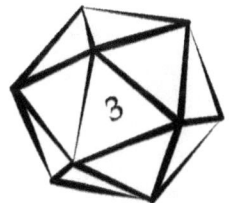

*T*he disconcerting thing about the Shadowrealm is how similar it is to the Middlerealm. Not even similar. Precisely the same. Eddy keeps expecting cracks or sepia filters or lens flare. She's up to an hour in the Shadowrealm, replaying her Middlerealm timeline, an exact rerun of her workaday existence, or it would be if she could perfectly replicate her actions from the first go around. Her body is locked securely in François' lab, her mind equally safe in either realm.

Eddy's still uncertain with the Instances, and, working alone, she has a shudder of terror that she's done something wrong. Not moved at all, or sent herself back too far and she's trapped in the Shadowrealm for years, Eddy van Winkle, waking up to find all her shows were cancelled seasons ago and Tumblr is full of spoilers. Eddy checks her watch. She'd bought herself a new one with François' grant money: a diver's watch, black face with a red and blue bezel. It looks like a Pepsi can, but it's presumably meant to represent something about running out of oxygen. Most people care more about breathing than they do about snacks.

She's got fifty-eight minutes left. She appreciated François' help, but he's already spent more time beside her than she expected. He doesn't have time to linger with individual researchers as they learn the equipment. She should ask one of the grad students to work alongside her, if she cares about following the *laboratory safety regulations.*

The point of today's experiment is establishing baselines. Spend as much of the hour as Eddy can manage in comfortable boredom. Eddy remembers sitting in dentists' waiting rooms as a teenager, before she had a cell phone, the same songs repeating on the radio, magazines with dating advice that even then she recognized as counterproductive. But Eddy's a m and she's long since acclimated herself to the glorious present where patience is a lost art, so watching the clock is mind-numbing. Last time she tried this experiment, she fell asleep almost immediately and ruined her null signal. She's determined not to do it again.

Eddy checks her watch. Fifty-seven minutes. She stares at the black face, at the silver hands counting down the minutes on the red and blue bezel. She should have bought a stopwatch, or a dive computer, but she likes the analog device, solid and regular on her wrist. She's trying not to think about Wahid muddling his way through his first paper revisions without her, about who got stuck with her marking when she quit in the middle of term, about getting back to the Middlerealm and spending the rest of the day with conducting gel matting her hair. fMRI signals are more granular than EEG and they leave the subject less sticky, but even François can't magic up funding to buy an MRI without pilot data. Maybe Eddy did something wrong after all, and time's moving more slowly than usual. A second ticks by, and Eddy's convinced it took too long. She watches another go by, and another.

Eddy brought a notebook and pen to the weekly group meeting, and tried not to be too obvious that she was doodling rather than taking notes. The PhD student with brown hair in a ponytail was presenting, but it would be unkind to tell her to stop talking to her feet, so Eddy focused instead on her artistic rendition of a City Council meeting in the Shire. The Sackville-Baggins were presenting a petition. Eddy kept erasing and redrawing their papers, unsure how many signatures they'd get. They weren't very popular in the Shire, but the Goblin tariffs on pipe-weed was an issue that affected everyone. She added an extra spiral of parchment and considered the effect with a discerning eye.

"Have you encountered this before, Eddy?" François asked. He must have realized she hadn't encountered the idea this time — he'd been watching her sketch all meeting, his eyes trailing her hand across the page — but gently shaming the inattentive group member was fair play. A necessary part of a strong research culture. Eddy looked up at the overly wordy PowerPoint slide and replayed the last five seconds of talk in her head.

"Not this exact scenario," she said, playing for time while she waited for her thoughts to cohere. "But some questions aren't answered by studying real-time responses. We might need to consider environmental determinants of health." The unfortunate presenter — Lydia, that was her name — looked panicked, eyes wide as she tried to muddle out a connection between Eddy's words and the occasional side effects in her stage one trials. François' brows furrowed, momentarily flummoxed by Eddy's word-salad diversion, and Eddy was going to pull this one out of the fire. François was clever, would see through her feint in a few seconds, but none of the students would know a thing. "Have you collected any data on the background of the participants? Even their postal address and whether they're students or not might tell us something, though socioeconomic status would be better. We'll need to go through Ethics to get approval to use the data." In retrospect, volunteering to collaborate with a first-year PhD might have been a somewhat extreme response to the risk of slight embarrassment. Now was the time for frantic backpedaling. "But I think you're worrying too much, Lydia. The side effects are minor and barely above statistical noise when you compare them to the placebo. Besides, this is why we test their reactions in the Shadowrealm first." Eddy used her soothing, teacherly voice, and hoped for the best. Francois' mouth curled upwards with a hint of a smile, and for a moment she thought she'd amused him enough to get away with it, shivered in delight at her success.

"It's worth investigating," Francois approved, nominally addressing

Lydia. "She's right, you should go ahead with the study. But if the participant data exists, why let it go to waste?" Eddy, striking out with François, yet again.

"We could broaden the study," Owen suggested, and Eddy knew she was doomed. If Golden Boy seconded the motion, it carried. "If we have to do a new Ethics approval, we could get it to cover all the drug trials in our group instead of just Lydia's."

"Did anyone see last night's episode?" Owen had to be talking about *Night Beats*. It was the only thing anyone still watched on syndicated TV. Eddy focused intently on her laptop screen as she filled in an Ethical Approval Application. No foetal material. No recently dead. No vampire/werewolf non-canon pairings. Last night's episode was queer-baiting, PG-13 soft-porn trash, and Eddy was here for it and she would brook no dissent. "Jordan's backflips with handcuffs on, seriously. I need to try that."

"You'll break something," Lydia countered. "He's got a stunt double. Regular people aren't that flexible." Lydia was more confident when she was wrong about television than when she was right about her project. Someone needed to talk to her about imposter syndrome.

"I'll be a stunt double then," Owen agreed. "My second career." Oh, to be young and naive enough to believe in careers. Owen was the type to make it, if anyone could. Though not as a stunt double for Jordan.

"The actor trained as a gymnast," Eddy informed the ignorant Youths. She hadn't meant to use her teacher-voice. "He's got more range in his hips than his facial expressions." Lydia, at least, laughed at that. Even die-hard Jordan stans ought to acknowledge that he was a bit of a blank slate. "Jane's got a stunt double, you can see the height difference sometimes." Eddy could list the episodes and scenes, if anyone doubted her. Probably not the timestamps.

"I want a stunt double." Lydia sighed wistfully. "She can write my proposal for me." Lydia was unnecessarily terrified of a ten-page write-up, including figures. She was horrified when François wouldn't define the corresponding word count — it took her nearly a day to recover. "Or an Evil Twin."

François walked in, with perfect timing, or it would have been if he was a twin; Eddy mentally chided herself for inconsistent characterization. "Sorry I'm late," he said, not offering an explanation. He wasn't usually, which made it forgivable. She gave him a once-over, assessing. A powder-blue collar peeked out underneath his cadet-grey sweater. Black slacks and leather shoes made it a perfectly ordinary Tuesday outfit. A video conference, maybe, or he got distracted editing.

"What did you think of the episode?" Eddy asked without preamble. It wasn't exactly a test, but he claimed to watch. He should know what she meant.

"Mara liked it," François hedged. Eddy frowned at him. Coward. He relented at her glare. "The Doppelganger plotline covered the same ground already, and it was better. They foreshadowed the switch that time."

He was right, but Eddy didn't want to admit it. "Last night had Brent. Ghostly shenanigans?" She looked plaintively at him, an expression which had so far failed to get her into his pants or out of writing an Ethics Approval Application, but which might be sufficient to change his mind about an hour of television.

"It did," François agreed. "His pun at the end justified the whole thing." François wasn't typically one to pace. His meandering ended behind Eddy's chair, close enough that she could imagine the wool of his sweater brushing against her arm as she typed. She didn't lean back, didn't press against his chest. Didn't feel it rise and fall behind her scalp. "Have you made any progress?"

Eddy wasn't sure if he meant her project or the one she now shared with Lydia. Probably the second one, given the context, but the answer was the same either way. "I don't think so?" Paperwork didn't count as progress.

"What's the problem?" If François was standing unusually close, surely Lydia or Owen would've noticed, would have said something. It crossed Eddy's mind, for an instant, that if she re-lived this moment in the Shadowrealm, she would have the courage to turn around and see for herself. She abandoned the thought as quickly as it occurred. François had made his intentions clear. Rejection in an alternative timeline would still be rejection.

"Lots of things." That phrase covered this situation and every other situation in Eddy's life. Efficiency was a blessing. "I'd like to work without administrators looking over my shoulder, if you don't mind." She could feel his silently shared amusement, not to be let on to the students. "Oh, and hook me up with the local hospital so I can get access to an MRI machine. There's only so far an EEG can get you."

François pulled out the chair to sit next to her, opening his notebook. "I'll see what I can manage."

A series of unremarkable 8.5 by 11 printouts sit on the bench in front of Eddy. She doesn't know the specifics of each image. If there's one thing computers are good at, it's randomization. Her head itches, knowing she's not to disturb the electrodes conducting between her brain and the detector, and she's already bored. If at first you don't succeed, repeat your failure twice more so it's statistically significant. The initial EEG results were as rubbish as Eddy predicted, but not in any useful way. Eddy scratches her head, getting goop on her hands, disturbing the sticky by her ear and pulling her hair in the process.

The images are designed to be neutral, whatever that means. A crisp, perfect red apple floating in a black background. A rack of shirts in a messy closet, an Edison bulb, and then, impossibly, a baby's head and limbless torso in a jar — formaldehyde — a worn strip of white fabric tight around the neck, her eyes as wide as its own. The image in just enough colour to highlight the whiteness of his skin, and Eddy's hand, mindless, automatically flips to the next image: Christmas lights across an orchard, a stack of tires, it doesn't matter, Eddy's eyes glaze over the next pictures without seeing them.

The photo shouldn't have been in the database. It shouldn't exist. Someone fucked up. Or, François added it to the database deliberately, but Eddy doubts he has the technical ability. He has a key to the lab, and he could have physically added the photo to her stack. Anyone in the group could have, but Eddy can't imagine anyone other than François would. It's one more data point towards elucidating what he actually hired Eddy to investigate, what François wants but won't ask for. What secrets he needs the Shadowrealm to reveal.

The thought prompts Eddy to the computer. She glances at her watch. Not enough time for a proper synthesis of the data through ten thousand Bayesian replicates. The raw data is accessible but meaningless, squiggles approximating intention, the sum total of her existence as a dozen points sliding along an arbitrary baseline. She can see the blip where she moved the electrode, and she does it again to be sure.

Eddy stares at the lines, willing them into meaning. She's looking for a jump, something loud enough to stand out against the noise. She imagines the black squiggles forming into eyes, glassy and black, almost doll-like, staring back at her, no blood, no hint of a struggle. Do babies struggle for life? Maybe they do. Maybe, buried deep in the random fluctuations, there's a pattern. She can't know for sure until she gets back to the Middlerealm, but it's worth testing.

"Mara!" Eddy's volume when she caught sight of Mara in the departmental foyer was inappropriate for the workplace, but Mara flashed a grin at her. Worth it.

"I'm heading to the office," she said, slowing enough for Eddy to join her. She resumed her pace when Eddy caught up and patted a quilted dusty rose Hermes purse. "François forgot his meds."

"I didn't realize he was sick," Eddy remarked, more curious than concerned. She'd have sensed it if François was dying. Blood pressure medication was consistent with the demands of his position and the occasional tremor of worry Eddy felt off him. Besides, Mara was determined rather than tense or scared, slate-blue kitten heels landing at regular intervals on the worn departmental carpet.

"Migraines," Mara told her, sighing. "He works too hard." She spoke with the same tone with which one might describe days shortening in winter or brown-outs in summer, an immutable law of nature. Mara fumbled in her purse for a second, steps not slowing as her hand moved, and emerged with a slightly crumpled white sheet. "I hoped I'd run into you. I brought you stickers."

Eddy beamed. Mara had remembered. More than that, the stickers she'd picked for Eddy were amazing, brightly coloured, anime-ish cats with word bubbles saying things like, 'Good job' and 'You're a star.' Eddy had great taste in women. "Thanks. Did I tell you I've got a cat?"

Mara shook her head, a bob of black hair falling around her pale face. "Can I see a picture? After I give François his meds. He brought the wrong bottle to work and no amount of vitamin C is going to make the aura go away."

After François recovered, Eddy would laugh at him. "He won't catch a cold, anyway."

Mara acknowledged the joke with a gentle nod, also not laughing. She turned the door handle of François' office to reveal him sitting in near darkness. He looked utterly miserable, hunched over, vulnerable in a way Eddy had never imagined him. Eddy would have gone to him, smoothed his hair and lied that it was all going to be fine, but of course that's why Mara was there. "Zeeskeit, darling, I'm sorry," she said softly, lovingly, two white pills in her palm. Mara glanced at Eddy. "Can you get him a glass of water?"

"Her name is Lilith," Eddy explained as Mara scrolled through an embarrassingly long album of cat photos on Eddy's phone. "Vee and I lived in an old house that was converted into apartments, in a postage stamp on the ground floor. There was no AC so when Vee was in the field I'd leave all the doors open for a cross-breeze. And one day Lilith walked in and started meowing at me for attention. I opened a can of tuna and we've been together ever since. Lilith, not Vee." Eddy hadn't seen her ex since she got the job in Fort McMurray, but occasionally Vee messaged demanding status updates on Lilith.

"She's beautiful," Mara said. Clearly Mara also had good taste. "You'll have to introduce me." Her brow creased and she added, "I meant to ask you over for dinner with me and François and Joseph. I don't know — you can bring Lilith I guess? Does she like smoked salmon? I can get tuna instead. I don't know very much about cats except they like boxes. You probably shouldn't bring Lilith. I do want to meet her, though. She looks soft."

Eddy managed to keep a straight face through the onslaught. She put a steadying hand on Mara's forearm. "I'll have you over some time. Lilith is a bit of a shut-in."

Mara relaxed against Eddy's hand with a slow breath out. "That's good. Are you busy next Saturday?"

Eddy's nonexistent social life, rebounding to her benefit. "I'm all yours." It was past time for Eddy to move back and she reluctantly withdrew her fingers, half-convinced she could see the imprint of shared warmth through Mara's raw-silk sleeve.

Tinder was a dangerous app for an academic, but Eddy wasn't a professor anymore, and she'd rented an apartment miles from the student district for a reason. She only hesitated a little at picking a photo with her face in it, smiling brightly at the camera while holding a drink with an umbrella in it for someone's birthday. She needed something to balance it out so she didn't look like an alcoholic. A book signing, Eddy and friends beaming next to an exhausted Ryan North, showing off copies of *Machine of Death*. An alcoholic nerd. She tried to find one of herself outdoors, or failing that, in natural light. Maybe Eddy was a vampire. Or maybe she'd lost any semblance of hobbies, or work-life balance, or balance at all, really, and suddenly devoid of responsibility she was floundering for meaning in an absurdist reality. She found one from a con, taken under fluorescent lights but technically shot in the daytime, the picture only a few years old. Eddy was a vampire, but a hot one, dressed like Lilith from the season four finale in steamtrollop dress with a bustle and corset, Jordan collapsed at her feet with puncture marks on his neck.

What was she even looking for? Someone who wouldn't get her fired would be a nice start. She tried to read meaning in the manufactured photos, an intentionality to lure her in. Jessie liked climbing and skiing, presumably to escape the Russian spies hunting him down after he turned double-agent. Kim looked soulfully at the camera in a low-cut black evening gown, confident that the poison was in her companion's champagne flute. Eddy swiped left on her too.

"New plan, Lilith," Eddy announced. Lilith, a grey puffball with one white sock, flicked her ears at her name but gave no other indication that she was paying attention. It deeply affronted her dignity when Eddy picked her up and held her like a baby. "I've kept you in kibble and litter for eight years. Your turn to make it in the big wide world, I'm going to be the shut-in who sleeps til eleven, screams at the walls, eats some lunch and goes back to bed." Lilith had climbed up Eddy's sweater like a tree and perched on Eddy's shoulder. A pirate cat. It was patently unfair that dogs were allowed in the workplace but Lilith wasn't. Not that Lilith needed the Shadowrealm to live blissfully free of any conception of consequences.

Kyle was Hollywood plain-looking, a poorly defined jawline consigning him to life as a sidekick, hair just shy of true blond. All his photos were of activity, cycling without holding the handlebars, water polo, ultimate frisbee. Team sports, even. They'd have nothing in common. But then his bio said he worked at Bed, Bath, and Beyond, and Eddy thought of an excellent joke from Tumblr, so she swiped right. It seemed as good a reason as any.

Eddy frowns at the collection of bottles on three benchtops in front of her. "No eating in the lab," she tells herself sternly, not that she worries about Health and Safety shutting her down in the Shadowrealm. Or in the Middlerealm. University administration is as inept here as anywhere Eddy worked, reliable only in its consistent lack of ability. Poisoning herself with residual something

from the grad students' pharmaceuticals is more likely. Unless it's fast-acting, consequences won't carry over to the Middlerealm. Maybe not even then. The public's favourite question about Instances, still unanswered. If you die in the Shadowrealm, do you die in real life?

What Eddy is worrying about is what she, in her infinite wisdom, has assigned herself for this afternoon. Eddy needs signal to drown out the noise, and she's fresh out of photos of murdered babies, no thank you François, though Eddy hasn't mustered up the courage to ask if it was him in any Realm. It didn't even work, to her Middlerealm self's disappointment, and there's only so much suffering she'll endure without a data-point as reward. What Eddy does have is hot sauce. Endless bottles, scores of flavours. Lydia's mom is an aficionado and Owen pitched in. Eddy recognises Owen's contributions, Tabasco sauce, Frank's, sriracha. She's never even heard of the things Lydia brought in. Ignorance was bliss.

There's a metal spoon on the lab bench next to the bottles and Eddy imagines it corroding, melting under the onslaught of '1 million Scoville units of agony.' She imagines her esophagus following suit, bubbling and boiling away, tendrils of smoke rising up at the contact with stomach acid before the flames consume her, a modern-day Joan of Arc. She's being ridiculous. No one's ever died from hot sauce.

No one has before, and no one will today.

"Nope," Eddy declares firmly to the empty lab. "Fuck this." She sweeps the bottles to the floor with a wave of her arm. Disappointingly, none of them break, though one of them rolls to oblivion underneath the far lab bench. RIP, Acid Rain. All the bottles are now consigned to oblivion when Eddy's Instance is done and she returns to the Middlerealm. Acid Rain will face its destiny alone, in the dark, and Eddy doesn't feel the slightest bit sorry.

This experiment is doomed to failure, but Eddy will come up with something else to try. She has the impeccable track record of an academic who's faked her way through interviews, paper revisions and grant applications, everything up to tenure review. She'll think of something. She always does. What she's thinking of right now is the 150,000 word Cosima/Delphine fanfic that she stayed up 'till four AM to read and didn't finish. In the Shadowrealm, there's nothing to stop her *from going to François' office, sitting in his leather rolly chair, and drinking his Nespresso while she reads.*

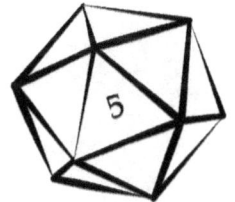

E ddy wasn't going to win a staring contest with Lilith. Defeated, Eddy collapsed on the bed beside her cat and rubbed the spot where her tail met her back. Lilith accepted her tribute with purrs as a cloud of pale fur rose from Lilith's undercoat to settle on Eddy's black dress. There would be a Lilith-shaped patch on her chest all evening, assuming Lilith ever agreed to stop sitting on her outfit and let Eddy put it on. The spot would be plenty soft, but there was no way Eddy could convince Mara to pet it.

"It's not a date," Eddy explained to the skeptical Lilith. "I know that. I'm going to wear a black dress, but it's not little. It's plausible-deniability hot, not date-hot. A scoop neck but I'm flat enough that it's respectable. You know I own a dress made entirely of leather. If you don't move, I'll wear that instead."

Lilith watched her intently, not blinking. Eddy's bluff had been called. She needed to change tactics.

"You can shed all you like on this one. I've got backups. Most of my closet is professional-hot black dresses. Not that it matters. Normal humans don't invite you for a first-date threesome with their husband, and Mara is a perfectly normal human." Eddy reconsidered her words. Inadequate and unfair characterization. "Emphasis on perfect," she clarified for Lilith. "You'll like her."

"I brought wine," Eddy said. She'd done her research on the bottle. Châteauneuf-du-Pape, ranked 91 on a website where nothing Eddy bought for herself rated above 79, no offense taken, *Wine Spectator*. Wahid's revisions had taken less time than the selection. But Joseph had opened the door, not François, and he looked young enough to make Eddy reconsider her stance that undergraduates were babies. That would make Joseph barely a fetus. Eddy couldn't give him the bottle. He was hardly old enough to be trusted with juice.

Joseph reached out his hand, a gangly confidence in his movements, and Eddy passed over the wine despite herself. He carried himself with François' self-assurance, an expectation that the established order of the world would conform to his preconceptions, and Eddy could only wish she'd had half as much certainty at fourteen. Or forty. Maybe the world was kinder to boys with rich parents. "Mame's in the kitchen," he explained. "The roast's cooking slow." Had Eddy misjudged the time? François had passed on Mara's request for 6:30. Mara was probably panicking, eyes glued to the meat-thermometer, quietly debating the risks of turning up the oven temperature. Or maybe something had been lost in communication and rich-people society dictated a fashionable half-an-hour late to dinner as well as to cocktails. Joseph's nonchalant demeanour gave no hint of what state he'd left Mara in. Maybe everything was absolutely fine, and Eddy was the one freaking out for no reason, or more accurately, for the reason that it had been a very long time since Eddy had been on a first not-date. Unless Kyle counted, in which case it had been seven days exactly. It would take an expert in classification to determine if what Eddy and Kyle did last Saturday met the legal definition of a date, or not-date, or both. "I can take your jacket."

The plan was for Mara and/or François to see Eddy in her leather rocker jacket and be overcome with desire, or mildly intrigued with desire, or at least appreciate her rad outfit. But Joseph had already opened the closet door and gotten a hanger, wine in the crook of his arm. "Thanks," Eddy said helplessly, thwarted again.

Joseph's social obligations fulfilled, he placed his free hand on the wooden banister, facing upwards. "Dad!" he shouted into space. "Someone's here!" He grinned at Eddy, who found herself unable to resist smiling back. "He'll be a sec." Joseph scuffed at the floor with a black-socked foot, looking for a topic of conversation. He eventually came up with, "Do you like *Night Beats*?"

"Everyone likes *Night Beats*," Eddy said. "If aliens come to Earth, they won't ask to meet the President, they'll ask to meet Jane." Much as Eddy loved Lilith, she'd make a terrible emissary. "Or they'll ask to meet Jordan, and we're all doomed."

Joseph considered her point, examining it carefully. The kid probably fancied himself a Jordan. Most men did. "Why?"

Eddy was rescued from attempting to explain the intersecting concepts of benevolent prejudice, exceptionalism, and soft xenophobia by the emergence of François at the bottom of the staircase. Like any monarch surveying his realm, he assessed the situation before him with a critical eye and found it wanting. Eddy'd failed to style a pixie cut that had grown to the wrong length of short, her eyeliner wings were uneven and flightless, and she had too much leg showing even with tights. Warm blood rushed to her face as she waited for his verdict. His gaze finally rested on the wine she'd irresponsibly handed to Joseph. "Eddy's a guest," François said mildly, and Joseph sighed dramatically, judging his luck, before vanishing upstairs. François watched him slip away, then turned his attention to the bottle Joseph had passed over before departing. "This is a good one."

"Thanks," Eddy said, definitely not smug about her victory over the elitism of the sommelier industry. "It was this or California's finest Strawberry Zinfandel. Two bottles for twenty-four bucks." She'd spent a few more dollars than twelve, but not so many that she'd make things weird. Less than he must have spent on their drinks that first night.

François smiled, the corners of his eyes crinkling. His face had lines, worn-in creases, and there were flecks of grey dotted through his black hair. François had the poise to carry off 'distinguished' rather than 'tired.' Eddy tried to convince herself that an objective analysis would conclude that Kyle was hotter. Scientists were supposed to be objective, or was that journalists? Despite Eddy's internal protest, as she stood inches away from François, her pulse raced, suggesting it was journalists.

"Joseph would prefer that. He's a long way from developing taste. But Mara will like this." François' approval shouldn't matter to Eddy outside the lab. "I'll decant it while we wait for Mara. She won't be long."

"No," Eddy said decisively, waving a bun more emphatically than she'd intended. At least there were no celery sticks around to torment her. "Jane absolutely should not join a wolf cult to get in touch with her canine side." She put the bun on her side plate, white with a geometric pattern in silver, and reached for the butter. It was hard to believe anyone could be this wrong about anything. That was the Youths for you.

Joseph stood his ground, metaphorically. Literally, of course, he was sitting at Mara's dark-stained oak dinner table, which was laden with enough food to make Eddy fear for its structural integrity. "It's her true nature. She needs a pack." Between answering the door and arriving at the table, Joseph had changed out of his black hoodie and baggy jeans, into a forest green polo shirt. He still wore jeans, but this pair didn't look like Mara had bought them with room for him to grow into. Somehow the outfit only made him look younger, a boy play-acting at adulthood.

"The werewolf pack eats people," Mara pointed out, uncertainty in her voice, in the quick movements of her hands. Their motion was echoed by the long-flared sleeves of her sky-blue blouse. "Is it okay if she eats people if they threaten her pack?" Mara's outfit reassured Eddy about her own: smart-casual, attractive, but suitable for an evening not-date with a completely platonic acquaintance. The shirt billowed around

Mara's top and the buttons were done up to a perfectly respectable height for a dinner with a friend, Eddy noted regretfully.

"Werewolves are an endangered species. Dr. Lou Garoo said they need to look out for each other." Joseph had no time for moral ambiguity.

The situation was ridiculous enough when Jordan was the one describing it, but it was impossible not to snort when it was Joseph. Eddy tried to cover it with a cough, which went terribly wrong somewhere and ended with François leaning to his right and patting her on the back. It wasn't hard enough to be effective if anything was actually the matter. Still, the nearness of his physical presence drowned out the sensation of choking on nothing. His touch was gentler than she'd expected. "Guess I failed my Constitution Save," Eddy said in a feeble attempt at humour.

François chuckled. "Fortitude Save." Eddy fell silent as she attempted to work out which of them was right, and, more importantly, how he knew Dungeons & Dragons well enough for a rules challenge. "Eddy works with me on time loops," François said, filling the conversational dead space. "She could probably answer your questions about them, Joseph."

Joseph had taken advantage of his moment to pile more mashed potatoes on his fork than physics allowed. While he chewed and swallowed the gravitational black hole of carbohydrates, Eddy contemplated her fate. She'd done outreach events. Typical questions included: How can you tell if the Instance is real? When will Instances be affordable for the general public? If you die in an Instance, do you die in real life? You can't, quite possibly never, and no one knows, respectively.

"Why don't they work for the future?" Joseph asked. "What's the difference between the past and the future?"

Smart kid. Eddy found herself liking him. Fourteen-year-old Eddy, a creature of solid disdain, would never have shown this much enthusiasm in front of one of her mom's friends. "They should work," Eddy admitted. "Probably some kind of manufacturing defect in the equipment. Engineers cutting costs."

"I'd hate to see the real price tag if I bought the cheap version,"

François said. "I assumed the difference was entropy." Most people did. Well, they would if most people bothered to think about it. Eddy's years of teaching suggested virtually no one did unless prompted by an exam question. Even then, a solid forty percent of the class wouldn't bother. It was a miracle of lowered expectations that anyone passed.

"Nope," Eddy replied, secretly pleased. She liked being right. "It is in the Middlerealm, but the terms cancel out in the Shadowrealm. Everything is reversible." She shrugged. "The math works, so the physics works. If in doubt, blame the engineer."

"How would you fix it?" François asked, momentarily transitioning from object of desire to manager, and Eddy was not prepared to admit that version of him was hot too. More to the point, Eddy needed to stop volunteering for more work. Mara, sympathetic, poured the remainder of the bottle of red into Eddy's glass. The third bottle was already open, breathing beside the second. The first was but a distant memory.

"I'm not an engineer," Eddy countered, but she picked up her glass. At least they didn't expect her to suffer while thirsty. "I'll read some papers." She'd almost given up hoping François might forget which things he had asked her to do. It had worked on her first postdoc supervisor.

"I'm good with computers," Joseph said. This must be another rich-kid thing. Most of Eddy's first-year students struggled with drag-and-drop. Surprisingly, the number of undergrads who failed to locate the save function when they were programming was uncorrelated to the difficulty of the assignment. Eddy had run the stats to prove it. "I'll have a look at the code. I can try some things and see what happens."

"Only if you write it down," Eddy informed Joseph with mock severity. "That's what makes someone a scientist instead of an ordinary weirdo. We take notes."

After dinner came Scotch, a test Eddy was preparing to fail when she discovered, to her happy surprise, that she did like whiskey. At least, she liked what François had served her, a bright gleam in his grey eyes as he handed over the glass. "This doesn't taste like a campfire."

"I've got that too," François offered lavishly, gesturing at the liquor cabinet where Inuit soapstone carvings flanked rows of bottles. "My father preferred that. Mara doesn't." Mara was sitting beside him and partaking in a healthy volume of Balvenie, as if to verify François' statement. Joseph drank wine with them at dinner but hadn't been offered any hard liquor and was working on a glass of Pepsi instead.

"Maybe I should try drinking that in the Shadowrealm. I can't make myself drink hot sauce." Eddy admitted her failure to inches of amber, watching the patterns of light as she turned the cut-glass tumbler. "Peaty Scotch isn't quite as bad." It seemed like a waste to drink expensive alcohol she hated, though price wouldn't matter in the Shadowrealm. Or to François, given his generous pour. And the landscaping around his house.

"Why are you drinking hot sauce?" Mara asked, and that was a question. Eddy knew the answer she and François had worked out for lab group and grant applications, and it was close to the truth, or at least close to what François told Eddy the truth was. But Mara had deep brown eyes, brilliance unobscured by glass lenses in thick frames, and Eddy didn't want to tell her half-truths.

Eddy took a sip instead of answering, playing for time. She liked her job. Most days, it was more fun than the one she'd left behind. She liked her group, and she had any number of feelings about her supervisor. Eddy could tell Mara all sorts of things, and if she did Eddy could find out exactly how much of his life François shared with Mara — but no one endeared themselves to their boss by threatening the comfortable foundations of his marriage. And no one survived on short-term research contracts unless they endeared themselves to their boss.

"She's testing responses to stimuli in time loops," François answered for her, when Eddy's silence dragged on too long. "She's having trouble generating responses above baseline."

"Hot sauce sounds awful," Mara said sympathetically, confirming her status as the best. "Have you tried cake?"

Eddy had tried cake, and ice cream, and fudge. Applying grapefruit-scented moisturizer, playing *Universal Paperclips*, sitting in the sun and rereading *Shards of Honour*, every small pleasure she could think of. François laughed when she suggested sex and didn't take her up on it. "Yeah. Vee suggested cute aggression but that didn't work either."

"You should rob a bank," Joseph suggested with far too much excitement. "That's what I'd do."

"Banks are too stuffy." Eddy wasn't risking her freedom for anything as mundane as money in any Realm. Joseph shouldn't either; cash was too heavy to physically steal a meaningful amount when his family was already rich. "Art, maybe. If it's really good."

"Like the *Voice of Fire*?" Mara asked whimsically. *Pingouin and Bomb* hung behind the couch, suggesting that at least one member of the Gagnon family had too much taste to allow *Voice of Fire* into their house. As she spoke, Mara pushed a strand of hair along the side of her glasses and behind her ear and if Eddy was on her deathbed, the sight of it would've revived her. "If you steal *Sleep of Reason*, you can give it to me. I like Goya."

Instantly, Eddy started plotting. Could she hide in the bathroom as the gallery closed? Would there be laser alarm systems? Where could Eddy get a catsuit to wear when delivering her loot? All evidence suggested that Eddy was quite drunk. Inhibitions lowered, Eddy went for playfully coy as she asked, "What's the most intense thing you've experienced, Mara?"

Mara grimaced, which was the wrong answer. "Childbirth, but I don't think that helps. It would take too long and besides, you can't go in the lab when you're pregnant."

Eddy liked to think there were lines even she wouldn't cross for science, but it took several contemplative moments before Eddy said, "No, that wouldn't work." Eddy was drunk and her responses were slow, that's all.

"You need to find something unexpected to try." François didn't elaborate, but the reminder was enough to kill Eddy's buzz, or at least knock it off its feet and rough it up a little. Someone had found a way to get a dead baby in the lab, or at least the image of one, its glassy stare fixed in solvent. Eddy scowled, finished her drink, and tipped her glass towards François. He graciously refilled it. There was no way Eddy was writing a grant application in the morning. If she was really lucky, she might get the laundry done by the end of Sunday.

"I can't surprise myself," Eddy argued. "It's literally impossible. Like tickling yourself." Eddy had clear unadulterated logic on her side, and all François had was signing authority over her paychecks. "Besides, last time you tried a sudden shock, it didn't register on the EEG in the Middlerealm." François didn't react to her statement, either the part about the shock or the part where she implicated him in it, but a good poker face hardly absolved him.

"Oh," Mara interjected, startling Eddy. No one was talking for her words to interrupt, but Mara's words were too energetic, given everyone else's post-dinner lethargy. "I meant to ask! What are you doing Thursday night?"

For once, Eddy had a prior commitment. And her mom used to say Eddy never did anything fun. "I'm busy." It was a shame, but some things couldn't be helped.

"I know," Mara agreed instantly, speaking without her usual hesitation or nervousness. Mara was drunk too. "But do you want to watch *Night Beats* with us?"

As long as there had been universities, there had been journal clubs. And as long as there had been journal clubs, a single rule remained sacrosanct. No one picked a paper longer than ten pages. Eddy found one that was five, with figures, and no supplementary material. She'd won the lottery, and her lab group got to share in her winnings. It was even well-written.

"*Schrödinger's Catnap: Charcot-Wilbrand Syndrome Sleep Therapy Through Transcranial Quantum Entangled Magnetic Stimulation*," read François off one of the copies Eddy had printed for the meeting. "The title could be worse. Nini lost her argument with Reviewer Three."

"What?" Lydia asked. Eddy suppressed her laugh so Lydia wouldn't think Eddy was making fun of her. The Third Reviewer was always the evil one.

"The first version she submitted was along the lines of *My Study Was So Boring It Cured Insomnia*," François explained. "Most people don't keep up with the literature these days, and the first impression you make with your title determines if they'll read through to the abstract. Unless you're writing about drilling holes, don't include the word 'boring' in the title."

Eddy rolled her eyes. Only François could work a pun and a Teachable Moment into the same statement. "People who can't dream can't use Instances. You need an intact parietal lobe for both." A particularly useful finding, if one was attempting to run brain scans with minimal success. It suggested a target for Eddy to focus on, a trail of breadcrumbs leading her deeper into the forest.

"So Instances are fake?" Marcus asked, though he barely deigned to put the question mark at the end of the sentence. Eddy refused to allow herself to be trolled by a Masters student in his fourth year. It was hard to resist, though. "Really expensive dream simulations." Marcus was surly and unbearable since Kit defended, according to Lydia. Marcus had started his Masters before Kit had started her PhD, which was a good explanation but a pathetic excuse.

"No." Eddy took the bait. "That interpretation only makes sense if this is the only study on Instances you read. Everything on information transfer suggests that the results are reproducible." Plus Eddy's lived experience, and François' healthy grant funding. Katie, Bao, Lydia and Payton exchanged meaningful glances; all their projects relied on Instance technology in one way or another. This was hardly the right audience to suggest it was all smoke and mirrors, but Marcus showed no capacity to read the room. Still, François looked more irritated than he should have. It was practically a scientific law that a subset of underperforming grad students would regress to sullen teenagers.

"The authors suggest Instances are experienced as dreams," offered Owen-the-peacemaker. "If the temporal information is processed by the same brain functions as dreaming, then expensive dream simulations provide valuable real-world insights." Owen sounded like he was composing his next conference talk in his head, and François nodded, clenched muscles in his jaw loosening ever so slightly. It offered Marcus a graceful way to back down, so of course he didn't take it.

"Or you think they do. Maybe it's just stuff your brain makes up when you get back."

"Same thing," Payton said with perfect nonchalance. "It's all shadows on a cave wall. It doesn't matter if they're real, as long as they're useful." Payton was an imposing ginger who Eddy could easily imagine charging down the Highlands with a claymore. They were also hopelessly in love with Owen, a situation compounded by Owen being 'literally, the best housemate.' Eddy could sympathize with their predicament. Back when a younger, less cynical Eddy was in grad school, her randomly selected housemate, Vee, showed up to move in at the end of Vee's first field season. All Vee's possessions were in an enormous backpack nearly as large as her own body and she was drenched like a half-drowned rat because she was congenitally incapable of remembering her umbrella. The two of them had spent at least fifteen minutes with all of their clothes on and it had been a tense quarter-hour. Payton's two years of unresolved pining was unimaginable torment. Eddy wasn't into slow burn. "I still like the multiverse theory best."

"You just want Magneto to be real," Owen teased, and Eddy felt for Payton.

"Of course I do." As if everyone wanted a traumatized superpowered dude lashing out in their universe. Though if the dude was Michael Fassbender, it tipped the scales. "Which is why if I ever act especially crazy, you need to film it to prove that I'm the Payton from another reality and I've taken over this 'verse's Payton's body."

"Can you think of a controlled way to test your hypothesis?" François asked, his eyes narrowed, redirecting the conversation to the established path with all the subtlety of a snowplow. "Marcus' dream theory is wrong, but the important thing is that he's demonstrably wrong. When Payton gives identical treatments in and out of an Instance, the subject responds the same way." He might try to hide it, but François was in a touchy mood. He wore a jacket and a silk tie with chevrons that matched his curtains, proof of a morning spent in an industry meeting. Maybe it had gone badly.

Eddy frowned, mulling over a thought. "So far as we can tell." The tests all worked, but they were designed for the greatest probability of success. They hadn't tried to maximise the chance of failure. "There's no way to export data on nuances of responses. Maybe we're ignoring the subtle differences." Eddy had an idea, which was the best thing a scientist could have. She needed some time to sit with it, sketch it out on paper, discuss it with Lilith, before telling anyone else. But it had promise. She wasn't expecting the grad students to follow along with her meandering thoughts, but she looked to François for his usual nod of encouragement. It was not forthcoming.

"That's what your project is for, Eddy," François said, and Eddy downgraded his mood from 'touchy' to 'grumpy'. Eddy didn't miss her days as an assistant professor courting industry partners, attempting to coordinate the pace of research to the demands of quarterly financial reports. She did miss life on hard money, or even her first postdoc contract with its guaranteed two years of funding, instead of this three-month renewal nonsense. Still, research positions didn't grow on trees. She was lucky to have this much, for as long as François kept her industry funders satisfied. "Independent verification. As soon as you get your first data point."

Bad day or not, that was below the belt. Reminding someone of their experimental failures was up there with house arrest on the list of inappropriate ways to treat a scientist. "I tried the replicate you wanted. I was right. It didn't work the first time and repeating the test didn't work either." Eddy shouldn't have acted belligerent in a group meeting, and François shouldn't have acted like a dick. No one was being their best self.

François shrugged dismissively. "Try something else."

"I've got some ideas," Eddy said, speaking fast enough that her limited self-preservation instincts reached her mouth only after the words escaped. "I could steal Defense Department procurement proposals and read them in the Shadowrealm. It wouldn't matter if I got caught since no one in the Middlerealm would know." Case in point, Middlerealm-François didn't know about Shadowrealm-François' mysteriously dwindling coffee supplies; they reset each Instance, and so did he. "Maybe I should collect blackmail material on the other profs, you know, while I'm there anyway. I'm trying to work out how to manage insider trading from the Shadowrealm, but I might need the forward Instances for that." Said out loud, none of Eddy's wildest speculations seemed the slightest bit excessive. Eddy spent two years of a Master's and five of a PhD learning to recognize outliers. François wanted something from her, and it wasn't a paper in *Scientific Reports*. Eddy had formulated plenty of hypotheses during her time in François' group.

François, for his part, endured Eddy's rant with more grace than he'd shown during her bout of enthusiasm. He furrowed his brows, thinking, and Eddy knew she wasn't getting fired, at least not that day. "The Forwardrealm?" François tried experimentally, then shook his head, clearing the air and restoring order to the universe. "That's terrible. You'll need a better name when you discover it."

"Upperrealm? Flamerealm? Mistrealm?" All popular fan theories for the name of the unrevealed Third Realm in *Night Beats*. The actress who played Titania improvised most of her lines, meaning that her episodes had the best writing and the most plot holes of the show. Eddy had long since given up on canon explaining what exactly the Middlerealm was supposed to be the middle between. *Night Beats* didn't content itself with panning to Chekhov's gun on the mantelpiece; they cleaned it, loaded it, pulled back the safety and then left the firearm on the couch, completely forgotten, ignored even when the family sat next to it to watch TV. "It doesn't have a name on the show." There was the Mirrorverse, but that was an unrelated geographical phenomenon to the Realms, a land of leather bodysuits and goatees.

"Then it's a race between you and the *Night Beats* scriptwriters. The Fae haven't made an appearance in a while so you've got some time." Not as much time as he thought. The actress for Titania was under contract for five episodes this season, which meant the Shadowrealm would be back, even if the plot holes therein only got deeper. Matter settled, François turned back to the paper they were there, theoretically, to discuss. "Did anyone find inconsistencies in the work?"

"The paper focuses on the inability to dream, but the individual suffered from agnosia as well. It's the same region of the brain." Owen did the reading and then some. He earned his status as Golden Boy. "It's in Table Two but they never mentioned it in the text." The line was highlighted in lime green on his printout. "It would help if they had more than one subject, with variation in symptoms."

"It would, but the whole study was an accident. Maybe in ten years Instances will be cheap enough to run screening tests, but this research only happened because Nini got lucky with a grad student." François surveyed his loyal subjects with a discerning eye, but it was tempered by benevolence. If his gaze rested longer on Eddy than his students, it was momentary, too fast to mean anything. "I'm not endorsing any of you getting traumatic brain injuries. You have no idea how much paperwork Nini had to fill out, and it didn't even happen during work hours."

There was general laughter, and the lowering of tension was enough for Lydia to ask, "What's agnosia?"

"You can't recognize familiar things. The patient couldn't remember faces or places," Owen explained.

"So maybe it's a context thing? The brain can't process incoming information without a framework to put it in." Lydia, clever enough to come to the right idea, and brave enough to articulate it. Eddy felt a swell of pride. Formally, Owen was Lydia's mentor, but asking Golden Boy for help would've unnerved any first-year PhD student. Eddy was the one who edited the roughest draft of Lydia's proposal, recommended literature for her to read, watched her practice before her first lab tutorial. Lydia's success was, in some small way, Eddy's.

"Or something else entirely. Brains are complicated." Payton wasn't wrong.

"It doesn't sound like we're going to solve Instances today," François said, closing the meeting prematurely. Another industry meeting to prep for after lunch, maybe. François opened his notebook, a hard-cover book with a snowy scene on the front binding, inside an itemized list in neat handwriting. "Anyone who wants to attend the seminar at York needs to email me today, or pay the fee themselves and claim back the money. Thank you to Bao for organizing the lab cleaning this week. It looks much better now. Let's try to maintain that." A forlorn hope, but supervisors were obliged to ask. "Lydia, Owen, we should meet tonight to finalize plans for the blood sampling. We need to be ready for storage and preliminary analyses on Monday." François checked his calendar on his phone. "At six, if you can make it."

It was a glass half-full situation for them. On one hand, Lydia and Owen were young, and they might have plans on a Friday night that they hadn't felt the need to run past their supervisor or post on the group's shared calendar. On the other hand, convention stated that evening meetings happened at the pub, the supervisor bought drinks and sometimes dinner, and they wrapped up early enough to leave the bulk of the night free.

"Eddy, did you want to come?" he offered. "It's a bit far from your field of research, but I'm sure Lydia would appreciate your help on her allergy trials, and you've made good progress together on the socioeconomic study." It wasn't exactly an apology for being a dick, but after years in the university system it was more than Eddy expected. Lydia looked at Eddy, hazel eyes hopeful.

"I'm not busy," Eddy said, which was as close to accepting François' apology as he'd come to issuing it. "Sure."

In an uncharacteristic fit of generosity, François let Lydia pick the pub, which is how the four of them ended up drinking pitchers of sangria and eating poutine at an establishment clearly aimed at the more inexperienced crowd. The poutine was delicious, despite being vegetarian, but there might have been a whole glass of wine in the pitcher of sangria, if they were lucky. Lydia was happy, which was the important thing, given how tense she had been about the sampling on Monday. François ran Lydia through her biohazard handling procedures, the three of them threw a few hypotheticals at her, and they ran out of meeting before they ran out of sangria. There was no risk of running out of work though, and the conversation turned from one kind of shop talk to another.

"Someone left Wikipedia hyperlinks in their dream journal entry,"

Lydia told them incredulously. "They're supposed to be personal accounts. Did they not read the assignment, or did they dream about the Wikipedia article about chickenpox?"

"Is Dr West still running that assignment?" Owen asked rhetorically. "Marking those is a wild ride." He took a swig of sangria, a gesture that might have been more effective if the sangria had held more than a token fraction of alcohol. "I read so many essays about students writing exams for courses they never enrolled in that I started to dream it myself. Or they were forced to go back to high school for missing credits, or primary school — one student said he'd failed kindergarten and had to repeat colouring."

Marking dream journals was a rite of passage, and not a pleasant one. "When I was a TA, I had a student describe kidnapping and murdering someone in way too much detail. I was ready to go to student support services when Vee told me it was the exact same as that week's episode of *CSI*. We agreed I wouldn't rat him out for plagiarism but from then on all his journal entries were about *Highlander*. If I have to read about murder, there better be swords involved."

Owen and François laughed. Lydia chuckled, but it was closer to a sigh. "Some of them write really long assignments. I don't know why. I have to read them all and make comments, and it's never the funny ones that go over the word count."

"Tell the students you'll give them full marks if they volunteer for a research study instead of writing the journal entries," François suggested. "Ethan used to offer that before he had a TA doing the marking for him. Everyone needs more participants for their studies."

Eddy would've told Lydia to stop reading when she reached the word count, but François' idea was smarter. The world was a better place without first years delving into their own psyches.

By all rights, Lydia and Owen should've outlasted Eddy and François at drinking, the power of Youth on their side. Then again, Lydia and Owen probably had better things to do on a Friday night than hang out with their supervisor. By seven, the two students had made their excuses and Eddy and François were alone at the table as the pub filled around them and a cover band started their sound check. There was more than a glass of sangria left in the pitcher, but François put his hand over Eddy's when she reached for it. His skin was warm in the cool evening air. "Let's go somewhere where they serve the grape juice fermented."

Eddy released the jug. "Where to?"

"I wouldn't waste the Shadowrealm spying on my colleagues," François told her, his voice touchingly earnest. The tealights in glass-mosaic jars flickered weakly, casting shadows on his angled cheekbones, stubble-peppered chin, and sharp, grey eyes. He leaned in, lowered his voice to a deep whisper. "Most of them don't know about two-factor authentication. Besides, you can spear-phish anyone in academia with a request to review a paper."

Eddy kept her security settings up to date, and she ignored the obvious spam asking her to submit a paper on celery physiology or join the editorial board for the Journal of Singaporean Public Transportation Infrastructure, but François was right. Eddy rejected and accepted dozens of reviews during the months between meeting him at the conference and accepting his postdoc position. They all seemed legit, but they would. "So you've read all my bookmarked fics on AO3?" It was embarrassing not to have secrets more interesting than bad taste in straight ships.

"Charles is sleeping with an undergrad," François informed her, bypassing Eddy's question and the implications thereof. Charles was a reminder that there were fates worse than François catching her being boring. Given his field of expertise, Dr. Kennedy ought to have better internet hygiene than Eddy did, but most undergrad students had as much internet savvy as a toddler. The partner was probably the weak link. "Ethan's the one attempting insider trading, not me. Luckily, he's so bad at it that no court would prosecute. I keep telling him to hire an accountant and leave his investments alone."

Investments weren't a problem for Eddy, given the red hole of her finances. Her mother hadn't earned enough to have real savings, and even a basic funeral cost more than the estate could cover. François probably knew that too. "What about defense contracts?" Eddy leaned forward as she spoke, their voices barely audible over the classical music and chatter of other diners. François' lips, pale in the dim light, were inches from her own. It took a conscious effort of will to keep from moving closer.

His smile revealed a line of bright white teeth. "I don't work with DND directly. Or in the Middlerealm." He waved away the thought, or the waitress who'd turned up to refill their glasses. "That's all for me. I'm driving. Eddy, don't let that stop you. I'll give you a lift home."

Eddy didn't own a car. François probably had heated leather seats and a built-in GPS with a British accent. She nodded acquiescence to the waitress. Her crystal wine glass was large enough to make the increase in dark red liquid seem insubstantial, to minimize the differences between her drinking and François' sipping. "Thanks," she said to both the waitress and him. François could be relied on to drop her at her doorstep unmolested. He'd probably even wait 'til she unlocked the door before driving off. "It's the worst acronym."

"I'm sorry?"

"Department of National Defence," Eddy spelled out. "DND. They're less fun than fourth edition D&D, and that was when you had to keep track of cool-down times. And what's the point of calling a game 'Dungeons and Dragons' when you can't even play as a gnome?" In addition to providing safe transit, François could be relied on to pick good wine and to follow the spiralling tangents of Eddy's conversation, scientific or otherwise. Tonight's diversion into role-playing games was no exception.

"The Air Force could use some Sorcerers," François offered. "Magic is the only way they're keeping forty-year old fighter jets in the air."

"Sorcerers are just low-rent Wizards." Eddy hoped he hadn't played that class, or if he had, that he'd be open enough to acknowledge the truth in her words. "The military should hire double the Wizards and let the Sorcerers work for the private sector."

"Yes, but the Wizards all work for CSIS. They've got the Intelligence."

Eddy was about to protest that Rogues were a better fit for CSIS when she got the pun, snorted an unladylike laugh. "Druids and Rangers for the Ministry of the Environment. Where do the Clerics work?"

"They all quit along with the Paladins," François told her regretfully, eyes glimmering in the candlelight. "Quebec wouldn't let them display their holy symbols."

François told her to try something else. This is something. She suspects he'd be proud of her, or pleased with himself, or both.

This is Eddy's second attempt. The first time, she brought her costume change in a backpack, but they made her leave it in the lockers at the atrium. She went back to get it at five minutes to closing, hid in the public bathroom unnoticed as the ticket-sellers went home and the lights went off, but when she attempted to get back into the gallery, the glass doors were locked. Glass is hard to break on purpose.

This time, she's prepared. Eddy strips off her outer layer, a loose-fitting summer dress, black with white stripes and a bouquet of skulls over the heart. A bit garish for work but heist-appropriate. Underneath, black leggings are close enough to trousers, and a collared black polyester shirt, with the finishing touch of a blue apron embroidered with 'Canada Cleaning Care' & the accompanying logo of the company subcontracted to clean the gallery. Its deep pockets are full of spray bottles and dusters, among other useful items. Eddy worried about walking in with them. Even under a flowy dress, the bumps and bulges weren't exactly inconspicuous, and no one would believe she's spontaneously giving birth to a plunger. But no one looked closely or bothered to challenge her.

It would be easier to steal something off the walls. The gallery isn't designed as a maze, or if it is, it's a child's version of the puzzle, one entrance and one exit for visitors, and an obvious path to follow between them. Eddy passes Greenland Mountains, which her mother loved but was never Eddy's scene. Too barren. Looking at it is biting into an ice cube, flavorless. Maybe François would like it, he's got a thing for northern scenes. The Triptych of the Temptation of Saint Anthony, there's a painting that moves, that you sink your teeth into and they come out red. Eddy makes a quick detour to the Voice of Fire but can't linger. In another timeline, it would be ripe for some creative destruction, but Eddy's on a mission. She's there for the Goya, and that's in the vault.

Once she's inside the elevator, Eddy discovers it requires a key card to access the basement, which is a problem. Besides, something feels off about taking an elevator in the Shadowrealm. If this was a movie, the cables would definitely be cut, or it would stop between floors and she'd have to climb out. It's pure conceit — the elevator doesn't know which Realm it exists in — but Eddy presses the button to reopen the elevator door and makes for the stairs instead. They're guarded by the sum total of a rope with a laminated placard that says 'Staff Only' in Verdana. It's not an intimidating font, and Eddy steps over it without hesitation. The real difficulty starts at the bottom of the stairs, with another access pad waiting for a key card Eddy doesn't have, and an unyielding metal push-bar. Eddy can see hallways through the narrow window on the door, imagines moving shelves and unlocked cabinets just out of view, tantalizing her with their nearness.

Good thing she came prepared.

Nestled beside the plunger is a large knife, or a small short-sword, depending on whether the wielder is a halfling. It's less a well-crafted version of Sting and more a hunk of hardened steel produced by a devoted boyfriend during his blacksmithing phase, but that's exactly what Eddy needs right now. She straightens her stance, squares her hips and brings the blade down. The glass breaks with a satisfying crash, shattering outwards, and she emerges unscathed.

It's almost disappointing that there's no sirens blaring at the presence of an intruder. No one even comes to see about the window. Eddy removes her apron and wraps it around her arm, reaches through the hole and depresses the handle on the other side of the door. She's in.

It doesn't take much wandering to find a frankly problematic abundance of pullout drawers with flat works. There must be an organizational system of some sort, a Dewey Decimal equivalent for art, but whether it's based on the painter's last name, year of production, topic or colour, Eddy can't discern any order. She gets lost in a corps of Otto Dix prints and when she glances down at her watch, there's barely twenty minutes left before she's transported, safe and sound but sans artwork, to the Middlerealm. She grabs Assault Troops Advance under Gas and rolls it to a cylinder narrow enough to fit inside her paper towel roll. She's not confident it's Mara's style, realism rather than metaphor, but Eddy doesn't have time to travel to Mara's place after she escapes, cleverly eluding capture, let alone to find the Goya first. Next time.

Out is as easy as in until Eddy reaches the gift shop. Getting through the thick glass doors requires dozens of cuts with the blade and Eddy's shoulders ache by the end of them. She needs to practice more often in the Middlerealm. Unlike the vault, the gift shop is alarmed, blaring a warning as soon as Eddy breaks her first spindly crack. There's a metal curtain on the other side of the room, though it's been down this whole time, obviously shut during closing rather than falling dramatically as Eddy's presence was acknowledged by the system. Part-time jobs through undergrad taught Eddy that there's always a spare key for the curtain in the cash register. Eddy fumbles through opening the unfamiliar model until she tries selling herself something, a five-pack of fridge magnets with fussy paintings of New France. There's a satisfying click as the drawer swings out, and it's quick work to locate the key, but by then it's too late.

Waiting on the other side, arms crossed over their chests, is a trio of burly security guards dressed in black. One of them shouts at her, and Eddy's never liked men in uniforms, or men who think they can intimidate her by shouting. It's ridiculous. She's the one with the sword, after all. Not that she consciously thought about drawing it, but her blade is in her hand and the men are circling her. Eddy glances down. The bezel on her diver's watch gives her just under six minutes left.

The EEG readings are going to be amazing.

"He's a Jordan," Eddy told her cat once Kyle left. They'd had this conversation before, but Lilith didn't mind. Lilith was remarkably tolerant as long as the kibble arrived on time. "You think, oh, I'll message him for sex, but then afterwards you spend half an hour discussing brands of running jackets or else you feel like a bitch for not having an opinion on the positioning of reflective stripes. I bet Jordan talks to Jane about running jackets. Offscreen."

Lilith didn't pause in her careful attention to grooming between her toes. Lilith was a great conversationalist.

"I need more friends," Eddy said, sliding her head over so it was next to the cat. Lilith sniffed Eddy's nose, and then switched to licking that instead of her own feet. "Thanks."

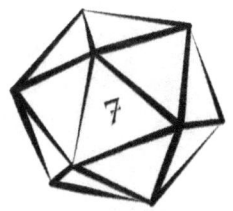

The beauty of nineties metal was its ability to obliterate everything around it — including, for example, the soft noises of someone breathing, the rustle of fabric as they shifted position, moving close enough to touch. Eddy pulled her headphones out of her ears and dropped them on her desk. Rob Zombie was still audible through the earbuds. No surprise she didn't hear François knock, if he had knocked, which she doubted. It wasn't his style.

"Hey." Eddy looked François over, searching for a clue regarding his intentions. He looked ragged, fraying around the edges. In a metaphorical sense, of course; his wardrobe was impeccable. His gray slacks and checked blue shirt were testament to Mara's skill with an iron, hair neatly combed, waiting for someone to run their fingers through it. But his posture was off, shoulders slumped, and the lines on his face were taut. Migraine, probably. His second that week. "You okay?" Eddy attempted a sympathetic pat on François' arm, but reaching his wrist required more leaning than she anticipated, and her motion was awkward and uncomfortable.

François didn't shrug off her touch. Eddy could feel the warmth of his muscle, tense under a thin layer of cotton, the leather outline of his watchband. "I'm fine." She doubted it. He looked less like a man who was fine and more like a man who'd had glass shards repeatedly thrust through his eyeballs. "Can you drive?"

"Since I was twelve. But I don't have a car." Eddy grew up in the middle of nowhere, Ontario, a car her only path to escape her mother's benevolent dictatorship. When Eddy had a growth spurt and got tall enough to see over the steering wheel, she begged her cousin to teach her and traded half her CD collection for the forbidden knowledge. "Ottawa's got decent public transit." Teenage-Eddy would've been horrified, certain that ownership of a vehicle was the clearest distinction between childhood and maturity. Adult-Eddy was less sure there was any meaningful distinction. She did her laundry more regularly nowadays and she didn't need a fake ID, but she didn't feel like a responsible adult, and a car wouldn't change that.

"There's mine, if you don't need to go to your place before *Night Beats*. Mara would love to have you for dinner, and she hates it when I drive after a migraine."

Eddy silently counted the fantastic elements in his statement. Six in two sentences, which might be a world record for maximum awesome per full stop. First, she was going to be driving François' Tesla. He lived outside the downtown core, which gave Eddy a fighting chance at clear roads to vastly exceed the speed limit. Second, it was Thursday, and Thursday meant *Night Beats*, and third, *Night Beats* with the Gagnons. Fourth, Mara was cooking, and fifth, Mara was going to be happy. Sixth, Eddy's guess was right, and she really enjoyed being right. If Eddy was a better person, she'd feel worse for François' suffering than she felt elated for her sudden windfall. She did feel bad for him. A person was capable of multiple emotions at once. "I can't let down Mara. Give me the keys."

The penguin plushie dangling from the rear-view mirror spun as Eddy sped around a corner and something finally clicked. The soapstone carvings, the family of Arctic-animal stickers on the car's back window, the WWF calendar hanging in François' office. Eddy called herself a scientist, and here she'd gone months without spotting the common element. "Penguins?" Eddy said, though it wasn't really a question. It was definitely penguins.

"I like penguins," François answered, but his tone was wrong, either too much emphasis or too little. He wasn't as good at lying as he thought he was. Eddy looked at him with the fixed expression she'd learned from Lilith-the-cat and, even with sunglasses as a defensive shield, he lasted less than a second before he broke under the pressure. Eddy could never withstand the Lilith-stare either. "I told Mara I liked penguins, back when we were engaged." It wasn't hard to imagine how the rest of the story unfolded. Penguin-print underwear at Christmas, penguin-shaped pasta on his birthday. François sighed expressively, leaning back into his seat. Eddy laughed and returned her attention to the road. The traffic gods had smiled on her drive and Eddy whizzed past trees and yield signs at a speed that deserved more of her focus than she was providing to it. "I wouldn't lie to Mara — I do like penguins. I assume everyone likes penguins." He turned to face her. "You like penguins, right?" There was a nervous edge to his question, as if he'd wanted to ask someone this for a long time.

"Everyone likes penguins. They're the motherhood and puppies of the fowl species. But I like penguins the regular amount." Eddy said, deploying her best teacher-voice. François brightened at her banter, despite his general state of exhaustion. "My house is full of nerd paraphernalia, like a regular person. You can find a sonic screwdriver, a Lilith plushie and a Panic Pete. No penguins though." The sky was cloudless and Eddy had all the windows down, wind loud in her ears. In another life, she'd keep driving until she got to the end of the road, and then she'd walk, not looking back. "Did I tell you that I got a hit?"

"You hinted." François radiated less warmth than the sun, but it was more focused, his delight in her obvious. "You didn't want to say in front of Lydia." A fair assumption, and he was probably right. Not a great sign, but Eddy didn't want to deal with red flags on a perfect day like that one. Amber flags at most. "How did you do it?"

"I broke into the National Gallery and pulled a sword on the security guards. Things got intense from there," Eddy said, deadpan, expecting him to argue or disbelieve her. Instead, François broke into a grin. She thought he might have high-fived her, practically kissed her, if she wasn't driving. More specifically, if she wasn't driving in a way that an unbiased observer might call reckless. Eddy had missed being behind the wheel. Besides, he almost certainly wouldn't have kissed her. "It's got to be something about the adrenaline rush. Maybe a threshold effect? I need fMRI to figure out exactly what's going on. EEG isn't precise enough. All I know is the signal passed baseline, not when or what."

"When we met, you said this was impossible," he reminded her. She tilted her head, considering. François wasn't challenging her, exactly. He was asking her to fit a new data point into an existing theory, to determine if they were compatible, or if the data point or theory needed to be discarded. It was part of the game. Having been wrong wasn't losing unless you let it be.

"Nothing is impossible," Eddy said flippantly as she thought. "There's no equivalent threshold effect in the Middlerealm. I guess it could be an attenuated signal between Realms. I should repeat the test in the Middlerealm, doing exactly the same thing, to see how the signals compare."

"Please don't," he said, his voice on the edge of serious. "Commit your crimes in the Realm where I don't need to bail you out of jail." Eddy nodded, conceding. "I've got a friend at the Ottawa Hospital who's interested in collaborating and he's got an MRI machine. You need to figure out exactly what tests you need to run, and what tests you'll tell him you're running." There it was, the holy grail, finally within Eddy's reach, and a thrill of excitement ran through her. "This can't be your only hypothesis. It explains this particular phenomenon, but it doesn't get us any closer to a unified theory of Shadowrealm weirdness."

"Unified weirdness is a lot to ask before dinner," Eddy protested. It might be achievable if he got her the equipment she needed, but that wouldn't happen before *Night Beats* aired.

Mara had muting during the commercials down to a fine art, not a note of background instrumental music lost and not a single chocolate bar slogan or acne medication jingle endured. Eddy couldn't remember if ads were always surrealist nightmares and she was more accepting in her youth, or if the world had changed, moved faster than she had kept up. It meant they got four-odd minutes of conversation between costume changes and dramatic reveals, not that Eddy timed the breaks. Mara's instincts were completely reliable, at least where the commercials were concerned. Less so for *Night Beats* plot points. "The poor father. He's so distracted by the insurance company reneging on his policy, he doesn't even realize his daughter is missing. I'd never forgive myself. And Jordan is so harsh with him." Mara, endearing as ever, even if her empathy was completely misplaced.

"The developer's in on it," François said with assurance. His guess matched Eddy's. There wasn't much foreshadowing in *Night Beats*, especially in Titania episodes, but it was the obvious twist. "Magic or not, there's no way he mistakes the uncanny valley changeling for his daughter." The CGI animation was bad, even by *Night Beats* standards. Someone in the animation department was expressing their creativity, and the long-suffering fans were subjected to a celery root which sparkled, had eerily big eyes and ears half the length of the misshapen body. Not to mention being introduced as the developer's newborn, but speaking in full sentences and being voiced by Taylor Swift. Continuity was not a problem for *Night Beats*. "He's working with Titania."

"Lilith works with Titania sometimes," Joseph pointed out. "Maybe she's the one who switched the babies." Mara had made Joseph put his phone away when Eddy showed up, which meant Eddy couldn't have hers out either, though Eddy was desperately curious who The Internet was blaming. Hopefully Joseph wasn't alone in his theory. Lilith/Titania made a great ship. "And maybe set the complex on fire. Lilith's done that before."

"Lilith is a terrible cop," Eddy admitted fondly.

"Jordan's worse, if he doesn't notice. How many times has Lilith destroyed evidence?" François asked rhetorically. The answer was four, five if you counted that she did it twice in one episode, when the leprechaun gold reappeared after sunset. "A responsible chief would have fired her by now. At a minimum she should have brought her in for a panel on misconduct."

"Maybe she's got a strong union?" Eddy suggested, secretly revelling in the Jordan-bashing. Joseph would have to learn the truth about his hero someday. It was for the best if it came in the safe space of his living room. "Lilith's got a few centuries of seniority by now."

Mara hit the unmute button at the perfect moment. The show resumed with Brent and Jane, he leaning over a microscope, she inserting a slide on the stage, but before they got to Brent's latest witticism, the television stuttered and went off. Along with the kitchen light and the gentle hum of the air conditioner. Eddy pouted, which felt a bit unfair when she was a guest and this was no one's fault, but her reaction was nothing compared to Joseph's start of outrage or Mara's soft, despairing murmur.

"I can check the fuses," François offered, half-rising, checked by Mara's steadying hand on his bare forearm, his shirt sleeves rolled up just below the elbow.

"It's no use, Zeeskeit. It's another brownout. The whole neighbourhood will be down," Mara said, gesturing at the outside world through windows closed to preserve the AC. François had installed a backup generator on the Instances. A few studies were published on mice and pigs caught in the Shadowrealm when the power was cut, and they'd found no evidence of harm, but no one had tried it on humans yet, and the animals couldn't report back on their experiences. There was a solid business case not to risk the lives or sanity of the grad students unnecessarily. There was no equivalent case for the Gagnons' home television. "I'm so sorry, Eddy. Can we stream it on my phone? There must be something we can do." Mara emphasized her words with her hands, as if looking for some way to fill them, something concrete she could do to make things better.

"It'll be online by the time I get home," Eddy assured her, hiding her dejection as best she could. Eddy tried not to be obvious about checking her watch, the silver hands on the black dial confirming her worst suspicions. "There's no point trying to watch it live anymore, we'll miss too much in the middle." Mara nodded, resigned. If Eddy left immediately, and if the buses were on schedule, she'd make it back only a few minutes after the episode finished, perfect timing for someone to have posted a download link with Korean subtitles. Eddy looked around the room. The penguin kitsch was easy to spot if you knew to look for it, family photographs from the Falkland Islands, an Inuit linoprint, a glass penguin sculpture on the mantelpiece. Mara worried at her lower lip in a way that called out for someone to kiss her nerves away, restless fingers moving across the pale blue fabric of the couch arm. François, ever the gentleman, would offer Eddy a scotch if the moment presented itself. Eddy wasn't ready to leave quite yet. "Or we can do something else while we wait for the power and finish the episode then."

Mara frowned, but with purpose, casting about for a second-best to *Night Beats*. Unfortunately, she came up with, "We've got Monopoly."

That was a solid no. Capitalism had wrought enough destruction in Eddy's working hours without bringing it into her downtime. There had to be an alternative activity that would satisfy Mara's hosting urges without destroying Eddy's soul in the process. "What about Dungeons and Dragons for a game? François, do you have any rule books? It doesn't have to be fifth edition." It was a shot in the dark, but an educated one. The dark knew an awful lot of lore for someone who claimed to be sophisticated and worldly.

"I kept my third-edition books," he offered without a trace of sheepishness. Good. "I haven't got any idea where they are, though." Mara instantly sprang into action, moving past Eddy towards the bookcase. Her sleeve brushed against Eddy's arm on her way, the sensation of silk against skin raising goosebumps along Eddy's arm that traveled all the way to her neck. Mara was clearly relieved at a task to accomplish, a goal to redirect her agitation at an evening no longer going according to plan. The house was Mara's domain, the location of each item inside it imprinted on her psyche. The Dungeon was now François'. Eddy couldn't conceive of a better Dungeon Master to direct their games.

Mara was gorgeous by moonlight, dark bob framing pale, nearly ghostly skin, eyes deep, nearly hollow in the dim glow of streetlights, any light reflected away by glasses before it could reach through. The bus stop was a fifteen-minute walk from their house, and she didn't need to wait with Eddy, but there she was, standing in the rich warmth of air that refused to cool despite the passing of sunset, waiting so Eddy wouldn't be alone. If it had been someone other than Mara, Eddy might have felt impatient for her to go so Eddy could scroll through online reviews of the episode. But it was Mara, and Mara could stay by Eddy's side forever.

"You like fiction," Mara said. "Do you want to come to book club with me?" Eddy tried to imagine herself surrounded by a group of polite women eating bite-sized low-calorie muffins and discussing themes. It was as absurd as imagining Lilith sitting around the coffee table discussing bestsellers. Lilith-the-cat. Lilith-the-vampire probably wrote graphic novels and convinced Jane to illustrate them. "We're reading *A Complicated Kindness* this month."

Fully impossible. There was no place Eddy wanted to be less than a book circle, and no one with whom Eddy wanted to talk about metaphors and queer theory more than Mara. A shared affinity for stories was such a thin thread to weave two people together. Eddy could imagine Mara feeling her way to a tie that could bind them, grasping at the skein for a loose end to pull on. "Sure, why not." Eddy aimed for a casual tone and Mara's eyes lit up with relief and delight. "If you come to a con with me." FanEx would be sold out by now, and Eddy would have to spend a small fortune to get a second ticket off an online scalper. This was what money was for. Her mother had complained that Eddy never saved for retirement. It was too late to start now, anyway.

"What's a con?" Mara was beaming enough to make Eddy feel churlish for her lack of enthusiasm about the book club. "I'd love to."

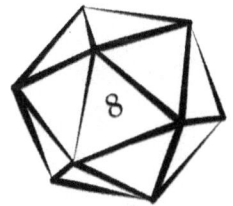

"What's your name?" asked Rose the Lawful Good Half-Elf Cleric, or technically, Mara the Lawful Good Human playing as Rose. Mara's conception of role-playing games involved an awful lot of her character being friendly to the Non-Player Characters that François created for them to interact with, but then it worked for her. So far, Rose's conversations had netted her a Handy Haversack, a Ring of Flighty Falling, and a Jar of Perpetual Mayonnaise, after Eddy successfully petitioned for the fifth-edition item in their three-and-a-half edition game. Plus, to Eddy's surprise and delight, François was gifted at character voices. "We've got a long wagon ride together. We should make friends?" Rose looked to Carmilla the Bard for a second opinion.

Carmilla was Chaotic Neutral, just like Eddy, but talking to the locals was just good sense, especially when François, as benevolent Dungeon Master, was in a mood to make it rain treasure. "I love making new friends," she said, smiling widely, her long canines visible for an instant. Carmilla should probably mention to her party that she was a Vampire. Eventually. These sorts of things needed to come up organically in conversation.

"I'm Bob," their driver said, looking back over his shoulder, giving minimal attention to the road or to his oxen. François tilted his head from side to side as his tongue wrapped around a South Jersey accent. "Pleased to make your acquaintance. We don't get many of your sort round these parts, you know." He offered a hand to shake, but Carmilla bristled and refused her own.

"Your sort?" Carmilla asked, affronted. She looked at the Half-Elf Cleric and the Half-Orc Barbarian sitting beside her, surrounded by a crop of recently harvested cabbages being driven to the local market.

"Adventurers!" Bob said cheerfully. Carmilla relaxed, giving his hand a firm shake. The three party members were the most heavily armoured people in the area, not to mention the only ones wearing dramatically flowing capes. Adventurers was a logical guess. "I was just saying to my cousin, Robby, that we needed a party to liven things up. And here you are."

"Bob. And Robby," Grogtar the Barbarian sounded appalled, demonstrating that Joseph was young and unschooled in the art of a Dungeon Master making up character names on the fly. "Wasn't the innkeeper Bob too? And the potion seller? And the armourer?" Grogtar stared Bob dead in the eyes, great-axe resting across his knees. "How many Bobs are there in this place?"

"I thought the potion seller was a woman?" Rose asked. Mara had a good eye for detail.

"Her name was Roberta!" Grogtar objected, banging a fist on a cabbage for emphasis. Bob winced at the damage to his precious cargo, but arguing with a Half-Orc rarely ended well for an NPC. "That's basically Bob!"

"Ah yes, that'll be my niece Roberta, a sweet lass and gifted with a potion. She'll see you right, our Roberta. And my uncle the armourer. We call him Old Bob, on account of his age. And then Tall Bob runs the tavern. We call him Tall Bob on account of his height, you know." Bob raised his arms in a wide placating gesture, reins sliding through his fingers. "But we're not all Bobs, mind you. You must've met folk what have other names."

"There's the Evil Necromancer we're hunting," Carmilla suggested with a smile. "Mortimer. That's original."

Rose shook her head and curled a twist of black hair around her finger before tucking it behind her ear. "Well," she said, clearly uncomfortable. Mara looked apologetically at François as she explained, "Mortimer isn't very original. My backstory is that I vanquished an Evil Necromancer named Morticia."

Grogtar groaned and buried his face in his hands.

Lilith walked across the keyboard, pausing to sniff disdainfully at Eddy's cup of coffee. Eddy let Lilith get away with it. She'd saved recently enough, and Eddy was the one disturbing Lilith's routine, not the other way around. Midnight was prowl-time, not PowerPoint-time. "I'm not making you a co-author, though. If you write me a *Nature* paper, we can talk." Luckily — or unluckily — the letters were meaningless gibberish, and Eddy Ctrl-Zeded them into oblivion. Computer-based destruction accomplished, Lilith settled on the corner of the desk Eddy reserved for her mouse. The cat had obviously calculated the exact position she could most effectively disturb Eddy's productivity.

"I would like to get to bed eventually, you know," Eddy complained, rubbing Lilith's chin. "I'm in charge of lab clean-up at 8:30, which means I have to be at work by 8:29 AM. Pre-caffeinated. And dressed like a grown-up. I need to wear clothes with buttons, Lilith. Save me." Unsurprisingly, Eddy's pleas made no impact on Lilith. Eddy should've adopted something with a more pliable personality, like a teenager. Or a rock. "With results. Or at least meaningless data points I can pretend are results. I need to justify my existence to François' industry collaborators before they notice that a PhD student's salary costs half what mine does. My contract is up for renewal at the end of the month. Again. Fucking soft money with three-month funding cycles. Cat food doesn't grow on trees, Lilith." She lay her head atop Lilith's bulk and listened to the rumbling. "I could offer to do a second PhD instead of a postdoc. At least then I'd have job security for four years." It was the worst idea that Eddy had ever had, and that was an achievement.

Lilith purred on, but after a moment Eddy lifted her head and took a sip of coffee. It was cold. She should down it and make a new one. Or she should accept defeat and go to bed, but that wasn't going to happen. Eddy was bad at giving up when she ought to. "I have one data point. I'm not supposed to tell the Board of Ethics about it, but how ethical is a defence contractor anyway? He's probably the kind of terrible person who would appreciate burglary of a charity followed by wanton violence." Eddy didn't want to tell a stranger about what happened at the National Gallery. She wanted to keep this secret, something for her and François, leaving the rest of the world out. She also wanted to keep her job. Eddy hated decisions.

Decisions weren't her responsibility anymore. Her fingers hesitated on the keyboard; she knew enough infosec not to put the question in writing. Instead, she sent François an email asking if he could meet her for a chat before lab clean-up. At 8 AM. It was an act of true desperation to have committed herself to being on campus that early.

"Are you going to show us?" the younger man asks, impatient. He's not a kid like Owen or Lydia — Eddy would put him at her own age, plus or minus a few years — but the grandfather-type accompanying him makes everyone else appear young in comparison. Besides, he's careless in the lab, touching vials and twisting knobs without the least concern for their contents or purpose, childish in the worst sense of the word. It's too late for Eddy to decide she hates him at first sight, but she certainly hates him now.

"She is," François says, face betraying neither irritation or amusement. "We're in her Instance." He adds an aside to the older man, "You won't remember what happens here, but she will." It's a warning delivered in a polite, conversational tone. Eddy's not sure who it's aimed at.

The younger man looks around, suspicious, alert for green screens or teleprompters, but the old man is unfazed. No. He's happy, jovial in a way that invites them to celebrate with him. The older man claps François on the back and says, "This is progress, my boy." It's not but Eddy smiles with him anyway. Keeping a complex bit of instrumentation running to spec isn't progress, but it's not easy, and besides it's nice to be appreciated by The Money. François is smiling too, at least with the upturned corners of his mouth; there's no warmth in it. Someone's on his best behaviour. If François' comment wasn't a warning for Eddy, his reserve ought to be. Eddy doesn't know what she's supposed to be afraid of. They're the ones locked in with her. She's got the better part of an hour to satisfy her curiosity on that question. "Tell me what you've done, but leave out all the jargon. Tell me like I'll tell DND procurement when we're ready to share our trade secrets." The old man is letting her in on the joke when he adds, "It might take a while. Some things you don't pay for with money."

Eddy looks to François, a motion she's sure the old man catches. It's François' show, but he's unreadable and gives her nothing to go on.

It's his gig, but it's her Instance. "When I'm done," Eddy hedges, not specifying a schedule, "I'll be able to watch what someone's doing in their time loop, if they're hooked up to a brain scan. The plan is to embed the hardware in the next generation of Instances." She assumes that's the plan, anyway. Now is a good time to find out, or it would be if anyone was in the mood to share, but Eddy is met with poker faces all around. Worth a try. "I'm on the right track — I got a brain scan signal to port to the regular timeline once." She tries not to sound begrudging as she adds, "The details were in my presentation." François' eyes flicker over her, evaluating her against some metric she still doesn't understand. Her cheeks burn.

There's a noise, and Eddy's gaze flits to the younger man. He's swirling a beaker of pills in methanol, holding it outside of the fume hood so he can better inspect the contents' dissolution in the light. "Leave it be, Norm," the old man says, and he does as instructed. "If you made it work once, why did you stop?" He turns to face Eddy directly. The question is for her, not François. "What would it take to see something from this Instance? Now?"

"Then," François offers the correction lightly. "Time travel is no excuse for bad grammar, Reid." Eddy's not sure François is right. Everything depends on where you place the observer.

Reid accepts his mistake, such as it is, with good grace. "Then, if you prefer. Can you do it?" He puts a hand on François' shoulder, quieting any further interjection François might make, and asks, "Can you show me?" He leans forward, and Eddy still can't think of a sustainable lie. This conversation was bad enough the first time.

When all else fails, there's always the truth.

"I don't know why it worked," Eddy confesses, and even in an Instance she can feel her funding shrivel up and die. "I stole something and got into a nasty fight — I thought it was the heightened adrenaline. But I can't replicate the signal, and I can't figure out what I did right that time." She touches her head but her fingers come away clean; there's only EEG goop on her hair in the Middlerealm. There's EEG goop, and there's Reid and Norm, watching her brainwaves, waiting for a measurable spike that Eddy doesn't know how to recreate. Eddy's out of time.

"Adrenaline," the old man repeats. It's not a word typically savoured like a cigar after dinner, like cold water on a sweltering day, droplets beading on the outside of the glass, rivulets sliding to stain the hardwood table below. "I can think of something to try, but you won't do it," Reid says with too much confidence. It's a dare, and Eddy never learned to back down from a head-on challenge. "He won't, either." There's a hint of derision in Reid's voice and Eddy wants to jump to François' defense, or to her own.

Eddy wished she could cry. She lay in bed, curled around Lilith, pretending it was dark enough outside to justify going to bed. The data was great. Eddy didn't have a scratch on her. Lilith was warm and soft and didn't object that Eddy was squeezing her too tight. Eddy didn't know how to cry when things went right.

François didn't hesitate. He didn't object or pull back or ask her to repeat herself. It was a very, very bad sign, and Eddy should have felt scared, not hopelessly, desperately lonely. Eddy's mom said that Eddy had the worst taste in men. Eddy touched her neck to find the skin unbruised, no hint of a blemish. Her mom was right.

Suddenly, Eddy couldn't stand the thought of being alone any longer. She was sick of it, sick of her closest friend living five hours away by bus, two long time zones between Eddy and Vee, and besides Lilith was the only one who would understand if Eddy attempted to explain. She picked up her phone. There was Kyle, who was decent in bed and laughed at Eddy's jokes and, most importantly, would be there if Eddy texted him. Flesh and blood and sweat and come, not some Shadowrealm Fae trickery.

“What if I don't want to get over him?” Payton asked plaintively. Eddy didn't understand how she ended up within ten miles of advising anyone about their love life. Thankfully Lydia was doing the heavy lifting.

“It's not that you totally get over him.” Lydia spoke with more assurance than she ever showed in front of François, or for that matter, Owen. “But if he's gonna do his own thing, you have to do your own thing.”

Payton sank into the chair and buried their head between their arms on the table. “I don't have a thing. My thing is having too many feelings. My thing is being the world's second-best roommate. My thing is accidentally walking in on Owen with a girl.”

Lydia put a steady hand on their back. “That sucks. I'm sorry.”

“I knew he was straight, but I thought he was single,” Payton moaned into their own arms. “It's different if I have to see him with someone else. What if she's really nice? What if the two of them are super cute together and they hold hands over homemade lasagna dinners? I need to move out.”

This was definitely outside Eddy's area of expertise. Monogamy was a foreign language, and not one she had particular fluency in. Lydia, on the other hand, was a gifted linguist in a dizzying range of social interactions. "If you've never seen or heard about her before, they're not serious. One makeout session on a couch is not true love. You can't move out for that. You'll feel stupid if you give your notice and Owen can't even remember her name in a couple days."

"What if he can?"

"We'll deal with that if it happens. But I bet it won't. Owen's been single basically the whole time you lived together. He got wasted and kissed a girl. Everyone does that sometimes." Finally, a sentiment Eddy could relate to. "I'll ask him."

"No!" Payton exclaimed, horrified. "You can't do that." Their face, peeking out between their arms, was as bright red as their hair. "Owen can't find out I told anyone."

"I'll be subtle." Lydia did not look like a person capable of subtlety. "I won't, like, do it in group meeting or anything." Eddy was only slightly relieved. The girl needed to focus on writing a talk for her next group-meeting presentation, not on finding a casual way to grill Owen about whether his intentions were honourable. François was significantly more interested in p-values than in his grad students' love lives.

Eddy groaned internally as she realized the obvious solution. "Leave it to me. Owen won't know anything happened." There was a small chance Lydia might be awed enough by Eddy's adulthood and possession of a PhD that she'd think Eddy was offering up her miraculous powers of persuasion. Payton's eyebrows went up. They realized what Eddy was suggesting, even if Lydia didn't.

"I think it's time I admitted the truth." Eddy paused dramatically, for ambience. "I can't hide my true nature from you any longer. I am," she took a deep breath, "a Vampire!"

Mara and Joseph exchanged a smile. "We know," Mara said. Technically, Rose said, but the distinction between player/character was a thin line at the best of times, and even more so for Mara. Her Lawful Good Half-Elf Cleric was armed with a preposterously large crossbow and a strong sense of disapproval for the enemy, but given how long it took to reload, she'd done more damage with the disapproval than the weapon. Outside of D&D, Mara didn't have any weapons, but Eddy would still hate to face her disapproval.

"Yeah," agreed Grogtar the Half-Orc Barbarian. "You demanded that we only adventure during the nighttime."

"I drink too much and need to sleep it off during the day," Carmilla said, not entirely sure why she was defending herself, but certain it was the thing to do.

"The 'wine' you drink is very red and very thick," Rose pointed out, with both audible and visible air quotes.

"Red wine is healthy. Prevents cancer. I like mine — extra red," Eddy said in a heavy, culturally insensitive Transylvanian accent. She held up her own glass as proof, though inside it was a very nice Pinot Noir. Close enough. Eddy's dice were clear, to better display the resin blood drops inside each plastic cube, but that couldn't be used as evidence against her; only the players could see them. Joseph complained that it was impossible to read the numbers on them, but he refused to use François' ornate brass dice instead; those always rolled low.

"You bite Monsters during fights, and when Rose used Heal to investigate one of the bodies the next morning, the Goblin was totally bloodless and had two puncture marks on his neck." Grogtar used Intelligence as his dump stat, and even he figured it out. Carmilla might not have been as sneaky as she thought.

"Okay, okay, I'm a Vampire, but I didn't want to tell you because of the exact same kind of anti-dead prejudice that you showed here." Carmilla gestured to the farmer's cottage, strewn with the dismembered corpses of a score of Zombies that used to be the farmer and his relations.

Rose frowned pensively, but Grogtar was outraged. "They attacked us! Without warning! You killed like half of them!"

"We didn't try to talk to them," Rose agreed, softly. "We broke into their home and started taking their stuff. No wonder they were upset."

Eddy should've predicted this response, but she hadn't. In third edition Dungeons and Dragons — technically 3.5e — Zombies were mindless automatons with all the sentience of a bowl of okra, if the okra was out to kill you. Eddy knew that, and François must have known, but of course Mara didn't, which meant Rose didn't. Eddy looked apologetically in François' direction, not that he seemed particularly devastated at the turn of events. François was excitedly writing himself notes behind his protective screen. The cardboard back was printed with a diamond pattern in the shape of an eye, hanging from a black, blue, and silver ribbon. Presumably he wasn't scrawling down a string of curse words. He smiled at Eddy over the screen's edge. Maybe okra and Zombies wanted to be friends, on their squishy insides.

"Being Vampired was the best death choice I ever made. Maybe they like being Zombified," Carmilla said.

"Can I ask the Zombies?" Rose, or Mara, said, reading over the list of abilities printed on her character sheet, finger keeping her place as she scanned down. "Do I know how? Is it a Cleric thing? I can do autopsies with Heal. It's not exactly an autopsy, though."

"You can Speak with Dead," François assured her, eyes twinkling. "But not these dead. You'll need a complete Zombie for it to work." Eddy would've let Rose fail and the party try to work out why, but François was a kinder DM than Eddy. Mara leaned over and kissed François with something more than gratitude. Presumably she wasn't trying to spy on the DM's notes, though one could never be sure. Grogtar averted his gaze, disgusted by Rose's out-of-character behaviour.

"Let's hunt some Zombies," Grogtar said with relish, banging on the table for emphasis, before reluctantly adding, "In a nice way."

"We could go to the graveyard?" Rose suggested. "A Zombie would be more comfortable in the graveyard than this farmhouse. The undead don't need to harvest potatoes and celery." She quickly added, with a glance to her left, "No offense, Carmilla, I don't mind what you eat. Who.

You can eat anyone you like."

The party decided, François led them on a tour through the deserted village, past the silent church bell, the vacant town square, and through a distressingly unfriendly nest of Pigeonbears who'd taken up residence in the abandoned City Hall, until they arrived, only slightly worse for wear, outside the graveyard.

"This befouled place was once a sacred home for those who had passed. Inscribed above the gates is the name it used to bear. *Oira Lórë*, it reads. Below it, in a shaky, barely legible hand, are newly painted red letters welcoming you to *The Six Feet Inn*. The air is heavy with the stench of decay and unease overwhelms you. You fear that coming here may have been a grave mistake," François intoned.

"Is your cat okay?" Lydia asks. It takes Eddy's brain a second to catch up, and Lydia gets there at the same time Eddy does. "Oh! This is your Instance. She's okay, then. I'm so glad."

"How far back did you go?" François asks, something more than mere curiosity, maybe. Eddy can't ascribe innocent motives to François' actions, even if he's got his fingers on the bezel of his watch. He bought a diver's watch when she did, gold and black, and he's twisting the counter on the edge to match her timeline.

"Five hours. I left the Middlerealm at 2 PM to get back to 9 AM in this Realm." It's the longest Eddy's spent in the Shadowrealm. She's not planning to mention it to Health and Safety, who have strict rules about maximum allowable lengths for Instances. Eddy asked François to keep an eye on her body before she left and he agreed without hesitating, even though it meant staying late on Friday night. Even though he knows the Health and Safety regulations as well as she does. His only question in the Middlerealm was the same one as he's asking now in the Shadowrealm, said with the same gleam in his eye. Eddy is the co-ed who goes into the woods to have sex, who drops the flashlight, who suggests they

split up to cover more ground. Eddy's not into survival.

"I'm sorry?" Owen is confused. Eddy has a flash of pity. Unlike lesser mortals, Golden Boy isn't used to being out of the loop.

"Lilith — my cat — peed blood, and I took her to the vet this morning." Before anyone can worry, Eddy finishes the story. "Lilith's fine, just dehydrated. She's at the vet overnight for fluids and I'm catching Lydia's talk in reruns. I told her I'd come by in an Instance if I didn't make it to the real version, and here I am." Eddy considers her words. "Now I am?"

"Thanks for coming, even if it's like this." Lydia's shoulders relax as she's reassured by the presence of Eddy in the room, and Eddy regrets she couldn't be there in the Middlerealm instead. Eddy should've majored in genetics and learned to clone herself. "I don't have much to show, anyway." Eddy suppresses a glare. She told Lydia not to put herself down.

"You've finished your pilot study of first-round participants and lined up a fleet of first-years for the next go. And simultaneously worked with me and Owen to run a neat little study linking low socioeconomic status to exposure to environmental pollutants and hypothesizing that as a cause for differential response to medication. That's not bad in less than a year." Eddy aims her tone for encouraging, not scolding. "We'll be ready to submit soon. You'll have your first publication before your Quals."

Lydia shivers at the reminder of Quals. "Yeah, maybe."

"Should we try to keep the experience authentic for Eddy?" Owen ponders out loud. "We could pretend she's not here."

"Only if you constantly compliment me behind my back," Eddy counters. There's a bit of friendly laughter. "I am here, you've seen me and talked to me, anything I'm going to affect in this timeline has already started. Schrödinger wins this round."

"It's hard to beat physics," François agrees. "I didn't realize you were that close to submission. I look forward to reading the draft."

"It won't be long, if you put aside time to edit in a few weeks. We should celebrate when the paper goes in. Go out for dinner." Eddy reluctantly remembers her obligations. It's uncomfortable and a breach of privacy, but she finishes the statement by saying, "With our partners. A table for five. Or six, if

Owen is bringing anyone?" Eddy can't name any restaurants in the city unless they specialize in delivery. François will be able to, when the time comes.

Owen shakes his head. At least Lydia will have this bit of good news to make up for Eddy missing her talk the first time around.

Eddy trails François to his office after the meeting, a puppy scared to be alone in a thunderstorm. She's got nearly four hours left to kill. Eddy needs to talk to him, in the Middlerealm, really, but she can't even broach the subject here, not yet. François is patient, waiting for Eddy to speak, not that he's got anywhere else to be in her Instance. No point in either of them wasting the time on writing. "Let's do something fun," she suggests, in lieu of the words stillborn on her tongue.

"What's your idea?" He knows something's coming. He knows her. He's not pushing, though. "An excursion to the art gallery?"

"Can we get a drink first?" It's barely eleven but it's been a hellishly long day for Eddy and it's not done yet. Eddy rubs at the left side of her head where the fuzz of her new undercut is starting to come through. "I'll buy."

"Don't be ridiculous," he says kindly. In retrospect, it doesn't really matter.

"I tried to steal the Goya for Mara last heist." The beer François selected is bitter and malty, too dark for summer drinking even in an air-conditioned pub. Eddy loves it. "I couldn't find it in the vault. I can't figure out how they organize the place."

"We'll need some help," François says. He's planning something, plotting maps and assessing contingencies in his head. "What's the security like? You said there were guards." He speaks with the confidence of a man who's done this before. It's undeniably hot.

"Only at the gift shop," she assures him. "Minimal to nonexistent for the vault, other than an access pad that wants a keycard."

"I need a name," he muses, pulling up the gallery's website on his phone, scrolling through. "Do you want to be donors or researchers?"

Eddy looks down at her outfit, selected on the basis of being the closest items to hand when she realized Lilith was sick. It's all black, which you wouldn't think could clash this badly, but diamond-patterned tights do not belong beside the Celtic knots on her miniskirt, or with an N7 hoodie covered in fur, washed and faded to the point that it's closer to grey than black. "Researchers." Eddy doesn't have the poise to carry off having Fuck You Money, but she's spent a lifetime working on her image as an Eccentric Academic.

"Dr Tristan Faulkner, then. Head of Curation." François finishes his glass before Eddy, possibly the first time that's happened. He's excited, eager for the game. "How drunk do you want to get before we do this?"

François takes a refreshingly head-on approach to heists. They're standing in front of the locked vault door, and he winks at her. Eddy grins back at him. Then, he knocks.

No one answers the first time, so he does it again. When a young woman in a badly fitting peach blouse opens it, François frowns at her, disapproving. "Thank you," he says, but his tone is more irritated than grateful as he steps over the threshold. "Can you find Dr Faulkner for me, please?" He's offering the woman a chance to redeem herself for her poor door-opening skills. She quickly accepts, practically fleeing the scene. Eddy feels bad for her, though given it's the Shadowrealm, soon it will never have happened.

Eddy follows François through the main hallway and into the open-plan office. Staff buzz around them, but without acknowledging their presence. They're a rock, and the river has adjusted to flow around them. They've been rendered invisible by simply existing where they shouldn't be. A Someone Else's Problem Field is a powerful tool.

François looks around until he spots the peach-shirt girl, who's frantically talking to an elderly man with a green polkadot bowtie. She takes a half-step backwards as they approach. "Dr Faulkner is in a meeting and can't be disturbed," she says, her voice too fast.

"That's a shame." François gives her a once-over and grimaces, as if she's met his minimum threshold for satisfactory, but only for lack of other options. "You can show us the Goya collection, then."

When he eventually deigned to meet with them, Dr Faulkner's capacity to pontificate under pressure was admirable, but he shouldn't have ignored Eddy while he did it. Sleep of Reason is rolled up and stuffed inside Eddy's hoodie. And they're safely out, eating victory ice-cream bars in the sun. The only fly in the ointment was Dr Faulkner's long-windedness. Eddy only has a few minutes left in her Instance; Mara won't be getting her Goya this heist either. Eddy still counts the expedition as a success. Before Dr Faulkner showed up, the intern showed Eddy where they kept the Goyas, a lathe-green file cabinet drawer in a closet-sized room at the end of the main hallway. Eddy will know for the next attempt.

Eddy looks at her watch, the movement causing almond-chocolate chunks to fall off the candy coating and onto the ground. Enough foreplay.

"When Reid was here, I went into the Shadowrealm. He was there." François nods, encouraging. His ice cream is melting too, drips threatening the sides of his hands. Eddy could lean over, catch the cool white liquid with a bright red tongue. "He came up with a way to — to get enough signal to drown out the noise." Eddy's words are failing her, but her watch gives her courage, hands inexorable, ticking her steadily through the red of the outer dial. "The readings were — incontrovertible."

"What do you need?" François asks her, a gentleness in his voice that can only be a trap. Eddy lets herself fall for it. She's a scientist. This is science.

One last, hopeful glance at her watch. She's on schedule. "There's eight minutes left in my Instance." Eddy looks François straight in the eyes, desperately embarrassed but somehow unafraid, and says, "It only takes three to die of oxygen deprivation." There's a touch of hysteria in her laugh when she adds, "Turns out, if you die in the Shadowrealm, you don't die in real life."

It feels like she does, though.

.

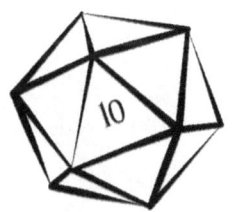

They were splitting a piece of strawberry cheesecake in the National Art Gallery Cafe, but it wasn't a date. Mara slid the side of her fork down the pink and cream marbled edge, shaved off a nearly translucent slice. Eddy liked watching Mara eat dessert, the deliberateness of each bite, carefully savoured. "They should theme the food for the paintings. Voice of Fire as a three-layer cake."

Mara smiled, hand steady with the fork. The cake curled in on itself as it fell. "Blueberry, vanilla, and strawberry." Her lipstick was a muted pink, shades lighter than the cake itself. "What else?"

"The room upstairs with the Quebec artists," Eddy gestured with her fork in the general direction, before cutting off a bit of cake for herself, though with none of Mara's delicacy.

"The Automatistes," Mara supplied helpfully.

Eddy nodded. "Them. The one with patches of white and pastels could be pasta with cream sauce and smoked salmon."

"I could make that. I'll cook you the gallery on Thursday." Mara's culinary talents were limitless, and Eddy had a standing invitation to dinner and games before *Night Beats*. François sometimes let Eddy drive the Tesla, and his NPCs were a delight. "*Voice of Fire* was as terrible as I remembered but everything else was wonderful. I'm glad you suggested we come here."

"We could improve it," Eddy suggested, idle speculation, probably. "There was a guy who vomited colours on bland artwork. Or we bring in strips of fabric and surreptitiously swap the order of the colours, see how long it takes for anyone to notice."

Mara's eyes lit up. "We'd get in so much trouble." Eddy's finely tuned senses could tell the difference between Mara's words and a refusal.

"We could do it in the Shadowrealm. No consequences for anything we do there." Mara's hand was resting on the table next to the plate, waiting for Eddy to take her turn eating. Eddy took a chance and set her hand on top, an arguably platonic gesture. She waited for Mara's reaction, a flinch or a retreat, but Mara met her sly smile with a questioning gaze. "Did I tell you I broke into the Gallery? With a sword?"

"Not yet," Mara answered. "You have a sword?"

"Of course I do. And you need one too, we have to get you one." Something delicate and sharp for Mara, a rapier, thrusting cuts instead of slashing. Equally deadly, but elegant. "We'll go to a proper weapons shop, the themed ones you buy at the mall fall to bits at the second cut." Eddy knew where to get a real sword in Toronto, but not in Ottawa. Her blacksmithing ex could ask around and recommend a place; he'd bought or made most of Eddy's sword collection, and he was the one who taught Eddy in the first place. Though Mara should probably start with a wooden weapon. "I'll train you in the way of the sword, and we'll deface *Voice of Reason* together."

"We'll come back to the Gallery in the Shadowrealm," Mara agreed. "But later. I've never even held a sword."

"It's a date." A girl could dream.

"Hey, Joseph." The kid was fixated on his phone and practically jumped at hearing his name. Eddy peeked at his screen. Someone had sent him the meme of a cat in a wizard's hat waving a magic wand, but Eddy couldn't read the text that went with it at a distance. "Didn't expect to see you here. You skipping straight from ninth grade to a PhD?"

Joseph perked up instantly and grinned at her, cat pictures momentarily forgotten. "I was at the uni library with Rory and Oliver. Studying for exams." He nodded at the brown Herschel backpack on the floor beside him. The seams were bulging. Eddy remembered when she'd finished the last course in her PhD, the feeling of relief that she'd never take another exam. Years later and she still had nightmares, dreams spent frantically searching for an exam hall to take a test on a course she hadn't meant to enroll in, clock counting down in fits and starts before she ran out of time. "Dad's driving me home when he's done his phone call."

Eddy looked at her watch. "It's nearly six." She'd last trawled by François' office at three, looking for a signature on the grant application form. He'd been on the phone then too, but Eddy started forging signatures in ninth grade to get out of phys ed, and François' handwriting was easy to mimic. She was only coming by now to tell François the paperwork was in. Academia was the sort of job where almost an hour past quitting time, Eddy was still at work, and so was her boss. "Wanna bet on how much longer he'll be talking? I'll buy you a frappuccino if he's out before 7."

"Deal," Joseph said with enough confidence Eddy was certain she'd be out $5.25, plus tax. "He said he's nearly done."

"Famous last words," she said, refusing to acknowledge the loss before it happened. A meeting going later than planned was like death and taxes, usually. "What's the exam on?"

"Geography tomorrow and math the day after. Then I escape grade nine." He was clearly delighted with the prospect.

"If you pass," she teased. The mere idea of Mara and François' son failing anything was unthinkable. It clearly never occurred to Joseph, who shrugged off the thought, completely unconcerned. "What're you doing with your break? I spent my summers peeling potatoes in a chip truck with no air conditioning. I don't recommend it." François could probably hook Joseph up with an office job with one of his friends. Reid might take Joseph on as an intern, assuming Oceania Holdings did anything they'd let a fourteen-year-old in on. For all Eddy knew, even their coffee orders were trade secrets, or vaguely illegal.

"I'm going to day camp," he informed her. "There's no air conditioning but there are horses." He must have been to the camp before, or spoken to someone who had, because he proceeded to regale Eddy with more horse facts than Eddy would've guessed there were to know in the world. Apparently, horse feet were a matter of grave significance, requiring constant vigilance to avoid frogs, thrush and colic, which devolved into a complex discussion of the inputs and outputs of a horse digestive system, and a long story about ways to scare off vultures which Eddy was unsure related to horses at all. All, seemingly, without pausing for breath.

Eddy kept her face as straight as possible during the onslaught, refusing to show ignorance in front of a Youth. "Cool." If it was *Night Beats* trivia, she could've held her own, but horses and Eddy had a troubled past. As a teen, Eddy had lost her first and only babysitting job over telling a child unpleasant truths about equids. "Hey. Did you finish your artistic rendition of Grogtar?"

"Yep. Wanna see?" He was already pulling up a photo of the drawing on his phone. His Half-Orc Barbarian was passed out with his head in a bowl of porridge, recovering from the first session's drinking games at the pub. Joseph wasn't allowed hard liquor, but Grogtar was. "I'm drawing one for Carmilla too, but she's not done yet." Joseph showed her the photo anyway. Eddy's Vampire Bard smirked as she unleashed a torrent of Vicious Mockery on the Kraken. "I'll give you the original when she's done."

"Thanks." Carmilla was perfect, from the ringlets peeking out from the hood of her cloak to her antique silver locket, shamelessly ripped off Lilith from *Night Beats*. Eddy intended to frame it and keep it on her desk. "I love her."

"One other thing," Joseph said. Eddy desperately hoped his next words wouldn't reference manure. "You know how you said Instances should work for the future?" Joseph's voice had the same keen enthusiasm as when he discussed how many hands a horse had. "I was thinking, do you have the assembly drawings for the instrument? I can't find them online. I thought maybe there's one-way parts. Like, if you had a worm gear instead of a belt drive." The kid had done his homework and was thrilled to show it off, but behind the excitement was more than a hint of nerves. Eddy remembered the first time she had gotten reviews back on a manuscript, the raw feeling as she looked at the neutral subject line of the email containing them, not knowing what feedback would follow.

Joseph didn't need to be nervous, though. He was a budding genius. Eddy said, "That's a good thought," and Joseph beamed at her, a thousand-watt bulb flicked on at dusk. "I don't have the specs but I bet François can get them for me." A little thing like trade secrets wouldn't slow him down.

On cue, the man himself emerged from his office. Eddy didn't need to look at her watch to know she'd lost the bet, but she did anyway, just to check.

"François, do you know how to make a bomb?" Eddy asks. If anyone in the department knows, he will.

He's utterly unfazed by her question, no raised eyebrows or batted eyelashes. "What do you need blown up?" If anything, he's enjoying himself, smiling at a new secret the two of them can share, at least for the duration of her Instance. "Mass violence is generally a pretty slow way to solve problems." François the dove.

"I want the specs for the instrumentation. I thought I could break into Sauro Sapun Industries, if I had a distraction." Eddy gestures at the machine, now in pieces on the floor of the lab. Disassembling it was harder than she thought it would be, tamper-proof screws and security fasteners defying anything gentler than a hammer. Smashing felt amazing, but it yielded less knowledge and more bits than she'd hoped. A heist would also feel amazing, and an explosion is the most satisfying kind of destruction Eddy can imagine.

François is making the face he makes when he indulges her, and Eddy scowls in return, though her annoyance is mostly performative. "You already have them," she guesses.

"Guilty as charged," he admits, hands up in surrender. "Was that everything you wanted?"

Of course not. "I want to find out what Reid plans to do with the Instances."

That gets a reaction, an intake of breath and a pause. "I wouldn't try a bomb around Reid." François is suddenly tense, muscles taut, eyes alert.

Eddy shrugs, an attempt at appearing nonplussed that François must see through. "It's the Shadowrealm. What can he do?" she asks, like she doesn't know.

"What happened last time he was in your Instance?" It's an honest question, not a rhetorical one, and Eddy wrinkles her brow in confusion.

"I told you." She feels a hand on her neck, but it's her own, index finger pressing hard enough she can feel her pulse beneath it. She must have told François. He's killed her five, maybe seven times? Her heartbeat is accelerating.

He shakes his head. "Not in the Middlerealm." There's compassion in his eyes, in his touch on her shoulder, and Eddy knows better but she turns toward him anyway, tilts her head, mouth slightly open, facing upward, yearning, and he pulls away, hands falling to his sides. He's killed her half a dozen times in the Shadowrealm but he won't fuck her in any timeline, and she's going to text Kyle when she's back in the Middlerealm. Again, and after she had promised Lilith it was the last time. François' voice is level, flat, when he speaks again. "Don't go after Reid directly. You want a mid-level employee. Someone with enough seniority to be a useful conduit, but not enough power to be high on his security's radar."

"Norm?" Eddy knows precisely two people who work at Oceania Holdings, and Norm has the added benefit that Eddy dislikes him intensely.

"Ideally someone lower-ranking, but Norm's an idiot." Even in her state of wounded feelings, it's nice to hear the derision in François' voice, to know he *agrees with her character assessment. "He'll do." François runs fingers through his hair, disrupting the neat arrangement of salt and pepper. He looks sheepish, or rueful, or something that conveys some version of regret, and Eddy decides to be mollified. "Did you still want my help to make a bomb?"*

"Why are we doing this?" Lydia asked dejectedly. Her nitrile gloves were yellowing with sweat and there were wet marks on the back of her lab coat. Eddy didn't imagine herself to be any more presentable. Even Owen looked uncomfortable, boiling alive in a lab without air conditioning so the university could claim it was saving the planet while coincidentally cutting costs and increasing staff misery. "A bot could do this."

Unlike Eddy, Lydia had yet to resign herself to the mindless drudgery that made up the bulk of academic life. Flow cytometry sounded cool when Eddy taught undergrads about optimizing dye lasers and analysing cells' responses to allergens. She left out the part where halfway through Sunday afternoon, someone realized they'd accidentally killed all the cells and everyone got to start over from the beginning. Still, it didn't even rank on her list of the least glamorous things Eddy'd done for a middle authorship. It didn't involve a constant awareness of the red in her tattoos while listening to the Einstürzende Neubauten-like assault of clanking and whirring produced by an MRI instrument, so it was a step up from Eddy's MSc days as a conscious, temporally present lab rat.

It would be nice to have an automated system to prep their solvents, but Lydia's plan had a fatal flaw. "A bot wouldn't do it for a PhD salary," Eddy pointed out. A postdoc on soft money had less job security even than a PhD, but Eddy's salary was higher than Lydia's, and Eddy wasn't paying tuition. Life was all about trade-offs. "Besides, if you get this step wrong, that's the end of your research career, or worse. I'd rather go to jail for my own screw-up than a bot's." Eddy was moralizing to the PhD students, like she was the killjoy supervisor instead of the supportive postdoc. She ought to be ashamed of herself. She ought to be giving out stickers as positive encouragement, but she wasn't sharing her bounty from Mara.

Lydia sighed. "It's still boring."

"Yep." That much, Eddy could wholeheartedly support. "If someone hadn't set off the fire alarm, we could've spent Thursday trouble-shooting, finished the run on Friday and spent the weekend at home like normal people." Well, the two PhD students might have done normal people things. A chapter dropped that morning on the Lilith/Brent omegaverse fic Eddy followed, and she was stuck in the lab instead of hate-reading, despite her disturbed fascination with how anyone could execute such a horrendous concept so well.

"It wasn't my toast!" Owen responded, surly and defensive. He was usually better at taking a joke, and this one was only three days old. It wouldn't get stale for another week, unlike his bread slices. Eddy wished François was there, so he could appreciate her pun and so he could swelter alongside them. "Crisp toast doesn't set off sprinkler systems."

"Your apartment is maybe a five-minute walk," Lydia said with a gleam in her eye Eddy hoped Owen was too obtuse to recognize. Lydia had a theory relating Owen's breakfast habits to ongoing developments in his and Payton's relationship status — or lack thereof — and she would not be stopped until she proved or falsified her hypothesis. "Why don't you eat your crisp toast there?"

"I had work to do," Owen said, not very convincingly.

"Did you get comments back on your ICIB abstract already?" It was easy for Eddy to play ignorant and change the subject. "Did François let you keep the statement about responses to Instances in participants with mood disorders?" The conference was in Kingston, which meant carpooling and shared hotel rooms. Eddy couldn't imagine what results she was allowed to share, and she didn't want to go, so she hadn't written an abstract. She considered it an experiment, testing François' attention to detail.

"Not until it's published." Owen wiped beads of sweat off his forehead with the arm of his lab coat. "How many do we have to go, Lydia?"

"A million," she answered flippantly, counting rows in her lab book. "Eighteen more, if we make the reagents right on the first try."

"We can survive eighteen," Eddy said with a smile that could pass for optimism, if you squinted and looked at it side-on. "This allergy medication better be life changing. I expect the test subject's white blood cells to eat their interleukins, Pacman-style."

"I doubt it," said Owen. "We gave them the placebo."

"I can't Cure Moderate Wounds for you again til sunrise," Rose told Grogtar, her face downcast. "Can you hang on for one more fight?" Given the rate that Zombies were emerging, one more fight was an optimistic estimate. Someone should have warned the party that a graveyard would be full of grumpy undead. Live and learn, though after a few more Zombie waves that would become an aspirational idiom.

Grogtar nodded. "I'm tough." His skin had taken on an especially pallid shade of ash which belied his statement, though his grip on his great-axe never wavered.

"This isn't working," Carmilla said. As one might expect, the root of the problem was François. He had taken it on himself to buy new dice sets for everyone. Eddy could appreciate the thoughtfulness that went into a carved-antler set for Joseph, a rainbow dichroic-glass set for Mara, and a cat-bum set for herself, but she wished François hadn't bought himself correctly weighted icy-blue resin dice to use instead of his low-rolling metal ones. "We need a new plan. What are our assets?"

"We have 545 gold pieces and three pieces of art," Grogtar replied after consulting his character sheet. "Legitimately acquired." He winked at his party. "And a Jar of Perpetual Mayonnaise if anyone wants a snack."

"Don't eat mayo straight from the jar," Rose scolded him, though she clarified her statement to one more context-appropriate and slightly less motherly. "Not during a fight. You'll lose hold of your axe."

"We could make the Zombies slip," Grogtar suggested, excitement replacing weariness as he strategised. "If we spread mayo all over the ground." He glanced at the handful of oncoming Zombies. They weren't the complete specimens the party was hoping for, though if you added up their parts you'd have enough bits to construct at least one full person, maybe two. The party hoped to find a less decomposed body in the crypts, if they survived the skirmishes on the way there. "Once they fall down, I could knock tombstones on them like dominos to finish them off. I wouldn't get close enough for the Zombies to hurt me." Grogtar gestured at the row of gravestones beside him, a lineage of Bobs from Boberta to Boberton, perfectly lined up by the grace of a benevolent DM.

Carmilla also eyed up the Zombies. She grinned wickedly. "Did you know that mayonnaise is flammable?" A Zombie, lettuce, and tomato sandwich, where the Zombie was nice and lean and the tomato was ripe. The greatest thing in the world.

"I'm texting Kyle," Eddy said to an unblinking Lilith. "You don't have thumbs. You can't stop me."

Lilith maintained her stare, not commenting on Eddy's proposal. Her silence was a damning indictment.

"It's not fair for you to complain. You like Kyle. You let him pet you when he comes over." Eddy rolled away from Lilith to stare at the dim outline of her phone, charging on the bedside. It wasn't going to do anything without her, but Eddy didn't want the responsibility. "I like petting too, Lilith."

The grey potato, now sitting behind Eddy instead of in front of her, said nothing.

"I can't sleep, Lilith. I'm fucking exhausted and I can't sleep and I've scrolled to the end of the fucking internet. I can't lie here and keep thinking any more. I can't think. I need to do something."

At that, Eddy stood up, which elicited an objecting meow from Lilith. Lilith was very attached to her routines. "I'm going out to chase a laser-pointer light. Don't bother waiting up."

"Thanks for coming with me," Eddy says to Mara. "To the bus stop." Eddy sounds ridiculous in her own ears. Flirting is hard. Eddy still feels tired, not in her body, six-hours refreshed, but something deeper she carried with her when she crossed into the Shadowrealm. "It's nice out tonight." The air is warm, rich with the noise of cicadas, starlight and streetlamps competing to illuminate Mara. "A great session and a great episode. The perfect evening." An evening worth repeating.

"I loved it." Mara is looking at Eddy with a curious intensity, as if she's the only thing that's real in a world of twilight. "The songs — I didn't expect them to sing." Softly, so no one but Eddy can hear, Mara sings the refrain from the night's episode.

"Swords and songs. The greatest episode of all time." Eddy mimes a cut, straight down on the head, and Mara steps to the side with her back foot, the invisible blade missing her by inches. She returns the blow with a thrust that Eddy only barely manages to block in time, and when Eddy tries to knock Mara's sword into the dirt, Mara twists it back around, brings the tip of the nonexistent rapier to rest on Eddy's breast, right in front of her heart. Mara's a quick learner. "Mercy! Grant me mercy!"

Mara drops her sword, letting it vanish back into their imaginations. "Always. You taught me."

They both see the bus emerging from a wind in the road, plastered in ads for pills to cure baldness, and English language lessons. Mara steps back, away from Eddy. "Goodbye, Eddy." She lingers over her name, maybe.

"I don't have to go," Eddy says quickly. "I don't need to get to work early." Eddy doesn't need to, but she will. She'll emerge in the Middlerealm, in François' hopefully empty lab, at 8 am, bright and early for the day's work. It's not exactly like pulling an all-nighter. "You don't have to work tomorrow. Let's go to the corner store and buy popsicles. We can run around the park like we're kids. Go on the swings and slides. Stay out all night."

Eddy said something wrong, she sees it immediately on Mara's face. "I have to make breakfast for François and Joseph. I have to make sure Joseph goes to bed. He'll stay up past midnight if I let him. François can't sleep if I'm not there. And the toddlers need me. I have Library Reading Hour tomorrow at 10." Mara waves at the bus driver, who's already slowing down for the women waiting at his stop. "I'll see you next Thursday, right? Or before, to practice swords?"

"Of course," Eddy says, stepping onto the bus. "Before, if we can."

"Raphael Gervex," said the Zombie. Or something like that. It was difficult to be certain of pronunciation, with his heavy French accent and parts of his tongue falling off as he spoke. "Though I go by my initials these days." He stuck out most of a hand to shake and Rose seized it firmly with both of her own. A bit too firmly, as most of his sleeve was unable to survive the onslaught and tore away, revealing festering, decayed flesh and a hint of bone.

"It's wonderful to finally meet you, Mr. RG." Rose spoke warmly, but Grogtar kept his great-axe trained on the newcomer.

"Please, please, call me Arg. Mr. RG was my father." Arg shook hands with the rest of the party, forcing Grogtar to single-wield his axe for a second. It would've been an ideal moment for Arg to stage a grappling attack. Unfortunately, no violence was forthcoming, to Grogtar's poorly concealed disappointment. "What brings you to the Township of Deadwood, where mortals fear to tread?" He made a slight bow to Carmilla, adding, "Excluding yourself, of course, mon petit chou."

Camilla returned the gesture with a deep bow, ribbons on her sleeves sliding along the ground. "We follow a quest of utmost gravity, upon which the fate of many lives hangs in the balance." Eddy rolled a blood-shot patterned D20 and frowned at the result. "Oops." Someone was heading to dice jail. Eddy should've rolled the cat-bum die instead.

"Mortal lives, ma cocotte," Arg rebutted, a degenerate elegance to his words, and indeed, to his overall person. He wore what was once a white silk shirt, now stained with dirt and a colourful assortment of bodily fluids, and the stench of death that clung to all Zombies was layered with a floral perfume. He might have used Axe, except Grogtar was the one with the great-axe.

Joseph rolled his eyes hard enough he risked permanent damage to his vision, and sighed the despair of a fourteen-year-old who knew he was infinitely cooler than his parents.

"All life is sacred," Rose said, not very helpfully. Not particularly convincingly either, given her body count. Hopefully no one had told Arg about Rose's growing crossbow proficiency.

"We were born mortal," Carmilla reminded him. "The mortals are our kin." She flashed a pearly white grin, her long canines showing, and added, "Plus, they make great snacks. I'd practically starve in Deadwood if it wasn't for my party."

Resin dice rattled behind François' cardboard screen and he jotted down the numbers without comment.

"The mortals are our doom!" Arg countered, raising his voice in agitation. "They invade our lands, attack without warning, kill without mercy. I know of your quest, mon beau bouchon. You seek to displace us from our ancestral homes so the living can reap the benefits of a city built by the undead!"

The party exchanged glances. "That's not the story that the mysterious stranger told us at the ale-house when we started our journey," Carmilla said, as calmly as she could manage given the passions rising in her breast. "Come to think of it, did the mysterious stranger even tell us their name?"

"When you put it like that, what we're doing doesn't sound very Good," Rose added. "Or Lawful."

"I just wanna smash stuff," Grogtar muttered glumly.

No one was booked on the shared Outlook calendar, but the Instances were in use. Apparently, the machine was unaware of appropriate lab group etiquette. Eddy double checked on her phone; Tuesday afternoon was white and unoccupied. Despite this, François sat motionless, mind elsewhen, chest gently rising and falling, movement barely visible under a cadet-blue shirt. His body, empty, was relieved of tension in a way Eddy had never imagined, lines melted, shoulders back. He looked younger, as if the speckled greys were a mistake, some kind of joke that François was conspiring with time to play on the rest of them. Heart racing, Eddy touched the yielding spikes of stubble on his cheeks, flecks of grey coming in there too. She half-expected his hands to lift, to close the distance between them as they reached for her throat, but of course he was still.

François should've booked, but then Eddy should've too. Eddy didn't want a log of how often she used the Instances, even for an entirely legitimate research trip like the one she intended that day. Mostly legitimate. Apparently, neither did François. There was no known safe way to bring someone back early, so Eddy's study was stymied for the length of his excursion. Unless Eddy hooked François into the EEG and measured his brain waves instead of her own. It was hardly fair that François got to look good at work while Eddy regularly attempted to clean EEG goop out of her hair in the women's bathroom. Testing on him was just, and more than that, it was scientifically justifiable. It was unlikely to produce any useful data points, but that wasn't why Eddy abandoned the idea. The thought of stealing François' secrets gave Eddy chills. She didn't want to know what happened if you died in real life.

François was due back in less than twenty-five minutes, according to the computer's timer. The lab protocols dictated no one went to the Shadowrealm without someone keeping watch over their flesh cage in the Middlerealm. They'd all broken that rule — some more often than others — but it was an excuse to sit beside François, carefully removing his glasses from their perilous slide down his nose and folding them neatly on the lab bench beside him, then settling in with the newest chapter of Lilith/Brent.

Tension arrived in François' face before recognition. He stared forward, eyes unfocused, until Eddy remembered his glasses and placed them in his hand, for him to return to his face. "Hey, François." There was something more than stress in his clenched jaw, hand gripped tight to the arm of the chair, breathing carefully controlled. Eddy pitched her voice at a whisper. "Another migraine?"

Francis nodded, not speaking yet. He took an orange-tinted pill bottle from the front pocket of his pants, opened the bottle with an ease borne of grim familiarity, and swallowed a tablet dry.

"I didn't know you could get migraines in the Shadowrealm," Eddy said. "Do you always?" His pocket bulged in a funny way with the bottle returned to it and Eddy restrained herself from asking if he was glad to see her. François didn't normally carry his meds, which meant he'd anticipated this pain. Overcome by a flash of empathy for his fate in the Shadowrealm, Eddy put a hand on his forearm. He ignored her touch, withdrawn into his suffering, and she left it there, unnoticed.

François shrugged minutely. "Often. Not every time."

"Half the time?" Eddy speculated. She shouldn't interrogate him, but François had taken his meds and there was nothing more Eddy could do to help him. Besides, this was for science. "Could you track it?"

"Maybe. If you want me to." He answered her questions, presumably in order. He ran his fingers through his hair, and seemed to take hold of himself. "Did I miss editing your abstract for ICIB?"

He'd nailed her, and two days before the deadline. Eddy looked away, as though refusing to make eye contact would spare her. "I'm on Lydia's." After a few moments, when the silence got more uncomfortable than speaking, she added, "What exactly did you want me to write about?"

"You got hits. Write about those." He sounded too sanguine about it; he must still think it was adrenaline that produced the signal. Had she never told him the truth in the Middlerealm?

She hadn't. She told him fresh each Instance. Each time they did it was his first time, and he never hesitated.

Eddy shuddered. It was exaggerated for effect, but not by much. "You want me to tell the scientific community that I broke into the National Gallery? And then I did it again for duplication?" More than twice, if she was being honest, which Eddy didn't intend to be at the conference. Her repeated failure to steal the Goya was getting to be embarrassing. Besides, only the initial heist gave her a signal above baseline, which more-or-less confirmed Eddy's suspicion about the blow to the head she got on her first attempt. Rest in peace, no-longer existent past-Eddy, turns out concussions are bad news.

François smiled — a thin smile, but genuine. "You were looking at crime-scene photography. It activates the same regions of the brain. No one going to ICIB is working on anything close enough to contradict you." François sat up straighter, eyes narrowing as they focused. Either the drugs were kicking in, or the problem was intriguing enough to distract him. "Break and entry does it for you? Not more general sources of adrenaline?"

Inception had heists. Bilbo was a burglar. B&E sounded tawdry and cheap in comparison. "Among other things," she hedged. Things that definitely didn't belong at a conference. "Who knows what evil lurks within the heart of man?"

François looked at her, through her. He knew there was more that she wasn't saying, that something was different between them now. His troubled expression could've come from the migraine. "Can you pad it out enough for an abstract? I already listed you as the second driver."

"I get Lydia," Eddy demanded. University regulations meant there was no point negotiating with François for an upgraded rental car. But she could pick her passengers. "And Payton. And not Owen, I don't want to spend three hours watching them flirt in the rear-view mirror." François winced at her raised voice. "Sorry," she said, and added, quieter, "I could present on using EEG to read people's minds while they're in the Shadowrealm, but I'd rather talk about something else." Anything else. "I could write about math? Payton's theory of Instance multiverses and Joseph's worm gear hypothesis." Eddy liked theory. Theory was neutral. Safe. No one had nightmares about physics equations. "I'll throw in a hands-on application. I'll say that after we solve quantum superposition, we'll use the insight to access Future Instances." She didn't offer a schedule for deliverables. "It's edgy for a bioinformatics meeting, but no one's rejected if they ask for a poster."

"You might as well try for a talk." He stood up, though he didn't look happy about it. "Did you want to invite Wahid? I'll cover his costs if you'd like."

"You're absolutely fantastic," Eddy says. She was never this enthusiastic about phys ed class, but that didn't have swords. Or Mara. "You need to work on believing me. And keeping your elbows in. But mostly believing me." Eddy grins mischievously. "If you don't feel flexible enough, we can go to the pub?" Mara is better at sword fighting when she's sober, but she's more confident in her abilities after her second glass of wine.

"I'm driving Joseph home from camp," Mara replies reluctantly. Her workout clothes are adorable: a two-layer sky blue tank top billowing out to reveal close-fitting fabric and skin beneath, and yoga pants sufficient to justify the existence of Lululemon. Eddy could tell Mara it's the Shadowrealm, that she can't get a DUI here, or it wouldn't matter if she did. Eddy tells François every time. She doesn't tell Mara.

"Don't go yet," Eddy pleads, glancing at her watch in dismay. Last time, they fought til the hour, sweaty from the heat and exercise, each of them victorious and defeated scores of times. Eddy hasn't found the words to make Mara stay. Yet.

"Of course not. It's not time. But I can't drink." Mara's always the responsible adult. She pulls out her sword and scabbard, together, up and forward. Eddy would have a broken nose if she didn't scamper backwards, if Mara's attack was any less controlled, if Mara couldn't pull short at a hint of danger to her partner. Eddy's lost her form though, and Mara's cut comes in fast, stopping next to the artery, a breath from her skin, close enough that Eddy can feel the wind from the blade and the cold of the phantom touch. That's the thing movies always get wrong about sword fighting. A real fight doesn't last through a musical number and four cuts on action. A real sword fight ends fast.

Eddy falls to the ground in surrender, hands up. Mara, not one to press an advantage, puts her sword back in the scabbard. Eddy's told her, over and over, never to do that until you're sure they're dead, preferably having escaped with their coin purse. Eddy lunges forward and pulls on Mara's calf, and Mara's down too, lying on the grass beside her, laughing. "Invite me over when you drive Joseph," Eddy demands imperially, as befits her status as victor. "We'll get smashed and assault watermelons." Watermelons make a satisfying and productive target, Mara discovered a couple Thursdays ago.

"I wish I could," Mara says, as if there's anything in the world stopping her. "What about Joseph?"

"I'm a great babysitter," Eddy promises, but instantly backtracks. "I only babysat once and I was so terrible at it, the kid's parents told all their friends never to hire me and I never got another babysitting job. Do not trust me with Joseph."

Mara giggles. "No," she says in what must be faux surprise. Mara knows Eddy well enough to believe it. Mara rolls over so their bodies are parallel, head resting beside Eddy's bare toes. "What did you do?"

"It was October 30 and Ash didn't have a Halloween costume yet. Her parents were going to pick up something pre-made at Value Village. Mara, Halloween is sacred to my people. Goths, I mean." Mara nods seriously at Eddy's words. "Ash *said she wanted to be a unicorn. So we made unicorn costumes for both of us and spent the night dressed up doing unicorn things."*

"What happened when her parents came home?" Mara is the perfect audience, enraptured.

"So maybe we went a bit overboard with the candles and salt pentagrams and I guess it was a waste to use her mum's Dior lipstick for the sigils, but we didn't want to use real blood and we ran out of ketchup pretty quickly." Eddy rests her head on Mara's shins. "No one understands, Mara. Unicorns are devastating agents of chaos."

L ydia knocked insistently on Eddy's office door, and the visiting
postdoc let her in. The postdoc was rewarded with a smile and a
plate piled with varying shaped pastries placed on her desk. "Happy Eid,"
Lydia said, pulling saran wrap off the delicacies. "My grandmother baked
enough to send the whole city into hyperglycemic shock."

"I'll sacrifice my pancreas to save the rest of you," Eddy said, nabbing
a cigar of baklava. She held it aloft and proclaimed, "For the greater
good," before taking a bite.

"Want any, Amelie? The cookies in the middle —" Lydia gestured at a
row of round, white pastries with spirals drawn on their tops "— don't
have any nuts, but they were made in the same kitchen." It was beyond
imagining how Lydia knew the dietary requirements of a researcher who
arrived maybe two weeks ago, when Eddy didn't even remember her
name until Lydia said it. Lydia had a superpower, and society could only
hope she used it for good.

Good or otherwise, Lydia certainly used it to great effect, given how
quickly she'd filled her pharmaceutical study with willing lab rats. She'd
made the stacks of consent forms to run the replicate tests in the
Shadowrealm seem trivial, a minor inconvenience in return for the
exclusivity of the study. Which was how Lydia had data — stage one data,

but still, data — in the first year of her PhD. Eddy was in awe. Lydia didn't believe Eddy when she said it, but it was still true.

"Tell your grandmother thanks," Eddy said, reaching with sticky fingers for her second treat. "Now, just leave the plate here and I promise I'll wash it before I give it back." The sweet was rich with butter and honey, a semi-coherent mass bound together in phyllo pastry. It also had the density of lembas, and Eddy was going to end up like Merry and Pippin.

"Bring the leftovers to group meeting tomorrow?" Lydia's words suggested doubt regarding Eddy's commitment to her eating goals. Probably justified, though more through Eddy's sheer physical weakness than her powers of self-control where rose water was concerned. "Do you know who's presenting now that Marcus bailed?"

Eddy didn't even know that Marcus had bailed on his group-meeting talk, not that she was surprised. "Not me. I'll ask François tonight." *Night Beats* had left them on cliff-hanger the previous week, an unexpected two-parter. Lilith and Titania were in cahoots again, Brad was wandering the Mirrorverse wearing a three-piece fishnet suit, Jane and Jordan were handcuffed to the wheel of a tall ship hours before the full moon, and Brent was too mopey celebrating his death-day to realize anything was wrong. If that episode wasn't enough to look forward to, Grogtar and Arg were bonding over a shared love of senseless violence. Last session, Grogtar showed off his collection of dinosaur teeth to an admiring Arg, and they agreed to go on a hunting expedition together when they vanquished the villains of Deadwood, though of course that was delayed by their newfound uncertainty over who those villains actually were. "Oh, congrats on getting a talk for ICIB."

Lydia frowned. "Thanks. But I didn't — I mean, I haven't heard anything yet."

"I thought you told me?" Eddy said, recollection trickling back as she spoke. It wasn't Lydia who had told Eddy; it was François. He knew the session chair and had gotten a heads up early. Eddy and François had been talking shop in the Shadowrealm, not quite flirting but not entirely professional, before — before Eddy had left the Shadowrealm. "I got one too. Wish me luck. I barely started the work I put in the abstract."

Lydia looked quizzical but didn't contradict Eddy. Moving to surer ground, Lydia informed Eddy, "Owen and Payton are sharing a room at the conference. I'm sharing with Katie. She's buying me earplugs. Who did you get paired with?"

"No one." Being a postdoc came with some perks. Privacy was one of them, at least in François' group. Eddy took a cookie. It was a foregone conclusion that she would make herself sick. "Are you more excited about your elaborate plan to hook up Owen and Payton or your first talk?"

"I definitely didn't tell you about my elaborate plan," Lydia said suspiciously. She looked at Eddy, too much insight in her hazel eyes. The space between Realms was cracking and Eddy was falling into the abyss between timelines, and that was fine, it was all fine, as long as Lydia didn't know about it. Lydia was too young to share Eddy's weariness, but if she could see through Eddy's lies, there was nothing Eddy could do for her. Then Lydia grinned, and Eddy realized she was joking. "Wanna hear?"

"A person isn't an object," Carmilla explained. "Even the living." She winked at Arg who nodded in response.

"Bien sûr, mon saucisson," Arg agreed, frowning gravely. "If Rose wishes to sell out our kind to the living, she cannot use Locate Object in her quest."

"I would never," Rose objected, her voice soft but determined, her hands clasped together. "Carmilla's in our party. You too Arg, if you come with us." She looked at him with wide, earnest eyes. "Maybe we don't need to fight. If I can find the living and talk to them. Carmilla is a Bard. They'll listen to her."

Grogtar made a sound of disappointment at the prospect of a non-violent solution, and Arg groaned. "You may try," Arg agreed. "But I fear some conflicts can only be solved by the sword." He gestured at Carmilla's rapier, still sticky from the cotton-candy spiderwebs they'd chopped through to get into the crypts, and she tried again to wipe the blade clean.

"Thank you for your trust, Arg." Rose scanned down the list of Cleric spells. "I can Scry the living? But that's not until fifth level. And I need to meditate before I cast anything."

"Ninth level," François corrected, but he kissed Mara's cheek to soften the letdown.

"We can use Locate Object, if we can think of an object only the living would carry." Carmilla gestured to Mara's spread of snacks. "Wine and cheese?" Thankfully there was no celery in sight of either Eddy or Carmilla. "The living might carry a Jar of Perpetual Mayonnaise." Carmilla gestured at Rose's haversack. "She does."

"That's really useful," Grogtar countered. "Anyone would want that in a fight."

Arg raised his eyebrows, or what remained of them. "I think not, Grogtar. Zombies and mayonnaise are not such great friends." He shook his head sorrowfully, losing an ear in the process. Rose was quick to retrieve it from the floor, though she was temporarily out of spells; his ear wasn't going back on that night. Given its partial mummification, it wouldn't worsen before she recharged.

"Bandages," Carmilla suggested, watching the scene unfold before her. "Advil. Sutures."

"Nail clippers," said Grogtar, displaying excellent out-of-the-box thinking abilities. "Orcs use our axes but I bet we can find a living Human who carries nail clippers."

"I know something you don't know," Eddy said in a singsong voice, standing at the edge of François' office door, not quite crossing the threshold. A vampire needed to be invited in. It was daytime and there was plenty of sun streaming through the single-pane windows, but Eddy was wearing a black dress with lace sleeves and red seams. Close enough.

François put down his espresso mug. The problem with Nespresso machines was they couldn't brew a pint of coffee in one go, but someone had done their best to make up for it by giving him an adorable wee mug, happy penguins dancing along its rim. Mara, surely. "Tell me?" he asked, playful. "Or do I need to guess?"

"Guess," she demanded. "Three guesses, or I get a coffee if you can't get it." She'd had two cups off him in the Shadowrealm already, but they didn't count towards Eddy's blood caffeine level.

François reached for a mug as she said it, this one with a polar bear making a snow angel, and a matching tiny plate. "*Night Beats* spoilers leaked and you know who the Final Guardian is." He added two cubes of white sugar to the dark liquid and stirred with an equally undersized spoon. "I don't keep milk in the office," he said apologetically, like Eddy didn't know that. He tilted his head and lifted the cup in her direction, and she entered the office to take it, fingertips brushing against his. Eddy shivered at the touch of his hand, but if François noticed her reaction, he gave no sign of it.

"Nope. Closer to home." Eddy took a sip, though it was too hot to drink properly. "Guess again."

François grinned at the challenge. "Joseph convinced you to buy a horse." Eddy had decided that horse-camp was a circle of Hell where parents sent children to learn to speak in tongues. Theoretical physics keynotes made more sense to Eddy than Joseph on a horse-related monologue. Eddy glared at François suspiciously, and he radiated innocence back. She suspected he'd been encouraging Joseph's discussion of cannon bones last Thursday, which Eddy considered the least interesting kind of canon.

"Nope. Guess whose voicemail password is '1234'?" Eddy drained the cup, ignoring the heat. The sugar at the bottom never fully dissolved, a hit of sweetness to counter the bitterness of the coffee.

François took her cup to start brewing her another. "Half the staff of the Department," he said with a gleam in his eye. "Who did you get?"

"The most irritating human in defense contracting." If Eddy was exaggerating, it wasn't by much.

He laughed. "Surely not. Even Norm wouldn't be stupid enough to leave the factory settings on his phone. Reid makes his senior employees attend infosec workshops." There was a certain resignation in François' voice, as if acknowledging that education was wasted on Norm. That man possessed a firm conviction that he already knew everything the world had to teach him. Their last meeting with Oceania Holdings, Norm had tested even the boundless limits of François' poker face. None of the students had noticed, but Eddy had caught Reid's eye and they'd shared a smile, which was enough to reassure her that Norm's antics wouldn't keep the adults from getting on with the real work, and that Reid had a sense of humour, even if Norm didn't.

"But what if Norm was exactly that stupid?" Eddy smirked and took possession of her second (fourth?) coffee. "He mentioned a Winston. Who's that?"

"Norm's son. He's a year younger than Joseph, but they're in the same group at Sterling Acres. The counsellors intended Joseph to be a good influence on Winston, but it's more likely to be the reverse. Boys their age are raptors testing the fences." There was no judgement in François' voice, only bemused acceptance.

"Girls too," Eddy said.

"What did Winston take this time, Norm's car or his ID? Or did he spray-paint frogs on Norm's car again? Last time Winston did that, Norm couldn't get a rental before the golf weekend."

Eddy had a fair bit of sympathy for occasionally commandeering a parent's car, though she'd relied on her older cousin when she wanted anything that required proof of age. No one would've confused teen-goth Eddy with her blonde, hippie mother. "Neither? Reid said he'd talk to someone on the Board of Trustees at Sir John A Macdonald Academy about getting Winston a place. He said the grade nine class shouldn't be full this early in the summer."

"I'm surprised Norm bothered to apply for Winston." François didn't sound surprised. "Winston doesn't have any of the attributes they look for in a pupil, and Norm doesn't have the ones they look for in a parent. But Norm doesn't like hearing no."

"Could Reid get Winston in?" Eddy asked. Reid sounded confident in the voicemail.

François shrugged. "Probably, given how much they value their alumni, but I don't know why he would. I didn't need to for Joseph, and my name's on the lacrosse trophy in the lobby. I suppose we'll find out in September."

Eddy looks at the waiting guards, and realizes, too late, that she fucked up.

Every time Eddy breaks into the National Gallery is a bit different, the pattern subtly changing. A Gentileschi exhibition instead of Hans Holbein, the girl in the peach blouse replaced by a stern-looking man with a beard, Toronto Moose in the City plushies appearing in the gift shop. A true experiment, run in triplicate, would have Eddy going back to precisely the same instant — back an hour, then back two, then four. It's longer in the Shadowrealm than Health and Safety would allow, but Eddy means to try it eventually. She's a diligent scientist. Going back on different days, different months, sometimes, is replication, but it's not identical. It ought to be enough to get the Goya, though. That was Eddy's plan for today, rigorous science be damned.

Her plan isn't going to work.

The National Gallery security guards wear black, and they shout, and they occasionally throw punches, but they're not armed. It was only the first time they got close enough to do anything, and Eddy's learned from experience. She watches her distance now. The guards might call for backup, but by then Eddy's back in the Middlerealm and they don't exist anymore.

These guards wear pale blue shirts, nearly grey, with what must be bullet-proof vests on top of them, and they look at her with a mixture of concern and disdain. Eddy's not used to seeing guns. It feels discordant, like something out of a movie, not real life. She's not sure if this counts as real. They're shouting at her — there's always shouting — but Eddy's not listening. She's trying to think, figure out what she missed, what was different this time.

A string of black SUVs pulls up, five at least, tinted windows and miniature Canadian flags. Eddy's brain is stuck, she knows she'll get it in a second, if they would only keep quiet for long enough for her to think, to pause instead of to react, instinct taking over, the short sword comfortable and familiar in her hands. It's a bad idea, she knows it's a bad idea, and the noise of the gunshot arrives after the bullet does, pain swifter than she's used to, sharp and sudden, excruciating, and then, nothing.

Lydia had her lab coat on. It was entirely unnecessary for the negligible dosages they gave out in the Middlerealm during the stage one trials, and doubly so since they delivered the medication as pills for ingestion, not via dermal exposure. On the other hand, it instilled a sense of confidence in the patient and reduced long-winded questions by fifteen percent. Technically, there was no way for either the patient or Eddy to know if it was the Middlerealm, or if they were living through Lydia's Instance. Eddy would've asked, but she had her principles, and those included the double-blind experiment. "Thank you for coming, Travis."

"No probs, Lydia. You said I'd get to time travel plus a gift card to Tim Hortons." Travis had slicked his hair to the side, like he'd already time travelled from the 1990s to get to the lab. He was watching Lydia's face with a ferocity reserved for first-year psychology students who recently learned about microexpressions. "And marks."

"Yes, but you can't use the gift card on campus," Lydia corrected him firmly. "And term's over. I can't give you grades for doing this instead of your dream journal." Lydia pulled a plastic bottle from a row and ticked off the serial number on a list. Before opening the safety packing, she asked, "Did you still want to participate?"

"Do I get to time travel?" Travis said, though any bartering was ineffectual at best. The study parameters were long-since fixed and detailed minutely in the form Lydia handed to him, along with a university-branded pen. He got to keep the pen, which was more than literally nothing.

"Lydia gets to time travel, and you'll be along for the ride," Eddy offered, handing him a plastic cup of water. Even that sounded more glamorous than the reality of not-experiencing someone else's Instance. "But you can tell people you're saving lives and the gift card's ten bucks."

The air is sweet with the smells of freshly mown grass, magnolia, and wisteria, and the Gagnon's windows are open to let the summer suffuse the house. They have fly screens, of course, but those yield to a pocketknife or the jagged edge of a key. Mara's in the living room, reading, lost to the world in a story. Eddy watches her from the edge of the room, the soft rustle of the pages, the rise and fall of her breathing, and then Mara looks up.

When Eddy sees Mara's still face, something not-quite afraid, she knows she's miscalculated. It's only the Shadowrealm, but it's unbearable to know she's hurt Mara so deeply. To know that Mara's learned how to wear this much pain with so little to show for it. Breaking into their house was a mistake.

It's only the Shadowrealm. Eddy will get it right next time.

"Are you his midlife crisis?" Mara asks calmly, voice devoid of bitterness. She barely even sounds surprised. "Did he give you a key?"

Eddy shakes her head. "No. François would never." She doesn't say what, exactly, he would never do.

"They all — I thought he might be different. He's not perfect. But he's different. I thought so, anyway." Mara is drawn in, coiled so tightly that Eddy sees no edges or cracks in the surface. Eddy longs to reach out and hold her, to bury her fingers deep inside and pull until she grasps Mara's still-beating heart in a trembling palm. Eddy wonders, absurdly, what François does with her body when she's gone.

"He's different," Eddy says dryly, the understatement of the timeline. *"But I'm not his midlife crisis."* She smiles and steps forward, until she can smell Mara's nutmeg and honey scent, until she can feel the weight of Mara's eyes on her. She reaches for Mara's hand, resting on the open pages of her book. *"I'd like to be yours."*

"Right," Grogtar called, on his hands and knees, eyes near parallel to the ground so he could distinguish the muddy footprints left by complete shoes from the myriad of Zombie marks on the pavement. "They turned right here, and then they went up the stairs — there's someone in the bakery." He took in the weeds around the door, the fallen sign resting by the boarded-up window. "Ex-bakery," Grogtar said in the dejected tone of a man realizing he was not going to be eating sweets that day. In stark contrast to his character, Joseph was making solid headway through a bowl containing the eight different flavours of gelato François had bought for Mara.

"Alas, us Zombies, we are not natural bread-eaters. The bakeries, they are not so profitable now as once they were." Arg punctuated his words with a heavy sigh, bits of his lower lip sliding down his face with the force of his exhalation. Rose handed him a handkerchief and he mopped them up before they made it past his chin. She waited until he was clean to kiss him on the cheek. "Merci."

"There's something tastier than baguette in there," Carmilla said excitedly. Arg was a good friend but a terrible snack, and Rose only escaped anemia through regular applications of Lesser Restoration. Fresh blood would make an excellent addition to the menu. "Someone's alive."

"Not for long," Grogtar said enthusiastically, standing up and brandishing his great-axe.

"We need information," Rose reminded her action-oriented party. "We're here to talk to them, that's all. They might be perfectly nice and only here by accident."

Arg raised most of an eyebrow. "A settler, here to invade the lands of the dead, cannot be nice."

"We were," Rose said, patting his forearm. With a combination of Mend and Inflict Minor Wounds — which had the reverse effect on a Zombie — she'd patched up most of Arg's shirt and the flesh beneath it. "It was a happy accident that led us here." She looked slightly embarrassed and added a mumbled apology for the many Zombies they'd murdered along the way.

"The deserted bakery is dim. Only the merest glimmers of moonlight pierce the cracks between the wooden slats that lie over the window frame, and you bring your torches close to the walls to investigate. The shelves are full, moldy cupcakes and stale muffins telling the tale of an impromptu flight as bakers abandoned ground once fortified and well-defended. Just Desserts has fallen on hard times, and you fear its owners may have fallen on harder." François paused for effect, or, more likely, so they could appreciate how awful his pun was.

Grogtar took the opportunity to ask, "Can I Search for cake?"

"Roll a D20," François replied optimistically.

"Try not to roll a one," Eddy advised him. "If you do, they're lying about the cake. Or it's made of neurotoxins."

François laughed and allowed that Grogtar's six was enough to locate some, though it was only carrot cake, and the cream cheese icing had developed a decidedly hostile shade of green. Grogtar ate it anyway, claiming it reminded him of his grandmother's baking, but then again, his grandmother was an Orc. He rolled a nat 20 on his Fortitude save to resist stomach-ache. During Grogtar's Search, he also discovered a crumb trail leading to the kitchen, which interested the rest of the party far more than the potential for food poisoning. They gathered in the nearby hallway and held silent for a moment. Over the noise of Arg's dripping bodily fluids, they could hear the unmistakable sound of munching, as though someone had recently located a jar of chocolate chips.

Carmilla charged in, heedless of danger, only to hear a young man's munchkin-like whine, "I send Magic Missile on the darkness!" While the attack failed to cause any physical harm to the darkness or to Carmilla, it succeeded in rendering Eddy paralysed with laughter and unable to retaliate. It also set the bakery on fire. The young wizard had obviously neglected his potions lessons and failed to appreciate the explosive properties of flour, particularly when combined with torches moving at high velocity. Grogtar followed close on Carmilla's heels, axe held high, then Rose and Arg. The corridor was so narrow that the four party members ran into each other as they closed the distance. Rose reached out her hand to Inflict Wounds on the threatening mage.

With all the excitement, it took the party several seconds to realize they were dissolving.

Eddy's body is heat and agony. Unbearable, the kind of pain that makes her want to fight, to escape, to — momentarily — live. She's not meant to resist, but sometimes, unbidden, her body remembers the lure of breath and her arms swing of their own accord, elbows reaching for tender places. François is behind her this time, there's nothing to connect with. She twists, tries to make space between hands and neck, but he holds on, steady, inexorable.

The hallucinations are a relief, as always, a kindness of kaleidoscope lights and ecstasy that elevates the suffering but provides no respite, the juxtaposition accentuating instead of relieving the turmoil of her body. It lasts longer than she could have imagined enduring.

And then, mercifully, it stops.

When Eddy came back, François was watching the EEG scans, watching her, lines of concern drawn across his face, as winding as the patterns on the screen. "You told me it was adrenaline," he said. She had, when it was him, Reid, and Norm gathered around her readouts, imagining what the rise and falls of her brain waves could mean. Believing her lies, or pretending to. And she told him that again, each time he asked her in the Middlerealm. "But that's not what happens, is it?" They'd danced around it long enough, his questions, his acceptance of her refusals to answer. He wasn't letting her get away with it this time.

Eddy looked down at her hands, twisting in her lap. "I died. It's the only way to get a signal." The counter on her diver's watch was still set to midnight, as if that was when she ran out of air, not now, not then, whenever 'then' belonged to when she reset it each Instance. "I'm fine now." Embarrassment was unfortunately not fatal. "It's fine."

"You died for every data point." Despite all the time together, Eddy couldn't read François' tone. She wasn't intending to look him in the eyes. This wasn't the sort of thing laughed off with a joke about 5 pm in Australia, and if Eddy fucked up this conversation, François would cut her off from the Shadowrealm.

If you die in the real world, do you really die?

"I said that I'm fine. The algorithm isn't ready to distinguish my response to eating a Metro coleslaw versus Mara's brisket." She pushed the words out and put some force behind them. "Did you get Lydia's revisions done or do we need to ask the editor for more time?"

"How do you do it?" he asked, ignoring her attempted diversion.

When she told him in the Shadowrealm, she was telling him the future. Here, she was telling him the past. Eddy couldn't find the words, couldn't think of anything that wasn't ridiculous, and he waited her out until with a hysterical giggle she finally said, "I don't. You do."

He flinched, maybe, or maybe she wanted him to.

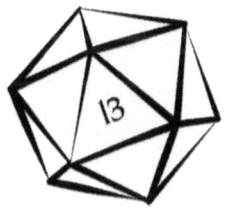

August was hot and slow, a sticky haze that seemed determined to go on forever without interruption. Eddy, not privy to the rationalizations of the upper class, couldn't explain why the Gagnons had thrown a garden party when they were fortunate enough to have AC. Not that Eddy considered declining the invitation, despite the heat, despite her opinion of parties. Mara had nervously tucked an invisible strand of hair in place behind her ear as she asked and thus rendered Eddy incapable of resistance. And so Eddy found herself wearing a black polyester maxi dress in the blazing sun, tendrils of hair sweat-stuck to the right-hand side of the back of her neck, sunburn imminent, trying to work out what had gone wrong in her life that led her to this moment. Luckily, Mara turned up with a flute of of champagne, wearing a green A-line dress with a white flower pattern and a narrow bow at the waist, and Eddy remembered exactly why she had agreed.

"I should introduce you to the guests," Mara said brightly, though Eddy had grown out of her 'meeting new people' phase in grad school. "You know us, of course, and there's Charles and Ethan and Herbert from the Department, Colette from book club, and you know Reid and Norm from your work with Oceania, though Norm is late so there's no one Joseph's age. I hope he gets here soon." Joseph looked perfectly content, animatedly talking to an elderly man Eddy vaguely recognized as a Tory politician, though she had no idea which one. The man couldn't have been interestingly bad, or Eddy would have remembered. His hat, on the other hand, was endearingly terrible, a fabric attempt at a fedora that had lost most of its shape decades of washes ago, a tan memory of its former colour. He listened to Joseph with an earnestness that suggested kindness rather than political opportunism, particularly given that Joseph was too young to vote and was probably talking about horse camp again. Maybe he was one of the good ones. The less bad ones. "Do you want cake?" Mara added abruptly, turning suddenly in the direction of a snack-laden table. "I made you *Voice of Fire* cake again, with red velvet and blueberries."

The cake was a successful lure, drawing Eddy to a gazebo-covered table with chocolate-covered strawberries, meringues and, amongst the sweets, a forlorn vegetable tray. Eddy pretended not to see the celery taunting her with its greenery and promise of health. Mara presented Eddy with a china dessert plate piled high with multicoloured layers and a miniature fork to eat it with. Certain logistical problems presented themselves in holding both her cup and her plate and using a fork at the same time, so Eddy reluctantly followed Mara to a glass table surrounded by wicker chairs and adults bemoaning the state of the world.

"That's Tobias, and Lucy, and Colette," Mara said, tilting her head in the general direction of each person, an introvert's version of an introduction. A generous introvert, who didn't expect Eddy to remember anything about anyone she met at book club. If Eddy had to sit at the grown-ups table, she was happy to do it from the periphery, Mara filling in names and backstories, Eddy's attention mostly focused on devouring a Grogtar-sized portion of cake and reflecting on whether Lucy's dress, a red Bardot with a neckline precisely on the near side of appropriate, was also stealth-goth. Of course, it couldn't last.

"You made it," Reid exclaimed, and Eddy smiled back at him despite herself. "You must meet my wife. I can't let you think my life revolves solely around tormenting you and François with action items and deliverables." Reid indicated the stately woman on his right who wore a broad, white hat with netting across the top. "Eddy, this is Alycia, my better half."

"We're lucky you have her," François agreed easily. "Alycia has a humanizing effect on our Reid." Reid acknowledged the truth of François' words with a slight lift of his beer glass, full with amber liquid and lazy bubbles. "Alycia does great things for the arts, while Reid gets his hands dirty." François nodded across the table to Tobias, who was sweating his way through a short-sleeved dress shirt. "As does Tobias, though politics is his vice of choice."

"You're misrepresenting me, François. Objective journalism only looks like politics to people who have a side," Tobias pontificated, and Eddy made a mental note to avoid getting trapped sitting next to him. Mara said his wife was an opera singer, which checked out. Lucy could break into song as a cunning diversion the instant Tobias opened his mouth.

"Everyone's got a side," Lucy said, more astute than her husband, the print journalist. Both of them were the last of a dying breed, a dodo married to a passenger pigeon. There was something romantic about lost causes, about refusing to look reality in the eye.

"The truth doesn't have a side," Tobias objected. "If my work makes progressives angry, that's because they don't like what my investigations reveal. They should focus on changing the future, not my stories."

"Tobias reveals the truth to an unwitting public, Alycia fixes society's attitudes towards it, and I work hand in glove with the Department of National Defense. It won't be long before we're the ones deciding the future," Reid declared. "François, on the other hand, only changes the past."

"For now," Eddy said, more confidently than the data warranted, but no one won grant applications and industry collaborations by hedging. Eddy knew the game, had reached Assistant Professor, nearly gotten tenure before her luck ran out. And, after speaking, she knew she shouldn't have, that she ought to have let François defend himself. François looked pleased though, something close to smug but not quite making the distance.

Alycia airily waved the conversation away. "No science shop talk. I absolutely forbid it." Her words were soft but there was steel in them, the hardness of a woman used to being obeyed. "Lucy, rescue us."

Lucy obliged, relating her director's heartwarming but unfortunate attachment to his wife, who, at 60, was no longer the dancer she was at 20. "She dances well for her age, or she would if she was in her 80s," Lucy said, darkly sorrowful eyes at odds with her mischievous tone. "Dorothea doesn't belong in the same postal code as *Don Giovanni*."

"Her dancing is better than the Commendatore's singing," Tobias replied. "Who choreographed Valentín singing and sword-fighting at the same time?"

"I love opera," Colette ssaid smartly, but then torched any goodwill she might have received: "*Phantom of the Opera* is my favourite movie." Lucy's answering wince was more mournful than hurt, and went entirely unnoticed by Colette. "It's so romantic. I wish I was Christine."

No one seemed quite certain how to respond, and for once Eddy was grateful to see Norm, if only to break the momentary silence. He looked like a parody of an Abercrombie and Fitch ad, khaki pants too tight, a monochromatic sweater tied around his shoulders in such a manner as to utterly negate the purpose of the garment, if it had any place on a sweltering August day. His son followed in his tow, freckled face wearing a sullen expression familiar to Eddy from her own teenage years, when she had been the kid obliged to make an appearance at her mother's parties. The boy instantly disappeared to find Joseph, and regardless of frog-related transgressions, Eddy silently wished him well.

"Sorry I'm late," Norm said. He accompanied his brusque words by handing Mara a bottle of something Eddy didn't recognize, but which got a nod of approval out of François. Mara took it graciously and busied herself getting him a beer to replace it. "Coors Light tonight, I'm driving, thanks."

"Did you really future-proof the Instances, Eddy?" Colette asked, her words brimming with enthusiasm, though not with scientific accuracy. Mara had said Colette worked for Alycia, but Eddy was unsure how the perky gymnast-type in a pastel blue sundress fit into a charitable foundation for the arts. That question would have to wait until Eddy and Mara were alone together, rather than during this time of shared suffering. Hell was other people, and those people were extroverts. "That's amazing."

"I'm working on it," Eddy said, smiling, giving nothing away. Not when The Money was in the room.

The Money raised his eyebrows. Eddy didn't know if Reid thought she was lying that she could or that she couldn't. "Of course you are. Talent like yours, you're wasted in academia. I'd have you on my team working against Russian expansionism." Reid looked at François, eyes twinkling with mirth, before he fixed his gaze back on Eddy. "Let me know when you're done with The Cathedral and your vow of poverty. I'll be waiting."

Eddy felt her veins burn hot, blood scalding, something too familiar in Reid's half-mocking expression, in the tone of his dare. Eddy remembered her first conversation with Reid, the one that never happened for anyone but her, and her hand involuntarily moved to her throat, slid along a black choker of beads that complimented her dress and matched her earrings. Her skin felt impossibly far away, as if it were someone else's body that Eddy had no claim to. She forced her hand back down, picked up her champagne flute and took a sip, waiting for the sensation of liquid gathering on her tongue only to discover her glass was empty.

"Do you want more champagne, or I can make you a cocktail? I made rhubarb simple syrup for the Old Fashioneds," Mara interjected, reaching for Eddy's cup. It took a conscious effort for Eddy to relax her fingers enough for Mara to retrieve the flute.

"Mara said it was you." François cornered Eddy by the snacks table. She had constructed an elaborate pyramid of chips, cheese, and Nanaimo bars, undeterred by the non-uniform shapes involved in using party mix as a building material. In an ideal world, rich people would use normal-sized plates for snacks, but even in this world, the only things holding Eddy back were gravity and cowardice. At François' words, Eddy tried to maneuver her face into an innocent expression, whatever that looked like, but she could only maintain it for a second before her lips twitched upwards.

"Southeastern Australia makes some excellent wines," Eddy said, bluffing. Her month of free membership to *Wine Spectator* had long since expired, and she wasn't paying money to impress François. "Mara likes a good Shiraz."

"She thought it was very sweet of you to get Little Penguin." François was equally incapable of maintaining his severe expression, instantly lapsing into a grin. "You must realize that everyone gifts me from that winery. Thank goodness it's drinkable or Mara's roses would be alcoholics by now." Eddy suspected as much when she bought it, but she wasn't letting other people's behaviour stand in the way of her trolling. François' stance shifted to straight, suddenly serious. He put a hand on her arm, ignoring her sheen of sweat, a mixed pleasure in the shared warmth of touch. "Reid can be a bit much. Are you okay?"

Eddy nodded, like there was any timeline where she told him she wasn't.

Lucy bent down to sniff a rose, her long, pale fingers drawing the stem closer, the red of her lipstick more intense than the flower. "They're lovely," Lucy told Mara. "And the koi pond is charming."

"I worry about them in winter," Mara admitted. "But it's seven years now and they're still alive. They have babies every year, but then they eat most of them."

"It's the state of nature," Alycia said. There was something surreal about the pure ivory white of her shift dress, as if even grass stains and mud deferred to her authority. "It can't be helped."

"We could teach family planning classes to the fish?" Eddy suggested, and was rewarded with a mixture of polite and genuine laughter. Sunlight bounced off a golden scale, shadow momentarily transformed to brilliant colour by a changing angle. "Only ninety-three years til one of them turns into a dragon, if the stories are true. You'll need a bigger pond." Eddy eyed up the back yard. "You could link it to the pool?"

"Where would we go swimming?" Colette asked, utterly devoid of imagination. She would have been a perfect fit for Norm, but Mara said Colette was married and Norm hadn't dated anyone since his messy divorce.

"I'd swim with a dragon," Lucy said, arms fluid in a motion equally swimming or dancing. She was as elegant and alluring as a dragon, but it was the wrong species for her.

"When you transform, you'll become a siren," Eddy foretold. "The beauty of your songs will lure countless to their doom, and they'll recite your praises as they crash into the rocks."

Lucy accepted the compliment with a gentle shrug. "And you? What do you become after a hundred years?"

"I'm a unicorn," Eddy told her, like a young girl declaring herself a fairy princess. "But not a safe unicorn. You can't trust the stories." Lucy laughed, a throaty, intoxicating sound, and Eddy wondered why she'd never been to the opera. "Mara, let's go see Lucy's opera. I have to hear her sing."

Mara was frowning, biting her lower lip, and she ignored Eddy's statement entirely. "Colette, I'll get you a towel and you can go swimming." Her movements were abrupt and Alycia looked at Mara with concern.

"I'll come with you," Alycia promised.

Eddy's mother hated eavesdroppers. She said nothing good came from learning other people's secrets. Used to say. Eddy was done filling glasses with champagne for herself and Lucy, she should be back at the pond by now. But Alycia was talking, her whispers audible from the edge of the drinks table, and Eddy listened, despite herself, despite knowing her mother was right.

"I can't imagine what it's like for you," Alycia said, sympathy crossing the border to pity, hand on Mara's shoulder. Mara's pull was irresistible, making everyone who met her determined to protect her. "Not knowing what your husband is up to when he says he's at work."

Eddy started at that. Alycia couldn't have known. François didn't tell Reid what he did to Eddy, let alone telling Alycia. Reid had known at one time, but only in the Shadowrealm. And none of them would tell Mara the truth.

"I didn't go to university," Mara agreed, voice low, wavering. "François explains his research in simple words and I try to follow along. I think Joseph understands more than I do." Mara sighed, giving Alycia the opportunity to relate to her inadequacies. "Is it the same for you, with Reid? But, of course, you're so much cleverer than me. You figure things out."

Eddy needed to leave before she heard any more, before she got caught. Still, the only reason she moved was that Joseph appeared at her side, unsteady on his feet, eyes wide with panic.

"I need your help," Joseph said. "I screwed up and my parents are going to kill me."

Something cold and unwelcome settled in the pit of Eddy's stomach. "What can I do?"

In Eddy's experience, puke on the living-room carpet was not grounds for filicide. At worst, a stern talking-to and an attempted grounding. Joseph might be cooperative enough to abide by parental punishment, teenage-Eddy had not been, but then teenage-Eddy had never gotten drunk on seventeen-year-old Ardmore. Joseph swayed, feet and head providing him conflicting information about the precise location of the floor, but he was still better off than Norm's son. He sat on the floor next to the vomit, unable or unconcerned to move away, head hanging down, face pale. "Get him some bread and a glass of water," Eddy ordered Joseph, but kindly. She had never been young enough to panic when someone got plastered, but from the expression on Joseph's face, she imagined it was a frightening experience.

Joseph disappeared, leaving Eddy alone with Norm's kid. Luckily he didn't have any hair to hold. "I'm Eddy," she said awkwardly, eyes searching the room for an emergency garbage bin, or, failing that, a decorative bowl. Even a vase in a pinch. "You okay?" Small talk was the worst part of crisis-management.

"Yeah," the kid lied, not very convincingly. He seemed equally at a loss for conversation, finally adding, "I'm Winston." The misery on his face increased and he said dejectedly, "Are you gonna tell my dad?"

"No." It hadn't even occurred to her.

Winston perked up at that, if only marginally, and he accepted a slice of white bread and glass of water from the returning Joseph without complaint. Joseph followed Eddy's directions as much as he could, clearly grateful not to be the one making decisions. He didn't know where the carpet cleaner was, but he got Eddy a trash bin, dish soap and paper towel, then mouthwash and more water for Winston. Eddy was done with the bulk of the cleaning by the time Joseph sat beside her, knees up.

"Thanks," Joseph said, embarrassed. "Sorry." He had the same plaintive expression as Mara, and he was equally impossible to be angry at, if Eddy had minded an excuse to abandon the party.

"Did you know I have a cat?" Eddy asked. Joseph shook his head and Eddy continued speaking. "Her name is Lilith, and ninety-nine percent of the time she's the softest, best cinnamon roll of a cat. The last one percent she's the kind of cinnamon roll that chases a bat behind a framed print of Saturn Devouring His Son and screams incessantly at it to come out so she can murder it." Joseph laughed, and Eddy passed him the bread bag. "You should eat some too, and drink as much water as you can. Mara's smarter than Norm." Joseph took a bite and chewed it deliberately. "I had to free the bat who was clinging to the wire loop as if their life depended on it and then Lilith was devastated about her failure as a hunter, but she's forgiven me. Or forgotten. The bat's probably forgotten too." Eddy smiled encouragingly at Joseph. "If the carpet dries clean and Winston doesn't puke in Norm's car, this never happened."

Eddy feels at home in the hospital lab in a way she never does in François'. She's collaborated with hospital labs since her PhD, even if this time it's François that got them in the door, rather than her research profile. There was a comfort to find in the bleach-white walls and chipped linoleum floors, before her mother's illness made the place too familiar. Eddy hadn't thought she'd find it again. She hadn't thought of a world existing after.

The lab tech is more excited about playing with the equipment for the Instances than setting Eddy up for an fMRI, and Eddy doesn't blame him. She's been to the Shadowrealm dozens of times and part of her still wonders at suddenly existing now, instead of then. Reading someone's mind — badly — pales in comparison.

François is overdressed, navy jacket reappearing for what he must think is a significant event. It will be if the data's any good. He's frowning, lines etched across his forehead, and Eddy wants to flick his tie over his shoulder, to make him laugh. He arranged this for her but he doesn't like it, doesn't like that they're here, unfaithful to his lab. But he hasn't won enough money from any granting agency to buy her an MRI machine, and she's getting antsy working with EEG. Eddy is a high-maintenance date.

Eddy suspects she knows why he doesn't want her in the hospital labs, experiments monitored by near-strangers bound by ancient oaths to long-dead philosophers. It's not exactly jealousy. "It's okay, François," she explains, a conversation she still feels unable to fully engage with in the Middlerealm. "Even if the fMRI picks out what we do here, I made sure I'm the only one with access to the data. The most any watcher can do is make sure my body doesn't die."

The lab tech looks alarmed. He lifts a hand and observes it closely, reading the lines across a weathered palm. "Are we in an Instance now?"

"No," Eddy lies, but François can always tell, the corners of his eyes wrinkling in amusement. She succeeded in getting him laughing. There's no sense to it. Eddy can lie to him in the Middlerealm, sometimes, and he can't remember what happens in Eddy's Instances to fit together a pattern, but he always catches her in the Shadowrealm. She should ask him what her tell is. She should kiss him. Maybe it doesn't count as cheating on your wife, in a different timeline.

"Rich is going to spend the rest of the day in an existential crisis," François chides her playfully, then addresses Richard. "She's winding you up."

"Sorry," Eddy says, and Richard blinks at her, unable to make sense of the undercurrents in the room. François is mostly right. Richard is going to spend the next few minutes doubting his own existence, at which point he's going to stop existing. Richard fumbles with the controls on the MRI, nervous at the routine motions he conducted with unconscious confidence in the Middlerealm. His concentration is further broken when François glances at his phone, mutters something about emails and deadlines, and tells Rich to give him and Eddy twenty minutes alone to deal with an incoming minor crisis. All the while, Eddy counts down the time on her watch, seventeen minutes left in the red zone of the bezel before this world ends, if her theories on the Shadowrealm are correct. If Eddy's wrong and Payton is right, then in a parallel universe, a parallel Eddy is about to die.

François catches the gleam in her eyes as she approaches him and shakes his head in a no. It was worth a try. "Ready," she whispers, voice low and throaty. She clasps her hands together behind her back and focuses on taking slow, regular breaths, calm and collected. Her pulse is racing at the thought of his touch. François puts a hand against each of her shoulders, thumbs resting on her arteries, and presses down.

The party blinked in the sudden brilliance of gas-lamp lit streets, the unexpected bustle of humans mingling with dwarves, elves, and dozens of other species. After so long in Deadwood, most of the party marveled to see people moving unencumbered by the squelching of decaying organs or the drag of slowly detaching limbs. Arg frowned at the sight. "I mistrust this place," he declared, as though being unwillingly teleported by a mysterious Sorcerer to an unknown location was insufficient cause for alarm.

"Don't let the neighborhood put you off," the young man said hastily, unlocking the reinforced wooden door. "Even a unicorn startup can't afford a shop on Chrome Street. But you didn't come all this way to see the outside of the store." He ushered them in with a wave of his hand, closing the door behind them. "Welcome to *Adventure Capitals*, the latest in tourism technology!" he said with a bow. Inside the shop were rows of brightly coloured brochures advertising weekend getaways, shelves of potions for teleportation sickness and a rack of witch's Tilly hats. "Bobbie and I are your tour guides, your hosts, your daring duo of adventure capitalists." As promised, Bobbie was a unicorn, complete with an iridescent horn, a dark flowing mane, and a feather pen held firmly between his front hooves as he made out traveller's cheques.

"You kidnapped us," Grogtar said bluntly, hefting his axe with one hand, biceps bulging. "That's not how tourism works. You don't kidnap people and call them cruise passengers or say it's a camping trip." Joseph had dice out, poised to roll for initiative, but it was too soon in the evening to swing weapons. Plot first, then dessert.

"Why not, though?" Carmilla asked with a mischievous grin. Grogtar opened his mouth to object but closed it again, unable to think of a response.

Arg nodded in agreement. "Bien sûr, ma petite miette. It is best to find a captive audience for one's business."

The young Sorcerer looked distressed at the Zombie's words, shaking his head. "Erm. That's not what — I didn't mean —" he floundered. He took a deep breath, smiled weakly and grabbed a handful of postcards.

"On the house!" he said as he passed them around. Bobbie sighed at his colleague's action, letting the air out in a whinny.

Rose examined the picture, a dragon roasting a village of thatched-roof cottages. "Evil Dragon Empire: Wish You Were Here," she read, then placed it in her Handy Haversack. "Thanks." Her pointed eyebrows narrowed together quizzically. "What did you mean to do? Who are you?"

"Teleportation!" the man replied enthusiastically. "I'm Robert the Constructor. I'm an Innovator! Bobbie and I pioneer disruptive teleportation magic. Move fast and break things, that's our motto." True to his word, the phrase was written in friendly Papyrus underneath *Adventure Capitals* on a series of storyboards resting on easels in a corner. "We're workshopping our advertising campaign."

"No, we are not, you short-nosed biped," Bobbie said gruffly. He sounded a bit hoarse, but then he was almost entirely horse. "Customers expect all their internal organs to teleport with them, you legless wonder, and who's going to explain to Auntie Bobbins that Grandpa made it to Tramura but she needs to come by the office to collect his spectacles, derby cap and spleen from spiderhooves here?" Bobbie put down his feather pen to glare at Robert. "It won't be me, roundears."

"Is there gonna be a fight?" Grogtar asked. It didn't take an average wisdom stat to read the room. He tossed his great-axe from hand to hand experimentally. "Whose side are we on?"

"No, no, no, no, no, no," Robert said, hands waving frantically. "No need to fight, I'm fixing it. My spell is going to be lit." He looked frantically between the party and Bobbie. "That's why I brought them, they've got what I need."

"I can't help you teleport?" Rose said, more a question than a statement, checking her character sheet. "That's not a Cleric thing, I think. Can Bards teleport?" She smiled at Carmilla. "Bards are good at lots of things besides singing."

"But also singing," Carmilla responded, knowing full well that she was setting herself up and unable to think of a single lyric that wasn't straight out of the *Night Beats* musical episode. Carmilla was powerless when Rose smiled like that, corners of her eyes crinkling, face soft and round.

Robert coughed. "Actually. I need your Zombie. If you give me the body, I'll give you a 50% off voucher on the next expedition to Bellstrom." Bobbie scowled at the suggestion and mouthed something about "hornless fools" that Robert wisely pretended not to see. "Everybody wins, no one gets hit with an axe."

"I don't win," Grogtar mumbled, his mind slowly working its way through Robert's statement. The ticking of gears in Grogtar's brain was metaphorical rather than audible, and there was no literal stream coming out of Grogtar's ears, but there might as well have been. Grogtar took his time when he was thinking, but he got there in the end. "Arg doesn't win either. You can't dismember someone in my Party! That's illegal! That's worse than forcing someone to go on a walking tour!"

Robert backed up several steps, til he stood beside an exceedingly reluctant-looking Bobbie. "There's some mistake. I'm not calling you an ignorant, undereducated Half-Orc, okay. But everyone knows Zombies aren't sentient. It's just a meatbag." He glanced uncomfortably at Bobbie and licked his lips. Bobbie stamped a hoof on the floor and whinnied an eerie, otherworldly neigh.

Rose gritted her teeth as she pulled back the string on her crossbow. "Don't. Say. My. Friend. Isn't. Sentient." She wrenched the bolt into place and stared down Robert. "Take it back."

Robert shook his head, concern and disdain fighting for dominance on his face. "You're making a mistake." He reached into his sleeve and pulled out a round vial. Dark red flames danced around its circumference, licked at the stopper, waiting for their chance to escape. Robert rolled the sphere nervously in his palm. "We should talk. I have medical scrolls."

Rose picked up her glass dice, rainbows flashing across her palm. She rolled a twenty. Robert rolled a one.

E ddy held out a pair of dog ears on a plastic headband. "For you," she
offered. "If you want? You can be Jane." Eddy had plastic vampire
teeth in her own mouth and stage blood running down her chin. Her
cape was tied around her neck, purposefully failing to cover a shockingly
low neckline in a spiderweb-lace black dress, but she'd left the top hat
sitting on the back seat of the car. She'd put it on when they got to
Toronto. Eddy's prized possession, a genuine silver replica locket, hung
between her breasts invitingly. If only she wasn't trying to seduce a
werewolf. "Like the Halloween episode."

"Okay," Mara said, sliding them in place over her hair. Eddy worried
Mara might balk at the full furry outfit required for werewolf-
transformation Jane, but Halloween-episode Jane required minimal
props.

Eddy grinned, showing off her fangs. "I made us a road trip playlist.
Don't worry, I only put the soundtrack from the musical episode on it
twice." Assuming the timing on Google maps was accurate — highly
unlikely but not utterly impossible — they'd pull into the Air Canada
Centre with *Titania Triumphant* blaring through the rental car's speakers.
"It's mostly metal so far but I'll give my phone and you can add stuff if
you want." Mara's comfort was more important than Eddy's elaborate

plan, but Eddy's DJing prowess was thwarted by a complete inability to figure out what music Mara would be into. "Or we can play the radio?" Eddy wasn't going to insult Mara by suggesting CBC 2, but then it was more plausible than Mara adding Aqua to the playlist.

"I like metal," Mara said, brightly and potentially naively. She touched the faux-fur of her brown, floppy ear. "Thanks, Eddy. It's nice to get away for a bit." Mara placed a rolly grey carry-on bag in the trunk and smiled gamely. "This is going to be fun."

"Everyone, this is Mara. Mara, this is Eliza, Raine, Anna, Felix and Aisha." Eddy pointed in turn at Asami the Genius Inventor, Korra the Magical Jock, Ibuki the Tardy Ninja, Ian the Uncivil Wizard and Aisha the Spoilsport. The five of them sat around a table with con-food of sadness: pizza that contained more grease than flour, nachos with a cheese-like substance indistinguishable from the plastic container it arrived in, and chicken tenders that deserved neither of those words. Eddy and Mara had stopped at a Timmies on the way in and ate something that resembled actual food, and they hadn't needed to mortgage Mara's house to pay for it. "Nice outfits, guys. Minus Aisha."

Aisha smiled in response. She didn't need plastic enhancements to make the expression a threat, sharp and pointed. Aisha would've made a great Titania, if anyone dared bully her into dressing up. Eliza had ventured as far as offering to buy Aisha a red-panda onesie so she could cosplay Jamila, but was met with steely rejection.

"Thanks," Felix said, a well-chewed pencil emerging from nowhere in his hand. He flipped over his pizza plate and started sketching on the slightly less dirty side. "I wanted Raine to go as Entrapa. She could dye her braids purple and put wires in them. But Eliza wanted a canon ship for their couples cosplay." His eyes flashed up from his drawing to Mara, but he resumed his artwork without any comment on Eddy and Mara's costume choices. "Eddy said it's your first con. Anything you especially want to see? Particular fandoms?"

"Eddy said *Night Beats* is here?" Mara answered, voice rising to make it a question rather than a statement. Eddy nodded encouragement and Mara continued. "She said we can get pictures with Lilith and Jane?"

"With the whole cast, if you want to spend two days standing in lines, but Eddy gets a photo with Lilith every year. I guess Jane is your fav?" Felix handed the paper plate to Mara with a flourish. He'd done a good job at a labyrinth, considering how quickly he drew it. He must have practiced. Mara accepted the oily artwork gratefully. Maybe they read *Cascade* in book club and Mara recognized the reference. Though *Sleep of Reason* didn't exactly match the awareness-campaign tone of book club, and Eddy couldn't imagine Mara reading it to toddlers for Library Reading Hour. "Jane's actress is a sweetheart. Everyone loves her."

"The photo opportunities start at one. We need to head over there in ten minutes if we want to beat the rush," Eliza said with the confidence of a woman who memorized the program and worked out an algorithm for the fastest routes between events.

"They timed it right this year," Aisha said approvingly. "It's late enough Lilith should be awake but early enough she might not be coked up yet." No one pretended to be shocked at her words — even Mara took it in stride. Wildly irresponsible behaviour was on-brand for Lilith and equally so for her actress.

Anna giggled with a certain amount of pride. "I snuck into a cast party a while ago. I have seen things." She pushed her mostly eaten nacho tray into the centre of the table, where it was beset by Raine and Felix in a manner similar to a pack of ravaging wolves. Anna stood and pulled Eddy into a hug, and Eddy held Anna tight enough to feel the cotton on Anna's cat half-mask soft against her neck. "Hey, it's good to see you, Eddy. We missed you."

"That panel was everything," Raine gushed, and she wasn't wrong. "No one on that session checked any of the Twitter hashtags before they got there. The fans have been planning this for ages and they just walked into it. Seriously, running a panel on *Women of Night Beats* when there's only ever been one recurring WOC and they're still bringing her to panels, like, three seasons after they fridged her — what did the producers think would happen?" Artists Alley merch tables held no particular appeal for Raine, leaving her attention free to relive the highlights of the afternoon. Raine would sneak back later and get something for Eliza, but she'd select from the myriad of items Eliza would gaze longingly at over the course of the afternoon.

"Jane knew what was coming. She looked like she was ready to gnaw off her own leg to escape before they even finished introducing the panelists." Felix, on the other hand, was on a mission, grey-contacted eyes scanning each booth, grey-painted fingertips assessing quality. His costume wasn't complete yet. "Or she was the only one who could read the room. I've seen friendlier crowds when I recited Vogon poetry," Felix said. When Felix contacted bookers, he described his band as 'innovative.' Occasionally, he pushed his luck and called them 'creative.'

"Ona felt it too," Aisha pointed out. "But she was looking forward to it." Aisha was rolling together the pseudo-inspirational posters she and Anna purchased: gorgeous photographs of star systems and nebulas covered with extremely sarcastic quotes from *The Expanse*. It was a good thing for humanity that the two women didn't share an office, lest the world be destroyed by excessive cynicism.

"The writers deserved it," Raine argued, though no one was disputing her. "After the Extra Special Gay Episode —" heavy finger quotes were required to express the strength of her feeling "— was about a corpse who held hands with another guy in a vision-induced flashback. *Star Wars* has more queer content than that."

"There was the episode Lilith bit Jane," Eliza offered. *Night Beats* directed that scene with all the subtlety of the prologue to a Herminone/Snape fic, but Eddy was over handing out cookies for subtext. "Or the episode with the cursed swords, where they fought and made up." Eliza spoke from deep inside a rabbithole of 'Adora declares her love' fanart. Eddy counted two mugs, a canvas bag, and three separate prints laid out on the table in front of Eliza, not to mention the cell phone case and keyring. Eliza grinned sheepishly at Eddy's gaze, though someone holding as many *Night Beats* plushies as Eddy couldn't throw stones. She'd drop a plushie if she tried. "I can't decide. Aisha, help me."

"We could get swords, Eddy?" Mara suggested. "For our costumes. They wouldn't be real swords for fighting, I know. But maybe someone here sells fake swords for Jane and Lilith like in the episode." She pushed her fuzzy ears back, as if checking they still rested on her head.

"They do," Aisha confirmed, holding a mug in each hand and eyeing them speculatively. "Three rows back, at the end of the aisle."

The pub was crowded with fans, noisy enough they could barely hear the questions, but Eddy and Eliza were an unstoppable force where *Night Beats* trivia was concerned. "Everyone knows Jane's from Newfoundland," Eddy said with disgust. "Why even ask that?"

"They could have meant the character, not her actress," Eliza responded nervously, pinching the damp edges of a Rickard's Red coaster. "It's Toronto in the spin-off comics, but that's never addressed in the show. Not everyone agrees the comics are canon."

Aisha gave the MC a once-over, taking in his *Supernatural* hoodie and ill-fitting jeans. "He doesn't read the comics," she said decisively. "Put Newfoundland." She scanned down the sheet. "Someone double-check the answer on magical pregnancies, and I'll turn it in."

A fervent debate emerged on whether Bigfoot as the father inherently made the pregnancy a magical pregnancy, if a traditional mode of impregnation was employed. During the uproar, Anna appeared with a strawberry daiquiri in each hand. She handed one to Eliza and sipped from the second. "Hey, Eddy, I gotta give you the room key. I met someone." Anna pulled a plastic card from a pocket that shouldn't have been physically possible to fit on her costume. "Room 414. I think. Aisha knows. I'll dish in the morning." With that, she disappeared back into the crowd.

Eddy wasn't exactly surprised. Back in the early years, when they were all saddled with student debt, they didn't bother booking a spot in the hotel for Anna and saved the money. It meant the occasional overcrowded bed, but they got away with it more often than not. Eliza beamed at the interaction, and Eddy looked at Felix suspiciously. If there was a set-up, he was in the middle of it.

"There's two beds in the room," Felix answered Eddy's unspoken question. "You know that Anna hogs the blankets. We didn't want Mara's memory of her first con to be the night she spent preventing a caterpillar from making a cocoon." He didn't say that Eddy and Mara got a private room while everyone else shared, but it was implicit in his words. Eddy and Vee never got a private room back when they were a couple, but of course Eliza would see this con as an opportunity to bring to life her Lilith/Jane fanfics, and of course Felix would be in favour of the plan. Raine must have lobbied hard for the second bed, or Aisha booked it and made it a fait accompli.

"Seven," Aisha declared, settling the argument. "We're counting Bigfoot and we're counting Jane's Shadowrealm pregnancy that vanished when she got back. We're not counting Wendy's pseudocyesis or meeting Jordan's daughter in the Mirrorverse." She adjusted their answer and picked up the page before making her way towards the MC.

Without the restraining influence of Aisha, or any more trivia questions to debate, Felix pulled out the final addition to his costume, a laser pen with a juvenilely rendered cock-and-balls filter. He shone it at the middle of the table with pride. His grin was more delighted than cocky, but his grey skin, hair and eyes made a dramatic contrast to the forest green of the booth behind him, and he could've been a Charmer, almost.

"Ian Mallory is a massive dickhole," Eddy recited, before anyone else could say it first. She reached to her hip and grinned.

Drawing a sword in a crowd required precision, straight upwards in a single fluid motion, but Mara caught Eddy slipping to her feet to improve the angle and drew only a beat behind her. The swords were only painted wood, but they were solid, better quality than most of the metal props Eddy'd seen, and they made a satisfying clunk when the blades met over the table. The crowd was too dense to give the women much space, spectators sliding only a couple steps away, phones out to capture the battle. Mara and Eddy's cuts were tight, their movements restrained, a twist of their hips and a shift of balance all the defense they required. Mara pressed an attack, slashes to the face, chest, gut, then a thrust. Eddy blocked the first cuts but at the last one she turned to let Mara close the distance, and reached, not with her sword but her mouth, plastic fangs resting lightly on Mara's neck, Mara's blood hot and impossibly fast beneath her teeth.

"You win," Mara whispered.

"Fuck Lilith, marry Jane," Eddy said without hesitation. "Wait, no, that leaves me killing Titania. I will not, you can't make me." Eddy was more used to the 'slow burn/fake date/enemies to lovers' version of the game that Eliza preferred, but introducing fanfiction tropes to Mara was a conversation for another night.

Mara laughed, drunk, cheerful and, unfortunately, sitting on the second bed in the hotel room. "Okay, not Titania. Jordan?"

"Jordan," Eddy confirmed. "I could kill him." She bared her teeth, though she'd taken out the fangs before she brushed. "Back at you. Lilith, Jane, Jordan?"

Mara groaned. "It's so hard. I love all of them." She looked towards the dark of the ceiling. Only the bedside lamps were on, and that was primarily mood lighting. It was well past two and hypothetically they were going to sleep. "Same. I can't kill Jane, and Lilith is hotter than Jordan." She giggled and turned back to Eddy, light blue silk housecoat sliding as she twisted, rose-gold fish pattern rippling down the waterfall of Mara's shoulder, revealing folds of a white linen nightdress and pale skin. "Arwen, Galadriel, Eowyn?"

"A classic," Eddy said approvingly. "Fuck Galadriel, marry Eowyn." She shrugged a tank-top covered shoulder, the rainbow unicorn-skull print hopefully as appealing as Mara's outfit. "Sorry, Arwen. You're cute, but Eowyn's a badass shieldmaiden and marriage to her means I get *de facto* marriage to Faramir in the bargain. Two for the price of one."

Mara frowned and pushed her glasses further back along her nose, a disapproving librarian, which was its own kind of sexy. "That's not how the game works." It only took a moment for her to add, "Besides, Arwen comes with Aragorn."

"I'm really into my partners bathing on a semi-regular basis, and Aragorn looks like he's never washed his hair." Eddy couldn't put into words what she wanted in Eowyn, but she could articulate exactly what was wrong with Aragon. "Besides, Eowyn is hot in armour. You've got to admit it." She grinned at Mara, confident in her assessment, and Mara nodded her agreement. "Jadzia, Ezri, Kira."

"Marry Jadzia and I would kill Ezri. So, fuck Kira, I guess." Mara gave the obvious answer, but then it was an easy one — hardly Eddy's best work. Mara spent a moment in thought before suggesting, "Scar, Armstrong, Roy."

"You've seen *Fullmetal Alchemist*?" Eddy asked, trying not to sound too surprised. *DS9* was always playing in reruns, but even then, Eddy wasn't certain Mara would recognize the names til she answered. Anime — old anime — seemed a step too far for her wildest fantasies.

Mara looked down at the tacky comforter, her fingers picking at a stray thread in the stitching. "When Joseph got the flu, we watched a lot of Netflix," Mara explained in warm but somber tones. "Joseph likes anime." As she again made eye contact, the kimono returned to its place of modesty on her shoulder.

"He's the stunt double for Fausto," Anna explained in a matter-of-fact tone. She was still wearing her Ibuki costume from the previous day but without the mask, and her makeup was, somehow, pristinely on point, despite her toiletries spending the night in Room 414 with Eddy and Mara. "His name's Mathieu and he does really funny impersonations, if you're into that, and he's got an insanely high pain tolerance." Anna lived so far over the line of TMI that she couldn't see it in the distance. Eddy could only hope Anna wouldn't show Mara photographs. "He's a dick but I bet I'll call him back."

Eliza looked troubled but didn't object. "Did you get any breakfast? We smuggled granola in case." Anna accepted the transfer of a used yogurt container of cereal unearthed from its hiding place underneath dirty socks in Raine's canvas satchel. There was no way to subtly eat it, but Anna had brazened her way through worse. "We've got coffee too, in a thermos."

"Coffee," Eddy demanded, arms out like a zombie. "The diner said it was bottomless, but it doesn't count if the waitress is too busy to fill your cup more than twice. And they were practically kid-sized mugs. Coffee for babies." Eddy took the lidful gratefully, but offered it to Mara after her first sip, the two passing the drink back and forth as they waited for the show to start. Con mornings were inevitably torture, though today's was significantly improved by the Advil that François had packed for Mara. "This part is pure suffering. There's ages of hiatus left. They could show spoilers where Jordan dies 'cause werewolf-Jane eats him, and we wouldn't know what they actually meant til next season."

"You don't have to watch," Aisha pointed out. Not that any of them considered moving. They paid good money — plus got up unnaturally early after a late night — to get seats for the *Night Beats* infomercial that was *Behind the Scenes & Sneak Peeks*. They were guaranteed the Rube

Goldberg-like machinations of Brent and Jane pranking each other, a blonde corpse-of-the-week gushing about how friendly everyone was, and Jordan practicing backflips, cartwheels or somersaults to demonstrate his manly gymnastic prowess. "Or you can revel in believing Jordan bites it until the next season snatches that joy from you. Again."

"Jordan is invincible," Felix confirmed. He added an aside to Mara, "Eddy falls for it every year."

Mara smiled at Eddy sympathetically. "I'm glad. That he lives, I like him. Not that you get fooled."

Eddy grinned as the music started to play. "Nah, not this time. Instead of lies about Jordan, I'm planning to believe this season they finally reveal the Third Realm to us." Eliza's eyes widened in hopeful excitement, though she knew full well Eddy was joking. "My bet is, that's where the Final Guardian rests."

Eddy doesn't want the weekend to be over, doesn't want to be home. Doesn't want to be parked on the street, trunk popped, waiting for Mara to undo her seatbelt and get out of the car, for the con to disappear into nothingness. It's late and it's dark and Mara's not moving but Eddy's too burnt to think of anything to say, so Eddy reaches for her phone and scrolls through her music til she finds Blind Guardian. Mara's musical education was as lacking as Eddy suspected, but she's taken to metal as quickly as she did to swords.

Mara smiles and undoes her seatbelt, the click barely audible under the music. "This was really fun, Eddy." In the darkness, Mara is all shadow, a silhouette that moves cautiously but deliberately, hand finding Eddy's cheek and then mouths together, a jolt of energy as they meet.

"Wouldn't that kill you?" Owen asked. "If you set a bomb off? Even in an Instance." He frowned, as much at Eddy as at the cell cultures he was photographing under a microscope. Between the furrowed brow and his tweed jacket and bowtie, he was practically ready to be a professor. There was no explanation for Owen's outfit besides that it was Friday. Owen and Payton had a running gag on Fridays, which Lydia attempted to explain to Eddy and which Eddy didn't attempt to understand. The tweed was a bit excessive for Owen, who was too young and, most days, too enthusiastic to pull off British knobhead academic, but it was less absurd than his three-piece suit from the previous week, blue-striped tie twisted into a Windsor knot.

"It only goes off fifty percent of the time," Eddy said, flippant to disguise her discomfort at discussing the possibility of her own death with the students. "It can't be a big explosion, anyway. I can't take a fifty-fifty risk in the real timeline. It just needs to be observable."

"I thought the bomb was the one doing the observing," Payton remarked, which was a discussion for the quantum theorists, and even then after a few pints. Following the logic behind the Elitzur-Vaidman bomb-tester hypothesis was easier with reduced sobriety. Payton was sitting beside Owen, not doing any work at all. Hypothetically they were watching Lydia's body while she was in the Shadowrealm, which Lydia was insistent on, but Owen and Eddy could have managed it between them while they were already in the lab. On the other hand, Eddy couldn't have appreciated Payton's commitment to the full dress kilt, complete with sporran and high socks, if they hadn't been slacking in the lab instead of working in their office. Not that bare knees were lab appropriate, but Eddy was in a generous mood. Payton wasn't technically breaking the rules as long as they wore close-toed shoes. "You're only there to write it up."

"The most important part," Eddy said. "Papers are what separate scientists from ordinary weirdos."

"Conference talks too," Owen protested, probably because he got one for ICIB, or because Payton had too. François' group was embarrassingly well represented for an international conference. "Kingston's in a week."

"Conferences matter," Eddy agreed. "But all the important work happens at the breaks and dinners. Nothing productive happens without coffee or wine." She stretched, then gestured Payton to her computer. "Can you check my specs while you're here? My light-sensitive bomb isn't going to optimize its own physics."

"This job looks fun," Carmilla said, consulting the parchments nailed to the 'Help Wanted' board outside the Town Hall. "'Intrepid adventurers needed to gather valuable magical reagents and alchemical compounds! Botanical alchemy experience a huge plus. See Beastmaster Bob, Heart of the Forest, for details.'" She grinned at Rose. "I'm sure a grateful client wouldn't complain if we liberated some material components for your spells while we were helping him out. A girl can always use more material components."

"Or this one," Grogtar suggested. "'Help! Farm is overrun with aggressive radishes! Able-bodied warriors needed to exterminate pests and deal with angry Druid. Please contact Farmer McBobble ASAP.'"

Grogtar considered for a moment, as deep in thought as it was possible for a Half-Orc to be. Shallow in thought. "Can we do both?"

"We should let Rose choose," Arg offered with a low bow, hair sliding forward with his scalp. He readjusted it to a fashionable swoop, and Rose uttered an Inflict Minor Wounds to lock it in place. "Go ahead, Rose. Treat yo half-'elf." He gave Rose a dazzling smile as he said it. Joseph groaned, which was typically more Arg's thing.

"Um," Rose said uncomfortably, eyes on a third parchment. "I don't like this one." She read aloud, "'Fire Marshall José LesBurney seeks qualified adventuring party to round up arsonists responsible for the destruction of multiple city blocks. Culprits will be forced to pay all insurance fees.'"

Grogtar gulped loudly. "I don't like it either." He clutched their bag of gold close to his chest with one hand, rested the other on the haft of his axe. "I don't like it at all."

"Kyle looks like he's not done baking yet," Vee said. Eddy imagined Vee zooming in on Kyle's neatly trimmed blond hair, plaid shirt, fit-for-his-age physique, and frowning pensively as she came to her final assessment. The point of the picture was for Vee to see Lilith walking across Kyle's shoulder and fulfilling her destiny as a pirate-cat, not for Vee to critique Eddy's hookups from four thousand kilometres away. "Ottawa's got a million people and you picked him?"

"You're a lesbian!" Eddy protested futilely to the cell phone charging on the beside. Speakerphone was a glorious thing. It was too hot to use the skull-pattern duvet, but Eddy lay under burgundy cotton sheets coated in a thin layer of grey cat fur. "You don't get a vote!"

"I am objective," Vee responded, a statement that would not have held up in a court of law. "That's more than you can say. You're biased cause Lilith likes him."

"Lilith has good taste." This was demonstrably untrue, given Lilith's opinions on squirrels, bats and Temptations. "She's a good cat." That part was true.

"Lilith likes anything or anyone that might involve food. We need an impartial judge. I'll send the pic to Aisha." There was a pause, short enough it could have meant nothing, and then Vee added, "Aisha said your girlfriend is cute." It was universally acknowledged that Aisha had a sixth sense about other people's partners. Though, with the notable exception of Felix, not about her own. Eddy could almost hear Aisha's response to Eddy's thought, the acid in her voice as she commented about stones and glass houses.

"Mara's not my girlfriend," Eddy sighed, stretching her arms in the emptiness of solo occupancy of a queen-sized bed. "Not yet, anyway."

Vee harumphed at that. For a woman who absolutely refused to attempt long distance, Vee was highly skilled at vocalizing her feelings over the phone. "What's wrong with her? Does she speak really slowly and you're only at 'ye' and it might be a couple months before you get to the 's'?"

"She's married? To a man?" Eddy offered. It didn't seem like as much of an obstacle as before, if only Eddy could manage a rerun in the right timeline.

"Does she know about poly? Talk to her about poly. I'll write you a script." Vee cleared her throat before launching in. "You now have options! It's your choice! Did you know that sex that could save your life is now available within the bounds of wedlock, thanks to the relationship strategy called polyamory? Let this be the year you stop all your heteronormative bullshit, and prevent or treat whatever nonsense you and your husband get up to! Don't let concerns get in your way. Talk to Eddy — she's a doctor! Now you have options! It's your choice! Let's do this!" In a deeper voice, Vee finished, "This has been a PSA."

It took Eddy some time to recover from her laughter.

When Eddy quieted down, Vee said with a sniff, "You're not gonna talk to her, because you're a coward."

"Unfair characterization. I am not a coward."

"Sure, but you're not gonna talk about it. What's her husband like anyway? Can you tell him you're into threesomes? Men like those. I read it in a magazine." Eddy barely heard Vee's second question, already lost in the answer to her first.

François was unrelenting force, broken blood vessels where fingertips met neck, pressing, inevitable. He was the last deep breath, the smell of red brick, cypress, and rust lingering when other sensations had evaporated. He held her together when she fell apart and he never told her it was going to be okay.

François was sharp edges, pain quick but not fleeting, languid panic as she bled out, fear omnipresent and yet impossible to draw into a single moment of action. They'd tried knives a few times. Eddy wanted to test different signals, see if she could pick them apart in the data. It was her idea but François didn't argue. He encouraged her, drew her onwards in this as in all things. Except for the one.

François was smiling, chatting afterwards, bad puns and obscure nerd references, windows down in the car to his place for *Night Beats* on a Thursday, knowing he didn't remember, knowing it wouldn't change anything if he did. Eddy suddenly wondered if François killed her in his Instances too. Maybe she was a coward, because she knew she'd never ask.

Eddy was taking too long to answer and Vee would notice. Besides, the distilled essence of the problem was easy enough to sum up. "François is my boss."

"I wasn't sure which I should practice with," Mara says, a wooden sword in each hand. The paint on Jane's sword won't survive the wear and tear of battle for long but it's safe in the Shadowrealm. Eddy taps the Night Beats replica with the tip of her own blade and Mara grins, placing her bokken on the back porch. Mara is wearing a pale pink crop-top hoodie, high waisted black leggings and

bare feet, toes free in the grass. She twists her wrist, spinning the blade by her elbow, stretching.

Eddy joins her in lunges, then practice cuts, maintaining her distance as they track each other across the yard. "I figured out the plot twist for next season. They're finally killing Jordan."

Mara looks at Eddy in disbelief, nearly misjudges her distance in shock. Nearly lets Eddy get too close. "That's not what happened in the Sneak Peeks. Lilith was kissing him." Her blade whooshes as it makes for Eddy's head, meets the edge of Eddy's sword with a clash.

"There were teeth!" Eddy objects. After eight seasons Eddy knows better than to hope. Mara's got to be right. Still, Lilith had an awful lot of very pointy teeth out for an affectionate peck. Eddy changes the game, steps off the line, knocks Mara's blade slightly to the left. Mara retreats along the line, raises her sword and Eddy slides past her, reaching for Mara's gut as she moves. Swords are more fun if you pretend antibiotics haven't been invented yet, though even in the twenty-first century no one wants to be eviscerated. Mara blocks, goes for Eddy's hamstring and they switch feet in unison, an elaborate dance. It's a draw, or it would be, but as they raise again Eddy's the one to get the distance wrong, not enough space to swing and Mara dips under Eddy's aborted strike, grinning as she kisses then gently bites Eddy's lip.

"See?" Mara whispers against Eddy's cheek, "Teeth."

L ess than ten minutes after introductions, Lydia had commandeered
  Wahid's drink tickets and dragged him along to the early career
researcher pizza party. It was nice to see her PhD student again, but Eddy
wasn't going to complain about a temporary reduction in babysitting
responsibilities. There would be plenty of time to catch up during the
conference. Eddy and François' version of a pizza party involved
considerably more prosciutto and roasted garlic and considerably less
networking; they'd ordered takeout from Wooden Heads. They ate from
cardboard boxes, sneaking sips of Four Roses bourbon out of François'
flask, feet dangling over the side of the Time Sculpture as they watched
sailboats on the lake. It was among their least-illegal activities together,
but it was still a milestone. "To our first joint crime in the Middlerealm,"
Eddy proposed, lifting the flask. They only had the one drink between the
two of them, but François met the flask with the edge of his slice of
Sicilian and they toasted.

It tasted of vanilla and burning oak. Not as smooth as the Scotch, but
Eddy wasn't complaining. "You've got a bird fixation," she remarked,
examining the pheasant on the flask before passing it back to him. "Or is
this Mara's fault too?"

He sighed, contentment rather than annoyance. "My ancestors are to
blame for the heraldry, but Mara bought me the flask." His lips shadowed

hers on the mouth of the bottle. "Mara would have given us a penguin, but whatever French king assigned the Gagnons our coat-of-arms lacked her imagination."

"A penguin, and holding a fish instead of a leaf," Eddy suggested, reaching for another slice. She wasn't exactly hungry anymore, but she wasn't ready to be done eating. "And driving a Tesla."

"Edith Courant," he said, nearly a question. Eddy made a face at her full name, which existed only on conference abstracts, published manuscripts, and — before — to Eddy's mother. "Any knights in your family?"

"No one told me about any. And I don't think I'd make a good knight. My chin isn't square enough." Eddy contemplated François' chin. It was square but too narrow. Between that and the angled cheekbones, he'd never play Captain America. Not that Chris Evans was particularly Eddy's type, or even her preferred Chris.

A seagull hopped towards them, head tilted hopefully. Eddy, always a sucker for an animal with a sob story, tore off a bit of crust and threw it. Lilith would never forgive Eddy if she knew about her betrayal of mammalian solidarity, but all the best relationships were built on a foundation of prevarication and evasion.

François handed Eddy the flask. His grip was firm, yielding as he released the bottle, clipped fingernails and smooth fingertips. Eddy kept noticing his hands, kept imagining them against her skin. "The seagulls won't leave you alone now," he commented, warding off the seagull from his own slice with a stern glare. Not that the seagull paid him any attention. Even François couldn't earn a seagull's respect without an offering of carbohydrates.

"I will be their Seagull Queen," Eddy declared, tossing another morsel of crust to her loyal subject, and then several more to the flock of seagull compatriots which instantly materialized at the possibility of a free meal. Seagulls were worse than grad students. Eddy couldn't taste the memory of François' mouth on the flask, only astringent metal and the sweet, textured weight of the bourbon. "They will love me and despair."

The important thing was to drink no more than eight cups of coffee in any twenty-four-hour period. Eddy was safely at two after breakfast, giving her two for the morning coffee break, two for lunch and a two-cup buffer for emergencies. The conference coffee was predictably terrible, but Eddy clutched the white ceramic mug against her fingers, a talisman of protection against the overly enthusiastic air conditioning in the hall.

"Your group is intense," Wahid observed, a matching cup of coffee in his hands. "I think they went to bed at three, maybe four?"

"They are. But none of them are presenting this morning." Eddy was, which had meant an early bedtime, leaving François to network and the kids to get drunk without her. Eddy could only imagine that a temporary burst of insanity had compelled her to ask for a talk instead of a poster. Wahid had a talk, but then the role of supervisors was to force their underlings to apply for oral presentations. Hypocrisy wasn't illegal yet. "Where did you all go?"

"The Pilot House til they kicked us out, then Lydia demanded we all go to these weird cylinders by the lake and play tag in them." Wahid took a deep breath and started, "There was some kind of drama."

Eddy took a sip of coffee and wished this was happening to someone else. Unlike Season-3-Halloween-Episode-Lilith, Eddy's wishes rarely came true. "Don't tell me," she said firmly. "It's not my role. I'm their supervisor." Clarification needed. "Your supervisor. I'm not on their paperwork." Further revision requested, but Eddy would appeal that one to the Editor.

Wahid looked plaintive, but Eddy was resolute. "Should I tell François, then?" he asked.

Eddy restrained herself from groaning. The urge to confess was strong in this one, and Eddy was confident he hadn't even done anything wrong. "Was it an academic dispute? An argument over p-hacking or the role of citizen science?" Wahid shook his head slowly. "They're adults." A look at the likely culprits — Lydia's shoulders slumped in her pale mint blazer, Owen engaged in serious conversation with whoever François had introduced him to and decidedly not making eye contact with Payton — and Eddy doubted the validity of her statement. They were children, completely unprepared to make rational decisions about their lives, but then what was the alternative? Eddy might be older, but she couldn't claim to make better choices in her own. Though she hadn't drunk-texted François during the night and she'd paired pinstripe slacks and a black cardigan with burgundy flats in the morning, so maybe she had gained some wisdom over her 41 years. "They'll figure it out with time."

Wahid shook his head again, but he didn't push the point.

"Wine, Eddy?" François offered generously, the lip of a green bottle poised over her glass. Like he needed to ask. The two complimentary bottles on the table had been surreptitiously regifted to Nini's grad students, and a more acceptable vintage purchased from the redcoat-clad waiter providing ambience to the conference dinner at Fort Henry. Between François' wine selection, Wahid's new contacts, and the full room for Eddy's talk, conferences had a way of making it all seem worthwhile.

In a less heartwarming turn of events, Payton and Owen were seated as far apart as the table would allow with something close to geometrical precision. Eddy wanted to throw bread rolls at both of them. Instead, she turned to François, determined to focus on the positives in life. For example, on the deep red Eddy swirled around her glass, watching for legs. "Thanks."

"Nice talk, Eddy," François told her, loud enough that the rest of the group could hear him over the general din of the conference dinner. "Well done." He smiled, a king bestowing favour, and it shouldn't be hot,

Eddy's insides shouldn't be melting in squishy delight at an utterly deserved compliment. More of an observation, really. "I'm sure Lydia will represent us just as well tomorrow."

Lydia looked less confident than François in this statement. Eddy willed Lydia not to contradict him, to believe in her own self-worth or at least be scared enough of François not to argue. "Owen was good," Lydia deflected, nervously twisting the straw in her vodka soda. "You dealt with the questions really well, Owen." First conferences were bad enough and Owen was a hard act to follow, even two days later. Not that anyone besides Lydia was comparing the two. Eddy didn't envy Lydia her cortisol levels.

"Thanks," Owen said, presumably unwilling to commit multiple words to any conversation which might come to include Payton. Eddy's fingers curled around the seeded bun. She'd even buttered it. If Eddy was especially lucky, and Owen was especially unlucky, it might stick when she threw it. Payton was staring at their glass of wine as if determined to volatilize the liquid through sheer force of will. In the true spirit of principled investigation, François completely ignored the unmistakable tension between his students.

"He did," François agreed. Lydia's shoulders relaxed as François' attention was transferred to Golden Boy. "Questioners aren't typically that hostile at ICIB, but Wyatt and I have professional differences." François' tone was dry. The code was easy to translate; François had rejected one of Dr McCormick's papers and the review process was less anonymized than advertised. Still, only a complete dick took their feelings out on someone's students. "He's convinced he'll find inconsistencies in our statistical modelling."

"He won't," Eddy said disdainfully. Dr McCormick hadn't found any in Owen's work and he wouldn't in Lydia's. "This isn't our first time. We know what we're doing."

"Wyatt doesn't. Lydia, if he tries to challenge you during the Q&A, tell him you checked for induced correlation and didn't assume normal distributions." Wisdom dispensed, François turned his focus to Bao. One of Nini's PhD students had given a talk on a topic perilously close to Bao's research, and François double-checked Bao hadn't given away too much during his poster session.

A topic of such intensity required reckless gesticulations from Bao. These had the unfortunate consequence of knocking Payton's glass over, spilling ruby liquid over the table and threatening the white of Payton's shirt and green of their kilt. Bao and Payton yelped in unison and Eddy leapt into action, napkin at the ready, but a single square of fabric was insufficient to the task. The rest of the group joined her, tossing napkins into the fray. When Eddy looked up from her task of crisis management, she realized that Owen was standing a foot away. He must have come over to add his napkin; it was too far to throw with any kind of accuracy.

Payton saw Owen a moment later. It was the kind of moment Eddy read fanfic about, Lilith/Jane or Cosima/Delphine, but it felt awkward to watch in real life, something almost pornographic about the intensity of their happiness. Eddy sat back, took a sip of wine and pretended not to notice Lydia staring.

After dessert, the Youths were distracted by two parallel needs: to groove to the DJ's '80s dance mix and to gawk at the senior academics attempting the same thing. And so Eddy and François slipped away, under the darkness of the new moon, like Cryptids.

François led Eddy to the first threshold, a solidly built black door, the paint smooth under Eddy's fingertips. The lock was black too, and archaically large. The knock-off Swiss Army knife François pulled from his trouser pocket turned out to be a set of lockpicks. Did he always carry them, or had he planned for this exact moment? Both options were ripe with possibility. The flashlight on Eddy's phone barely pierced the darkness of the tunnel on the other side of the wooden door, illuminating less than a metre of stone walls brushed with white. The air underneath Fort Henry was thick with damp and smelled of mold. Eddy didn't hesitate, and neither did François.

"Turn off the light," François said. Their shadows danced uneasily over rough surfaces as he closed the door behind them. "I'll tell you a story."

"What kind of story?" Eddy asked. She did as bidden without waiting for his answer. The outline of the door shone more faintly with each step deeper under the fortress' dry moat, fading to a soft memory of light. Eddy reached out her hand to be sure of the wall. Even in the heat of the summer, it was cold to the touch, like a body long dead.

François was a dark presence moving behind her. He put his arm on her shoulder, somehow sure of his movements in the near-darkness, and she stilled. "A ghost story, of course." His voice was low, a whisper, and closer than she'd expected.

"Tell me."

"Won't you be scared?" he asked playfully, as though Eddy wasn't terrified, as if she couldn't taste her heart pounding in her mouth, as if her skin didn't burn with electricity, fingers in the socket, feet wavering at the edge of a tall cliff. Eddy had tied herself to the railroad tracks and she finally felt alive.

"Never," she promised him, as if he couldn't see the lie in her words for the darkness. His hand slid down to the small of her back, a gentle pressure urging her onward. As soon as she took a step forward, the warmth of his hand was replaced by the chill of the tunnels.

There wasn't a lock on the door at the end of the tunnel, but then, why would there be? It opened to a small room, or series of rooms, with narrow, angled windows and low ceilings, archways bulky and oppressive. The dim light afforded by stars and moon through the windows shone brightly, but not for them. Another closed door at the end of the series. "Another burglary for you," he told her, as if he'd designed the fort and the tunnel and perhaps the entire British colonization of Upper Canada purely for her enjoyment. "Do we turn back here?"

"No," Eddy said simply. "But this isn't a real door handle." Her fingertips inspected the metal imposter. "It doesn't turn." The metal was smooth and unbroken where a keyhole might sit. "You always have a plan. Tell me what we do next."

"The hinges aren't real either," François informed her. "Tourists aren't meant to get any farther than this." It was hard to place noises in the murky black but if Eddy closed her eyes she could feel François' presence beside her, waiting, patient. Eddy glanced down to check her watch, a nervous tic, but she couldn't read it, couldn't even distinguish the black face from the surrounding gloom. "It would be easy to shift the entire door out of the way." She could hear the grin in his voice as he asked, "Shall we?"

The other side of the false door smelled like wine gone acid, like loam and rot, like something that used to be alive and would be again. There was something different about the blackness as they kept moving, as even the last echoes of light were lost behind a bend in the tunnel. Eddy's eyes played tricks on her, perlin noise of synapses firing, phantom images of her own motion, lies her mind told her in the absence of information, and she nearly stumbled over the smooth dirt floor. Her hand went out, found cotton and then flesh instead of wall to stabilize her, and and it was François' steady hand she squeezed as she pulled herself to her feet. Her pulse raced, unsure where his persistent fingers would travel, but instead of moving, he started to speak, to tell her the story of a violent death and a man hanged, thrashing on the noose as the crowd watched his breath fail.

Eddy drove too fast for the more cautious François, leaving his car in her dust somewhere around Smith Falls. There was an empty seat in the car on the way back; Lydia had stayed in Kingston to see a friend. Eddy's remaining passengers were passed out, Morgan in the front seat, Katie from the drive up traded for Owen, who was curled against Payton and letting out gentle snores. Eddy peeked with the rear-view mirror and was treated to a confirmation of her suspicions; they were holding hands. Payton's right arm rested around Owen's shoulders and the fingers of their left hand were intertwined with Owen's. Eddy, freed from the need to project an aura of professorial indifference in front of Wahid, smiled. She was right. Some things just needed time to sort themselves out.

"Not yet!" Mara says in faux horror. "We're not making cookies. You can't eat the dough." She looks at Eddy sternly, but her brown eyes are twinkling. "You shouldn't eat cookie batter either. You'll make yourself sick with raw eggs." Eddy makes for the tea towel covering the ball of dough but Mara swats her hand away. Mara's got good reflexes. "It needs to rest. We have an hour. And longer til anyone from book club shows up."

Eddy is not known for her patience, but she'll make an attempt for Mara. "Did you like the book?" she asks. Mara's ability to bake themed snacks has proven uncorrelated to her enjoyment of the monthly dose of literature. All Who Go Do Not Return *wasn't exactly Eddy's taste — not nearly enough dragons or unicorns — but it was a compelling story nonetheless, and Eddy's not expecting Mara's frown at the mention of it, her body slipping into uncertain edges, suddenly fragile. Mara's fingers smooth invisible wrinkles on the fabric edges of her apron — sea blue with green stripes and a bright yellow fish on the pocket — and without thinking about it, Eddy hugs Mara. Mara furrows her brow at the spontaneous gesture, as if unaware of the intensity of her own feelings, unaware what she might have done to provoke this response. It should be awkward but instead it's comfortable, holding Mara, and Eddy doesn't let go.*

"Lucy's coming back to book club today," Mara says, soft in Eddy's arms, folding herself into the creases of Eddy so there's no space between them, no space that isn't them. Her words seem like a non sequitur, but Eddy isn't going to object. "She took a break during the opera's European tour, and then the American one. She'll be early. She always is. But not before lunch."

"Are the others coming too? Alycia and — the rest of them?" Eddy is terrible

with names, can't remember anyone else from the garden party, but Alycia is too grand to permit herself to be forgotten.

"Oh, she doesn't come to book club. Alycia is so busy with her charity-business." Mara speaks softly, but there's something determined in her voice. She pulls back far enough to examine Eddy's face, loosening Eddy's grip but not breaking the hold entirely. "You've got flour on your nose. I knew you needed an apron."

Eddy's worked in enough labs to know better than to touch her face with contaminated hands, and besides, an apron is entirely useless at protecting a person's face. Still, she submits meekly to Mara's fingers on her nose, then along her jawline, a gentle caress that wouldn't remove even the lightest dusting of flour. Mara's mouth is next, kissing along the line she's drawn, but Eddy interrupts to meet her with lips and tongue. Eddy's hands slide down to untie Mara's apron, then up under Mara's silk blouse, revealing pale stomach and dusty-rose lace.

"Is everyone done shopping?" Rose asked, looking around the party. "Grogtar, did you get all your black-market weapon enhancements? Carmilla, do you have the illegal mushroom spores? And the powdered pearls and roc eyes?" Rose collected items from each of them to add to her bulging Handy Haversack. "We are never going back to Yr. We can't risk the fines."

"Not without a small army," Grogtar said. His axe sparked and flickered eerily in his hands, brighter than the candles and gas lamps which illuminated the nearby shops. "Or a few extra levels."

Arg's linen shirt was new, and fittingly swashbuckling for his status as an adventurer. It had fewer bloodstains than the previous one, but other than that Carmilla thought it looked good. He coughed to get their attention, composed himself, and began. "Rose, mon lutin, I misjudged you. All this time, I mistrusted the living, but you — you have been the most loyal of companions, the most loyal of friends, to a Zombie such as myself. I delight each day that I have learned your true nature, and that despite our differences, despite the hatred our history calls for, that you have learned mine." Arg took a knee, though Carmilla wasn't sure he would be able to put it back. François pulled a bouquet of roses from behind the DM's screen and presented them to Mara. "Take these Vampyre Roses as a sign of my affection, ma mie, dearest Rose, the most glorious of flowers."

Mara smiled affectionately as she took them and kissed François. "Thank you, Zeeskeit." She ran a finger along a perfectly formed red petal.

Arg coughed again. "Erm, I might avoid overmuch physical contact with the roses, if you are not ready to join me among the dead."

Rose withdrew her finger quickly. "I'll get a vase."

Arg reached behind the screen again, this time revealing a pair of high black leather boots. Joseph's eyes lit up, so it must have been a horse thing, more's the pity. "Grogtar, the most violent of Half-Orcs, with such irregularly shaped teeth, each one more jagged and protuberant than the last, what tyrannical philosophy, what brutality —"

"You're embarrassing me," Grogtar said, arms outstretched. "Give me the boots already."

"These are Boots of Fleet Foot," Arg explained, handing them over. Joseph immediately reached for the zipper to try them on. "And you, Carmilla, my fellow undead, a friend to both the dead and the living, I have not forgotten you." François handed Eddy a folded sheet of 8.5 by 11.

Eddy grinned. The grant had come through and François was buying an MRI for the lab. Eddy's days of suffering through EEG goop in her hair were behind her. Her mind began to formulate experiments. They'd have the resolution for visual stimuli, if there was any value in capturing oxygen-deprivation based hallucinations. Eddy firmly squashed that line of thinking as inappropriate for a Vampire Bard. "What is this, Arg?"

"A magical instrument," he told her, eyes twinkling, and Eddy knew a pun was forthcoming. Joseph was too distracted by his new footwear to scowl. "Play it for ten minutes, and it casts Zone of Truth upon friend and foe alike." Arg's voice took on a serious tone. "It is called a lyre."

"How long are you comfortable spending in the Shadowrealm at one time?" François asked. Eddy jerked back at his hand on her shoulder, skittish in a way that would have given him entirely the wrong impression. He withdrew it, resting his palms on the lab bench. There was no way to explain the conspiracy of fear and need that etched along her bones, dissolving in concentric rings of acid, rippling out from where he'd removed his hand. She longed for it back. She put her hand beside his on the black countertop, little finger brushing his, a mere accident, a coincidence of touch. "If you ran the same Instance as Lydia, but went further back than she did, you could replicate her experiment multiple times. You'd have to tell me which revision we were on, of course, and even if we play fast and loose with Health and Safety rules, you can only spend hours there. I don't want to have to call your next-of-kin." He spoke with a calm bemusement which should've been the thing that frightened Eddy.

"I'm not Monica Keeling," Eddy promised. "And my cat hasn't figured out how to work phones yet." She didn't dare slide her fingers closer. They were on a cusp, a transition from one steady state to another, and if Eddy held very, very still, they would cross the tipping point and fall into the Mirrorverse.

François straightened, a smooth motion, betraying no tension. "I have something I need you to do in the Shadowrealm."

"'Course," Eddy said. This was what she expected, from the moment François hadn't propositioned her at the conference. "Tell me."

"Fuck," Eddy swore, too loudly, closing the cupboard door harder than she'd meant to.

Kyle looked up from his phone, bewildered. "What's up?" Eddy could see his screen. He was looking up the weather, of all things. Kyle could just look outside the window like a normal person.

And Eddy could get a grip on herself. "I'm out of coffee grounds. I'm so sorry, Kyle."

"S'okay," Kyle answered, unconcerned. He bounced to his feet. "I'll get Timmies before work. What do you take?"

François had a Nespresso machine in his office, white ceramic shot glasses, a tawny red-tinged crema floating on each espresso it pulled. So far, Eddy had only helped herself in the Shadowrealm. What could François do if he caught her, anyway? He needed her.

What could he do that he didn't do already?

"One sugar." Eddy kissed Kyle on the cheek. "Thanks."

Time passed slowly and occasionally nonlinearly. Any given day might contain an incidental backwards digression, but in the end, it moved in a substantively forward direction. The nights became shorter and cooler, and the Brent/Lilith omegaverse fic went on hiatus while the author started back at college and got a handle on her fourth year. Eddy had been a postdoc for long enough that one class of data points wasn't enough to satisfy her anymore.

By any reasonable metric, it was too late in the day to be still working, but Eddy was determined, staring at squiggles on her laptop screen as if enlightenment came from direct examination of raw data and not from the smooth operation of a well-designed algorithm. When insight failed to materialize, Eddy bit the head off a gummy worm. Lilith pawed hopefully at the bag it came from but it failed to transform into a bag of kibble, nor did it run away and hide under the bed in an entertaining manner. Lilith glared balefully first at it, then at Eddy.

"Nip?" Eddy offered in partial appeasement. Leaving her data to its own devices, Eddy trekked the handful of steps to the kitchen, Lilith tight on her heels and occasionally fully underfoot. "Not my substance of choice, but this is a judgement-free zone." Eddy sprinkled a healthy portion of catnip on Lilith's scratcher and placed a rainbow fabric mouse on top as a garnish, and Lilith dove in headfirst.

"You're welcome, Lilith," Eddy said, since acceptance of dues rightfully paid was the most thanks anyone ever got from a cat. "I don't suppose you're willing to do me any favours in return? Wanna debug my life, rubber-duck style?" It shouldn't be funny to gently shake the can over Lilith's head so it was raining catnip on the delighted animal, but Eddy was easily amused. "François upgraded me to fMRI, but there's no point if I can't find correlations between my brainwaves and visual stimuli. No, asphyxia-related hallucinations don't count, they're not replicable, you know about replication Lilith. That's why you knock Panic Pete onto the floor every night, instead of just doing it once and leaving the poor stress toy alone." Lilith was attempting to simultaneously roll in, eat, and inhale the leaves, which resulted in adorable cat sneezes. Lilith's scientific pursuits were limited to repeating her bad decisions, and not to learning from them.

"Speaking of things I can't discuss in mixed company, got any advice for starting the conversation with Mara in the Middlerealm? I can't just go, hey Mara, remember when we discussed our favourite pastries, well, guess what you've been eating lately?" Eddy sighed. There were some conversations she could only have with Lilith.

As the nip kicked in, Lilith's already poor sense of scale got worse. She grabbed the mouse with her front paws, back paws kicking furiously at the air in a futile but adorable attempt to eviscerate the furry imitation. "Getting with Mara in the Shadowrealm is like the exact opposite of masturbation." Eddy reached down to rub Lilith's fur, cautious lest her hand become the next item of prey after the mouse met its inevitable fate. "Kyle does whatever I tell him in bed. I should like that, right? A sane person would like that better."

Eddy glanced down at her watch and groaned. "I don't want to wake up in seven hours, Lilith. I don't want to go to group meeting in —" she checked again, as if willing the time to pass more slowly "— eleven hours. You don't understand what it's like, Lilith, because you're a cat. You only care about time because I won't feed you before 6 AM. No, not even if you scream as if you're starving. You're not starving."

Lilith took no notice of the pointed comments, but suddenly her lack of sympathy didn't matter to Eddy. "I thought of something to try, Lilith," she explained as she walked back to the computer. Eddy was a woman on a mission. "When you're done with your post-nip nap, I'll tell you if it worked."

Lydia, the very soul of discretion, scrawled a note in her lab book and slid it over the desk to Eddy. It was a foregone conclusion that François would see the movement. Eddy would pay for her sins in the group discussion after the talk, but as long as she made a couple insightful comments François would let her off with minimal public shaming for the distraction. Eddy looked down at the page, read the message and groaned internally. 'Owen told Payton that he's ace.'

Responding to bad behaviour was condoning bad behaviour. Even though she knew that, Eddy wrote a message back in her own notebook and pushed it towards the young woman. 'Why are you telling me this, this is not my business, do not tell me this.' In retrospect, Eddy should have added a smiley face to soften the blow. Lydia didn't seem overly upset, though, frowning over her page and crossing out the offending statement. She replaced it with an equal number of words and turned the book back towards Eddy.

'Owen and Payton are dating now.'

Eddy didn't want to hear about the details of Owen's sex life, or lack thereof, but good for those two crazy kids finally working it out. She smiled despite herself and Lydia grinned back, mission presumably accomplished. The two of them should have focused on Marcus' talk instead of gossiping, but it was pretty thin gruel. Enough to pass his defense when he gave it for real, but only because François selected

Marcus' examiners very carefully, and Eddy should have an opinion on that but she couldn't remember what it was. The important thing was that Eddy could get away with offering Marcus generic feedback and even François would accept it.

Everyone applauded politely when Marcus finished presenting. Eddy suggested he make the text larger on the captions, include the full referencing on his figures and add slide numbers. Owen offered some restructuring advice, and Katie, only a few months away from her own defense and feeling a misplaced level of camaraderie, pointed out each time Marcus changed fonts and every overused semicolon. Marcus complained about administrative hiccups — it was even odds whether he hadn't filed his paperwork correctly or the secretary had taken a dislike to him — and François promised to sort it out.

Eddy dawdled when the rest of the group left until it was just her and François in the empty classroom. Eddy tried to speak quietly, but it was hard to contain her excitement. "I can see the numbers on my watch," she told him. "On the fMRI. It's the last thing I look at before each death, and I thought, maybe if I looked at the networked signals from the prefrontal, parietal, and inferior temporal regions associated with maths and numeracy — I wasn't sure if it would work, since the stimuli that causes the measurable signals happens after I look at my watch, but then the whole point of Instances is they're timey wimey, so why did I assume they only ran linearly and forward?" Eddy paused her onslaught of words to consider their effect. If possible, François was more thrilled with her discovery than she was, pride and admiration in equal measure.

"Is it related to those regions of the brain? Or an interaction of the stimuli broadening the observation window?" He wore a pistachio-green shirt, sleeves rolled up past the elbow, a skeletal leaf print revealed on the inside of the cuffs. It was new, not that Eddy had his wardrobe memorized, and tailored. A gift from Mara, maybe. The important thing was he'd understood her point, when no one else in her life would have untangled her mess of jargon and fandom.

"My guess is the second. I haven't found anywhere else — anywhen else — with the watch showing up in the scans, or numbers at all." She swallowed, excitement suddenly overwhelmed by nerves. "There's so much more to discover. We have so many tests we need to run."

"The Franklin Expedition is just the beginning, my boy," Reid proclaimed with a wide grin, slapping François on the shoulder. "We're creating history. Alycia clears the ice with a reminder of our heritage, I follow in her wake. It'll take a military base to secure the Arctic, but soft power comes first." He wore a dark suit, somber colours fading into the background, though no one could miss Reid in a room, even if anyone else had been wearing a monocle. The Gala was gothic-themed, which nearly everyone other than Norm had understood to mean severe black suits for men and not Hot Topic. Though even Norm didn't outshine the man who took the Franklin Expedition inspiration literally and arrived in a period-authentic replica sailor's uniform.

"You'll never convince the Liberals," Tobias said with the predictable level of objective journalism for a *National Post* reporter. "They won't spend a dime to secure us against the Russians." Even if the Liberals were open to being convinced to arm up, Eddy was unsure how replicating a doomed expedition would be a selling point in favour of the plan. Doom seemed unlikely this go around, regardless of how much a long walk would add to the aesthetic. The impact of climate change on high latitudes gave the New Franklin Expedition a head start on getting through the ice, and Alycia had conceded to modernity enough to let them bring lead-free cans, based on the advice of Colette, who'd graduated pre-med though she'd never gone all the way. Still, re-enacting the Expedition made for an excellently themed charity gala, if you pretended that 'restoring Canadian greatness' was as charitable as Alycia claimed on the tickets. Mara paid for Eddy's entrance as a thank you for the con, though Eddy suspected there was an order of magnitude difference in the price.

As Tobias continued to expound on the vital topics of national sovereignty, deficit spending and — somehow — Louis St. Laurent's statue, Eddy examined the art Alycia had selected for the Main Hall of the National Gallery. The Group of Seven were unsurprisingly prominent, but Eddy was disappointed to find so many depopulated landscapes, not a penguin in sight to torment François. A few of the European pieces were worth looking at, and Eddy let her gaze linger on *Man Proposes, God Disposes* while she waited for Tobias to run out of words. The man must do cryptic crosswords.

"They don't think they need to," Alycia said, bringing the conversation back to national defense. It seemed Alycia and Reid's penchant for arming Canadian governments was more than a business venture; it was a lifestyle choice. "They think the Inuit presence is enough." She shook her head, more in sorrow than anger. "It worked for Pearson, but they shouldn't count on it again. You can't rely on those kinds of people."

"Liberals are so well-intentioned," François said, offering the less-uncomfortable interpretation of Alycia's statement. "You wouldn't put one in charge of defending a bird feeder, but it's endearing." François had replaced his typical diver's watch with a pocket watch for the event, silver fob dangling from his wool jacket. At the reminder, Eddy glanced at her own wrist, moved by force of habit more than concern for the time or the Realm, but she'd also abandoned her watch at home as not sufficiently thematic. "Do you really think the northern borders are the ones we need to worry about?"

"The Americans aren't sending their best," Reid agreed. "If the Liberals hadn't scrapped the Safe Third Country Agreement — but then we couldn't expect anything else from them." Eddy took a sip of her wine to cover any face she might be making and looked around the group. Everyone else seemed to take it in stride. Mara was frowning, distressed, but then Mara always looked distressed at parties and Eddy couldn't kiss the lines from her forehead, run hands along Mara's shoulders until they relaxed down and Mara smiled. Not yet, anyway. Eddy took another sip, or perhaps a gulp, judging by how much remained in her glass when she was done. She needed another drink. Maybe a bottle.

"Give them a chance," François argued, waving his glass of red. "Once they integrate, there's no real difference. Talent finds a way. Think of Steve Jobs or K'Naan." François needed to be careful with that glass; Mara was wearing white, cotton lawn so delicate it was practically sheer, a high lace neck ringed with a loose strand of pearls. Most of the women wore black — Eddy did, a loose ruched skirt of a thick fabric and a corset top — but there were white dresses as well, variations from Alycia's stark-white tea dress, thin fabric draped modestly off her shoulders, to one of François' doctor friends wearing a burnt off-white dress with an irregular hem. Only Lucy wore red, a deep burgundy as rich as blood.

"You can't build a country on exceptions, my boy," Reid explained, a teacher giving extra help to a promising student. "You need a strong foundation." He turned his benevolent gaze to Eddy next and she looked straight back at him as if she wasn't afraid. "I wouldn't have hired just anyone for her job. I don't hope for the best. I make it happen."

"No," François agreed amiably. "I wouldn't do that either."

"Of course not," Reid said, still looking at Eddy. Looking through her, as though Eddy's skin had been exquisitely flayed, tendons peeled, blood washed away to reveal ivory white bone. She should have been screaming but her throat was missing. "Eddy's good stock. I could work with her."

Suddenly she was anywhere but there, anywhere but standing beside Reid, her body still calmly smiling back at him but only an empty shell, mind purged, voided in silent, painful heaves and Eddy was going to be sick. She needed to leave before she threw up but her body couldn't move when her consciousness hovered two meters above her head. Eddy could barely handle knowing what they needed her to do, a hot ember of a thought that she hid at the back of the fireplace in her brain, took out occasionally to see if it had cooled only for her fingers to be burnt anew. She could barely handle imagining her future, and that was with François beside her. The thought of Reid instead, his jovial grin, chin tilted upwards, his avuncular tone pitted against the meaning of his words, filled her with dread.

François put a hand against the small of Eddy's back, a point of stability as her mind vapourised and floated away. Something real.

Something now. Eddy closed her eyes and let herself feel her weight against him, listened to her pulse pounding, louder than the chamber music playing in the background, louder than the chattering voices of the conversations around them. But not her group's conversation. It had gone silent. Eddy opened her eyes to see everyone looking at her. She took a sip of her wine and pretended not to notice.

François stepped into the silence. "People can surprise you. Norm's son got a place in Sir John A Macdonald Academy, and you know they only take the best." François' expression was a cipher, blank as if they were talking about the weather or construction. It was Mara's sudden rise in tension, Mara, who didn't even know what François' words meant, that tipped Eddy off to look at Reid's face, bright red with anger, shining in the dim light.

"Joseph is so happy to have Winston at the same school as him," Mara said, voice nervous and fast as she rushed to fill the conversational space before Reid could speak. "The boys are friends. It's a shame Joseph is a year older. They would be in the same grade, otherwise." Mara's eyes were wide and beseeching as she looked to Alycia.

Alycia touched Reid's arm and shook her head ever so slightly. Reid took a deep breath. As he released it, he seemed to deflate, just a little. There was still colour in his cheeks, but his voice was as genteel as ever. "Indeed." He smiled, but it didn't come close to his eyes. "A round of Old Fashioneds next. Unless the ladies prefer something gentler?"

"Whatever you like, Reid," Alycia said approvingly, giving his arm another pat. "But quickly. Lucy's singing from *Der Rosenkavalier* next and you don't want to miss it."

Where Eddy sees black uniforms protecting the National Gallery, Mara sees boys. Eddy sees it too after Mara points it out, the college kid hidden inside the security guard's outfit, claiming a poorly fitted authority, shoulders shrugging to

keep it in place. "They're waiting for someone to tell them what to do," François says, and Mara nods.

"They're hungry. Boys are always hungry." Mara smiles at them warmly and they respond in kind. "They're watching the dessert table but they don't get any." She's right. The guards seem much more interested in the marzipan-white topped cakes than any of the glacial landscapes hanging on the walls. Eddy sympathizes. "I'll bring them a plate."

Kindness proves an effective distraction. Either the guards don't notice the trio slipping past them or they don't care, attention fully devoted to pastry-related concerns. François' up next, and he must always carry the lockpicks because he makes short work of the lock on the vault door. Eddy lingers at the opening, peering into the rich darkness, appreciating what she's finally going to accomplish. This time, Eddy can't fail to give the Goya to Mara, can't run out of time, not when Mara is right beside her, eyes bright with mischief, smile as wide as Eddy's own. They've passed the Final Guardian, ready to step over the last threshold.

"François, is this where you've been hiding all this time? I've been looking everywhere for you." Alycia's voice rings out, cutting through the music and chatter of the party upstairs with an unrelenting clarity. Backlit, Alycia radiates like an angel, sheer gloves tucked beneath starched cuffs, lace trim of gathered white skirt caressing the floor. "I want to talk to you about the Academy."

François makes a rushing motion at them lest they be seen as well, though he must know what Realm they're in, and that it doesn't matter if they're caught. Mara slips through the door without further hesitation, and Eddy follows after.

Laid out on a lightbox, The Sleep of Reason Produces Monsters is even more gorgeous than Eddy expected. Maybe it's the thrill of the hunt. Maybe it's the etching itself, owls, bats and a lynx staring them down with surprise and hunger. The two of them don't have anything to hold down the corners except hands, their arms criss-crossed as they examine their prize, quiet for a satisfied moment, and Mara brushes Eddy's cheek with a soft kiss.

"Can we get it out?" Mara asks, lifting her hands and letting the corners of the paper curl, smooth white gloves a sharp contrast to the dark fabric around Eddy's waist, Mara's fingers running over lines of boning. "They won't ignore us carrying it, not even for profiteroles." Eddy turns to kiss her, mindful that the Goya doesn't crease as she raises her hands, but Mara slides away. Eddy's approach is too fast, too intense. "Careful of our makeup."

Mouths are to be approached with caution, but there's no embargo on hands. Mara's fingers tease the waistline of Eddy's skirt where the fabric's edge hides underneath the black dip of her corset. "I snuck a plastic sleeve under my top to protect the Goya. We just need to secure it under your skirt — your bustle is bigger than mine."

Mara laughs at this, a deeper, throatier noise that Eddy's ever heard from her. She reaches with covered fingers for the laces on the back of Eddy's corset, ever so slowly undoing the ribbons. Eddy watches Mara work in the mirror, fascinated at the deliberate, slow pattern of Mara's touch up her back.

"I don't remember a mirror in the vault," Eddy says quietly. She's breathing fast, shallow breaths and there's no air in her lungs left for talking. She's been to the vault more times than she can count, but there was never a mirror before. And there was never Mara.

Mara pauses in her work to close the distance between them, chin resting on Eddy's shoulder, lips breathing out words against the bottom of Eddy's ear. "The exhibit on decorative arts. Alycia made them move it for her party." Mara steps back and pulls the ribbon out from the remaining loops, catching the corset before it falls. It's not cold that makes Eddy shiver, nipples hard, and Mara's pulling at her skirt, down, leaving bare legs and ridiculous shoes. "We should investigate. There's teacups and lamps and a chaise longue. There's beds, Eddy, one with a headboard round like the sun, one rounded and lined like a flower." Mara smiles as her hands move up. "I think you'll like them."

"If we're on a side quest to find the missing mighty steeds of

Proudloch," Grogtar said with unshakable determination, "I can go on a side-side quest to find a snack to go with my mayo." He glared at his party, lest anyone dispute his claim. "I can't just eat mayonnaise."

"The jar makes lots of things," Mara explained, not for the first time. She'd written the full list on Rose's character sheet. "You keep asking it for mayonnaise."

"Mayo is great," Grogtar said. Logic was not a Half-Orc's strong suit. Strength was a Half-Orc's strong suit. "I bet it goes great with pie."

"Ugh, living food is disgusting," Carmilla objected, sharing a forbearing smile with Arg and sipping on a glass of a nice red. Wine, not blood, but an MRI machine wasn't a one-for-one with a magical lyre either. It was about the willing suspension of disbelief. "Go ahead and eat your fleshy nonsense, I'm going to busk for coins." Eddy would never make it as an opera singer, but she could carry a tune. Carmilla got out the lyre and started singing "Where the Wild Roses Grow."

"There's blood pudding on the menu," Rose pointed out. "Do you want some, Carmilla?" She smiled winsomely at Boberta the Hag, who ran the local pie shop, All You Knead. The Hag scowled back at her, which was in character for a Hag. "An order of blood pudding, hold the pudding, please. And something a Zombie would like. What do you suggest?" She reached to squeeze Arg's hand.

Metal dice clattered behind the DM's screen. "Brains," the Hag replied slowly. "From animals. From one specific type of mammal. Mammal brains. Non-ruminant. It could be any species. But it's not. It's one very specific species. Of non-ruminant mammal." She shook her head violently as if attempting to loosen her own brains. "I'm trying to describe our Zombie specials, which are the brains of one very specific type of non-ruminant mammal." Boberta's expression turned to loathing. "You!" she shouted, pointing at Carmilla. Carmilla continued strumming on her lyre, her face studiously fixed in her most innocent expression. It wasn't very innocent, but then Carmilla was a Vampire. "How are you doing this to me?"

"You're killing the horses for pie ingredients!" Grogtar exclaimed, catching up to the plot. He dipped his remaining pie in mayonnaise, took a last, enormous bite, brushed the pie crumbs from his beard, and narrowed his eyes. "You fiend! Horses are majestic animals and you are a wicked criminal!" Pie disposed of, Grogtar grabbed his axe.

"Honestly, I don't see the problem," Carmilla responded, but she drew her rapier anyway, to be sociable.

"If you're not comfortable, there's no rush. Time is something we have." François tells her, and maybe it's meant to be reassuring. Eddy looks at her watch. Four hours to go in this Instance, though that's not what François is talking about. She could back out. She's certain François will let her. He'll smile at her like he's not disappointed and tell her it'll be easier next time. But if Eddy can't do it now there won't be a next time.

She's got a job to do. She's not paid to like it.

Eddy longs to run her fingers over the creases in François' face, wrinkles from smiles and worries, each imperfection a story, each confirming he's human after all. But this is not permitted. "I'm fine. It's the Shadowrealm. It doesn't matter."

He smiles at her like she's passed a test. Something hard settles in the pit of Eddy's stomach and she knows it's not going to leave, not this Instance, or when she's back, or ever. Eddy's bound like vampires on Night Beats, *Lilith's silver locket is a brand denoting a covenant made, but instead of jewelry, François got Eddy an anxiety disorder. Everything plays better on TV. "I'll do it, if you like," François offers.*

"Yes," she agrees. She doesn't say thank you. It's her either way.

He should call her a coward for this pretense. He won't.

The worst part isn't watching the volunteer on the other side of the glass as

she starts to feel the effects, a tickle in her throat, as easily chalked up to hypochondria as to the dust. Besides, the woman doesn't want to disturb the scientists in pristine white lab coats holding clipboards as they watch her. It's only an allergy trial. The volunteer knows she might get the placebo, she's been warned she might feel uncomfortable, but the scientists told her that the pills she's testing are safe.

They're honest; the tablets are safe. The water François handed her to wash them down is not. Eddy watched him mix it before Lydia or Owen or the patient arrived, and Eddy stood beside him as he poured precisely 150 mL into a dinky plastic cup, and Eddy did nothing as he handed it over. Eddy doesn't tell herself that François is working on developing the cure, not the disease, or that the real version of the woman is safe in the Middlerealm, because semantics don't matter when she sees her gasp for air.

François goes in, oozing charm and Eddy would believe herself well too if he talked to her the way he's talking to the patient. He's listening to her, really listening, writes down each thing she says as he promises to look into it. There's glass and distance between Eddy and the words but she knows exactly what the woman is saying. It was nothing, she's telling François, voice getting thinner. She's fine. François admires the woman's hand-made loose-knit cardigan, she always gets so chilly indoors, even in the summer, but she's fine, really, she didn't mean to trouble him, just a tickle in her throat. Just the dust. When François rejoins them on the other side of the glass he looks at Eddy with an expression that's a cousin to compassion.

Eddy's job is to watch. That's all; watch and report back on later so they know how far François' research on the antidote has progressed. The creature in Eddy's gut has laid eggs, each as heavy as its mother, and they're clawing their way out of their shells and through Eddy's flesh. But the worst part isn't watching the woman, floral capri pants and baby pink flats, watching her scratch her throat, watching her struggling for air, invisible hands around her neck. It isn't that the woman is dying alone, terribly, hopelessly alone, something François would never do to Eddy.

The worst part is watching Lydia.

At each twitch of discomfort, François makes a note on his clipboard. The *consistency of François' movement serves to reassure Owen, who nods along with each tap of the pen. This is science, and science is its own justification. It's not enough for Lydia. Lydia is scared and confused but she's certain, somehow, that something is wrong, Eddy can see it in her face, in the nervous way Lydia touches the glass, rests her fingers on it, testing how far she dares go. Lydia's jaw clenches, and she looks to François, then back to the woman and shifts her feet. Lydia wants to go in the room, scientific rigour be damned, she's moments away from walking in and attempting mouth-to-mouth. Lydia, the only one of them who retains their humanity. Eddy's almost jealous.*

François turns to Lydia, his tone almost kind. Almost, but not quite. "Can you get a hold of yourself?" Lydia shrinks under his gaze. She lasts a minute longer until the woman starts moaning, then frantically mumbles something about the bathroom and bolts. She won't be back.

Eddy envies her now.

François stands beside Eddy, certainly too close, but then Owen is gifted at not-seeing. François murmurs against her ear, "Are you okay?" and Eddy nods, sharply, not trusting herself to speak.

At the end, when they're alone and François wraps his hands around her neck, Eddy leans in.

François was waiting for her when her mind got back, his eyes fixed on the fMRI signals emerging on the desktop beside her body. He shifted to face her at the first sign of consciousness, when Eddy's eyes focused and her fingers curled. Her stomach came alive at the same moment she did and she bit back nausea, bit her lip until she thought it might bleed, an offering of blood to the fallen but nothing came because Eddy was already sucked dry, shambling forward as her body fell apart around her.

"Are you okay?" he asked, in the exact same tone as last time he said it. Eddy tried to nod again but the tears came first, and any chance at dignity was lost as she cried. François leaned down to hold her and she buried her face in his grey shirt. "What do you need, Eddy?"

"Lydia can't be there," she said to the cotton as it turned dark with tears. "I can't do it again if Lydia's in the room when we run the test. I can't take it with her there. I'm sorry, François. I thought I could — I tried. I'm sorry. Not again."

François smoothed Eddy's hair; his hands were her lodestone and she followed their motion across her scalp, letting them lead her in rhythmic patterns away and then back into herself. "It's okay, Eddy." His voice was caring and steady. "We don't need her there. Next time we run it, I'll send her to work somewhere else." It sounded so logical when he spoke.

Eddy shook her head, not hard enough to make him lose his touch on her. "What about her project?"

"Oh, Eddy. You're too good." Eddy closed her eyes and let the movement of his hands on her head, the warmth of his body, encompass her world. "Lydia's got the Middlerealm and her own Instances. She doesn't need yours too."

François waited until she'd stopped crying, breathing returned to even, before pulling away. He gently brushed the hair back from her face and looked her in the eyes. "Tell me if it's too much. There's no rush, Eddy. Can you promise to tell me?"

It was the easiest lie she ever told.

Mara's not home.

Eddy's lonely. She can't talk about it, she can't speak at all, her throat is collapsing and she's wearing a maroon turtleneck sweater to hide bruises that don't exist anymore — never existed. Eddy needs to see someone, touch someone, to get out of the lab and out of her skin. It doesn't take a lockpick's skill to cut through fly screens but as soon as Eddy does she can feel the emptiness. The house is Mara, and Mara isn't home. Still, Eddy ventures onwards. Maybe she's wrong. Maybe it's Eddy that's empty, and the house is fine.

There's a noise, upstairs, and Eddy heads towards it. She's not sure what she's going to tell Mara this time. This is a bad idea, she's going to hurt Mara again, and the Shadowrealm doesn't count but Eddy shouldn't, anyway. Not when it's Mara she's hurting. Eddy keeps walking. The bathroom door is ajar, and it doesn't take much to push it open, as effortless as a thought.

The situation is both obvious and makes no sense. The sound is Joseph, home when he should be at school, head carefully positioned above the white toilet bowl. The seat, tilted upwards, is shining clean, and it occurs to Eddy that Joseph must have washed it for this exact occasion.

"What's going on?" Eddy asks, as calmly as she can.

Joseph looks at her. He's impossibly far away. He's kneeling on a neatly folded faded blue towel, and beside him are a handful of empty meat packages, black styrofoam streaked with blood, saran wrap balled up on top of each. "What are you doing here?" She can't tell if he's panicked or relieved to see her. She can't understand anything anymore.

"It doesn't matter," Eddy replies. Maybe it does matter, but not compared to the scene in front of her. "Is everything okay?" The answer is self-evident, and she tries a different question. "Joseph, why?"

"Grade 10," he says simply. "Grade 9 was hazing. Grade 10 is my turn." His voice catches on the last words. Eddy's stomach twists. There were benefits to being an untouchable loser in high school. "Don't tell anyone?"

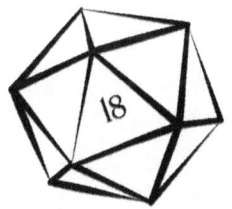

"Bad CGI," François suggested, brows furrowed in contemplation. "More coffee?" He already had her cup in his hands. François was nobody's fool — not when it came to Eddy's rampant caffeine addiction, or when it came to *Night Beats* finale bingo.

Eddy frowned, considering the implications of his words. "How bad? Does it have to be worse than the episode with the horrifying Paddington Bear-esque CGI, which I guarantee they only scripted because they got so much hate for the Cursed Indian Burial Ground plot line, but writing an Indigenous person transforming into a terrifying example of why amateur taxidermy is a dangerous business is not a replacement for actual representation, especially in a nominally Canadian TV show." Francois probably thought Eddy was gonna pause for breath at some point in that sentence, but Eddy wasn't weak. "Also yes please." Eddy took the tiny, penguin-rimmed espresso mug from François by the miniature handle. She held the vessel out to him so he could place two cubes of sugar in her cup, straight white edges dissolving as he released them into the black. He passed her a spoon to stir them. "Thanks."

"We need a threshold," François said, pulling a second cup for himself. "They wouldn't have a season premiere without Brent, and when Brent's on screen they always apply the soft-edges filter to demonstrate his spirituality." He waited for Eddy to groan appreciatively and she happily complied. "But we can't expect a second taxidermy bear.

That was a once-in-a-lifetime event."

"I thought Joseph might fall off the couch laughing," Eddy agreed, smiling at the memory. She added 'Notably Bad CGI' to Mara and Joseph's bingo cards. They'd agreed on 'Shadowrealm' and 'Mirrorverse' as separate squares, of course, though Eddy lost the argument about 'Middlerealm' and had to compromise by writing it on the free space in the middle. François let her get away with 'accidental Toronto cameo' and 'deliberate Toronto cameo' as separate squares, so she was reasonably content with her lot in life. Plus, it was barely 3 PM, which meant Eddy was still on the clock and François was paying her to sit in his office and plan their season premiere watch party. He wasn't the worst boss she'd had. She took a breath, ran a finger along the edge of her Edwardian collar, and refused to let herself reconsider that assessment.

"Jordan dies," François teased her and with a deliberate effort of will, Eddy released the tension she was holding. She assumed his suggestion wasn't serious, though he pulled off a good deadpan.

"I've already got that on everyone's card," Eddy pointed out. It might have been the first thing she wrote. In all caps. Underlined.

"Jordan could die twice in the same episode." François was definitely teasing. The corners of his lips quirked upwards and there was warmth in his grey eyes. "Three or four times, if the writers get lazy." Eddy laughed and François relented. "We could include a murder weapon on the bingo."

"Lilith's teeth," Eddy said instantly. If Eddy blushed at the thought of her, François didn't remark on it. Presumed heterosexuality was good for something after all.

"François," Mara said softly. She sounded tired. "It was Ahlai on the phone. Elkanah's computer is dead and he needs one for university."

François put a hand on her shoulder and Mara sighed, her body collapsing against his as she reclaimed her place beside him on the couch. He kissed the top of her head, between the dog ears on her headband, and put an arm around her. "Get him a MacBook this time. Poor quality costs more in the long run."

"Tante shouldn't call during *Night Beats*," Joseph complained, sensibly enough. Even apart from the transgression occurring during the sacred hour of *Night Beats*, no one should phone anyone, ever. If humans were meant to call each other, humanity would not have been blessed by the invention of texting.

"She doesn't watch, Joseph," Mara said. He looked suitably chastised, though Eddy suspected he was moved by Mara's sorrowful tone rather than her words. "What did I miss?"

"The best part," Joseph explained, eager to redeem himself. "After Jordan reads the cursed horoscope he's gored to death with a bullhorn, so Lilith bites him to turn him into a vampire." Against her better judgement, Eddy had gotten Joseph a faux sheriff's badge so he could cosplay Jordan for the watch party. Etsy sold pins declaring the wearer to be the 'World's Least Interesting Man,' but that was too much truth about Jordan for a fifteen-year-old boy to endure. Joseph's life was hard enough.

"Unrealistically," Eddy said. The prior commercial break had featured Joseph and Eddy loudly debating whether Eddy got to cross the top-right corner off her bingo for 'Lilith's teeth' if Jordan was already well on his way to corpsehood when Lilith bit him. "Lilith wouldn't save Jordan's life. Not when she didn't even try to turn Jane when she was dying." Eddy wore the same top hat and locket as she had at the con, but also her leather dress. If anyone asked, she was dressed as Mirrorverse Lilith. Minus the goatee.

"Lilith knew Jane was gonna be fine," Joseph argued. "The scales that fell on her head weren't made of silver."

"It was a weighty concern," François intoned in a reasonable impression of Brent. He wore the skeletal gloves Eddy brought him, black with glow-in-the-dark phalanxes and carpals. A sheet over the head was a more appropriate costume for Brent the Ghost, but it would have been a waste of François' cheekbones. Eddy was willing to make some concessions on accuracy for a good cause. "The scales of justice are always balanced."

Joseph sighed despondently and pointedly looked away from his father before resuming his plot summary. "If Jordan can't steal his soul from the Final Guardian in the Astralrealm before midnight he's trapped as a vampire forever."

François' puns were high quality, completely worthy of Joseph's disgust and Eddy's high five. The *Night Beats* plotline did not merit equal commendation. "That's even more unrealistic. Jordan should want to be a vampire." After his turning, Jordan spent a long scene tastelessly bemoaning his fate as a Cryptid with an irredeemably tarnished immortal soul to anyone soft-hearted enough to sit still and listen, which meant it was Jane who endured the tirade. Either Jordan, or the writers, or both, had forgotten that Jane was a werewolf. Jane's actress dealt with the situation by mouthing sympathetic platitudes about original sin and forgiveness while gazing at the holes on Jordan's neck with obvious avarice. In a just universe — or in a half-decent fanfic — Lilith would have turned Jane and left Jordan to die. "I don't mind Astralrealm as a name for the place after the Middlerealm. Even if they did beat me to discovering it."

François took a moment to catch up with Eddy, but he managed to follow her tangent to its logical conclusion. "You've been busy," he said kindly. Eddy made a face at his excuses.

Mara's hand was on the remote, finger at the ready, signalling the imminent resumption of Jordan's trials and tribulations. Eddy had the perfect opportunity to casually introduce a topic right before the end of the commercial break and she wasn't going to waste it.

"Joseph, are you still interested in helping with my lab work? You had some cool ideas about the Astralrealm — Future Instances — before." Eddy casually surveyed the adults in the room. "If you support Joseph getting involved in after school science enrichment activities?"

"Does *Night Beats* even exist here?" Grogtar asked, poking a stick into the fourth wall, unconcerned that it might crumble and shower them all in debris. François said no as Eddy said yes, leaving Rose caught in the middle and unwilling to commit.

Carmilla stared down her party with unwavering determination. "*Night Beats* exists in every 'verse." As a Bard, Carmilla was prepared to break into song if anyone challenged her, but after a moment's hesitation, Arg shrugged in acquiescence and Joseph rolled his eyes in surrender. "If Rose hadn't killed WhatsHisBob the Sorcerer, we could have asked him to transport us to a performance. Too late now, unless anyone's got a reincarnation spell?"

Rose examined her character sheet, Arg cleared his throat in the decided manner of a man intent on making a plot point, but Grogtar interrupted before either of them could speak. "Maybe Bobbie can take us. Do Unicorns get Teleport?"

Mara put a gentle hand on Joseph's arm. "Bobbie's dead, Grogtar. I'm sorry." Her voice was soft and empathetic. It was slightly unsuited to the situation, given the precise manner of Bobbie's demise and Rose's participation therein, but Rose was kind-hearted. Besides, a Cleric couldn't be blamed for trying to do the right thing, even if it came a bit late.

"We never saw the body!" Grogtar protested, a technicality but more than sufficient for Marvel. It remained to be seen if François held himself to a higher ethical standard than the Disney Corporation.

"We burned down six city blocks," Carmilla reminded him. "Most living sorts of people don't survive being on fire. Not even peasants." She flashed a grin at Arg, who nodded sagely.

"C'est vrai, ma crevette. Flame is among the mortals' greatest weaknesses. The living are not like us." He bowed to Rose, adding, "Though they are not all bad. And in truth, us Zombies are not so fond of fire ourselves." He left a pregnant pause — somewhere around eight and a half months, with triplets — giving the Party a chance to ask follow-up questions, an opportunity which Grogtar immediately squandered.

"If Robert and Bobbie are both permadead, and we finished the side quest, and Mort the Necromancer might be the good guy, what do we do now?" Grogtar asked, a question he immediately revealed to be rhetorical by answering, "We should go to the pub." He punctuated his statement with a resolute bang of his great-axe on the ground.

"That won't help us get to a *Night Beats* stage play," Carmilla suggested, grinning wickedly. Unlike Joseph, whose trolling was probably accidental, Eddy knew exactly how much DMs enjoyed it when players decided to take initiative.

François looked hopefully at Rose. She twisted a strand of hair behind her ear, distractingly indecisive, then rested her crossbow on the cobblestone road and considered their options. Grogtar waved his axe around threateningly, in case any of the nearby trees got any ideas while Rose was disarmed. "I'm not sure," Rose admitted. "I'm not sure who we're supposed to be fighting anymore. We could go to the pub and look for the mysterious stranger who told us about Mortimer? Maybe they'll have an idea."

Grogtar's eyes widened in excitement. "I'm gonna gamble all our gold at the pub. No, wait. Half-Orcs are pretty bad at math. Maybe just some of our gold." He hefted his money sack and eyed the size of it speculatively. "All our gold, but I'll cheat so I win."

François wasn't laughing, but it was a near thing. He'd failed a DC 15 Will saving throw to resist total plot derailment.

"I need that for baking!" Mara scolds with mock disapproval. She's used to Eddy's thieving in both Realms, and she still lets Eddy in the kitchen. "It's semisweet baking chocolate. It's not for eating." Her breath is hot on Eddy's ear, and she presses a kiss against Eddy's earlobe.

Eddy twists around to look Mara dead in the eyes and pops the shard in her mouth. It isn't Coffee Crisp but it is chocolate. Never let the perfect be the enemy of the good. "Counterpoint. I'm eating it right now." Eddy sticks out a chocolate-covered tongue, a cunning distraction as she reaches for another piece.

Before Eddy's fingers can close on the sliver, Mara gently raps her knuckles with a wooden baking spoon. "I already weighed that!" Eddy closes her hand instead around the French rolling pin lying next to the bowl of dough and slips out of Mara's arms to make distance. She taps the end of Mara's spoon, tempting her to lower her guard, but instead Mara giggles and raises a cast-iron frying pan as a makeshift shield. "Wait until it's done!"

Eddy steps off the line to the left, reaches for Mara's wrists with the rolling pin, but Mara wields her sword and shield as a seamless unit and there's no opportunity for a clear strike. "You'll get tired eventually," Eddy warns Mara. "Frying pans have terrible balance."

"Not like your steel sword," Mara teases. Conner, Eddy's ex-boyfriend, made the weapon for her with great enthusiasm, but it really was a terrible sword. Short, unbalanced, and unable to keep an edge; it might manage a painless kill on the first strike, but by the fourth cut, it was more suited to a life as a bludgeoning weapon than a slashing one. The point was consistently sharp if a piercing weapon was required, but chainmail had gone out of fashion in the 17th century. "Actually — can I borrow it? I need to defend my baking."

"Of course," Eddy promises, though she's acting against her own interests. She shifts left again and catches sight of something impossible. Nestled in a black shadow box, above the white table in the breakfast nook, hangs The Sleep of Reason Produces Monsters.

It's a print, of course. Mara likes the aquatint so she bought herself a copy. It is a good quality reproduction, and not a matter of further concern. Eddy's brain is rationalizing faster than her body can respond and Eddy's already turned her wrist before her mind can scream at her to stop. Eddy's run past the edge of a steep cliff, and as soon as she looks down she's going to realize she's standing on nothing, and fall.

Eddy looks down.

The bezel on her diver's watch was at the neutral position, home at midnight, same as it was when Eddy had bought it. Same as it always was in the Middlerealm.

Eddy stared at the face long enough to see five seconds tick by, to hear them tick in the otherwise silent kitchen. She twisted her arm experimentally but the bezel didn't turn on its own. It only moved when she twisted it. François told her to get a good quality timepiece when she started the job.

"Is everything okay?" Mara asked, concerned, implements of baking-related destruction abandoned on the counter. She put a hand on Eddy's forehead then cheek. "You're flushed. I'll get you apple juice."

"I can't believe we're finally starting Phase 2 Trials," Lydia said with delight, snapping the buttons on her lab coat closed and redoing the green elastic on her ponytail.

Eddy could believe it. A dozen participants. A dozen tablets, a dozen dinky little cups of water, a dozen consent forms with a line on the bottom asking for a signature. A dozen faces Eddy didn't want to see again. Eddy twisted her arm and scratched her elbow, the movement of a person who was simply itchy rather than a person with a loose grasp on reality surreptitiously checking her watch for the hundredth time since lunch.

Middlerealm.

François was there too, navy jacket and grey chevron tie. It was a big day for Lydia. He joked about finally getting some quality data out of her and Eddy laughed along with the rest of them. There was a volunteer with a jean jacket, faded and worn to precisely the same shade of baby blue as her pants, and Eddy wondered if she always wore them as an outfit, if they'd started equally bright and paled together. A man with a Poirot moustache that he curled with his fingers before he signed the page. An undergrad who argued fervently that she should get both the dream journal marks and the gift certificate for enrolling in the study. Eddy stepped in at that.

"Give them both to her, Lydia." Eddy sounded tired. It wasn't hot in the anteroom but she wiped nonexistent sweat off her brow with the sleeve of a dark blazer.

Middlerealm.

A dozen people is easier than just one. Eddy memorized each twitch and gasp, each desperate wheeze of the first woman. Now she's too busy to keep track. The window of visual transfer stretches back long enough from her own death that she doesn't need to memorize the information; all she needs to do is look at her records shortly before the end. This requires careful note taking. It's easier to endure with a job to do, easier to see them as symptoms: cyanosis of the lips, localizing pain to the throat, nystagmus. When there's a dozen, it's easier to forget they're people. As each one falls, Eddy looks at her watch and carefully writes down the time of death.

Shadowrealm, every time.

Eddy couldn't sleep. Eddy wasn't sure if she'd ever be able to sleep again.

Lilith was asleep. She was curled up in a perfect circle at the foot of the bed, snoring little cat snores, and Eddy resented her for it. "I could wake you up," she said to the sleeping lump. "You do it to me all the time. It would be justice." In Eddy's experience, cats didn't put much stock in justice.

"I can't call Mara." Mara set clear boundaries and they did not include middle of the night booty calls. "Not til the morning." Lilith wasn't even awake to refuse to comment on Eddy's indecision. "I could go to the Shadowrealm and see her there, though." Eddy shivered under the blankets, a visceral response to her own words. Her arm felt naked; she didn't wear her watch to bed. The alarm clock flashed the time but Eddy knew it was wrong. She hadn't bothered to reset it after the most recent power outage. Maybe it was for the best that Lilith withheld judgement on Eddy's life choices.

Eddy fumbled at the nightstand for her phone. "I'll text Kyle."

"No one understood why you left," Steve said. Eddy, not entirely devoid of manners, didn't roll her eyes. Technically, Eddy had known Steve was coming. François had warned her before inviting one of her old colleagues. He'd spoken with conditional phrasing, to make it clear he'd find someone else to be Marcus' external if it bothered her to run into a professor from her former department. At that point, Eddy thought nothing of it. Her life had unfolded in unexpected directions, but she was fine. Her life was fine.

Now, setting up a snacks table in the lounge for Marcus' defense, there was no way for Eddy to avoid Steve. It was too late to get him uninvited or, failing that, fake her own death to avoid him. Eddy looked down at the sparkling apple juice — there would be alcohol that evening at the Gagnon's house, but not on campus — and didn't answer.

"You abandoned the job in the middle of term," he continued. "I had to cover all your marking, you know. On top of my own. I had to get two extensions on my *PLoS ONE* revisions. And for what? Soft money?" Steve, never the most stable of academics, was taking on a certain volume. He'd been fun to sit next to in meetings, a man with a poorly developed filter between brain and mouth. They hadn't collaborated or socialized outside of work, and they hadn't stayed in touch. "You better be getting a string of *Nature* papers. It doesn't make any sense, Eddy. You're not stupid."

Technically, it counted as praise.

Eddy shrugged. Steve needed a haircut and a new pair of jeans without a hole in the wallet-pocket. Same as when she left. He needed a PA or a wife, really. François was lucky to have Mara. There were no holes in Eddy's black-and-mulberry skater dress, but she had less demands on her time than Steve did. "We're millennials," she said, not that Steve thought about himself in terms of the social forces that constructed him. "There's no job security for any of us."

"There's tenure. You were a year away." It was touching, the earnestness in his voice. Maybe he knew something Eddy hadn't. Or maybe the reverse. It was too late to second-guess now.

She didn't owe him anything, but Eddy caught herself apologizing anyway, unable to meet his eyes. She stared at her disorganized mess of a cheese platter instead, a pale imitation of what Mara could produce. Eddy: nearly good enough at a wide range of tasks. Passable in the short term. "I'm sorry, Steve." She cast about for something she regretted, to finish the thought. "For the marking."

Mara gasped in surprise as she scrolled through pictures of Lilith on Eddy's phone. "This is not a cat picture."

"Oops," Eddy said, suddenly remembering the other set of photos in her 'Recent' folder. "Sorry, nope, that's Kyle asking if I want to come over." Eddy couldn't remember if she went. "Keep scrolling."

Mara's finger didn't move, eyes fixed on the screen. At least she wasn't zooming in. "You've got a boyfriend."

Technically, no, and Mara had a husband, but offering excuses seemed like poor form. "I should've told you." If this was the Shadowrealm, Eddy would tell Mara that Kyle was meaningless, that she had loved Mara from the moment they had met. Eddy's watch rested on the bedside table, too far away to check.

"I thought you liked women."

Eddy, who came out in her teens, thought that she'd passed the phase of explaining the concept of bisexuality to the bewildered. But then, she thought she passed the phase of dating girls who claimed to be straight, and yet here she was, in Mara's bed. Mara and François' bed. Presumably on François' side, though there was nothing on the bedsides to denote either. "That too." Eddy reached for Mara's chin, tilted her head for a kiss. "Same as you." Eddy slid her hands along Mara's arms and felt her shiver at the touch, before taking back her phone from Mara's unresisting grasp. "Is it okay?" Kyle would be cool with Eddy having a girlfriend, might want to watch, but Eddy wasn't going to tell him. She hadn't asked if he was seeing anyone else and he hadn't volunteered an answer.

Mara closed her eyes, framing the words in her mind. "I thought François and you were having an affair. Before this." She opened her eyes to gesture at the bed, at their naked bodies, at the memories therein. "That picture isn't François." She took a deep, hard breath. "But there could be other pictures." Mara left the follow-up question unspoken, but Eddy could still hear it.

"We're not." And then, because while honesty might not be the best policy, it was a policy, and Mara was hard to lie to, Eddy added, "He said no." Over and over until she lost count, in every Realm.

Mara made a sound that could charitably be called a laugh. "He's a good man."

Eddy let that one go. "I'm not here for him. I'm here for you." Eddy reached across Mara and rested her head on Mara's chest. "Tell me something I don't know. About you. About anything you like."

"I don't know." Mara did, though, and Eddy could feel it, feel the words waiting inside Mara's chest. "When I was little I wanted a pet, but my parents said no. We couldn't afford it, there were too many kids in the house already. Revkah had tropical fish and her family was bigger than mine, but Revkah's Tate was a doctor. She showed them to me after school." Mara's energy was all inward, her body a black hole, her story the only thing which could escape.

"Revkah got me a goldfish for my twelfth birthday. We named him Benny. Ahlai — my sister — helped me hide him in my sweater drawer. I wanted to get him special food and a bigger bowl but Ahlai said no, she said that goldfish can live on breadcrumbs, that they only grow to fit the size of their bowl." Mara brought her knees up to her chest, wrapped her arms around them, as small as she could make her body. "I went to the pet store anyway. They sold me this liquid to add to his water and said I needed to clean his bowl every week. As soon as I did that he started to shake. It didn't take him very long to die. I didn't tell anyone what happened."

Eddy reached for Mara, draped herself over Mara's stiff edges. "I'm sorry," she whispered. Mara was crying silently, face red but no sound to give her away, and Eddy had no consolation to give, no wisdom to dispense in the face of tragedy. In lieu of solace, Eddy offered absurdity. "I heard that thing about goldfish growing to the size of their tank but I always thought it meant something else. I thought they grew to match the shape of whatever you put them in. Like you could have a perfectly spherical goldfish or a giant square one. And you had to keep moving them to bigger and bigger tanks as they outgrew each one."

Mara lifted her head and spoke with certainty. "That's not how fish work." She'd stopped crying to stare at Eddy in baffled wonder. "I have koi in my garden. Do you think they get too big for the pond? Do you think wild koi grow into whales?"

"I dunno," Eddy answered honestly. "Maybe they turn into dragons."

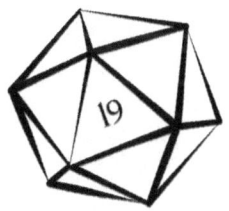

In Eddy's mind, afternoon tea at the Chateau Laurier was a sophisticated affair, an event where the upper crust of society wore perfectly tailored flowing gowns and sharp-lined suits, or at least clothes that fit and didn't have holes. Eddy didn't stand out as overdressed in her purple-and-black argyle fitted shift dress, but then Colette didn't stand out in a pink miniskirt and thigh-high suede boots, and their table was arguably the best-dressed at the restaurant.

Alycia recounted each and every change that the inevitable passage of time had forced on Sir John A Macdonald Academy in the years since François had been a student, or in the millennium or two since Reid had been one. She covered the financial necessity to accept international students, long since acquiesced to, and the political one to accept female students, still steadfastly resisted. "And then there are the darker times the school weathered," Alycia said with obvious relish. Her opal brooch shimmered in the afternoon sun, iridescent smooth surfaces contrasting the herringbone-white of her skirt. Alycia dressed like Eddy's conception of rich people from before Eddy had met so many of them.

Eddy shook her head. "Tell me," she said, like she knew she shouldn't, like she knew Alycia meant her to. Beside her, Mara radiated unease, perched on the edge of her seat, eyes darting around restlessly.

"It must have been, what, thirty years ago?" Alycia asked, apparently rhetorically, since she answered her own question instantly. "Twenty-eight. Reid was on the Board of Trustees, and it was such a scandal, they worried it might close the school. Of course, no one talks about it now."

Mara reached for her cup of tea and held the rose-patterned ceramic tightly.

"Reid asked me to console the young man's mother. He tries, bless him, but he doesn't know how to talk to women when they're emotional, and it was such a delicate situation. She wanted all the boys involved arrested, or at least expelled. The loss to the Academy — the loss of all those bright futures, with so much promise — some things are best handled quietly." Alycia's hands rested neatly in her lap as she spoke, dignified and self-contained, the very picture of civility.

"What happened?" Colette asked in breathless, fascinated disgust. No one could bring themselves to look away from the mangled bodies and twisted wrecks of a car crash, but it was polite to pretend dismay.

"It was the Labour Day weekend before the semester started. One of the boys' parents was away and their son threw a party to introduce the new students. They were roughhousing — boys do like to wrestle — and one boy held a chokehold too long. These things happen. The important thing is that we move on, instead of getting lost in the past." Alycia's lipstick was bright red. It stood out like a wound against her fair skin and the white of her straight hair, tied back in a bun. "His mother's name was Jeanette. I don't remember the boy's name. The victim, that is."

Mara nodded from behind her teacup, took a cautious sip before speaking. Her hands shook as she tried to place her cup back on its saucer and she missed the rim of the plate. The black tea spread, a dark stain across the clean tablecloth, and Mara stared at it, helpless. When she spoke, her voice came out low and trembling. "There are accidents. Boys make mistakes."

"Exactly, sweetie," Alycia said, patting the top of Mara's hand. "No one's life should be ruined for a bit of recklessness." She took a sip from her own teacup, hand perfectly steady. "But you already knew this story."

Luckily, the NPC they sought was an alcoholic, and a well-heeled one at that, visiting every pub along the way from Yr to Proudloch before waiting patiently at a combined tavern-and-shrine, The Pub-ish & Parish, for the party to arrive. On second meeting, details about the Quest Giver that initially went unnoticed — or that a rusty DM forgot to disclose early in the D&D campaign — became obvious to the party. She had a startlingly large body, filling half the tavern, a pleasantly symmetrical face and eight legs. The Spider-Elf sipped on a mojito and knit, but she still had more than enough arms and eyes left to play cards with the party.

"Another round!" Grogtar declared happily, dealing out hands for a variant of Texas Hold 'Em designed by characters who had absolutely no knowledge of Texas and only slightly more of poker. Grogtar initially wanted to play Magic, but even he acknowledged that they couldn't play without a Wizard, or this far from the coast. He'd managed to lose an impressively large quantity of gold in an impressively short time, but he continued betting undaunted. He had, as he loudly whispered to his party members, a plan. Rose looked concerned at his words, but it wasn't like she was winning many hands either.

"Verily," replied the Spider-Elf in an accent that sounded like an alien species had watched too many Britcoms and thought that an amalgam of those mouth noises was the best way to blend in with humanity. "Mayhaps, as we partake in this feebleminded entertainment, I might enlighten my new companions regarding the quest to which I have pledged mine life?"

Grogtar failed his Intelligence check to figure out the meaning of 'feebleminded', which was for the best, all things considered. He agreed with the stranger's plan despite remaining unsure of the exact contours of her suggestion, and ordered another pint of mojito.

Rose seemed less convinced. "You haven't told us your name yet," she pointed out. She pushed a handful of copper coins towards the centre of the table, nervously twisting a strand of hair around her finger and then behind her ear. "How do we know we can trust you?"

"Forsooth, t'was a mere oversight! May I take this most fortuitous moment to introduce my humblest self. I am the inestimable, most esteemable Charlotte Miriam Webster," she said, offering a low bow to the company. Charlotte fixed a stern glare on Carmilla, who quickly turned her laugh into a cough. At least the Spider-Elf wasn't another Bob. "If I might commence mine tale without further interruption or concern?"

"If you cannot be prevented," Arg replied, unnecessarily moodily, but he claimed to hate pubs ever since his zombification had turned him bone-dry. Arg casually rolled up a newspaper and began idly thwapping at the table in a way calculated to be not-at-all intimidating to a creature who possessed many of the same squishable elements as a spider.

"Newspapers don't exist," Grogtar complained, his ability to suspend disbelief still wounded by the plethora of puns earlier in the session.

Arg casually rolled up the town crier, then thought about what he'd just done, unrolled him and let him get back to his work informing the public. Arg leaned over and put a hand on Rose's shoulder. "Pay the Spider-Elf's words no heed, mon trognon," he told her, not bothering to moderate his tone to be inaudible to the spider-elf in question.

"Thy words art artfully deceptive, Zombie, and moreover, thou art void of breath. I declare thine comments meaningless and thus, declined. Zombies speak only lies, or rather, speaketh not. Tis another who speaketh through thee." Charlotte drew a card as she spoke and made a high-pitched chittering noise of delight. "Two pair, ace high," she informed them, laying her cards face-up. "My most amiable newfound companions, I must win again."

Rose kissed the back of Arg's hand where it rested on her bare shoulder, causing a thin yellow film of adipocere to adhere on her lips. She placed her own cards on the table. "Royal flush."

"That's impossible," Grogtar argued. "You can't both have aces in your hands. I already have all five aces! You both need to stop cheating!" He winked broadly at his party and Rose sighed. "We'll call this turn a draw." He gathered up the cards to shuffle and re-deal, accidentally dropping two jokers out of his sleeves and another from his coat pocket.

"If I mayest recommence my tale," Charlotte said, her tone brooking no objection. "There exists a necromancer of direst evil, whomst goeth by the diminutive of Mortimer." Her lips curled over the word as if it was a particularly distasteful fly. "His solitary objective is to drive forth the living from this plane and remake this land solely with the undead!"

Arg cracked his knuckles, and Rose muttered a hasty Inflict Light Wounds. "How long must we listen to this drivel before Grogtar raises his great-axe?" Arg asked.

"How long must we endure the voice of Mortimer!" Charlotte cried out passionately, her voice rising out to the heavens. "This Zombie is but an abomination, void of thought, mindlessly parroting the words of its maker who even now watches us from afar! It possesses no life, no feeling. This lump of flesh is nothing more than an automaton in the shape of a man!"

Rose stared Charlotte down without an ounce of compassion or mercy. It was one of the hottest things Carmilla had ever seen. "I don't like it when people say that."

"Five projects, including everything?" Eddy counted on her fingers as she went. She always forgot something. Joseph had made the mistake of asking her about her research, and she was not going to let him escape the conversation topic before she finished answering. François, equally trapped, was conversational collateral damage. "Lydia and I are working on testing allergy meds together, plus I'm testing meds for François' industry contract. It's the same idea both times — placebos in the real world and the medication in Instances. Cuts down on side effects." The trick to a good lie was keeping it close to the truth. "He hired me to figure out if you could use brain scans to record what someone was thinking when they were in the Shadowrealm —" but there were very good reasons that Eddy really wasn't supposed to talk about that work, particularly to impressionable Youths, and she needed to deflect as quickly as possible "— but that project's on the backburner now. My publishable first-author work's going to come out of the physics side. Testing quantum states — there's something there. François gets migraines half the time he goes in Instances, and there's the coin flips I'll do with you, Joseph. Fifty-fifty chances scream quantum interference. I have an inkling that physics is the route to discover Future Instances so maybe I should count that as only four, but I might be completely off-base and need to count that separately. So, five." Eddy paused for breath, and to glance at François. His expression said she'd forgotten something. "Six? I guess so, if you count the publication with Lydia, but please don't ask me to work on a follow-up. The research wasn't even about Instances. Take mercy on me."

François wore a button-up plaid shirt, sleeves rolled to his elbows, a relaxed look for take-your-kid-to-work day. "That's not the one I meant. You're still working with Wahid."

Eddy wrinkled her nose in objection. "He's rewriting in thesis format so he's not doing original research right now. Wait, you're right he is, our collaboration with Dr Augustine is ongoing. They'll throw me somewhere in the middle of an author's list for the code I wrote before I started here. I'm on six active research studies. Unless I missed any or you give me more." She shrugged helplessly at François.

"How do you do it all?" Joseph asked with a kind of awe, still young enough to imagine multitasking was a skill set rather than a survival strategy.

"Badly?" Eddy offered. Honesty in a methods section, for once. "Don't tell my boss."

Joseph grinned back at her. "I won't."

"I can tell when I'm not wanted," François said, taking the opportunity they gave him to gracefully escape. At his level of seniority, he was neglecting a lot more than six projects to hang out with them in the lab. "Call me when you've got some results."

Joseph waited an hour, ensuring that François was safely engrossed in meetings, before he broke and started talking. No one could resist the lure of a confessional, of no longer being alone with their sins. "I thought Winston was gonna die," Joseph said, eyes bright with tears. "It's bad shit but no one is supposed to die." Eddy put her arms around him. His life was another planet to Eddy, and besides no teenage boy wanted advice from a middle-aged woman, but she could listen. "It's just stupid shit to toughen up the new kids at school. We all did it in grade nine. They tape mickeys to your hands and you have to drink them, stick your head in a toilet, that sort of thing. Rory bought this raw meat and left it out so it stank, it smelled so bad, and the new boys had to eat it. Winston tried, he did everything we told him, but he couldn't eat it and he started to choke — I did it last year, Eddy. It was my turn last year, I wouldn't do anything bad to Winston, I wouldn't hurt him, but I did it last year and I was fine.

"Winston started to clutch his throat and his lips were turning blue and no one did anything, Eddy. We all just stood there and watched. It was like it was happening on TV. I just stood and watched." Joseph took a ragged breath. "He coughed it up and Oliver gave him a beer to kill the taste. But I can't stop thinking about it." He'd started crying, face screwed up in a hopeless attempt to contain the tears. "I keep worrying that maybe I didn't actually do it last year, I mean I did, I went to the parties, but maybe it wasn't as bad for me. Maybe everyone went easy on me. People like me and they don't like Winston. I need to know I could handle it as bad as it was for him. I need to know that and I can't find out." He took a step back and looked up at Eddy for absolution but she had no grace to give. And she'd thought their lives had nothing in common.

"I'm sorry, Joseph." She was as useless to him as she'd known she would be. "You can't go back a year in an Instance to find out. You can't even go back as far as the party with Winston." Everyone thought time travel would solve their problems, but self-recrimination transcended dimensional boundaries. "Your body would die, like Monica Keeling died when Instances were newly invented. Instances can't — I can't fix anything for you."

Joseph was a smart kid; he already figured out that adults didn't have any special insight into the world. All Eddy had to offer was platitudes and she wouldn't condescend to him like that. "I know. I just wanted to talk to someone, you know? And I can't tell — most people."

Eddy knew. Eddy was an expert in keeping secrets. "I can listen. And science is a pretty solid distraction." Everyone used the same black fabric chair in the lab for Instances. The butt indentation was permanently worn in and the arms were missing bits of plastic where nervous students picked at them as they waited to go backward through time. Eddy gestured at it enticingly. "Your Instance next, or mine?"

One of the volunteers is still breathing. Eddy can see the laborious rise and fall of his chest, orange muscle shirt and dark skin standing out against the grey-flecked carpet. He's passed out, but he's not dead. Dead people don't breathe.

Owen and François are on the other side of the glass from Eddy. They're checking on the patients, anxiously searching for signs of life, for scraps of information that Owen can tell François, and François can pretend to communicate to the paramedics on a phone call he isn't making. For scraps of information François is actually conveying to Eddy so she can write on her clipboard. Owen's always too distracted to ask why Eddy doesn't join the two of them in tending to the fallen.

They're both too far from the breathing man, too busy with bodies already lost, and Eddy has a moment of panic that he'll die, or she will, before anyone can measure his vitals. She needs to get François' attention and explain but Eddy can't speak, as mute as the man she sees struggling for each gasp of air, and she can't cross the threshold into the room of the dead, she just can't. Eddy tries tapping on the glass like François is an exhibit at Ripley's Aquarium and she's an unruly toddler. François doesn't notice.

Eddy is being ridiculous. If ghosts can haunt her across Realms, they can find her one room over. And if Eddy can't track the symptoms, the man's transient sacrifice will be wasted. She tries reminding herself they're working on a cure, but her feet remain stubbornly unmotivated.

The man's breaths are shallow but steady. Black hair in a tight curl, ACAB tattooed on his left bicep and a pin-up girl on his right. François gave all the volunteers the same dose but this one responded differently. It's a clue. Add in Eddy's real time observations, and they might learn something, something they can use to make things different next time.

Eddy checks her watch once more and steps into the room.

"Eddy, what happened?" Mara's rose-painted fingernails traced the edges of the sharp red lines on Eddy's shoulder and down the front of her chest. Her thumb detoured for a moment to trace a circle around Eddy's nipple, eliciting a pleased moan. "Are you okay?"

Eddy looked down, half-expecting a ring of bruises, but of course she couldn't see her own neck, and there wouldn't have been anything to see if she could. "Oh, that's just Lilith scratches," she reassured Mara, catching Mara's hand with her own and bringing it to her mouth. "We were playing 'Who's a Tree' and it was my turn to be the tree, and then there was a noise." Eddy kissed the tips of Mara's fingers. "I'm always the tree."

Mara laughed, then gasped sharply as Eddy caught the tip of Mara's thumb between her teeth. Eddy applied gentle pressure, nothing that could leave a mark. "Cats are dangerous?"

"Everything is dangerous," Eddy said darkly, and Mara giggled. Eddy propped herself up on one elbow, her hands following her eyes as they searched for distinctive patterns along otherwise smooth skin. "You've got one too." A thin, silvery line traced across Mara's stomach, a scar long faded and forgotten. "Is this from when you escaped prison? I recognize the razor-wire pattern."

"No!" Mara protested, but without moving, allowing Eddy to kiss her way along the line.

"A bar brawl?" Eddy persisted, her mouth moving down, along the crease at the top of Mara's thigh. If it were a movie, Eddy would have heard footfalls, the creak of the door, a glass dropped in surprise. "Or were you frolicking with unruly unicorns?" Eddy expected a chuckle or a sigh, amusement or pleasure. Instead, Mara's sudden stillness, a rabbit frozen in headlights, was Eddy's sign that there had been a change, that something was terribly wrong. When Eddy turned her head to look up and saw François standing in the doorframe, it came as a shock, an incongruity, a mistake in the timeline.

He's wearing black socks, no shoes. He doesn't want to track dirt in the house. He runs his fingers through salt-and-pepper hair, mussing the shape of it, and the only thing he's looking at is Mara. Mara's knees come up and she wraps her arms around them, her body as small as she can make it. Her head is down, face buried. "I'm sorry."

Eddy picks up her clothes, slides her way past François, and flees the scene.

*E*ddy should start the conversation in the Middlerealm, but she doesn't, because she's a coward. Maybe it is the Middlerealm. Eddy knocks on François' office door, and it sounds the same as ever. The counter on her watch is deep in the blue, three and a half hours left. "Hey," she says, turning the handle. François looks at her for a second, barely long enough to register her presence, before dismissing her with his eyes.

"Not today."

"It's the Shadowrealm," Eddy explains. What they do here doesn't count, doesn't follow on from the real timeline. Those are his rules. "I have experiments to run." The words are corpses on her tongue. He's not coming.

"Run them yourself, or skip them."

If he was looking at her, it would be embarrassing how she stiffens, how her face freezes, pale and bloodless. Small mercies. She can't think of anything to say but she can't force her feet to carry her away, so she waits for him to speak, too long, silence stretching into a new kind of agony, a heaviness that collapses her organs and burns out her senses. She'd rather fall out a window, given the choice.

Crying in front of a student was decidedly unprofessional behaviour, but this wasn't the aberration that would get Eddy fired. Besides, it wasn't as though Eddy had invited Lydia to the pity party. The young woman simply emerged in Eddy's office with a cup of tea, heedless of Eddy's conceit that she was crying silently. In an ideal world, Eddy would be home with Lilith, but there was no point running an experiment if she didn't log what little she remembered of the data afterwards, values safely listed in alphanumeric codes, intelligible only to François and her. It was hard to type with a keyboard slick from tears, though.

"Did you wanna talk about it?" Lydia asked. It was more restraint than Eddy expected from the girl. "I can keep my mouth shut." Eddy eyed her dubiously through tears and Lydia played at affronted. "I can! You don't know all the things you don't know I know. You have no idea."

Eddy ventured a smile at that, but it didn't change her mind. Lydia was a student, even if she was the one holding the Kleenex box. There were lines for a reason. "There's a lot going on," Eddy hedged, as close to the truth as she dared. "I need some time." That part was less true than Eddy'd hoped. François wouldn't talk to her in either timeline. Even if he did, what could she say? A politician's apology — sorry that François' feelings were hurt — was unlikely to reinstate Eddy in his good graces. Mara, too, was lost to her, didn't text back, didn't answer her phone when Eddy worked up the nerve to call. Eddy would try the house, in the Shadowrealm. Tomorrow. She'd maxed out on rejection for the day. Today, she'd go home and hug Lilith, drink most of a bottle of wine, maybe text Kyle if she could stop crying long enough to fuck. "I'll be fine." In the end, everyone always was, if the definition of fine was broad enough.

Lydia's eyes fell. "Are you gonna quit?"

That was one of the questions Eddy most wanted to avoid. She took a sip of tea to stall before saying, "I don't know." Realistically, Eddy doubted it would be her choice to make. A postdoc on soft money was let go if the account ran dry, if the funders failed to renew the contract. It was a shame, but financial realities were inescapable. Lydia didn't need to know that.

It was long past time for Eddy to get out, anyway. She was too old, publication record too thin, there was no future for her in academia. A holding pattern of short-term contracts until she fell through the cracks, until someone decided to hire a PhD student with youthful promise instead of a lifer postdoc. All it took was a month of unemployment and she'd never get back in, her research career as good as dead. Eddy had transferable skills. She could get a job as a technician at a hospital lab, or in industry processing big data. It was the smart move. It had always been the smart move, even when she was offered a tenure-track position and everything seemed possible.

Further conversation was interrupted by the sound of the door opening, one of the other postdocs greeting the visitor. Eddy futility wiped her eyes, traded tears for a dark smear of eyeliner and shadow on the back of her hand.

"Hi François," Lydia said, her tone considerably more polite than the death glare she was directing his way, arms crossed over her chest. If François noticed Lydia's body language, he ignored it, attention focused solely on Eddy.

"Eddy, can you take the bus tonight? I'm leaving work early." François asked the question like a decree, leaving no possibility Eddy would refuse. Except for the minor consideration she had no clue what he was talking about.

"The bus?" she repeated stupidly.

"For *Night Beats*," François explained patiently, no trace of annoyance, not in front of Lydia. He nearly smiled and Eddy's heart shattered. "It's Thursday."

François wanted to talk to Eddy in his study so Eddy followed him up the stairs, an obedient puppy. He'd stopped smiling as soon as they left the front hall, gotten out of sight of Mara or Joseph. Eddy watched him close the heavy wooden door behind her, heard the click of the mechanism falling into alignment. Her mouth was dry and her heart was pounding, body unaware that it was safely the Middlerealm, that François never touched her in the real world. She ran through the events of the day in her mind, weight resting on the balls of her feet, and it had to be the Middlerealm, the timing didn't work otherwise. Eddy could've checked her wrist, but she didn't.

François' study was dark and tasteful, oak bookshelves containing tomes with leather binding, heavy wooden desk with a green banker's lamp and — Eddy winced — a child's ceramic penguin mug holding François' fountain pens. Joseph must have made it for him, years ago. Neither of them had spoken since they left the uncomfortable welcome of the family unit at the door and Eddy wasn't going to cry. Wasn't going to scream. No one would hear her if she did, fabric wallpaper and thick carpets absorbing sound, muffling footfalls as François moved purposely around the room. No one would hear except François. He put a CD on the sound system, an anachronism; it should have been a record player from which 'Summertime' rang out."

He approached her then, stopping just shy of touching her, and Eddy was suddenly calm and unafraid, a void where her emotions used to sit, her mind placid and clear. She'd done this part scores of times. He was more nervous than she was, now, sweat beading on his upper lip. Eddy wanted to lick it off, bite down until he bled, lock her jaw and refuse to let go, refuse to accept any version of the story where he drove her away. Eddy did none of this. Eddy stood still and waited.

"Mara talked to me last night," he said, opening lines, hands forward, palms towards her. Eddy knew François' hands well. "She said I needed to get over myself." He laughed brittlely, stepping through a thin layer of ice. "Those were her words exactly."

Eddy nodded as if she understood the point of his statement. There was no need to interrupt the flow of his words when he was finally speaking to her. She could ask him to explain in the next Realm.

"If you're still interested, of course," François added when she failed to react. He stood his ground, neither advancing or retreating, looking at her with the same intensity that always drew her in, as if she was a planet caught in the gravity well of his star. Ella's voice filled the edges of the room, smothered Eddy in sound, and this moment could have lasted forever. "Or we go downstairs and watch TV." The offering was clearly an afterthought, François smugly certain of her desire for him, despite everything, and that was what it took for Eddy to understand what he was suggesting.

She could've been pissed at him for his cockiness, for every boundary he set or broke for the both of them, but it seemed like a waste of time when she was finally getting what she wanted, when relief and need mingled into a new kind of fear, overwhelming, blood on fire, burning her alive from the inside. The serenity gave way to something else, an undercurrent of electricity, heart pounding against her rib cage, struggling to escape, and Eddy could hear its echo through every vein in her body. This time, when Eddy leaned forward, François didn't pull away. He tasted like every bad idea Eddy had ever had and kissing him felt like falling. Eddy did it again, to be sure.

François touched her with a familiar confidence, the same certainty that he showed in the Shadowrealm. Eddy's body was alive with anticipation, nerve endings firing alerts, synapses screaming warnings, her mind and skin trained to expect different outcomes from fingers pressing into her body with unyielding determination. Different, but parallel. The French called it *le petite mort*.

François' breathing was as ragged as her own, his desire for her objectively confirmed. Eddy undid his pants and helped him pull off her dress. He would've started slower, some attempt at foreplay, mouth running kisses along newly bared skin, but she snarled with impatience, tugged at his hips, and he acquiesced. After so long, it felt good to finally be right.

He took her to the desk and leaned her over the writing surface in the middle, between neat stacks of paperwork. He'd moved the laptop to make space for her, put a box of condoms in the drawer with the stationery. What a gentleman. She couldn't see him, couldn't guess what he was thinking. She could only feel him moving deliberately inside her, fingers gripping her sides, his nails brushing against her skin. Francois dictated their pace, slow and measured, savoring the tension breaking between them. Eddy could feel the curved edge of the desk biting into her hip as restraint gave way to fervor, and this was the Middlerealm. This would count.

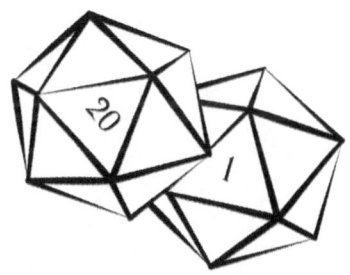

The morning's group meeting was distilled, highly refined agony. François' deadpan fell just short of a Buckingham Palace guard, microexpressions flitting across his face too quickly for Eddy to consolidate a firm thesis on his emotional state. His cheeks twitched up as she entered the room and he might have been pleased to see her for the briefest fraction of a second. Or Eddy might have been fantasizing images on a Rorschach test, imagining two dogs with their skulls split open where a normal person saw a butterfly, visual delusions sufficient to convince any psychologist she'd gone mad. François avoided eye contact, for the most part, but Eddy expected a few moments with the two of them alone together when the meeting finished. Time where he'd have to look at her. He'd have to say something more than bland generalities which satisfied the grad students but were a torment to Eddy's oversensitive nerves. But it never came. Lydia stayed too close afterwards, refusing to leave for her office before Eddy did, an overprotective mother bird refusing to let a predator within a ten-foot radius of her chick.

At least Lydia kept her voice down when she started her interrogation. "Are you okay?" Lydia demanded, a question that Eddy was entirely unqualified to answer. "I know you're not okay."

Hypophora was Eddy's favourite rhetorical device. "I am," Eddy lied. Lydia, who had no poker face whatsoever, was obviously unconvinced. More lies were required. "Everything is okay, Lydia. I had a hard morning yesterday, but I'm fine now." Eddy could rephrase the statement as many times as necessary until Lydia believed her.

Lydia shook her head. The smart students were always the most trouble. "Eddy, what happened?"

"Lydia, it's not your business." It came out sterner than Eddy intended. "I'm fine, I'm not quitting, that's all you need to know."

Lydia looked at Eddy plaintively and Eddy's resolve weakened. "Please," Lydia said. "Please tell me. I won't tell anyone. I need to know that it's not as shit as it looks. I can't just work on my PhD and pretend that he's not your supervisor too."

That was an unfortunately convincing argument. While she wouldn't advocate it as a primary course of action, as a last resort Eddy occasionally appealed to the truth. Though phrased in as PG a manner as possible; Lydia remained a student. "François has a traditional attitude towards marriage. His wife has a — more flexible attitude."

Lydia's jaw dropped. She was more expressive than Jane when she found out that the Final Guardian was a time-travelling version of Brent. "You and Mara?" she asked.

"Yeah," Eddy confirmed, wishing she had half François' ability to pull off inscrutable academic. Her cheeks heated as Lydia stared. She'd settle for a quarter. An eighth.

"And François?" If Lydia kept looking at her, brown eyes wide and gaze fixed, Eddy was going to fake her own death to escape. That Halloween episode of *Night Beats* was widely acknowledged as the best one, anyway.

"He was upset when he found out," Eddy allowed. "We talked about it —" fucked about it "— and he's okay now."

"You and Mara," Lydia repeated. "Holy shit. You absolute legend."

There must have been a dating-advice book or magazine article which covered how many glasses of red wine a woman should drink on a date with her boss who was maybe angry with her but definitely intending to sleep with her. Unfortunately, Eddy had never read it, and she got bad-decisions drunk. Arguably it wasn't a significant difference from her sober state, besides the stained tongue, and that didn't put François off kissing her in the elevator on the way up to the hotel room. Her place was close but embarrassingly messy, and he had money.

Eddy slid her hands under his grey shirt, feeling the skin of his stomach, til the relative confinement of his tailored cotton became too much and she started to work at the buttons. Buttons were unnecessarily difficult while drunk, a breathalyzer test to get laid. François' fingers moved to help her, brushed against hers and she felt a familiar thrill of fear at the feel of them. She'd barely gotten to kiss him before, not properly, all this time and she didn't know the feel of his stubble against her cheek, his teeth on her lips, his tongue against hers. She wanted to savour the moment and she wanted him inside her immediately and she bit him on the shoulder, hard enough to leave a bruise, ran her thumb over the saliva-slick indentations as if she could hardly believe they were hers.

"Bed?" he suggested, his mouth nuzzling her throat, her pulse staccato quick under the pressure of his lips. It was an easy one to acquiesce to. They tumbled down together into a sea of white sheets and she leaned over him, a hand on either side of his chest, and then it was simpler to just straddle him. Her hips pressed against his while she kissed him, black hair with red tips falling over her eyes, momentarily hiding him from view. She tucked it away behind her right ear and everything was over, as suddenly as that.

At first Eddy was determined to revive the moment, brashly

confident, but as seconds ticked by she felt her cheeks burn at her continued failure. François let her try until long after it was awkward, then tried at last with his own hand, critically surveying her naked form while he worked but finding her wanting, nothing to arouse or provoke interest. When he finally stopped, the admission of her defeat came as a relief. "Sorry, Eddy," he said helplessly. "It's not you."

She slid down to lie beside him, staring up at the smooth cream ceiling. It was a very nice hotel room to not get fucked in. She didn't ask if this happened with Mara. "Next time," she said, tone as neutral as she could manage.

"Next time," he confirmed, a heavy presence at her side. Eddy willed herself to fall through the bed and the floor into the room below. Her attempt at phasing was about as successful as the sex had been. "I won't drink," he offered, as though she couldn't count his drinks as well as her own, as though she didn't realize exactly how sober he'd stayed while she got trashed. He cupped her cheek with his hand, very gently, and it only made everything worse. "Do you want me to drive you home, or are you going to sleep here?"

"In this lab, we do not risk a cat's life. Schrödinger was an unconscionable jerk." Eddy looked sternly at Joseph as she spoke. He took her frown almost as seriously as Lilith did. "If a cat goes in a box, it's because she fits."

"It's not real," Joseph attempted to argue. "It's just a thought experiment about quantum." He still wore his school uniform, tan pants and a white collared shirt. Eddy restrained herself from teasing him about the tie. "I was reading about it. Flipping a coin isn't really quantum differences, is it?" He deferred to her sufficiently to make it a question instead of a statement, but he'd got her.

"Not really," Eddy admitted.

"Maybe that's why it's not working," Joseph continued, volume raising in his excitement. "You said it should be the same every time I go back in time and live the experience, or exactly fifty-fifty heads or tails, but that's for real quantum. With a coin, there's how hard I flip, and where I place my hand, and all kinds of things. It needs to be just one particle we change each time."

"I tried out the Elitzur–Vaidman bomb tester," Eddy admitted, feeling vaguely guilty, though she'd built a very small bomb indeed. A chibi detonation. If a CSIS agent found it, they'd yawn and move on. "It's the same idea as Schrödinger had, more or less, but the bomb's in the cat state instead. Much more humane."

"Does it go off?" Joseph asked excitedly, and Eddy knew she was moments away from teaching François' son how to operate a bomb. The kid had to grow up sometime. It didn't need to be this particular moment, and it didn't need to be Eddy holding the detonator, but science called.

"Some of the time," Eddy said, and Joseph's eyes lit up. "But not quite fifty percent of the time. There's two paths for the photon and it has to go down one of them. It should be fifty percent. But it's not." Physics was keeping secrets again.

"You said my dad had migraines fifty percent of the time," Joseph offered.

"I can't 'splode your dad," Eddy countered and Joseph laughed at the idea of it. "It wasn't exactly half, it was a bit more, but I figured his sample set was too small. I can't ask him to keep getting migraines to test a pet theory. I need someone else to test it with me." She glanced speculatively at Joseph. "We could upgrade from coins?"

"Exactly how many lemon-berry petit fours do I get to take home if I loan you my sword?" Eddy asked. Her moment of greatest negotiating strength was before she handed over the blade. Only then Mara smiled at her, soft and captivating, and Eddy remembered that any number multiplied by zero negotiating power was still zero.

"You can have anything left over after book club," Mara promised, which was enough to make sitting through an hour discussing *Poisonwood Bible* worthwhile. Unfortunately, Mara immediately rescinded her offer, eyebrows raising slightly, concerned. "Except I need dessert for tonight. Everything minus three." She reached for the ties on the scabbard at Eddy's waist, sparks of energy lighting up Eddy's skin beneath her touch, even through layers of fabric. Superfluous fabric at that; Eddy anticipated clothes would shortly become a moot point. A miniskirt was an atypical choice for the morning's sword practice, but a classic for seduction. Mara pulled at the swordbelt, and Eddy took advantage of her distraction to plunge a finger into the cake batter. Eddy looked into Mara's dark eyes and deliberately ate it, sweet and rich. "Eddy, you'll get sick!"

"You'll have to nurse me back to health," Eddy said, reaching in again. Mara caught Eddy this time, but too late, and ended up with batter on her wrist. Eddy helpfully licked it off, tongue traveling from sweetened lemon batter to salty fingertips. "You were right. I'm poisoned. I can feel myself growing weaker by the moment. Save me," Eddy said with an extravagant flourish which was intended to leave her in Mara's arms but nearly ended with her head banging into the counter.

Mara pulled Eddy back up straight, or at least as straight as before. "No more of that until I get these in the oven." Her fingers traveled the inside of Eddy's thigh as she smoothed the fabric of her pink-and-black plaid miniskirt, then set the locket back into place against her chest. "Ten more minutes. Then we'll have a half hour to ourselves while they bake." She frowned for an instant and added, "In the guest bedroom." Another moment and the expression was gone, replaced with a beguiling smile.

"I don't know," Lydia repeated anxiously, though she did. She knew the answer to Eddy's question ten minutes ago, when they were casually chatting about allergic reactions, but as soon as Eddy officially started Lydia's mock quals, Lydia was as ignorant about science as Jordan was about Miranda rights. "I can't do it. I'm gonna fail."

Qualifying exams were one of the harder mini-bosses of grad school, but Lydia wasn't going to fail. "Lydia." Eddy went for a tough-but-fair tone, and she stuck the landing; Lydia looked suitably chastised. "I believe in you. It's only a couple of hours. You can fake this." Lydia groaned and Eddy kept going. "Repeat the question back to me. It'll buy you a solid ten seconds."

Lydia nodded. "Okay." She retied her ponytail and took a deep breath. "Okay. You want to know what role interleukins play in allergy-related anaphylaxis?"

Eddy flashed back to the participants that morning — or yesterday morning, it must have been yesterday — three out of thirty, wheezing out desperate, gasping breaths, eyes wide with panic as their fellows died beside them, and Eddy did not want to know anything about allergy-related anaphylaxis, thank you. She nodded, hoping Lydia didn't notice her wince, or didn't take it personally.

Lydia was distracted writing the question in her notebook, and then jotting down some initial thoughts. Good. The kid had successfully wasted twenty-five seconds.

"The experiments are working," Eddy informed François as his lips found her nipple. Eddy gasped at the sensation, a bright, sharp point that extended radially out through every nerve, each synapse on alert. "Not great. Maybe one in ten patients survives now?" It was difficult to focus on shop talk with the things François' tongue was doing to her breast, but technically they were still on work hours. Eddy would hate to disappoint her boss when he let her clock out early. "But something."

François nodded for her to go on, or maybe that was his mouth moving over her skin, teeth lightly grazing, testing, a scientist's thrill at the unknown. Eddy was a pinned moth to be examined, a novel compound to be characterised, a participant in an experimental trial to be tested upon. His fingers slid inside her, his eyes on her body, gauging her response to his ministrations.

"If we could give them the antidote earlier, give them more time, before we introduce the infection —" Eddy paused, either at the shaking of his head or the curl of his fingers, and breathed out her need and her satisfaction. He withdrew his fingers, slick from her, and she mewled in loss, impatient as he opened the condom. Finally he replaced his fingers with his cock and pressed forward to kiss her, fingers inevitably finding her clitoris, and she tilted her head back and let herself be lost.

On reflection, the ceiling was as nice as she remembered it. François rested his head on her chest where he could listen to her heartbeat and whisper a cold hand over the peach fuzz on the short side of her undercut. Where she couldn't see the expression on his face. Eddy could have laid on the comforter while François pet her for the rest of the evening, but then they would have missed *Night Beats*. After far too short a time, according to her watch — bezel securely at time zero, she noted with a certain dark satisfaction — Eddy groaned and reluctantly stood up.

When she emerged from the bathroom, François had her clothes in a neat pile. He'd gone as far as attempting to fold them, and Eddy swore to herself that François would never see the inside of her apartment. "Thanks," she said, as if it was totally normal to retrieve and fold your lover's clothes instead of sending them home wearing your socks because they couldn't find either of theirs. This might have been the case with Kyle, once or twice, until he'd left enough over to have several on standby. At least François had the grace not to be particularly good at folding clothes, but the attempt was uncalled for. She kissed him on the cheek, and the mouth, gentle and open, and then he was running two fingers tenderly over her jawline as if she would break if he pressed too hard, and Eddy's body didn't know how to respond to the unfamiliar sensation from his fingertips.

"We need it as close to immediate as we can," he told her, and he waited patiently for the sex-fog to clear from her mind sufficiently for her to figure out what he was talking about. The softness of his touch on her skin felt like an insurmountable distance between their bodies. "Still, one in ten is an improvement. You've done well."

Eddy attempted to restrain her emotions so she didn't ruin the episode for everyone else, but Joseph was already in hysterics by the time they got to the commercials. "That's not — do you think they noticed — is it on purpose?" he managed to gasp out between fits of laughter.

"I'm sure they knew," Mara said, the triumph of optimism over experience, but even Mara didn't sound like she believed it. "Maybe the director thought a meat-packing plant was too gross for TV."

"A burger factory is gross, but a soy-burger factory is tasteless," François noted with a straight face. Joseph was sufficiently far gone that the pun only made him laugh harder. "Surely the location scout would have noticed the difference before they started shooting." He refilled Eddy and Mara's glasses with Tempranillo wine, leaving Joseph to manage his own intake of Sprite. "Maybe the werepig murderer felt uncomfortable at an actual abattoir?"

"Then he should have come up with somewhere else to hide a body," Eddy pointed out. "Did you see Jane's expression when they found the arm in a vat of soybeans and she had to pretend it made sense?" Joseph's eyes were watering from the exertion of his laughter. "Then Jordan confused the words porcine and porcupine and you could see Jane's entire career flash before her eyes."

"It's hard for the writers," Mara offered sympathetically. "Maybe they couldn't think of any other way to hide it. It's not easy." Mara clearly never read any *Night Beats* fanfic.

"Convenient explosion," Eddy replied.

"Bury it vertically, with a dead animal on top," François suggested, though it was highly unlikely he read fanfic either.

"Dissolve it in lye," Eddy added.

"Pour booze over the body and drive it out to the edge of town. It'll look like a drunk person froze to death," François said, rounding out Mara's options. Eddy considered a high-five at their impromptu Teachable Moment, but the risk of spilling her wine was too high.

"Kill them in the Shadowrealm and leave them there," Joseph proposed, excited to be part of the murder party. François and Mara both frowned at him, and Eddy winced at even the second-hand force of both Gagnons' simultaneous disapproval. Joseph looked down. "I guess that wouldn't work?"

It wouldn't, but the kid misremembering canon was no excuse for his parents' overreaction. The writers were unlikely to know any better than Joseph. "They wouldn't be dead in the Middlerealm. *Night Beats* established that in Season 4. But it might work in the Mirrorverse," Eddy explained. She ought to know better than to come between parents and their child, but she couldn't let misinformation about *Night Beats* stand, and she couldn't let Joseph wear that plaintive expression. "Even if it fails, then you're in the Mirrorverse with your worst enemy, and there's nothing like a good enemies-to-lovers in the Mirrorverse plotline." François transferred his gaze — and a portion of his disapproval — to Eddy, which made no measurable improvement to Joseph's mood but certainly worsened Eddy's. As a last resort, she could always change the subject; if she'd been smart, it would have been her first resort. "After this episode of *Night Beats*, we'll be pumped to kill any monsters we meet in the D&D session."

"We're not playing D&D tonight," François said, his tone final. "I'm not in the mood."

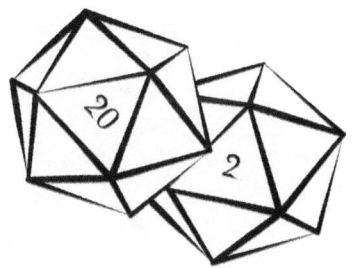

"You remind me of your father sometimes," Reid said, blue eyes twinkling. François smiled, the placid, controlled expression he defaulted to when Reid was in the room. Eddy wasn't sure if the words were intended as a compliment, but François didn't act insulted. "He had an engineer's mind. Always taking things apart to see how they worked. He wasn't afraid to think on a grand scale."

François nodded. "He was a great man." François wore a jacket and his grey-chevron tie, and Eddy had a collared blouse under her black blazer. It was less comfortable than her black-faded-to-grey 'Monster Manual or Waifu Catalogue?' t-shirt, which she'd nearly worn to work before she remembered her fate that day and reluctantly changed. Despite the buttons, meeting in the boardroom at Reid's factory was better than the alternative. No one had to clean the lab. As a bonus, Norm was with them at the meeting at the factory, which meant Norm was miles away from their experiments, which was where Norm belonged. Norm was less trustworthy in the lab than a fourth-year undergrad. "I'm not him." François opened his hands deferentially as he spoke, but he wasn't apologizing.

"You're more cautious than he was," Reid elaborated. That definitely wasn't a compliment. "Nothing of value was ever accomplished by the hesitant." This was Eddy's first time in Reid's explosives-manufacturing facility. There was something dissonant about the clean, orderly production lines, the repetitive motions as hands slid crisp-cut edges into place. Each one was a building, a neighborhood block, a violent death wrapped in tactical black and matted steel. Any human trace left behind was buffed away until sleek cylindrical housings reflected the sterile overhead lights.

"I know you want to move fast and break things," François replied, perfectly amiably. "But you brought me in to design you some glue." He glanced at Eddy, who gave him her best confident, supportive expression. She was going to let François stand between her and Reid, which was kinda like having François' back. Chivalry had to be good for something. "You told me you needed a proof-of-concept for my cure or you'd find another way. We've done it."

"Ten percent survival?" Norm said derisively, looking at his notes. "If Reid deploys his bioweapon, only ninety percent of the people who get the antidote die. What an achievement."

"There's four of us here," Eddy speculated, "so statistically, one of us might make it, if we hit the inside of the Poisson distribution." The tail end of the distribution where all of them survived had bad odds, but there was no need to look at the glass as 99.985% empty. "A proof-of-concept shows we can succeed, with the application of time and money." Her time, Reid's money. François' moral support. "If this was easy, you'd already have done it. Without us."

"There's no good alternative to having a cure in hand," François followed on seamlessly from her point. "You can't deploy until we've got an acceptable survival rate. There's no way to be certain you only target the enemy." Semantically incorrect — Reid shouldn't deploy. But Eddy appreciated François' point too much to correct him, much as it pained her to agree with Norm on anything.

"Dr François Gagnon, cap in hand, asks for another vial," Reid intoned, and for a second Eddy feared the worst, but Reid brightened and slapped François on the back. "You've done well, my boy. I wasn't sure you had it in you. I'll give you another aliquot of fresh microbes, and I'll give you the time. It's no hardship when I see progress." He smiled knowingly at Eddy, who remembered too late why she'd planned not to draw attention to herself. "And I'll supply money, for anyone motivated by such petty things. You know," Reid added in a not-terribly-private aside, "François could pay your salary himself if he didn't prefer to keep his work at arm's length."

Eddy could do basic math. She'd figured that out after she saw the Gagnons' house. "That's François," she said, shrugging. "Lawful Good at his core." Lawful, anyway. "I've had bosses with worse character flaws."

Reid chuckled as if she'd made a joke, and a funny one at that, but Norm only scowled. Reid didn't notice his expression or chose to ignore it.

Norm touched Reid's arm to get his attention, the gesture casually intimate, and Reid took a second to remember to look irritated. Eddy's undergrad dating experiences included enough closeted girls to recognize the bit of theatre, and she felt a pang of unwelcome sympathy for Norm, at least until he started talking. "The antidote isn't developing fast enough. If the Russian delegation gets their way on oil rights in the Arctic, we've got to respond. The drilling rigs showed up in Finland fast after those negotiations. You said we don't want an international incident. If we have to dispose of Russian crews on our land —"

"I know what I said," Reid told him sharply and Norm pulled back. "I haven't given up on influencing our government. But if the Liberals are inclined to hear out the Russians," Reid sighed and didn't finish the sentence. "Not all problems have elegant solutions." Reid closed his notebook and stood, gesturing at the others to rise as well. "But we can hope for the best, even if the timeline is not entirely within our hands. How much longer do you need, François?"

"The research would go faster if I wasn't being kept in the dark," François said. "It's easier to design a cure when you know the biology of the disease." Reid's impatience seemed to roll off François, leaving scientific curiosity as his prevailing concern. This was clearly a matter they'd discussed many times before, and reached the same conclusion each time. "We might already have your antidote if you let us collaborate with your microbiologist. But you're committed to keeping us apart." The group followed Reid to the man's office, full of sleek, airy furniture with artistic schematics decorating the walls; Eddy recognized the blueprints for Fat Man and Little Boy hanging behind the minimalist desk. "You'd get further if you were more trusting."

"I trust my microbiologist," Reid replied. He pulled up that day's passcode on his phone, keyed the nine digits into a small, unassuming gunmetal-grey box and opened the safe, pulling out a vial closed with a bright yellow crimp seal. After a moment's reflection, he took a second vial out of the safe. Eddy's breath caught at the casual way he handled the thin glass, but then he'd never seen what happened when the things inside got out. Eddy had, and she would again, if moments that never existed counted for anything. "But I'll give you two, this time. Because I like Eddy."

The antidote needs to work before geopolitics or Reid's mood go awry. Eddy knows enough of both to find that unsettling. At least the experiments are going well. Grim consolation, but she takes what she can get these days. François shows up in Eddy's peripheral vision at the thought, the perfect example of comedic timing, or dramatic irony, or something a Film Studies major would know the name for.

"Three patients are unconscious but breathing, and a fourth is responding favourably to Owen's CPR," François reports, as though he sees this every day. He doesn't; he'd have more migraines. He waits for Eddy to write his words on her clipboard before he resumes speaking. "You said you had a good feeling about this cohort."

"Yeah." Eddy shivers and wraps her arms around herself, her left wrist in her peripheral vision. Shadowrealm. "I'm fucking up Lydia's experiments if I select patients with a common factor and don't tell her I'm doing it. But I thought

it would work on these ones. It's like the paper we published on socioeconomic status." 'Work' is an overstatement for a survival rate scraping twenty-five percent, and Eddy's not confident about most of their long-term prospects, if the volunteers had a long term, which they don't. They're in her Instance. She checks her watch again, conscious of François watching her intently. He won't remember in the Middlerealm. This François doesn't exist either. "Can you get her to discard the data points from this afternoon? Tell her it's an outlier or something."

"Of course," he assures her, hand on her shoulder, solid and reliable as always. François has his clinical detachment, Owen his saviour complex. Eddy stands among the dead and dying and tries not to dissociate. Plenty of time for that after François sends her back to the Middlerealm. Not now, not when she's got work to do.

"More penguins," Eddy demanded impetuously. "Every penguin!" Eddy waved a dress-shirt clad arm, subtle grey penguins on the exterior of the cotton, brighter blue penguins on the fabric inside. It was difficult to manage rolled up sleeves while displaying the penguin cufflinks to their full aquatic potential, but Eddy believed in herself, and in the transformative power of friendship, heart, and excessive thirst. "Bring forth the penguin underpants!"

Mara laughed gayly. "You're already wearing two pairs of briefs! I don't think he has more." She dug through the dresser as she spoke, triumphantly emerging with a set of black-and-white boxers with a beak positioned in an opportune location. "I forgot he had these. He never wears them," Mara said through giggles.

Eddy put them on immediately. They didn't fit, at least not the way they presumably fit François. In particular, the beak was somewhat bereft. "Does he have penguin-print pants? He probably doesn't. Boy pants are so boring." There was a mirror on the front of the oak wardrobe and Eddy considered the full outfit with a discerning eye, from the penguin slippers to the clip-on penguin bowtie. "I could wear this on the bus. I'm decent, and once I put on the penguin suspenders, I don't need to worry about the underpants falling down." Not that there was much risk of that regardless, what with the existence of Eddy's hips, but she needed to attach the suspenders to something.

"No," Mara protested, shaking her head. Her eyes glistened with tears. "No, you can't! Not yet." She took a deep breath and choked out the words, "Penguin winter clothes."

Eddy nodded solemnly. "I can't believe I forgot. Thank goodness you're here." She tilted her head down to kiss Mara, sneaking in a quick fondle while the woman was distracted by her near-hysteria, and then pulled away. "Onward. Take me to the hall closet."

Mara took Eddy's hand and led her along the hallway lined with family photos, down the circular staircase, and to the lawyer foyer where François was hanging up his grey wool double-breasted peacoat. He was clearly not expecting to see them, or, if he was, he was expecting to see Eddy wearing more of her own clothes and fewer of his. Eddy's breath caught. Mara stilled, laughter evaporating, her eyes searching François.

"I can explain," Eddy offered through the lump in her throat. Mara pulled her hand away from Eddy's in a slow movement, arm low and steady, like unsheathing a sword without drawing any attention.

François gave Eddy a very, very slow once-over. It was inconceivable he hadn't seen their hands, but he didn't react if he did. "I look forward to it."

"Eddy fell in the koi pond when we were sword fighting," Mara jumped in, words emerging in a sudden rush, and Eddy pet Mara's arm before remembering she wasn't supposed to. "She doesn't fit any of my things. She had to wear yours."

The corners of François' mouth twitched upward. "And the penguin items were the only ones you could find?" He looked at Eddy's feet. "How many pairs of socks are you wearing?"

"Nine," Eddy replied. "Mara said I only needed to wear five on one foot and four on the other to count them all, but I'm not a coward." She withdrew a foot from the plush slipper and wiggled her toes. "My feet are way too hot. And some of these are actually puffins." He grinned and she continued. "Also, Mara told me that penguins don't technically count as fowl. All of our puns are retroactively incorrect."

Mara looked faintly sheepish, but she didn't back down from her point. "Eddy has weird ideas about animals." François laughed at that, and Mara smiled back at him. A trepidatious smile, but there was warmth in it. "Especially about goldfish. Eddy, tell him about goldfish growing."

Arg gulped loudly. His lower half was immobilized by webs and Charlotte advanced towards him with a dagger in each of her closest legs and a menacing smile on her face. Her fangs dripped with a luminous green venom. Resin dice clattered on the table, and Arg's torso fell to the floor, thin strands of sinew and skin barely attaching the Zombie to his bottom limbs. Rose covered her face with her hands and Carmilla shook her head in dismay. Only Grogtar, lost in Charlotte's Suggestion, seemed unmoved by the scene unfolding before him. 'Tis merely a flesh wound," Arg said, not very convincingly. "I shall recover."

Charlotte Miriam Webster the Spider-Elf chittered in excitement, "The Zombie hath beingest a traitor, and bringeth gravest danger upon thine friends. Finish him, fearsome Grogtar! Unleash the greatest of axes!" She waved her front two legs as if conducting an orchestra, daggers serving as unconventional batons. Backlit by the fireplace, her silhouette made an eerie outline, casting long shadows around the room.

With a mighty battlecry, Grogtar raised his axe to swing at Arg, but before it fell, Carmilla began to sing in Eddy's best approximation of Titania's alto. She raised her hands — and her voice in Countersong — dramatically to the skies, finishing with a dramatic lilt and gave a slight bow to the remaining patrons of the tavern. They were mostly huddled under the remaining unsplintered table, hiding behind a bench they'd flipped onto its side, and looking apprehensively at the distance to the door. One of them offered Carmilla a hesitant clap, but stopped suddenly with a nervous glance at the Spider-Elf.

Grogtar looked torn, a glimmer of recognition returning to his eyes, hands trembling as his grip on the great-axe loosened and tightened, as if his own mind was battling itself. A throw of the dice, and he was free. Grogtar shook as if rousing from a slumber. He adjusted the angle of his swing downwards, away from the neck, instead slicing through the webs which bound Arg to the tavern wall. "I've done it," Grogtar cried triumphantly. "I've freed you! Get up!"

"Alas, mon ami, I do not think I will be rising this day," Arg said, tugging on his feet until the remains of thigh gave way and tore, ignoring the ooze of various fluids from the severed limbs. "These legs are past their walking days. But you must fight on, regardless of my fate."

Charlotte hissed at the collapse of her Suggestion. Rose gave a strangled cry and turned her attention to Grogtar, uttering a protective shield of Neutralize Poison around her comrade. Undeterred Charlotte reared up on her four hind legs and leapt forward. Carmilla had unsheathed her rapier, and, undaunted, Grogtar held his axe at the ready. Three on one wasn't good odds; a half dozen party members, each twice as high level, might've had a chance against a Spider-Elf. At their level, it was a miracle three of them were still standing to trade blows this long into the fight. The party rolled their hardest, but things were looking dire by the time Arg dragged his leaking body to the fireplace.

In the heat of battle, Arg's grasping shuffle went unnoticed by Charlotte. Heedless of pain, he reached with decomposing fingers for the bronze pot of Hot and Excessively Sour Soup hanging over the fire. With a single backward glance over his shoulder at his party, Arg threw himself against the cauldron and tipped it over.

The pub's chef had poor eyesight, and a penchant for drink, and this day was not the first he had misread the chemical labels in the kitchen and added hydrogen peroxide to his soup. Between that and the sulphuric acid — acetic acid didn't have enough of a kick for him — the dish was a WHMIS safety video waiting to be filmed. Iridescent orange liquid spilled out, bubbling and emitting black smoke where it met carbon-based materials. These included, in order, Arg, followed by the wooden floorboards, followed by Charlotte. Charlotte screamed, a high, shrill noise, as her feet, legs and finally torso began to dissolve. Arg simply gave them a thumbs up while his body sank into the remains of the floor.

Rose leaned over the puddle of soup and grabbed the thumb seconds before it met the same fate as the rest of Arg. "Grogtar, get the legs," she ordered. He instantly complied. "We need to re-Zombie Arg," she said, twisting a bit of hair behind her ear as she looked over her spell list. "Can I do that? Or Carmilla? I'm not letting Arg die."

"I don't know," Carmilla admitted. "There's Resurrection or Raise Dead, but I'm not sure what applies. Zombies aren't sentient in 3.5e —" Carmilla raised her hands at Rose's betrayed expression, calling for patience "— but Arg was, obviously. So we know normal Zombie rules don't apply to him."

"How are Zombies made?" Grogtar asked, picking up a leg in each hand and tossing them over. Neither Rose or Carmilla attempted to catch the gruesome objects. They fell to the ground with a splat, emitting a trickle of brown goo.

Camilla sighed. "I guess someone has to tell him eventually." She put on her best, thickest Transylvanian accent, and prepared to teach. "Oh, young Grogtar. When a Mommy Zombie and a Daddy Zombie love each other very much —" she began, only to be cut off by Rose.

"The Necromancer," Rose breathed in understanding. "Mortimer. He made Arg the first time. He can make him again." She pulled the Handy Haversack off her back and loosened the knot at the top. Rose kissed the tip of Arg's thumb, whispered it a Gentle Repose, and dropped it inside. "Help me with the legs next."

"It's the *Night Beats* 'verse, so everyone's a cop, but the only thing they investigate is the strength of their feelings," Eddy said expectantly. During the ten-hour pipetting marathon that was Wednesday, her brain power was fully occupied workshopping that line to perfection. Vee groaned appreciatively and it was all worthwhile. Not the pipetting — the flow cytometer gave up the ghost on the third sample and didn't acquire data for the rest of the run — but at least the joke went down well. "I always thought Jane would be an omega, but she's an alpha in the fanfic."

Vee groaned again. "Why are you reading this, Eddy? Why are you torturing yourself and now me?" There was a moment of silence over the phone as Vee considered the possibilities. "Eddy. Are you beta reading the omegaverse fanfic?"

Eddy snorted out laughter at the mere possibility of the thought. "Vee, you know I don't do fanfic. That's Felix's gig, and he's got Eliza to beta."

"Do you remember when we went to see *Alien vs Predator 2* and when we got home you searched Fanfiction Dot Net for Alien/Predator? You canonically have terrible taste in straights and I would not put anything involving a het pairing past you."

Eddy nodded sorrowfully, not that Vee could see. More than a decade later, and there were still no fics for her ship. "Look Vee, I just mind my own business on AO3. Maybe sometimes my idle wanderings take me past a Lilith/Brent omegaverse fic. And maybe sometimes I decide to drop in and see what it's about. I'm a curious woman."

Vee harumphed a disapproval too strong for mere words to express.

"It's longer than *Lord of the Rings* and loads smuttier," Eddy said, as if no one could resist such enticement. "It's bad but in the best possible way. Except that there's no way Jane and Lilith would have a dance-off to impregnate Brent when they could be poly with him instead."

"Eddy," Vee began, slowly and deliberately, and Eddy knew she'd said too much. "When we say 'poly instead,' just to be perfectly clear, cards on the table, are we still talking about the fanfic?"

"Um," said Eddy.

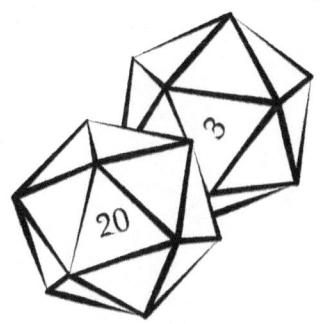

*F*rançois' teeth nip at her carotid artery and Eddy can't tell the difference between her fear and her desire. She's safe, her mind knows that he won't hurt her, that after François fucks her he holds her like a porcelain doll, like something precious and fragile. Her fingers, digging into his sides hard enough to leave marks, do not know this. "Should I get us a room?" he asks playfully.

Eddy looks around his office meaningfully, from the Anish Kapoor painting hanging over the Nespresso machine to the ugly beige bookshelves ubiquitous in university furniture. The wooden door is thick enough to be fireproof, and it's closed. "This is a room," she points out. The standing desk is new and will require more acrobatics than its birch predecessor would have, but Eddy's confident they'll manage.

François groans as Eddy works the front of his belt open. "People get fired for sex in the workplace. You have no idea how uncomfortable Charles' disciplinary panel got." People do, but not people like François. Consequences aren't for men like him. Besides, no one's around on the Friday before a long weekend, and the windows are high enough that no one would look in if they were. Also, the point is moot.

"It's my Instance," she reminds him. "Pretty soon this version of you stops existing." Eddy palms François' cock through grey fabric that fails to conceal his arousal. "Give me something to remember it by when I'm back in the Middlerealm."

He pushes her back against the closed door.

The inner workings of the hardware to run Instances were hidden from prying eyes behind metal panels secured with non-standard screws. Luckily, Eddy had the exact right type of non-standard screwdriver, not to mention the extremely proprietary schematics. Said schematics were open on Joseph's MacBook so he could guide her through the opening process without damaging the instrument. He was still young enough not to question how Eddy got her hands on these things, which was good. She would hate to implicate his dad and risk changing Joseph's opinion of the man. Eddy had been exposed to enough literature to know what happened when a young man lost touch with his father figure. Look at *Hamlet,* or *Oedipus Rex,* or *The Force Awakens.* Luckily, Joseph was more concerned with electrical impulses and diode arrays than petty questions of legal ownership or trade secrets.

"I'm the same as my dad, my tests in repeat Instances come out a bit over fifty percent," Joseph said, eyes tracing pathways on the screen. He frowned, comparing the PDF image to the reality in front of him in the lab, before tapping on the far-left corner to indicate her next move. "And you're under. But you and I don't get migraines and he does."

"It's a sample size of three," Eddy pointed out. Science was a harsh mistress. "And you're men from the same family. You have all kinds of similarities. For example, you both thought the episode where Brent got addicted to a cursed chat forum and Jordan had to use VR to save him was, and I quote, 'pretty cool.'" She punctuated her statement with finger quotation marks. "Maybe that's the common factor."

Joseph had stopped taking Eddy's diatribes seriously some time ago. "It was cool! Jane transformed into a wolf and hunted the leprechaun who was using the forum to transform people's souls into Bitcoins." As usual, Joseph's opinions about *Night Beats* could not be more wrong.

"What happens in dad's brain when he has a migraine?"

Eddy shrugged. "Do you think I know what happens in François' brain, ever?" Joseph looked at her with the same expression Lilith used when Eddy was slow with the kibble, and she relented. "Overstimulation of the visual cortex. Overexcitation of the brain." With a sigh, Eddy added, "Versus, I'm definitely under-excited. I don't get out much."

"There's something about energy," Joseph hypothesized, a hunch worthy of a child prodigy — if he'd come up with it on the first day, instead of after long sessions running through temperature, entrance speed, degree of attachment, and anything else they could think of, with occasional input from François. "Can we cut the power to the Instances?"

There was a point in a brainstorming session after all the good ideas were suggested, when all that was left was the absolute god-awful bullshit, and everyone pretended they were pearls of wisdom because no one had anything better to suggest. It was Eddy's favourite part of brainstorming. "I dunno, Joseph." She looked at the schematic open on his laptop. "Can we?"

"Are you lying to me?" François asks. It's not the question which is wrong — though it is wrong, he should know her better than to ask — it's the tone which unnerves her. Closer to pity than anger, and determined. Resolute. Things are going to be different this time, or François intends they will. Eddy's repeated the same scenes enough times to mistrust variation.

Eddy shakes her head in a no, her eyes watching his face and his shoulders for clues. He's upset, he's not even trying to hide it, but she doesn't know why.

"I know when you're lying to me, Eddy," he repeats. "I don't think you're lying now." The words bring him no pleasure. He's moving towards her, and she's too slow, all her sword practice and she can't bring herself to pull away when he reaches for her wrist. He holds her loosely and she's considering yanking out of his grasp when he asks, "Eddy, when are we?"

Eddy's breath catches and she doesn't answer.

"Do you know what Realm we're in?" His tone is kind, his touch gentle, as he lowers her arm to her side, out of view, and her chest tightens in pain to know she can't check her wrist. "Can you tell without looking at your watch?"

Eddy is a deer in headlights, staring down an oncoming car, nowhere to run in the bright lights. And maybe, even if she could escape, she wouldn't. "Did we kill someone?" Her mouth can barely form the words. François releases her hand and she twists her arm instantly, looks down at her diver's watch, countdown at zero and she was wrong about everything.

"No, Eddy," he told her and she choked out a sob. "No one died in the Middlerealm." François' arms came around her. Eddy buried her head in the soft grey of his cotton shirt, took in the scent of red brick, cypress, and rust, and pretended for one stupid, naive second that she didn't know what came after, that his next words weren't inevitable. The hardest part was waiting for the blow. "But you can't go back to the Shadowrealm."

Knowing it was coming didn't help, didn't make the words hurt any less. Eddy pulled out of his embrace to look him in the eye. "No. You don't get to tell me that. You don't get — I'm going back, François."

"Eddy." This time, when he moved to touch her, she jerked away before he could close the distance. "Eddy, it's not safe." He took a breath, then said, very softly, "Eddy, I love you. I can't keep killing you." His eyes were wide, his jaw tense. She'd never seen him afraid before.

"Fuck you, François." Eddy couldn't remember the last time she'd been this angry. "Fuck you and fuck your feelings." He recoiled as if she'd hit him. More than when she struggled in the Shadowrealm and she'd bloodied his nose once. "It's my life. I decide."

"Eddy." His voice was controlled, but she could feel the effort the restraint cost him. "Eddy, please."

She didn't know what he thought begging would accomplish. Maybe it worked on Mara, who was nice in all the ways Eddy would never be. "I'm not your wife. This is my job, François. This is science."

His mouth twisted as he worked out a reply. Eddy tried to imagine

François fighting with Mara, if two well-behaved adults communicating about their needs like some after-school special counted as a fight. Eddy let him suffer as she waited out the silence. "I'm your boss," he finally said. He must think arguments were won by logic.

"Sure. Because you're so concerned with your employees' health and safety." He laughed at her comment, a short, humourless sound, but Eddy knew she had him. "I'm careful when it matters. You can trust me." Her turn to beg. "I need you to trust me."

François was stronger than Eddy, could wear down her speed and agility, but physical prowess didn't matter here. After half a lifetime with Mara, he didn't know how to win this kind of fight. It took a moment, but then François leaned over to kiss her, running a hand down her cheek. "If you're determined to do this, make sure to run enough replicates that your results are significant." He bit the edge of her lip and she pressed into him, already lost. "Is that better?"

Eddy murmured assent against his cheekbone. "Much," she agreed. "I love you too."

"The holy water in the basin roils turbulently, as if displeased with the task. As each bubble evaporates into steam, the smoke begins to take shape, forms rising and coalescing in the mist before slipping back into nothingness." François rolled a D20. The resulting number was hidden behind the black, blue and silver diamonds on the back of his cardboard screen, and he examined it with his usual poker face.

Unperturbed, Rose dropped a roc's eye into the pool. She didn't pause her chanting as she released the gooey arcane material.

François smiled over the screen. It might have been encouragement, or he might have been toying with them before he made his Will check. Eddy's money would have been on the latter option. "It slides beneath the surface without a ripple."

Rose added a mixture of nitric acid, copper, and zinc, then double-checked her list of material components on François' cell phone. Her glass dice reflected prisms of rainbows as they rolled.

"The water hisses and spits like hot oil, and the smoke darkens to near-black, spreading to engulf the party, a fog as thick and dark as night, though no knight would dare enter its murky depths."

"I would like to run," Grogtar said, showing uncharacteristic wisdom, or his usual mistrust of puns.

"It's too late to run," the DM intoned, eyes twinkling with mirth. "All you can do is wait." He rolled again, metal dice thudding on the table. No one needed that many Will checks; Eddy suspected François was only doing it because dice noises were guaranteed to make players nervous. "As your eyes search the darkness, you start to see the outlines of a figure. A man stands before you, his unfocused gaze confirming that the scrying only goes one way. Mortimer the Necromancer is tall and slender. As he throws back his black robes and lifts a boulder with ease, you realize he is also surprisingly buff. He has broad shoulders, yoked muscles and a swole physique."

"Dad," Joseph said, visibly cringing. "Dad, no." The only thing a Youth hated worse than puns was an Old attempting slang.

"Go on," Carmilla urged him, ignoring Joseph's agony. "Tell me about the hot necromancer. For science. I can't use Clairvoyance until he gives away his location." Mara nodded in confirmation and Joseph buried his head in his hands.

"Mortimer walks a short distance to place the rock at the final point of the pentacle he's built on a grassy knoll. He looks at the tableau critically while he casually flexes, drawing attention to his stacked biceps. There's a skeletal evergreen near the pentacle and its bare branches must needle the young man, since he raises his hand, utters a spell, and the tree shakes itself back to life. Mortimer nods approvingly. The undead foliage really spruces up the place."

"No, no, no," Grogtar, or Joseph, moaned into his glass of ginger ale. "Make it stop. Rose, stop chanting. Break the spell."

"We need the spell," Carmilla objected. "We're gathering intel on our target, Grogtar. We need information and we're too far away to just axe him a question." François laughed and Rose grinned through her incantation, though she tried to hide it for Grogtar's sake. Grogtar slumped in his seat, despondent, though not too demoralized to nab a home-made blueberry macaron on the way down.

"The young necromancer sweeps his asymmetrical bangs out of his eyes, adjusting the frosted tips so he can see clearly through his fashionable monocle. He calls for his undead hawk, which lands on one of his black fingerless leather gloves. He shakes his head and mutters that he forgot something, that he needs to get the necromantic ambiance just 'rite'" — the narrator resorted to air quotes for the pun— "in case he has guests, which he won't of course because why would he be expecting someone, he's certainly not expecting anyone. With that, he strides with long, purposeful footsteps towards wrought-iron gates in thick stone walls. Next to the gates rests a hastily constructed wooden mailbox on a stake, an unfinished pine box which seems out of place next to the gothic horror he inhabits. Mortimer stops to check for mail, pausing beside the painted address on the side of the mailbox: 666 Graveyard Way. You sense your plot is about to get deeper."

"I'm dead," Grogtar said, picking up another macaron. Carmilla took a sip from her glass of blood — a nice Bordeaux — and nudged Grogtar, who handed her a macaron to go with the drink. "I died of puns."

"We might all be dead soon, or undead, or both," Carmilla agreed, taking a bite. "This seems suspiciously convenient. We'd better go investigate. At axe-wielding distance."

François holds the green ball out to Eddy as she wakes up, or she arrives, depending on which term is preferred by the reviewer. Time travel makes grammar hard.

Checking her watch in front of him is uncomfortable, but she needs to get over that. A minute and a half forward. "It worked." She lets out a high-pitched noise that defies description. Joseph lets out a deep breath, and high fives her. "It. Worked."

François and Joseph beam. "Welcome to the Astralrealm," François says, pride in his voice, in his expression, and she'll forgive him the pompousness just once because she feels it too. They did it.

François is looking at his own watch, setting his countdown to match her timeline. "Only ninety seconds here," Eddy tells him, though of course he knows, she told him before she left. "You'll be worrying about me in the Middlerealm." Joseph and Eddy needed François' help to turn off the backup generator so they could cut the power to her Instance, and he wasn't overly enthusiastic about risking her life in the Middlerealm. As if he had any moral high ground left.

"It actually worked. I don't believe it," Joseph says, delight heightened by relief. "I was so scared for you. You said we didn't know what would happen when we cut the power, and you wouldn't let me try it first, and I thought maybe —" He doesn't finish the thought. He's too perceptive for his own good, or at least for Eddy's good. Joseph smiles again, moving on. "But it worked. I can't wait to tell Mame."

Eddy shakes her head. "Sorry, Joseph, but no. We maybe stole some trade secrets and broke a lot of Ethics Board rules to do this, and besides if it gets out before it's published someone could scoop us. This is not a sharing story. Not yet, anyway." She smiles apologetically at him. "We'll figure out a version for public consumption, and then we'll publish. You can be a co-author on the paper?" If Joseph were Payton or Lydia, a free publication would be thrilling, but Eddy can tell that he's disappointed.

He puts a good face on it. "It's still cool we did it."

"It's incredible," Eddy agrees. Her time is ticking down. She plucks the ball out of François' hand. It's weird material, not quite rubber, and Eddy doesn't like the feel of it.

"Twenty-five seconds," François reminds her, glancing between her and his watch. "Do you want me to tell you any secrets from the future?"

It's a generous offer, or it would be if there were more than a few seconds left in her Instance. Eddy laughs it off. "I know all your secrets already." With that, she drops the ball.

Eddy's phone's sang out the rousing chorus of *Titania Triumphant.* Eddy glared at it. No one called her without messaging first. It was a telemarketer, or someone was on fire. Eddy wanted to ignore it, but the thought kept nagging that someone might actually be on fire.

Caller ID said it was François, which didn't make sense, because if there were a list of all the people who didn't call Eddy without texting, or call her at all, he would top it. "Hey?" she asked, more confused than concerned.

"Mara left a note," he said without preamble. His voice was choked and broken. "Mara — Mara left."

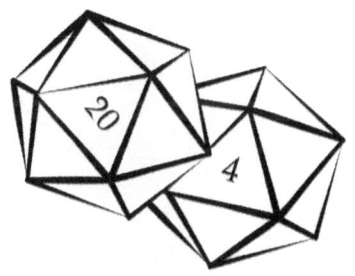

F rançois poured Eddy four fingers of Scotch and handed her the note. Mara wrote using airy letters with rounded edges; Eddy half-expected gen-pen hearts dotting the 'i's. She barely tasted the liquor as she read.

"Joseph told me everything. Joseph and I will be at Ahlai's house. I need space to think. There's leftovers in the freezer you can defrost."

There was no food on the table. François' caloric consumption for the evening was in liquid form. Eddy stared at the words, and François stared at her, and neither of them spoke.

Finally, Eddy said, "Joseph doesn't know very much."

"What have you told him?" François asked, too worn down for there to be any fire in the question. "She wouldn't — nothing I said to Joseph would make Mara leave." He gestured at the note in Eddy's hand. Eddy realized she was curling the corners of it between a thumb and forefinger, and placed it back on the table.

There was nothing, no timeline where Mara's note made sense. Eddy knew worse than she ever told Joseph, and Eddy couldn't imagine leaving. "I'm sorry, François. I don't understand."

François put down his glass, empty. He looked fine, in the same way that the American government looked fine: unmoored and on the edge of collapse.

The dining room light was the only bright spot in the house. Dark, the rest of the house felt barren, devoid even of ghosts. François couldn't stay there without Mara. He'd drown in the emptiness. "Pack an overnight bag," Eddy told him. He responded slowly, moving underwater, limbs slowed by invisible currents pressing against him.

Eddy picked up the bottle of Oban, still half full, and weighed it in her hand. They needed a sturdy brown paper bag if they wanted to drink it on the bus.

François didn't have a bus pass or tickets, fumbled for change before depositing a twenty in the box and heading to the back. He lasted until they were in Eddy's queen bed, an embarrassment of unwashed sheets gritty with toast crumbs and cat litter, before he fell apart.

Eddy held him as he cried. "Tell me where her sister lives," Eddy said once his breathing evened out. "I'll go in the Shadowrealm, I'll figure out what works — what Mara needs to hear." She leaned her head on his shoulder. "It's how I seduced her the first time."

The overhead lights were off but Eddy's apartment was dimly lit by the pale glow of streetlights, visible around the edges of the curtains and through holes poked by rogue claws. Eddy saw the outline of his body, his back against her white metal headboard, his head shaking a refusal. "She told us to give her space."

"She won't know if it's the Shadowrealm," Eddy explained, as if the intricacies of the technology were a revelation to François. "She won't know until I get it right."

"Eddy," François said, very carefully, "are we in the Shadowrealm now?"

Eddy's breath caught. The blanket was too warm, stifling her crossed legs. François was a dead weight beside her. Her watch rested on the bedside, miles away. "Are we?" she asked. Her voice sounded very small.

"No, Eddy." He sighed and eased himself down onto his elbows, the first step to lying down and, eventually, falling asleep. He wrapped his arms around her, his body urging hers to follow him. "Neither of us are going to contact Mara."

The morning was a misery of unsatisfied routines. Eddy scrounged for clean clothes through a heap on a chair, finally locating a pair of socks, or at least two socks that would pass for a matched set at a distance of five feet. François stared despondently in his overnight bag until Eddy, realizing the problem, dove back into the pile and found another almost-pair for him to wear.

He hadn't brought his aftershave either, or a toothbrush. He folded his steel-blue shirt when he packed it, but creases emerged by black magic, and Eddy didn't own an iron. She put it in the bathroom with the shower on hot, and they both pretended that made a meaningful difference to how presentable he looked. If he didn't like drip coffee, he was polite enough to hide the fact, but Eddy couldn't serve him off-brand children's cereal without milk, even if she upped the sophistication level by pouring it in a bowl. Carolans Irish Cream was technically dairy. Eddy tried to imagine what Mara must feed François in the morning. Freshly baked almond croissants with a fruit parade mar-ching down the side of the plate. Mara wouldn't be out of milk for more than a week, wouldn't need to wash dishes to conjure up two clean bowls.

"Let's pick up breakfast on the way," Eddy suggested. With luck — and the usual circadian rhythms of grad students — Lydia wouldn't be at work when Eddy and François strolled in together with matching styrofoam containers of food, with the exact same shade of grey cat fur on their respective black leggings and trousers.

François didn't answer, but at least his distraction was unrelated to his current state of sad bastardhood. Lilith occupied the bulk of François' attention, gently but insistently pawing at his leg, badness which he rewarded with a treat each time she reached for him. She deigned so far as to eat the Temptations out of his flat hand, raspy tongue licking his palm for crumbs. "She likes me." At least someone was having a good morning.

It isn't hard to find Mara's sister's address, even without François' help. Mara is better at infosec than Norm, but she's well short of two-factor authentication, let alone an encryption key. Eddy goes through Mara's emails looking for clues, for an explanation, not a house number, and when she stumbles on the address on a laptop warranty she tells herself she isn't going to go. And now she's standing on the curb staring at the salmon faux-brick walls of Ahlai's townhouse.

Before Eddy works up the courage to knock on the door, it opens. A gaggle of women, pre-teen to elderly, come out, voices overlapping, no pause in the cacophony of speech. Mara, walking at the edge of the group, is quiet. Mara looks fine. There's a nervous energy in the lift of her shoulders and the twist of her hands, she's not smiling, but she's fine.

As they approach, Mara meets Eddy's eyes, the deep brown of them obscured by the distance and her glasses. She shakes her head, and keeps walking.

The night air was cool enough that Eddy wished she brought a jacket, but between that and the darkness, the park was empty. She kicked at the sand underneath the swing restlessly as she spoke into her cell. "He uses my toothbrush. He's picked up clothes from the house a couple times but he always forgets his toothbrush." There were stray pink threads trapped between links of the swing's chain, and Eddy amused herself trying to pull them free.

"Buy him a new one," Vee suggested without a moment's hesitation.

"No. Tell him to buy himself a new one. Isn't he rich? Tell him to buy a pack of gold-plated toothbrushes. This is like, the one part of your life capitalism can fix." Eddy could hear the smug in Vee's answer. "Next."

Eddy shifted her weight to her feet so she could separate the links, but it was hard to hold her phone, lift the chain, and grab the threads all at once. She needed an extra arm. "He started doing my laundry. He folds it after." He hadn't asked where the laundry machines were. He could hear them through the paper-thin walls.

Vee snorted, which was not helpful. "This is the opposite of a problem, Eddy. You hate laundry."

"I'm forty-one years old and I haven't died from any pathogenic bacteria carried by dirty clothes. Maybe I need the filth to build up my immune system." If Eddy pushed herself forward, she could use the momentum to move the links rather than her hands. "I can feel him judging me," she confessed to the darkness and the cell phone. Eddy wished François left the apartment on his own sometimes so she could talk to Lilith instead of Vee. "He doesn't say anything but I can feel it."

"Oh," Vee said, not very sympathetically. Lilith was better at sympathy. "You could ask him to stop cleaning."

"How would that help?" Pressure released, the threads were instantly caught by the wind. Eddy grabbed for them, but they'd already floated away.

It's been enough iterations that the women's faces are familiar. Eddy sees fragments of Mara in each of them, in round faces, dark eyes, straight hair. In the sameness of their clothes, long sleeves, skirts past the knee, variations on a theme. Mara blends in, the perfect camouflage, another koi in the pond.

It's no good trying to talk to Mara here, so Eddy tails them. She doesn't have much time left in her Instance but they can't be going far on foot. A couple blocks and they turn into a square building with siding walls, Hebrew metal letters over the door. Eddy watches as the door swings shut behind Mara, as a handful of men wearing black suits and fedoras follow the women in. Eddy's wearing black too, but she doesn't think she'll make it in unnoticed.

Next time.

Of course François packed the note with him. Of course he was sitting at Eddy's desk with two fingers of Balvine in a glass, rereading Mara's words by the light of his cell phone instead of lying awake in bed like a normal person. He hadn't woken her — Lilith's screaming was responsible for that, and there better not be another bat in the apartment — but Eddy made a noise of complaint anyway.

His silhouette looked up from the paper. "Sorry," he said, an apology without an object. He must have memorized Mara's words by now. "Do you think if I quit —" François paused, and Eddy knew that she wouldn't like whatever he said next. "Do you think if I stopped everything, Mara would come back? Do you think it would be enough?"

"I don't know." Eddy used to think she knew what Mara wanted. François probably thought that too. "You'll have to ask her. When she wants to talk."

"I can't promise you my job when I quit, but I can get you an interview," François continued on. Eddy winced internally. Bargaining was the worst stage of grief, besides the other six. "They'd be fools to hire anyone else, but there are idiots in the department and nothing's guaranteed. You won't have a problem finding a postdoc position if you don't get it." Not with a letter from François, she wouldn't. If that was what Eddy wanted, back on the hamster wheel of academic progression. If Eddy even knew what she wanted.

Distraction is the best therapy. It's not an option for François, but Eddy doesn't get migraines, and death beats wallowing. Besides, it's for science. She's stalled out at 25 % survival rate for the patients, though her personal survival rate is somewhat lower.

"There must be another option," François muses again. She's sick of the repetition, but he doesn't realize, it's the first time for him every time. It's uncharitable to blame him for that.

Eddy makes a show of checking her watch. The countdown gives her another quarter hour but there's no reason to dawdle. Her notepad is thick with writing, symptoms, times, treatments. Patterns to be uncovered in the Middlerealm, not here. "I can't store all the information we need in my short-term memory. The fMRI records (will record? has recorded?) my visual stimuli in the minutes before my death. It's our only reliable way to transfer information between Realms."

He knows this. Knowing a thing and liking a thing have no relationship to each other.

"You're right," he tells her, calm and collected as always once he's made the decision.

Eddy smiles wryly. That's a sentence she doesn't mind hearing on repeat.

The *Night Beats* episode was good. It had everything: Titania, Brent, the Astralrealm, a queer-baitingtastic interlude with Jane and Lilith staring soulfully into each other's eyes and talking about how nothing would ever be the same. Eddy ordered Hawaiian pizza, and François picked up beer, and neither of them wondered out loud if Mara and Joseph were watching too. The twist ending didn't make any sense, but they were genre savvy enough that neither of them expected it to.

"I was right," Eddy said. François wasn't the person she wanted to gloat to, but he was closer than Felix et al. "Jordan's dead. The writers finally killed him."

"He's been dead the whole time," François confirmed. "The cure to being turned into a vampire is a stake through the heart, and the cure to that is your friends travelling to a parallel universe where you're not dead and kidnapping your alternate in his sleep." François looked bemused, or maybe his expression seemed crooked because Eddy's head rested on his lap and she was viewing him up and sideways. "I guessed they were holding something back during the season premiere, but I didn't see this coming." Lilith occupied the bulk of François' lap, a cinnamon roll with a leg stretched out, perfectly relaxed and unconcerned that she'd relegated Eddy's head to less than a quarter of the available leg-property. Cats weren't known for their financial prowess but Lilith must have figured out how much François' trousers cost; she was doing her best to unravel them thread-by-thread with her claws. Lilith wouldn't have wasted her time on anything less than a wool-blend. François pet Lilith's head, unconcerned with the inevitable fate of his pants or the unequal distribution of lap.

"Maybe because no one acted like anything was wrong," Eddy pointed out, stretching her arm towards the coffee table. Her beer was out of reach. She did her best Peter Parker impression and even went so far as to sit up and reach for it, to no avail. Lilith immediately shifted her butt to fully occupy the spot vacated by Eddy's head. "We're well into the season and no one even mentioned the swap before now. If his best friends don't bother to keep track of his version history, what hope does Jordan have?"

François handed Eddy her bottle of La Fin du Monde. Lilith turned her head to glare at him, silently berating him for his crimes against felinity, and he returned his fingers to the spot behind Lilith's ear. "They were waiting for the grand reveal. Now the situation is out in the open, maybe they'll be ready to discuss it."

"Nah," Eddy said dismissively. "I bet we never hear about this again." She'd put her money on bad writing any day. "*Night Beats* can't maintain a full episode of Jordan suffering through existential angst, let alone a season. This isn't literary fiction. He's gotta save the cat before the credits roll, and you can't fit clinical depression into a three-act structure."

François' ringtone sounded like the communicator on the TOS Enterprise, which was adorably nerdy. At the noise, Eddy's heart throbbed with the same hope she felt at every text message notification, with each refresh of her email, that this time, it would be —

"Mara," he said, half-choked, voice breaking at the word. He raised the volume on the call, then reached for Eddy's hand. She leaned her head against his shoulder, close to the cell so she could hear. "You called."

"Hi François." Mara paused. "Are you alright? And Eddy?"

Alright was a pretty generous marker, but they hadn't gone to bed sober since Mara left, so they failed to eke out a passing grade. "Yes,"

François lied. "How are you and Joseph doing?"

"We're okay," Mara said, maybe too quickly. "We should talk. In person. The three of us." She took a breath and clarified, "You and me and Eddy." Whatever calm Mara had at the start of the call was rapidly disappearing. "During the day, when the children are at school."

"We can come tomorrow," François offered. He was going to cut off circulation to Eddy's fingers at this rate. She squeezed back with whatever muscle strength remained.

Getting trash drunk in the wee hours of the morning before apologizing to a partner for crimes unknown was a bad look, and unlikely to induce the desired level of forgiveness. Eddy needed an alternative task to occupy herself until it was an appropriate hour for earnest conversations. Eddy didn't want to accompany François to his house on a quest to find the specific grey suit jacket Mara liked best, but she couldn't think of anything less awful to fill the time which wouldn't negatively impact her likelihood to be forgiven.

'I've looked everywhere," François told her, despondent, "and it's not here. I thought Mara took it to the dry cleaners. It looks like I was right."

To her credit, Eddy didn't ask why they drove twenty minutes if he knew it was a wild goose chase. "Then we'll go to the dry cleaners." It did not require two PhDs to solve this puzzle.

"I don't know which dry cleaner she uses, I don't have the claim tag to get it back if I found the right place, and I doubt they're open at this hour." He stared in dejection at his wardrobe. He had less than a dozen virtually identical suit jackets, so Eddy empathized with his anxiety. He might be forced to wear the wrong shade of grey, or to branch out into wildly garish colours like navy or black. "It's her favourite jacket on me." He reached to hug Eddy and she pressed her head into his collarbone. Eddy learned all her comforting tactics from Lilith. "What do I do without it?"

Mara's friends possessed a sameness, but even so, Eddy should have been able to pick her sister from the crowd. Ahlai had the same features as Mara, hourglass figure, pale complexion, but Ahlai held an exhaustion in her bones, as worn as her threadbare carpets. She gave Eddy a quizzical look, and Eddy wondered if Ahlai recognized her, or if it was Eddy's own guilty conscience seeing things. There was no question if Ahlai recognized François as she gave him a slow once-over. Ahali was half a foot shorter than him, but her stance said she didn't know that.

"Mara's upstairs," she said, turning her back on them as she headed to retrieve her sister. Ahlai hadn't invited them past the front hallway and they stood awkwardly, shoes still on, vampires unable to go where they weren't welcome. Eddy peered into the living room. Ahlai's home looked like the aftermath of a burglary, clothes on the floor, stains of mysterious origin on the coffee table, sneaker marks on the back of the sofa. Eddy tried to imagine Mara living there, a ghost floating through the clutter, anxiously reaching to tidy books that fell through incorporeal hands.

Noises upstairs. The creak of a door opening, muffled voices. Eddy tried to distinguish the two women's speech, to make out words, to sneak closer to the landing without François glaring her back into place. It was for the best that Eddy didn't get far since in a few moments Mara emerged, body tense, weight on the balls of her feet, a spring coiled tight. "Hi." Her voice was soft and nervous. "François. Eddy. You're here."

Ahlai escorted them to the dining room table, and watched eagle-eyed as they took their seats. Mara sat at the foot of the table, François to her left and Eddy beside him. "I'll bring food," Ahlai said and disappeared into the kitchen. They waited in silence for her to return with lukewarm instant coffee and lemon poppyseed cake. She spoke directly to Mara. "Az men est khazer, zol es shoyn rinen ibern moyl." Her words were sharp but there was love in them. Mara responded with a look but declined to comment. Ahlai sighed. "I'll be upstairs."

"What did Joseph tell you?" François asked once they were alone. "I don't understand what happened, Mara. I thought —" he glanced at Eddy, but refrained from any specific description, instead ending his sentence with "— I thought we worked things out." If there was accusation in his tone, bitterness or regrets, Eddy couldn't hear it.

Mara worried at her cake with her fork, broke off a morsel and ate before replying. "It's not that. It's nothing to do with that."

"Then what's wrong, Mara?" There was an intensity to François, his body leaning towards her. Mara, withdrawn into her shell, might have been in another Realm. "This behaviour isn't like you. You always talk to me."

Given her status as Mara's former unacknowledged mistress, Eddy doubted the accuracy of François' statement. It was a nice sentiment though, and worth expanding on. "We can't do anything if you won't tell us what's wrong." Eddy tried to sound earnest, like she was trapped in the climatic scene of a YA novel.

Mara's eyes were dark hollows behind her glasses, wide pupils and smudged eyeliner. "The things Joseph told me —" she gestured, open-handed, at the plate, at them, at the world, maybe. "You two keep so many secrets from me."

It was an unfortunately astute statement, and one Eddy was not prepared to deal with. Lying to Mara was outside Eddy's capacity, and telling the truth to Mara was the kind of bad decision even Eddy wouldn't indulge in. François was on his own.

"It's not like that, Mara," François objected, reaching for calm, for rationality. "We work together so we talk shop together. It's nothing that impacts you, but it's not a secret." It was technically true, by some definitions of technical, and some definitions of true. Eddy wouldn't have said it. Eddy couldn't have pulled it off with a straight face.

"I'm not stupid," Mara said, her whisper an indictment. "You think I won't notice. You think I won't understand. But I do."

François flinched. "I don't think of you that way. I know how smart you are."

"Why did you hire Eddy?" Mara asked, because François was right about her intelligence.

"If my work is the problem," François hedged, "I'll quit. I'll leave now — I won't even finish the term." He took a steadying breath. "We don't need to talk about the past."

"We do." Mara left no space for retreat. "I wanted Joseph to have a blank slate. You gave him your past. You let it hurt him." She always knew when her opponent's guard was down, when to bury her blade.

"What happened?" François asked instantly, one dread replacing another. "Is he okay?"

"He'll be okay," Mara promised, face softening at his concern. She put a hand on François' forearm, lying along the table. "Please, just tell me what's going on, Zeeskeit. We need to protect him. I can't do that if you don't tell me."

François took her hand in his. "There's so much, and it's all so tied together. I don't know how to start."

"He kills me in the Shadowrealm," Eddy said. Speaking the words was almost a relief. François stiffened but he didn't argue. Eddy didn't want to look at Mara. "We test medication on people there, and sometimes they die too." That confession hurt, burned like whiskey on her throat, filled her belly with fire.

"Why?" Mara asked, and her face held only pity. "Why do you do it?"

The coffee was horrible, and there was only so long Eddy could drink it to stall answering. "I don't know." She put down her empty mug. "François asked me to." Sometimes, depending on where you placed the observer. "Or I asked him." If Mara wanted the entire truth, even that wasn't enough. "I'm a scientist. He hired me for research."

Mara rested her head on her fingertips, wound a piece of hair around a finger and tucked it behind her ear. "Men zol zikh kenen oyskoyfn fun toyt, voltn di oremelayt sheyn parnose gehat." She sighed. "François, why?"

"Reid developed a biological weapon. If he deploys it before there's a cure, we have to trust he's clever enough to release it in a fully controlled environment." François shook his head. "I don't trust biology to stay contained and I don't trust Reid to try to contain it. If I work with him, I can delay him until the cure exists, and if I work in Instances, no one stays dead." Confession fell easily from François' lips. Eddy wondered how long he'd been waiting to absolve himself for his sins.

"What about Joseph? What experiments do you do with him?" Mara asked, showing the briefest flash of her hand.

"Nothing," François objected, repulsed at the thought. "I would never involve Joseph."

"We did," Eddy corrected him, unhappy realization dawning upon her, seemingly before it caught up with François. "He helped us discover the Astralrealm."

"We didn't involve him in the work for Reid," François clarified, defensive. "He's fifteen-years old. It's one thing with Eddy — I would never let a child participate in killing people, no matter the reason. Even if the deaths aren't permanent."

"You were fifteen once," Mara said, and François winced, absorbing the blow. "You can't think straight about these things. I don't want Joseph in your lab."

François nodded. "Okay."

"I withdrew Joseph from the Academy," Mara said after a moment of stillness, giving space for the weight of the conversation to settle. "I found a Waldorf high school. They let him start right away so he doesn't lose the term." She squeezed François' hand. There was an energy between the two of them, a spark of electricity, and Eddy wondered how she'd worried anything could keep them apart. "Everyone seems very nice there."

"A Waldorf school," François repeated, mouth catching over unfamiliar words. François was a smart man; he recognized the shape of a lost battle. "If you think that's best, I trust you."

Even Joseph failed at small talk on the drive home, even after Eddy deliberately mixed up horses and frogs in an attempt to draw him out. They dropped Joseph off at the Miyazaki film festival, and Eddy was happy for him to be making friends at his new school and not at all jealous that she wasn't invited.

"There's a Goya exhibition," Mara suggested from the passenger's seat, watching Joseph chat with a girl with enamel pins on her bag. "At the National Gallery." Her words were tentative as she tested uncertain waters, unsure how to navigate newly drawn borders after a tectonic shift. "We could go on a date."

Eddy frowned at *The Sleep of Reason Produces Monsters*, the picture resting on the gallery wall beside a half dozen of its fellow caprices. Concerned, she discreetly checked her watch. François caught her expression and put his hand on the small of her back, grounding her. Eddy relaxed at his touch, and more at his words. "It's an aquatint, and a popular one. There might be as many as dozens of copies of the print in the world. One of them is in the travelling exhibit."

Eddy liked the piece, but she was too goth to consider owls and lynxes as particularly terrifying monsters. "Billy Bragg implies that when Reason sleeps on the job, monsters take the opportunity to come out," she critiqued. "But I've always seen it the other way. Reason imagines monsters which escape from his dreams."

Mara stood in the doorway, gazing into the next room. "Goya's painting of the Spanish royal family is here," she said, pleased. She took a seat on the faux-leather bench across from the canvas and gestured to her partners to join her. "I like the children."

François joined Mara and put an arm around her. "The Black Paintings are around the corner," François said, consulting the gallery pamphlet. "We're getting darker."

Mara contemplated Queen Louisa's depiction at the centre of the piece, before shifting her gaze to the next painting: Ferdinand VII's portrait, fifteen years later. "I don't trust Reid," she said carefully, taking in Ferdinand's domineering figure. "You're right about him."

Eddy nodded and took a seat on Mara's other side. "What do we do about it?"

It took only a few minutes for the three of them to collect François' things from Eddy's apartment, given how unnaturally organized the place was. It wouldn't last. "You could spend the night at our place," François offered as he gave Lilith a goodbye pat, "if you'd like."

Tact was crucial in these situations. They didn't want Eddy there while they recovered from the day, her presence occupying the liminal space between guest and lover. They wanted to be able to fart, to cry, to fall apart without wondering what she thought of them. And Eddy was ready to have her home to herself again, to eat cream-cheese icing out of the can with a spoon, to play Rob Zombie at full blast, to put Lilith on something resembling a diet. Everyone needed an evening of normalcy. But Eddy shouldn't say that. "I've got plans," she told them. The plans involved catching up on the Brent/Lilith omegaverse fanfic, which would require Eddy's full attention.

Before he left, François touched Eddy's lips with his thumb, gently parting them, placed his hand on the back of her head and drew her close. Mara didn't hide her fascination as she watched them kiss, open-mouthed and hungry. When they pulled apart, Eddy half expected François to ask her again, but he didn't. Not this time.

"You and I, my boy, we're a breed apart." Reid's eyes twinkled. "When we achieve something, the world changes." He poured two fingers of amber liquid into each of their tumblers, in flagrant disregard of laboratory health and safety regulations. "To Eddy," he toasted, raising his glass.

Eddy watched the muscles of Reid's throat work, his Adams' apple moving as he drank. François lifted his own glass with only a second's hesitation. "Do I drink to myself?" Eddy asked, then shrugged and emptied her glass without waiting for an answer.

François smiled, tension lines on his forehead easing. "Eddy is your counterexample," he objected mildly. "There's nothing exemplary in her background, but she's the one standing beside us. She's proof that anyone can succeed." François pet Eddy's shoulder, relaxing into his role. Much like Jordan, François was a method actor. "Universities exist to elevate people with the capacity to learn."

Reid smiled, unaware of the turbid undercurrents in the room, or simply unfazed by Eddy radiating waves of anxiety in his presence. "You have good taste in bourbon," he complimented. "As you do in so many things." He followed Eddy's example, draining his tumbler and placing it on the black plastic lab bench. "You can't teach a man good taste."

"Unfortunately not," François agreed, and he'd overcorrected, was going to be the one who gave the game away if he couldn't tone his smug back down to an acceptable level of rich white bastard. He was usually a better liar than this, but then, it was usually only Eddy's life at stake. If they were lucky, if they followed the plan, Reid wouldn't want François in the room the next time they drank a toast (this time repeated?), and they wouldn't need to test the limits of François' poker face. "What do you intend to do with the Future Instances, now that Eddy's discovered them?" François' hands were steady as he tilted the bottle. Maybe he was doing fine, and Eddy was paranoid, terrified for a plan she wouldn't be able to experience herself executing.

"The Russian delegation," Reid said, savouring the words. "We're ready for a trial." His gaze was fixed on Eddy. She suddenly found it hard to remember how to breathe, to move cold air through her nose, to force her rib cage to swell and expand. Eddy glanced at her watch, though it was a pointless gesture. They were in the Middlerealm now, or they should have been, and besides her personal countdown timer wouldn't change if she was a side character in Reid's Instance instead of her own. Eddy tried not to picture hands closing around her windpipe, hyoid snapping, petechiae dotting her vision. No. Wrong Instance. Itchy throat, cyanosis of the lips, nystagmus. Keeping track of timelines was a nightmare.

"There are other methods to deal with the Russians' claims on the Arctic," François scolded him. "Even a Liberal Prime Minister is susceptible to reason." He looked Reid in the eye. "You didn't commission a virulent biological weapon so you could take out a score of high-status targets. Staging a conventional bombing is a comparably trivial matter. I'd be happy to help, if you need the assistance."

Reid waved away François' concerns. "Not a score of targets. One. After Salisbury, if the Prime Minister dies under suspicious circumstances, the Russians will be the only suspects. And when it comes time to release the bioweapon more freely," he lifted his glass, "it's always nice to have a fall guy in position."

"You can't risk it," François said, unperturbed, as if they were discussing buying an Ontarian wine instead of Italian, a refurbished laptop instead of a new MacBook, an NFT instead of an Anselm Kiefer. "The antidote failure rate is still 75%. If one of the Russian delegation ends up as a carrier, or you do — we're not ready to address an outbreak, Reid. You've seen the data."

"You and Eddy love to talk about statistics," Reid said genially, eyes fixed on Eddy as he spoke. Eddy shivered, and she was certain that Reid noticed the motion. Reid always saw weakness. "The odds of success are low, but there's a chance I roll boxcars. And access to the Future Instances means I can see the dice land before I place my bet." He shrugged, his smile unabating. "If it fails in the Instance, I won't run it in reality. That should reassure your nerves. Now, I suppose your vials will be past their best-before date. Pity. I'll get my microbiologist to prepare a larger batch." He beamed at François. "You might finally get to meet my microbiologist. It's a shame you won't remember the experience."

François was not smiling. "Do you expect me to go along with this? You know my stance on the matter," he said with restrained irritation. His voice rose, feelings reaching a peak as high as they would in a discussion on p-hacking or discarding troublesome data points as outliers, which, in a manner of speaking, it was.

"If that's how you feel, you don't need to be involved, my boy," Reid said. "I would hate to trouble your conscience." His attention swung to Eddy and she nearly stepped backwards. Reid tapped his head as if ready for cables to be run through it, for his brain to be downloaded, for himself to be remade, to be turned into a thing other than a man. "Eddy will manage everything for me."

"You're scared," François told Eddy, as though she might mistake the gnawing pit in the bottom of her stomach for an undigested bit of beef, a blot of mustard, without his keen eye for detail. "You don't need to be."

"What if the Astralrealm Eddy doesn't pull it off?" Eddy asked, as calmly as she could. Given Eddy's state of unresolved dread over what disaster her alternative-timeline self could have been perpetrating, Eddy could be excused a tremor in her voice. Hopefully, that Eddy would have enough consideration for her Middlerealm self to follow the plan. "Reid isn't stupid," Eddy said, because it was definitely Reid's willful nature Eddy was worried about.

"The man has blind spots," François calmed her. "He believed you when you told him he needed to be linked into the MRI to access the Astralrealm. He wouldn't have accepted the lie if I told it."

"He barely accepted it and took two beta blockers." Eddy fretted, pacing the semi-circle of space around François' standing desk. "Reid thinks it's adrenaline spikes that provide the signal. He only figured out it was my death in the Shadowrealm. But he's still suspicious."

François put a hand on her shoulder, and she stilled, steadying herself with the pressure of his palm against her. "Reid is always suspicious. He doesn't have any idea how granular the data is, and he doesn't realize that signals read backwards from the experimenter's death. It's going to be okay."

"But what if he figures it out when he gets back?" Eddy asked, and the worst part of being the observer stuck in the Middlerealm was unraveling Astralrealm grammar. "What if he realizes his death in the Astralrealm wasn't an accident?"

François pulled her close. Eddy rested her head against his chest where she could hear his heartbeat, constant, reliable. "You'll have died too," he reminded her. "Reid will have watched you asphyxiate beside him. He doesn't expect that kind of bravery from you. He has no idea what you're capable of." François smelled of cypress, of red brick and rust, and there was comfort in the familiar fear of his body against hers, his thumb drawing circles on her back and up her neck. "You're special, Eddy."

"I'm an idiot."

François laughed affectionately. "That too, sometimes."

He waited Eddy out then, refused to fill the silence any further, and she felt the pressure of words build inside, threatening to burst her at the seams. "What if the other Eddy doesn't want to die?" Eddy finally asked. "What if she can't go through with it?" She'd always had François' fingers at her throat, holding the knife, on the trigger. Pouring the glass. It was different when she had to rely on herself to break the vial.

François' voice was rich and comforting. "From the moment I first saw you at the conference, I knew you could do anything." His fingers brushed through the red tips of her hair, a soothing motion. "I love you and I trust you. Every version of you in every timeline."

The gates of the Necromancer's Tower swung open ominously and a red-splattered carpet unrolled beneath their feet. Carmilla smelled the rug experimentally, the nose of a connoisseur, evaluating the bouquet. "Is the colour from fresh blood?" she asked, gesturing for Grogtar to check. She licked her lips and put on her thickest Transylvanian accent. "It smells delicious."

Grogtar sniffed the air and rolled a Search. His eyes widened and he stared at the open front door in shock. "There's blood pudding in there. And there's cake!" He bounded forward, the carpet racing to unfurl beneath his hasty footsteps.

Mara hadn't cooked any ichor-related desserts for the session, but she had baked them the Necro-nom-nom-nom, a flat, rectangular cake with chocolate-frosting binding and a wide, hungry mouth. Mara passed around slices on white plates with silver edging. "Do you think it's a trap? Charlotte said Mortimer was an Evil Necromancer." Rose looked at her notes, second-guessing herself. "Charlotte was a jerk, though."

"It's a tautology," Carmilla informed Rose, her mouth full of cake and/or blood. "All Necromancers are Evil. Comes with the job description." Carmilla grinned at Rose. "It's a tasty trap. I'm falling for it."

Rose and Carmilla followed Grogtar through the ornate black door of the tower. "Welcome, fiends," Carmilla read on the wool doormat, written in friendly Papyrus. "That's what I expected from a Necromancer's lair. We're on death's doorstep." Grogtar groaned, equally dismayed by the DM and his punny collaborator.

After the party ate their fill at the dessert-laden sideboard in the entryway, they investigated the ground floor of the tower. The front-hall walls were lined with rich tapestries in colourful shades ranging from charcoal to jet, with positive messages written on each one, like "Rest your weary bones" and "Reduce, reuse, recycle."

"'LIVE, LAUGH, LOVE'," Rose read, tilting her head sideways to read the all-caps writing running up the fabric. "That doesn't seem so bad."

"You're reading the first word upside down," Carmilla corrected. "'EVIL, LAUGH, LOVE'." She considered the effect. "I like it."

On the right side of the short hallway was a closed door with a scrawled note nailed to it, reading "Fire Door: Do Not Block." Attempting to open the door posed some difficulty to the party, given the large quantity of skeletal remains and unidentified corpse bits piled in front of it. Grogtar guessed it would be a few hours' work to move them all, and he voted against tidying up someone else's mess, so after a quick deliberation the party decided to go left.

Left led the party to an open door and through that to a winding flight of wooden stairs which hugged the outer edge of the tower. The stairs climbed higher than the eye could see, flights upward visible through the empty space in the center of the tower exactly where a bannister or railing would traditionally be placed. There was an odd stain on the stone floor in the middle of the circle.

The stairway was clearly designed by someone who did not fear death or liability lawsuits. Each step had barely a foot's worth of space, and swayed at the slightest weight. To make things more exciting, the stairs were unevenly spaced. The elaborate bone candelabras lighting their path were beautiful, and the lavender-eucalyptus candles lent a homey air to the gothic structure, but maneuvering past them without falling to the now-distant floor required constant feats of Dexterity. The candles rested uncomfortably close to the thick damask curtains that billowed dramatically from black cherry wood window frames; the scene was to arson what a Gothic heroine's young sister writing a sorrowful letter and coughing was to consumption.

The climb seemed never-ending, and soon the cake was but a distant memory, as if the delightful pastry had happened to other people, in other lives. Grogtar's boundless energy waned, and even Rose was losing her optimistic bent, so Carmilla pulled out her lyre to sing an inspiring tune, "Handbook for the Recently Deceased," from the noble bard college The Damned Things.

Eddy used to imagine the future as an analog dystopia, *Mad Max: Fury Road* or *The Handmaid's Tale*. In Reid's arms factory, she saw a digital version of the apocalypse, *The Matrix*, or *Player Piano*. By night, it was worse, without even the presence of workers to humanize the automated lines, to put a living face beside the stacks of explosive ordnance designed to reduce people to rounding errors. Eddy was disgusted and fascinated by the gleam of chrome under the faint glow of their flashlights. Mara, no less intrigued, reached out and ran her finger over matte lettering. Eddy winced.

"I wouldn't worry about fingerprints," François offered. His words were probably meant to be supportive. "Our safety comes from Reid failing to realize anything's gone wrong. If he's suspicious enough to look for evidence, we're lost regardless of what he finds." It was the same logic they followed when selecting their heist outfits. François wore a black utility vest over a black turtleneck, black trousers and shoes, and Eddy had her blue apron over black skinny jeans, the one with the embroidered logo of 'Canada Cleaning Care' and pockets full of cleaning products. The two of them looked close enough to Security and Cleaning for a cursory glance, but nothing more than that. The odds of anyone watching the feed in real time were vanishingly low, and it seemed even less likely that anyone would catch up on old feeds in reruns. Besides, if a real security guard caught them on CCTV, they were both distractingly sexy.

Instead of relaxing, Mara tensed at François' words, shoulders rising, hands drawing back from the warhead, before she took a breath and stilled herself. "He won't."

"No," Eddy agreed. "We go in, we make copies of his notes, we add a few typos, we leave. Easy as that, right?" If François wasn't going to offer actually reassuring reassurance, Eddy would cover for him. "His recipes will still work, but with a bit less oomph. Makes it easier for future-us to design the antidote. As long as the bioweapon works on most people, Reid isn't going to calculate sample variance." The philosophical questions around whether Eddy's future self was the same person as her current version were too much to address mid-heist, and Eddy needed to focus on more important topics. For example, Mara's silhouette in black leggings, a matching blue apron hanging loose over her clingy black top. Mara was also distractingly sexy. "There's nothing to be nervous about. It's the middle of the night. No one's here."

"Yeah," Mara agreed, fingering the scabbard on her hip. It was probably a good thing one of them thought to bring a weapon, though a sword fight in a munitions factory was a bit gimmicky for Eddy's tastes. "Maybe I should stay at the front. I can guard the door."

"If you'd prefer that," François agreed. He put an arm around her waist and kissed her cheek. Mara melted against him, black fabrics indistinguishable, no distance between their bodies.

The safe made a satisfied, happy musical noise and released the door an inch. Eddy pulled it open without further fanfare, not quite believing the report of her own fingertips. She wrote the program to reveal his password from the MRI and yet it seemed impossible that it worked, that Reid's secret keeper yielded to such a petty thing as a scan of his mind while he died. That the randomized electrical impulses of a computer-generated number failed to be as uncertain as the path of a photon to a bomb, and thus the number was the same in both Realms.

The safe itself was an anachronism for Reid, paragon saint of cutting-edge technology, and it was too much to expect a hand-written lab book inside it. Instead, the lab manual was on a dismembered tablet, insides torn out, a gaping hole where the battery should be, bare wires instead of a wifi connector. There was a cord with a plug in the bottom of the safe, but even when they connected the device to the wall there was no way of copying the notes short of photographing each page. Compliance with infosec best practice ruled out Norm as the microbiologist, if he was ever in the running.

François' utility vest contained a slim camera, the size of a credit card, black with sleek curved edges. He pointed it at the tablet and pressed a button. "Next screen, please," he requested politely, and Eddy swiped right on the page. Three pages later, he asked, "Are Owen and Payton dating?"

"Yes. They have been for ages." She tried to match the neutrality of his tone, as though the ever-shifting fortunes of students' love lives were incapable of surprising her. As though François' interest therein was equally incapable of coming as a shock.

"Since the conference," he hypothesized, and she murmured agreement. "I'm glad." He smiled conspiratorially at Eddy from behind the camera, and she knew Owen and Payton would never have the faintest idea of François' feelings.

Eddy wasn't an expert in microbiology, but François was, or he faked it well. He ran his proposed changes by her despite her inexperience in the area. A few altered concentration factors in the standard operating procedure seemed safe enough, if you set the baseline for safety at all the other things which they got up to. Besides minor changes to the instructions, they left everything as they'd found it, or hoped they did.

They walked side by side through the factory. Eddy's nerves were on fire but she forced herself to walk, to match François' measured pace. Running would give the game away. Running would feel amazing.

As they rounded the corner, nearly at the front doors, François asked, as calmly as before, "Is that blood?"

Mara cried silently. Eddy knew this about her, though Eddy couldn't be certain when she learned it, what realm they'd been in when Eddy held Mara in silent companionship, when Eddy made Mara laugh through her tears, when Eddy was the reason Mara cried. Mara's face went red and splotchy, shoulders heaved, but she controlled her breathing, slow and rhythmic, and there might not have been anyone there for all the noise she made.

François reached her first, stepping through the lake of blood and over Reid's legs without hesitation. "Oh Mara," he said as she clutched for him, a drowning woman grabbing at a life preserver with red-stained fingers. Her hands dripped with blood as the metal blade slid out of her grasp and onto the floor. Her black ballet flats were drenched, bloody footprints where she'd circled the body, but her apron was clean, as if it repelled the storm to protect her. "What have you done?"

"Reid attacked me," Mara answered, words muffled as she spoke into the breast of François' jacket. "He wasn't supposed to be here."

Mara was right. They'd sat in the National Gallery, and they'd made a plan, and they'd agreed that none of the deaths would be permanent. Eddy tried to remember whose idea that was, who said it first. It could have been any of them. The important part was they'd all agreed. They would change the formula at night, and Reid wouldn't be in his factory, and no one would stay dead.

Reid looked smaller in death, reduced. Somehow his corpse looked good-natured, a smile gracing his lips, another across his throat, inviting them to be part of one last inside joke. Eddy didn't need to look at her watch to know it was real. She should feel something, fear or disgust or sorrow or maybe numbness. She should vomit or dissociate or cry. She'd done all those things in the Shadowrealm. But all she felt was scientific curiosity. Skim the methods section and focus on future work.

Reid's corpse posed almost as much of a problem as his animated body used to. Arterial spray was the sort of thing that attracted unwelcome attention. "A vat of lye would come in handy," Eddy mused. "I don't suppose you packed one, François?"

François' arms were tight around his wife. Her tears left dark streaks on the chest of his black vest, and her hands stained its back. He kissed the top of Mara's head. "Unfortunately not. If only we had access to explosives, and the expertise to make a detonation look like an accident."

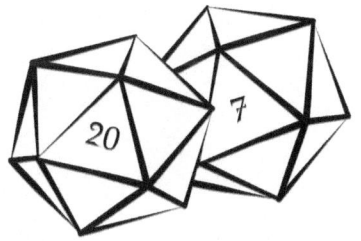

E ddy woke to the smell of unidentified baking. Butter and yeast, a
sour tang to the air. A pair of what must've been François' pyjamas
were neatly folded on the oak bedside beside her, next to the guest bed.
Her own clothes were nowhere in sight, and presumably never would be
seen again. RIP, black skinny jeans with miniscule pockets. She put on
the pair of red plaid pyjama pants and a t-shirt which declared her to be
the property of McGill University, and went on a hunt for the source of
the scent.

Her initial hypothesis was correct; Mara was hard at work in the
kitchen. Mara's face lit up to see her, though she didn't abandon her post
by the stove. "You're awake."

"We assumed you'd sleep like Joseph if you had the opportunity,"
François explained. "We weren't expecting to see you until noon unless
one of us woke you up." He was well trained by now and didn't bother
asking before brewing Eddy's espresso. He stirred in sugar, then paused.
"Should I froth milk for you?"

"This is good," Eddy said, accepting the cup and a kiss. It was the
briefest of contacts — a meeting of lips, no tongue — but François looked
at Mara for confirmation afterwards. Mara's eyes were wide,
mesmerized, though she returned her gaze to the cast-iron frying pan

when there was no follow-up. "Did you check the notes? Did we get everything?" Eddy glanced around, half-paranoid, but Joseph was presumably asleep and the Gagnons' kitchen was as safe as anywhere.

"We have the synthesis procedure," François told her. "Reid's micro-biologist didn't sign a name on the work, but there are other tells. It's only a matter of time before I figure out who." He spoke with confidence, self-assured as always. He wore grey checked pyjama pants, a stone-grey cashmere sweater with a tasteful monochrome penguin on the front and the sleeves rolled up. He was hot. A bit uptight sometimes, but hot.

Mara laid a handful of sprigs of dill on a driftwood cutting board and roughly chopped them. "I wish we knew. I keep wondering who's left." She shook her head at the herbs. "You can't stop the research if we don't know."

François frowned, considering the matter. "There's Norm, but it's hard to believe Reid trusted him with this." He ran fingers through salt-and-pepper hair. "Eddy, was there anything useful when you wiretapped his phone?"

Eddy shrugged, ignoring the shiver that went through her body at Mara's statement. "Reid and Norm were an item. Is that useful?" Mara moved to the fridge for capers and smoked salmon and Eddy seized the opportunity to grab a pastry from the pan and bite into it. Eddy hadn't realized it was possible to make English muffins from scratch, though of course they didn't emerge fully formed in plastic bags at the grocery store, someone must have made them the first time.

"Eddy, no," Mara scolded. She instantly negated her own admonishment by adding, "Do you like it?"

Eddy dipped the non-bitten edge in a pale lemon Hollandaise sauce. "Yes," she replied with a full mouth.

"We should get Norm a sympathy card," Mara suggested. She put down her knife to pick up a spatula and tend the remaining muffins. "And a fruit basket. I already got one for Alycia. And I'll invite Alycia to book club so she's not alone with her loss." Eddy stepped to the side, attempting to hide in Mara's blind spot, and slid her hand towards the cutting board where the smoked salmon was waiting. "Eddy!" Mara looked to François, eyes beseeching. "Zeeskeit, help."

François placed a hand on Eddy's shoulder and the other on her hip, pulled her towards him. Eddy's breath caught as she unbalanced. "You need to stop distracting Mara," he said against her ear, nipping at the cartilage with his teeth. Eddy tilted her head upward to kiss him, fingers tugging at the edges of his sweater.

Mara twisted a strand of dark hair around a finger and tucked it behind her ear, smiling at the scene.

Mortimer the Necromancer paced nervously around his cozy, hospitable Laboratory of Torture and Turning on the top floor of his gothic tower. He was scrawnier than he looked in the vision, muscles less pronounced, but then scrying always added ten pounds. The place was messier than they expected, too. Mortimer must have worked the scrying angles to avoid showing off the foaming vats of embalming fluids resting perilously close to surgical headlights, or the stacks of old newspapers littered across the Nain rugs.

"Hey," Grogtar said with inordinate disapproval. "Headlights and newspapers don't exist in D&D."

Mortimer must have worked the scrying angles to avoid showing off the foaming vats of embalming fluids resting perilously close to surgical torchlights, or the stacks of old town criers littered across the Nain rugs.

"That's better," Grogtar agreed. He sipped his ginger ale, which wasn't exactly real ale, but would do in a pinch, particularly given the exhausting climb. "Now revive Arg and we won't set you or your tower on fire." Half-Orcs were traditionally known for their blunt approach to negotiations, but in this case, Grogtar's words were sharp and coated with a thin layer of flaming mayonnaise.

Rose put a gentle hand on Mortimer's arm, her blue eyes gazing deeply into his black ones. "You are our only hope to restore our friend to life," she said, voice dripping with pathos, dice clattering on the table.

"Technically, to restore him to death," Carmilla corrected. The Area of Truth was still in effect so it was impossible for Rose to utter an outright falsehood, but apparently Carmilla's lyre couldn't prevent a mortalist slip of the tongue. "We want Arg back." She swirled the Pinot Noir in her glass, watching for legs, though Arg's legs were secure in Rose's Handy Haversack.

"I, erm, foresee some difficulty with, um, fulfilling your request," Mortimer hedged. He wiped a layer of sweat off his face with the sleeve of his black robe and glanced nervously at the lyre by Carmilla's side. Carmilla smiled encouragingly at him, showing off teeth which dripped red. "Arg, um, he was a Zombie." Mortimer paused, looking less like a strapping young Evil Necromancer and more like a fish out of water, flailing for air. "The thing about Zombies. Is. They'renotsentient." He stepped backwards nervously as he said it, nearly knocking over an ornate candelabra made entirely of teeth, holding rectangular white candles that smelled of peppermint.

Rose lifted her crossbow, bolt pointed at Mortimer's heart. "What did you say?"

Mortimer very slowly put up his hands, palms outward. "Zombies aren't sentient, Rose. But Necromancers are." He twisted the wrist of his right hand and bent his fingers. The corpse of a town crier, dressed in a fine red jacket with an absurd tricornered hat, sat up, losing an arm in the process. Mortimer twitched his index finger and the crier picked up the arm with his other hand and attempted to slide it back through the sleeve. When the arm was somewhat restored to its previous location, Mortimer waved as if conducting an orchestra, humming in concentration as the Zombie lifted a bouquet of Vampyre Roses from a cut crystal vase.

The undead crier bowed low, extending the flowers to Rose. "Mon plaisir quotidien," he said, a broken rasp which echoed the noises from Mortimer's throat.

Rose stared, motionless, the tip of her crossbow bolt poking through the buds. "Why?" she finally asked.

"Vengeance," Mortimer said, his voice a low growl. He hunched forward. A wall of town criers lurched to their feet at his motion. "Morticia was my grandmother. You killed her."

"Did I?" Rose asked, glancing down to her character sheet. "I didn't realize — I forgot my backstory. I'm sorry, Mortimer. I didn't realize she was yours." She rolled a Diplomacy check with shaking fingers. Metal dice clattered in unison behind François' cardboard screen.

Mortimer made a fist and the Zombies collapsed into viscera and embalming fluid. When the corpse with the bouquet disintegrated, nothing stood between Mortimer and Rose's weapon. He stared unwavering down the barrel of her crossbow. "My grandmother needs vengeance," he said, very quietly.

"Does she?" Carmilla asked. "If she's dead for real, does she even get a vote?"

"We could get vengeance on someone unrelated," Grogtar suggested. "Arg and I were gonna hunt dinosaurs together. Maybe a gryposaurus did something very wrong." He attempted to think up a crime sufficient to the occasion, a demonstration of how dedicated he was to Arg's memory; Grogtar didn't like thinking. "Tax evasion."

"I'm an Evil Necromancer." Mortimer's tone was flat. "I kill the living and I raise their corpses. It's who I am."

Rose dropped her crossbow and leaned forward to kiss him, their mouths meeting over the DM's screen. "Not us," she said. "You can kill everyone else. You go adventuring with us."

Alycia looked as stately in her mourning black as she had in pristine white. The women took turns to approach the pale-blue armchair she'd settled on and offer condolences, and Alycia accepted the well-wishes graciously.

"Mandelbrot?" Mara offered, holding out a silver-edged plate. Book club was at the Gagnon's house again and Mara matched her baking to the novel. Eddy must've lost track of time. She was reasonably certain it wasn't Mara's turn, not yet, but even a diver's watch couldn't anticipate the patterns of women who claimed to like quinoa.

Alycia took one and nodded for Mara and Eddy to take the chairs next to her, in much the same way an interrogator might to a prisoner of war. "Thank you, sweetie."

"I hope you like book club," Mara said, nervously tucking a misbehaving tendril of hair back into place. Her fingers brushed over her jade dragon earrings. "Even if you didn't have time to read the book. I'm glad you came." She lifted her hand, almost reaching for Alycia, then lowered it without touching her. "I can't imagine being alone in that big house."

"*Fiddler on the Roof* is a bit rustic for my tastes," Alycia said, "but it's lovely to see everyone. You're too kind." She looked over the gaggle of middle-aged women drinking tea and discussing yoga instructors, a queen surveying her subjects. Colette wore a black jumpsuit with a plunging neckline, in deference to Reid's death or the demands of fashion. She sipped kombucha, a recipe of her own formulation guaranteed to maximize healthfulness.

"It's old," Mara allowed, "but the world doesn't change. Men zol zikh kenen oyskoyfn fun toyt, voltn di oremelayt sheyn parnose gehat." Mara didn't translate her words, abruptly moving on to the next topic. "What are you going to do with the business?" Mara swallowed, and added, "If it's okay to ask. I'm sorry. It's probably too soon." She looked helplessly at Eddy, as if Eddy's experience of grieving her mother gave her any insight into this situation. As if Eddy wanted Alycia to take notice of her.

"You can ask." Alycia waved a pale hand, bestowing a favour. "There's the police investigation to endure before the company can get back to normal. Police always ask so many questions." Her eyes flit over Mara, assessing. Mara, restless and eager to please, was the same as ever, surely. "They want to see all the footage from the night my husband died. They suspect foul play."

Eddy's breath stopped at Alycia's words, her throat closed up, her diaphragm refused to swell. Her fingers dug into the linen arm of her chair. She shouldn't leave a silence, not Alycia's after a well-mannered, polite accusation, but she couldn't speak without air in her lungs, or without words in her mind.

"That's awful," Mara said, putting hand over her mouth in horror. "It's not Reid's fault his factory exploded. He made all kinds of dangerous things but he knew how to keep them safe. He wouldn't let any weapons fall into the wrong hands. Or be used in the wrong ways." Mara spoke softly, careful that her solace not carry beyond the three of them. "Reid was a careful man. The police won't find anything he did wrong."

Alycia shook her head, passing judgement. "Not careful enough, it seems." She took a bite of mandelbrot and caught the crumbs with a cadet grey napkin. "Unfortunately, the hard copies of the security tapes were lost in the explosion and Norm botched setting up the external feed. The police will find greener pastures elsewhere, and they'll move on." Alycia tilted her head and graced Mara with the hint of a smile. Eddy made herself breathe, a slow count of three in and five out, calm and collected. "They always do."

Mara nodded. "The police leave, and we clean up the mess." Behind her glasses, Mara's brown eyes were dark and sorrowful. Alycia's eyes were gleaming.

"They don't understand," Alycia said, gesturing away from their circle, at the police, at mankind, at the world beyond their three. "The work has to go on. They put obstacles in our way and we tear them down. We outlast them. We endure."

"My husband and Eddy were working with Reid," Mara offered. "Reid always funded her for only short contracts." Mara covered Eddy's hand with her own, just for an instant, before returning it to her lap.

"Reid was a good man, but he had no foresight." Alycia wore a single strand of iridescent pearls around her throat. Her red lipstick was a refined wound slashing through her powder-white face. It was impossible to imagine her crying. "What's next month's book?"

"*Hench*," Mara replied promptly. "You'll like it. It's much more modern."

The insistent knocking at Eddy's office door was, unsurprisingly, Lydia. Eddy let her in and the girl flopped dramatically on the empty chair in the cubicle nearest the door. "Nini invited me to do a three-month secondment with her group at the FDA. François thinks I should do it."

Eddy could translate that statement easily enough; François set it up for Lydia in a manner similar to a feudal king fostering out his children to strengthen an alliance. "Sounds like fun. Are you going to go for it?" It was important for the students to think they had agency in their lives.

Lydia scowled. "I dunno," she said, which meant yes. It took a strong constitution to deny the will of one's supervisor, and a lot more vehemence than Lydia's half-hearted imitation of reluctance. Besides, these things were great career moves, and Eddy wasn't lying to Lydia. They usually were fun. "I guess it would be good to meet new people. Maybe I'll find someone in Maryland who isn't part of Owen and Payton's polycule."

Eddy chose the wrong moment to attempt a sip of tea and ended up sputtering it over her keyboard, which saved her having to think of an appropriate response to Lydia's statement.

"Every hot person in this entire city is sleeping with Payton. Payton is getting more action since they hooked up with Owen than I have in my entire life," Lydia continued, exactly like Eddy wished Lydia wouldn't, because Eddy was the sort of mature professional who did not involve herself in students' love lives.

"Is the entire city exclusive with Payton?" Eddy's mouth formed the words without consulting her brain along the way.

"No, thank goodness," Lydia said with some relief. "But what's the point of dating someone if they hang with your co-workers and talk about university? I want a partner who has a real life, you know?" Lydia looked Eddy over with a critical eye, and Eddy should not have been the one blushing, trapped in this conversation with a grad student. "You do not know."

"Pass me the Sharpie, Zeeskeit," Mara called across the room. François tossed it underhand, and it landed in her open palm. Mara considered the brown box with a critical eye before writing "Costumes" in an open hand with airy, rounded letters. She should have written "Costumes + Lilith" but then Lilith's presence in an open box could be taken as read.

François was mid-way through constructing the next box, and true to form, Lilith ambled over to inspect his work. "How many *Night Beats* plushies do you have?" he asked Eddy, taping down the edges of the second merch overflow box. He didn't need to ask what the Lilith/Jane/Brent plushies were doing together in the *Night Beats* shrine; the answer was self-evident.

"Not enough," Eddy said without hesitation. Each time Eddy moved, she swore that the next time she'd hire professionals instead of bribing people with beer and pizza. Eddy bit into a slice of Hawaiian. François wanted La Fin du Monde, but Mara vetoed drinking 9% during packing, so they were enjoying Grapefruit Radler instead. "Next question."

"What's an ovipositor?" Mara asked, holding the tentacled tube and its packaging aloft for the world to see. Eddy felt an entire body's worth of blood rush into her cheeks at an alarming rate. François raised his eyebrows and Eddy contemplated the probability of all the molecules in the floor simultaneously disappearing so she fell straight through to the center of the earth. Apparently, Mara was packing a somewhat different box of costumes than Eddy had realized.

"Vee got it for me as a joke after we watched *Alien vs Predator 2*," Eddy explained in a controlled, adult manner, like the controlled adult that she was. The corners of François' eyes crinkled with suppressed mirth.

"What's it like?" It was patently unfair that Mara could look so innocent while asking that question. Mara pulled it from the clear plastic shell and balanced the device in her hand. "Can we try it?"

"You need to make the dissolving gelatin eggs in advance," Eddy said, a sentence she did not wake up planning to utter that day.

"Later, then," Mara agreed. She reached into the fibreboard drawer of Eddy's dresser and pulled out a succession of sex toys: a plastic set of vampire teeth with a pack of cherry-flavoured blood to accompany it, a strap-on, and a remote-control vibrator. The items were an order of magnitude less embarrassing than the alien dildo, but Eddy was still going to pass out from excessive blood flow to the face. "I like the teeth. You could wear your leather dress and locket with them. What else do you have in your closet?" As she spoke, Mara's fingers unconsciously traced the contours of the rainbow unicorn horn. Eddy put down her pizza and reached for her.

Mara ran a finger along Eddy's jaw, then kissed Eddy, mouth open and yearning. Her body pressed against Eddy's, her thigh a gentle pressure between Eddy's legs. When Mara broke contact, Eddy murmured her disappointment. But Mara's attention was focused on François, standing by Eddy's desk, watching with empty grey eyes.

"Sorry," she whispered, looking away from both of them. "I'm sorry."

"It's all right, Mara," François told her, but he wasn't smiling anymore. Mara was drawn in on herself, shoulders hunched, head low. He stepped over a pile of shoes and wrapped his arms around her. "It's all right," he said again, and kissed the top of her head. He held her for a long moment before saying, "I should get back to the office." Once he let her go, he stood beside her. Only after Mara kissed his cheek did he start to walk to the door.

"You don't have to leave," Eddy said. François turned to face her and she fumbled for words. It should've been easy. Vee said men liked threesomes. "You could spend the afternoon here. With us."

Mara looked at François with wide eyes, but she didn't say anything.

François shook his head. "Not yet, Eddy."

Eddy is dying again.

At least anaphylaxis is a novel diversion, and they say a change is as good as a rest. Eddy's throat itches. It starts as an annoyance, her maroon turtleneck sweater is too tight and she discreetly tugs at it, but soon she can't stand the pressure on irritated flesh. She tears at the collar until she finally gives in and pulls the whole thing off, lab safety and workplace etiquette be damned. Even that gives no relief. Eddy scratches at her neck, digs her nails in as if puncturing the skin could relieve the pressure. She's written about localized pain to the throat on countless patient summaries on countless clipboards — or the same clipboard in countless Instances — but she never thought about how much it would hurt. Eddy's thinking about it now.

François pushes a chair against the back of her calves and she collapses onto it gratefully. Tears blur her vision and she can't see anything when she checks her watch.

"Not long now," he reassures her, his voice soothing, his hand on her shoulder. She lifts her head to watch him but his figure is muddled, her vision won't snap into focus. His outline is cloudy and without form, a dark shape haloed by the fluorescent lights of the lab. His hand squeezes her shoulder and it's the only sensation left other than pain. "I'm here with you. It won't be much longer."

Only Mara would think that celery sticks were an acceptable food-substitute to bring to a housewarming party. Eddy was prepared to eat as many as one stalk, and only if Mara was watching her and she couldn't fake her own death to escape.

"Where are Lilith's bowls?" Mara asked, opening cupboards in Eddy's new, above-ground, multiple-roomed apartment. The excessive number of rooms might have made bowl-finding a challenge. For example, Eddy could have given Lilith a room to herself and put the bowls in there. She hadn't; the second bedroom was Eddy's office, and the bowls were in the kitchen, which was the sensible place to store cat bowls. But she could have. "I brought her smoked salmon and canned tuna and Temptations."

"Lilith has a lot to celebrate," Eddy agreed, handing over a black bowl with red paw prints. "Her short-term position got converted to a three-year contract, she upgraded her apartment, and her PhD student at her old job successfully defended his thesis." Eddy was confident she'd made a compelling case that she, rather than Lilith, deserved snacks without stringy bits. She followed up her words by attempting to grab a slice of smoked salmon from the Tupperware but Mara easily fended off the attack using the lid as an impromptu shield.

"Lilith's namesake won a karaoke contest against Titania and beat Jane in an arm-wrestling competition," François pointed out in her cat's defense. He carried a suspiciously cake-shaped rectangular white box which made Eddy confident she was not doomed to a life of vegetables. "We have something for you."

"Is it cake?" Eddy asked. Without waiting for an answer, she started lifting the tape holding down the thin cardboard top. "Also Lilith cheated on the arm wrestling. She knew Jane was ticklish." It was a fantastic episode, but the fanfic afterwards was the real star.

The cake was covered in white icing, with a drawing in thin black lines of chocolate: a sleeping man, with a lynx, owl, and bat behind him. "I did the piping," Joseph said with well-deserved pride. "Mame said you like the print in our kitchen."

"It's fantastic." It was almost too beautiful to eat, but wasting Mara's Italian buttercream icing would be a worse crime than defacing Joseph's artwork. "This is absolutely the best thing. I need to take a photo and then we need to eat it immediately. Joseph, the plates are in the cupboard by the sink. I can't believe you actually drew this."

Joseph grinned and went to collect Eddy's mismatched set of

dinnerware.

Mara, restless now without a task to occupy her hands, moved to François' side. He put an arm around her, drawing her close. "We have something else too," Mara said, tension in her voice.

"You keep destroying our flyscreens," François scolded Eddy, corners of his mouth quirked up into a smile. Eddy had thought she only broke into the Gagnon's house in the Shadowrealm. Apparently she was wrong. "It was easier to get a key cut than to keep replacing them."

The key was shiny steel with a round head, attached to an oversized keyring with the same ornate celtic knotwork as the one from when the Final Guardian unlocked the gate to the Astralrealm. Eddy ran a finger along the teeth, letting them dig into her skin so she could be sure they were real. "It's the real prop from the episode," Mara said, and it took all of Eddy's secret reserves of adulthood not to burst into tears in front of Joseph. He was too young to learn that grown-ups cried too, and besides, not at her house-warming party.

Mara hugged Eddy, and that was appropriate only if Joseph was too innocent to realize why his bedroom was moved to the basement and away from the guest room. Fatima — the enamel-pin girl Joseph hung out with now — did not strike Eddy as the naive type. Maybe she talked to Joseph exclusively about anime, and family living arrangements never came up in conversation.

"What's our next campaign?" Joseph asked as he cut slices of cake and placed them around Eddy's high table. Either he was as wholesome as a basket of baby Pigeonbears or he was willfully denying the obvious, and Eddy didn't care which.

"I haven't decided yet," François admitted with the delighted expression of a father about to troll his son. "You might meet a Lynx quest-giver named Bobtail and he tells you the sad tale of a Dwarven mining village overrun by Boblins."

Joseph paused in his consumption of cake to roll his eyes. "Goblins, dad."

"You don't know about Boblins?" Eddy asked, the picture of

innocence. Joseph's answering sigh was audible in the void of space. "If you don't like this quest, maybe we could fight a roving gang of root vegetables who attack travellers under the cover of darkness. They call themselves the Night Beets." Joseph buried his face in his hands, but even Mara laughed at that one.

Acknowledgements

I t takes a village to write a novel. There are so many wonderful people who are culpable for their part in producing this book. Their names have been recorded for future investigations.

To my partner, who is endlessly supportive in every way. Both this book and I would not be who we are without him.

To Rachel A Rosen, the best writing buddy anyone could ask for, who cheered when I was full of despair, brainstormed when I was stuck, and consistently told me to make it darker. This book is the worst parts of myself and she liked it anyway.

To Geoff, my marvelous publisher, who believed that strangers would want to read my weird little book, and then made it happen.

To the communities which supported me as I wrote. Fantasy Wryters, LGBTQI+ Critique Group, Spicy Peppers/Sad Joy Unit, Cats and Eldritch Horrors, and Night Beets. There are so many people who I need to thank within those groups. People who trudged through a long beta read, sometimes including multiple drafts, to tell me how each element of the story was landing: Saevelle, Eagan, Holly, Jess, Rohan, Emma, Rebecca, Marten, Rysz, Tucker, Renee. I can't possibly individually thank everyone who contributed ideas and partial reads and support over a very long two years, because it would double my word count, but you know who you are, and I know who you are. Thank you.

Finally, some character names (Reid, Alycia, Colette, Lucy, Tobias) and some character and place names (Fausto, Yr, Proudloch, Tramura), are used with permission from Rachel A. Rosen and Renee C. Carignan respectively. Charles is used with permission of Saevelle, and François' Dungeons and Dragons protective screen is used with permission from Renee. Thank you for sharing in the fun of shared creativity!

Night Beats is used under Creative Commons, and A Someone Else's Problem Field is taken from *The Hitchhiker's Guide to the Galaxy*. The line "Ian Mallory is a massive dickhole," is quoted directly from Rachel A. Rosen's *Cascade*.

About the Author

Zilla Novikov is the co-author of *The Sad Bastard Cookbook: Food You Can Make So You Don't Die*, written with Rachel A. Rosen, and the novella, *Query*. *Reprise* is her first novel.

Also published by
The BumblePuppy Press

www.bppress.ca

Rachel A. Rosen

• *Cascade: The Sleep of Reason, Book I*
• *So Human As I Am*
• *Blight: The Sleep of Reason, Book II* (forthcoming)

Carl Dow

• *The Old Man's Last Sauna*
• *Black Grass*
• *Wildflowers: The Women Who Made McCord Chronicle*
(forthcoming)
• *Beyond the Blood* (forthcoming)

Jules Paivio

• *Life Is Good: A Memoir* (forthcoming)

A. A. Milne

• *The Woke Winnie the Pooh*
(Forthcoming: Edited and with commentary by Geoffrey Dow)